EMPIRE STATE ENEMIES

An Enemies-to-Lovers
Billionaire Romance

Rosa Lucas

The following story contains mature themes, strong
language and explicit scenes, and is intended for mature
readers.

Empire State Enemies is a New York-based story, so its
narrative voice uses American English conventions for
grammar and spelling. However, the dialogue often
employs casual slang and contractions to capture
how people actually speak in their everyday lives and
relationships.

Photographer: Wander Aguiar
Paperback cover design by Champagne Book Design
Copy edit by Britt Tayler

PROLOGUE

Lexi

Tonight, I'm someone I barely recognize. A fraud in fake designer heels. A stranger in my own skin.

It's wild how just a few hours of craziness can flip your entire world upside down.

This morning, had you asked me about my grand plans for the night, I'd have confidently said I was destined for a glamorous evening sprawled on the couch, ready for a *Million Dollar Listing* binge-fest with my little sister, Grace. Decked out in my most tragically holey sweats and the kind of underwear that screams "here to support a full bush, not lure in a lover."

We'd be shoveling chips into our mouths, while we live vicariously through the disgustingly rich. Pretending just for a moment that we're the ones rolling in money.

But instead, here I am.

Pinned against a wall in a swanky hotel

bathroom by New York's most notorious playboy. Pulse jackhammering as I straddle the line between sheer panic and twisted arousal.

It's the kind of questionable decision you make when you're not thinking straight.

His muscular forearm presses against the wall, right next to my head. The graze of his dark stubble sends shivers down my spine as he claims my mouth ruthlessly.

I taste whiskey on his tongue, inhale his intoxicating masculine scent as he presses the full length of his hard body against me.

His kiss is rough, frenzied, fueled by some inner turmoil.

The kind of fierce lip-lock that electrifies every nerve in my body from lips to toes and all the good bits in between.

For a moment, I forget about wanting to knee him in the balls just minutes ago. Now, I'm struggling to resist as his skilled hands roam dangerously close to my underwear.

A groan rumbles through his chest as he grips my hips possessively, using his muscular thigh to force my legs wider.

Those rock-solid muscles imprint through my flimsy dress, his thick arousal pressing relentlessly against me. His rough hands, with their sexy veins, ignite dangerous levels of tingly heat on me everywhere they touch.

Our heavy breathing echoes off the walls, a hot and filthy soundtrack.

It's all too intense, too visceral.

He'd ruin me if he knew my true intentions. I've caught him in an unguarded moment, a slim chance to get what I need.

There's no time for guilt, no room for second-guessing. I just need to get in, get what I came for, and get out.

My shaking fingers slip into his pocket while my pounding heart threatens to give me away. Surely, he senses my fear. I'm one gasp from passing out into his sexy mouth.

I wish it weren't like this. Karma will surely savage me—she always collects her debts.

I'm not a bad person, I swear. Just a girl making questionable life choices in a shit situation. Like a cornered rat, or hopefully something cuter. Maybe a distressed raccoon, scavenging through life's garbage cans, searching for a decent meal.

My fingers trail his flexing back, distracting him while my other hand digs deeper into his pocket. Tracing those defined muscles . . . searching . . . until at last . . .

Jackpot.

I wrap my fingers around the small prize, prying it free.

I've done it.

Breathless, I break the kiss.

Tonight, I'm someone new. Someone I can never come back from.

Because tonight, I'm a brazen thief.

And when he figures it out, I better be long gone.

ONE

Earlier That Day . . .

Lexi

The first thing Grace and I see walking into Sunnyhill Assisted Living home is Sean Connery. Not the ghost of the legendary heartthrob here to charm the residents—rather, a life-sized poster of the classic Connery, sporting a red mankini, iconic mustache, and enough chest hair to upholster a sofa.

"Bet you ten bucks we can guess who put that up," I mutter to Grace.

We make our way through the beige lounge reeking of Glade plug-ins and meatloaf. Again, I question why this place costs us a liver and leg every month.

No amount of lavender potpourri can mask the depressing reality—this is Mom's "home." One we can barely afford thanks to her crap retirement planning and my perpetually broke status. It's a miracle I've kept her here this long, pulling money out of my ass.

I hear her booming voice before I spot her—another miracle given her fight with inflammatory lung disease, COPD. She's holding court smack in the middle of a group of paintbrush-wielding ladies, like she's the queen bee here. She's skin and bones these days, like a scrawny baby bird.

My guts twist with guilt every time I visit Sunny*hell*. Guilt that she's trapped in this place at sixty-five, instead of being home with us. Guilt I can't earn enough to care for her myself —especially with the high-tech babysitting her oxygen levels need, not to mention the whole nighttime oxygen therapy. Guilt that I harbor resentment for her crap planning dumping this on me. And then there's the deeper guilt, boiling beneath it all—a simmering anger that a lifetime of smoking has led to this, despite all the warnings she received

"*It was fashionable back then,*" she likes to tell me, as if that somehow absolves her from all responsibility. Now the damage is done, COPD stealing her freedom.

Mom should be sipping mimosas on a beach, flirting with a Sean Connery cabana boy doppelgänger. Not painting 'staches with Lynda who keeps forgetting her own freaking name.

I plaster on a smile, playing dutiful daughter, and shove my ugly thoughts down deep.

"My fabulous girls are here!" Mom rasps at top volume, grabbing everyone's attention. She turns to her painting pal. "Move it over, Tricia, darling, make room for my girls!"

She's telling, not asking, as she shoves Tricia's wheelchair aside with a noise that makes my teeth grind.

I cringe as Manager Lady Brenda glares across the lounge. Grabbing Grace's hand, we make a beeline to Mom before she causes a scene. Well, an even bigger one.

"Really, assault and battery today?" I force lightness into my tone.

She waves it off breezily. "Oh please, she's practically bionic! Right, Tricia?"

I give Tricia a consoling pat, but she just grins. "I'm tougher than I look, kiddo."

Mom beams, triumphant in her right to mow down rest home residents without consequence. I swallow down familiar emotions and paste on a smile as we exchange kisses. Happy face.

My gaze lands on the amateurish paintings —row after row of deranged half-naked Sean Connerys.

"Since when did art class go Fifty Shades of Connery?" I smirk. Knowing Brenda's anti-fun rules, I'm shocked she let this fly, especially since

Mom hasn't put any clothes on him.

"I told them no more daffodils, or I'll riot! How many damn flowers can a woman paint?" She points an accusing finger at the flowers. "I gave Brenda an ultimatum: it's bare Connery or Josh here gets to model au naturel. Her call."

Poor Josh, the nurse, doesn't know where to look.

One day I'll come in to find Mom leading a "Seniors Demand Orgies Now!" protest, bellowing "What do we want?" with the golden agers chanting "More sex!" while aggressively shuffling their walkers. "When do we want it?" "Right now!"

Mom breaks into another brutal coughing fit. It never gets easier to watch.

She takes a cautious test breath as the coughs subside, waving off my outstretched hand.

"Tell me everything," she rasps once it passes. "Grace, how'd your presentation go?"

Grace dives into her college presentation story. I try to stay tuned in, but it's tough. Half my attention's on Brenda, lurking like a vulture waiting to swoop. I sink into my chair, throat tightening. So not in the headspace for her today.

Meanwhile, Grace sneaks Mom a chocolate bar under the table that I elect to ignore. You've got to pick your battles.

But I can't help throwing out a warning as Grace wraps up. "You better be eating real meals too. Not just snacks."

She shrugs it off. "Managed the sloppy mac and cheese all right. We'll take those small miracles."

"It better be Michelin star slop for what we pay this place," I mutter, more to myself.

Her smile falters, and I mentally slap myself. Great job.

"I've told you, there's a much cheaper place in Utah," she says. "I'd love to live in Utah."

I summon patience as the familiar arguments circle. "That place looked terrible. We're not moving you to Utah," I say flatly.

"It's not right, you spending all your money on this place." Her frown shifts to a dazzling smile as Nurse Hottie Josh leans close to move art supplies. She nudges Tricia. "Our Alexa should be spending her money dating handsome men. Right, Josh?"

My face heats as Josh looks over, nearly dropping the bin.

"Mom!" I hiss through gritted teeth. He smiles uncertainly before moving away. I want to vanish into the floor. It's like dealing with a teen mom.

The second he's out of earshot I fix her with a glare. "Must you blatantly ogle the staff?"

Mom shrugs, unrepentant. "Oh, lighten up! A little harmless flirting never hurt anyone."

"Could you at least restrict the salivating to guys in your own age bracket?"

She barks out a laugh that dissolves into a

wheeze. "Have you seen the relics here? You don't suddenly want saggy old men just because you're older. At my age you learn all sorts of things about men you never wanted to know. Trust me, I know."

I roll my eyes. "I'll cross that bridge later. Spare me the details."

She lets out this big, dramatic sigh. "I should at least slip Josh your number. He's thirty, looks like he stepped out of a magazine, and he's a nurse. What more do you want?"

"Absolutely not. No matchmaking, please."

"Someone's got to take charge since you won't," she shoots back. "I'm living vicariously these days."

"I date," I counter weakly.

Grace snorts. "Yeah, right."

I huff out a breath. "Fine, not lately. But between work chaos and just . . . life . . . I don't have time to get wined and dined."

While my dating history might suggest otherwise, it's not like I've sworn off sex. I just don't have time unless it's efficient.

Gracie and Mom act like my nonexistent love life is a personal failing. Seriously, what do they expect—I go out with random Tinder guys and my credit score magically fixes itself? Bills get paid by the Dating Fairy?

That annoying little voice in my head reminds me about my last boyfriend. Always moaning about me being too busy, working late, or hanging out with Mom. Said I didn't pay him enough attention. We were heading for a crash anyway, but part of me wants to yell at that voice, "Maybe I'd have more room for love if I wasn't buried in bills from the care home."

Right now, my life's about scraping together stability. Until the choking weeds of debt loosen their grip, I'm basically in a dysfunctional relationship with my own anxiety.

I don't have the luxury of complaining or collapsing under the weight of it all. Because who the fuck else is going to solve it for me?

Mom's face crumbles as she clutches my hand. "I just want you living your best life, sweetie! I mean, look at this place. I'm surrounded by the nearly dead here."

I hold back sharp comments. Her dark humor's just her way of dealing with her health issues. Same way she coped when Dad's business tanked. And even more so after he passed away a few years later.

I spot Brenda making rounds. She crooks a finger at me, and my stomach drops.

"Back in a sec," I tell Mom, trying to sound casual.

She lets go of my hand, trying to look tough.

I walk over to Brenda, my sneakers squeaking against the floor like a bad horror movie. Brenda's just doing her job, sure, but she has this way of getting under my skin—the constant throat clearing, those judgmental eyebrows, that look like she's tasting something sour.

She dives right in, no warm-up. "Let's not beat around the bush. You know why I called you over."

I swallow hard. Yeah, I'm painfully aware. We pre-pay every six months, but with their insane price hike and my stagnant income, this time I'm short. Way short.

"I just need a few days," I say evenly, tamping down desperation. "You'll get the full amount by Friday. I swear."

"Tomorrow. Noon sharp." She spits out each word aggressively. "No exceptions, Miss Sullivan."

I'm pretty sure my soul just shriveled but I fight to keep my expression neutral. "Got it. Tomorrow."

Goodbye, groceries; I enjoyed our time together.

"And don't forget the late penalty interest," she tacks on, almost gleefully.

My eye twitches. I imagine Brenda moonlights as a loan shark. It wouldn't shock me if she's got a baseball bat tucked away under her desk. "Any chance you could waive the interest just this once? I'm always on time with payments."

Her response is colder than the Arctic. "Full payment plus penalty, by tomorrow, or your mother will need to find another facility by month's end."

I take a step back and force myself to breathe. No way in hell I can come up with it all in twenty-four hours. But I force confidence into my tone. "You'll get it. No need to threaten eviction."

Her eyes narrow. "Tomorrow."

"Yeah, I heard you the first time," I snap.

Heading back to Mom and Grace, I slap on the happiest face I can muster, stifling the panic. I need to figure this out somehow—good COPD care options in my budget aren't exactly overflowing.

For now, I'll channel my inner actress and pretend everything's sunshine.

Mom gives me that look, the one that sees right through me. "All good, honey?"

Part of me wants to laugh hysterically. When's the last time anything was just plain "good"?

I pat her arm reassuringly. "Ah, just dull admin crap."

"We were talking about Easter plans," Grace says, and I quietly bless her for the topic shift. "Maybe we could take Mom out for the day? Rent a car, head to the park if weather permits?"

"Sounds perfect!" I chime in, stomach knotting. That's assuming our Easter eggs don't come with a hidden surprise of an eviction notice.

I glance at my watch—we've got time left but I'm painfully short on fixing this looming catastrophe. "Got some things to handle, but we'll swing by on Wednesday, all right?"

We wrap up with hugs, and Grace and I escape. Hitting the streets, I take a deep breath, hoping for a miracle solution to smack me in the face.

It's going to be fine, I tell myself.

It has to be.

TWO

Lexi

I squint at my bank balance on my laptop, praying some fairy godmother dumped a shitload of cash in there. No such luck. It mocks me with the kind of numbers you'd expect in a two-year-old's piggybank. Between this shoebox apartment, Mom's care home, and utilities, I can barely afford Taco Bell.

I do quick mental math, feeling that familiar dread in my stomach. Payday's still four days away, and let's be real, my paycheck from Vallure PR isn't exactly a windfall.

Grace rummages through the fridge, humming tunelessly. Our "deluxe" open plan apartment means the kitchen's about three steps from the couch. I could flip a coin from the couch and probably knock over a pan.

If she breaks into *Frozen* one more time, I might snap.

Everything grates my nerves lately.

We've tried to make this cramped apartment a home, but it remains a certified shithole. The wallpaper's peeling, the floors are rising for some freaky reason, crap keeps breaking, and no amount of Target artwork or scented candles can disguise the fact that this apartment is two steps from condemned.

Home sweet home, *La Maison du Leak*.

Just last week, it was like Niagara Falls in my bedroom, thanks to the genius living upstairs. I'm pretty sure the building is haunted by a vengeful dead plumber. When I called the landlord, he was all *Stick a bucket under it until I get off my lazy ass*. At least that's what I heard. Any year now.

I must make some sound of frustration because Grace pauses her noisy fridge ransacking to glance over.

"You okay? Need a snack?" She offers me string cheese. "You're looking kind of tense."

"Just reviewing numbers," I reply tightly, gloom radiating from the screen. "Mom's payment is due."

Overdue.

"Ah." Grace spins around our sad little kitchen, avoiding the peeling floor like she's in some dance routine. She perches on our wobbly stool. "It's okay! I can pick up more hours at Stan's. You want some of that nettle tea I got? It's really soothing."

Nettle tea, yeah right. I need a fucking IV drip of Xanax. Or tequila.

Grace only knows the tip of the iceberg when it comes to our money troubles. A few shifts at Stan's Burger Pit aren't going to put a dent in this mess. Besides, she already juggles college and twenty hours a week at that dive.

She missed backpacking Europe with her friends, and I hate that she made that sacrifice. Just because I never finished college doesn't mean Gracie should miss out on life.

"Absolutely not," I say, probably too sharply. "Your only job right now is focusing on classes and leaving the money stuff to me. I've got this."

Except, I've "got this" in a way that twists my gut into knots.

My phone buzzes. The text is short: **Outside.**

Speak of the devil. Right on time.

Adrenaline spikes through me. Here we go again.

I grab my jacket and head for the door, bracing myself for another night of morally questionable choices.

"Where are you off to?" Grace asks through a mouthful of Lo Mein.

"Just a quick errand. Won't be long." I force a smile, feeling like the world's worst liar.

"You and your 'errands' at weird hours . . ."

I shrug, patting her shoulder. "Boring work

stuff. I'll grab something fresh for dinner on the way back. You know that Chinese takeout is ancient, right?"

She smirks. "Bet it's a secret boyfriend."

If only she knew. My own personal demon, more like.

It's better she dreams up romantic tales. The less Grace knows, the better.

I hop into Deano's flashy BMW, hands slick with sweat. It smells like an ashtray in here—if there's anything I despise more than Deano, it's cigarettes. For obvious reasons, not to mention they reek like garbage marinated in urine.

He swivels toward me, muscles flexing. He's the type of guy who gives pep talks to his biceps in the mirror. Just a nonstop parade of toxic masculinity and protein powder burps.

"Look who decided to grace me," he says with a smirk, manspreading aggressively.

"Hey," I mumble, only meeting his gaze fleetingly. Any longer and I might have to gouge my eyes out with a spoon.

"You just can't stay away from me, huh?" Deano purrs, his hand inching up my thigh. I swat it away, skin crawling. "People will talk."

"Cut the crap," I mutter, staring ahead. "You know why I'm here."

He tsks. "That's no way to treat an old friend, Sullivan."

Friend. Right. Young me thought he was charming. But age brings clarity, unmasking faux chocolates as the turds they are.

Deano thinks he's some kind of mafia kingpin, all decked out in his black vest, with hair styled like he's the Godfather and a beard groomed to perfection. But really, he's just a sad manchild playing dress-up, delusions of grandeur and all.

Self-loathing churns in my gut. I should tell him where to shove it and storm out, middle fingers blazing.

But of course, I remain seated.

"Fifteen grand this time, huh?"

"That's right." I keep my voice even.

He whistles through his teeth, leaning back with an exaggerated stretch, hand grazing my seat. I grit my teeth as he drags this out.

Just confirm the damn loan already so I can get out of here.

Finally, he produces an envelope, placing it on his knee. My focus zeroes in on that cash inside.

"Listen, for this amount," he drawls, "I'll need a little something extra. A special favor."

Is he asking me to sleep with him? Damn, am I desperate enough to consider it? I accidentally had drunk sex with him about a million years ago. Now I'd rather deep-throat a cactus.

He lazily taps his fingers on my seat as I eye the envelope. It's so close yet so far.

Desperation drives you to frightening depths, makes you consider sordid options. I've exhausted everything short of selling organs or starring in snuff films.

My credit cards are maxed to the hilt, useless lumps of decorative plastic that mock me every time I try to pay for something. I already work long hours at Vallure, desperately clawing my way up a corporate ladder missing crucial rungs.

A second job? I'd love to see where I could fit that into my schedule—perhaps in those fleeting moments between midnight email marathons and my one a.m. weeping sessions into the pillow.

If by some miracle I scrape Mom's fees together so they don't wheel her out into traffic, the credit card companies will be at my door next. Then I'll be right back here choking on panic in six months. It's a brutal, endless game of financial whack-a-mole.

Is this rock bottom? Because if so, it can go fuck itself sideways.

Deano's eyes scan me up and down like he's trying to figure out how much he could get for me on the black market.

I reflexively cross my arms, skin crawling, as he

smirks, dangling the cash. I'm not for sale. "If you think I'll sleep with you, think again."

"Still lookin' down that pretty nose, yet here you are beggin' for my help. Some thanks I get." He leans in, reeking of cigarettes. "Let's make one thing clear. I'm not interested in you."

"What's the favor, then?" I grind out.

"Just a little job. Some light entertainment for an evening."

My jaw drops. "Prostitution? Fuck off."

I can't believe I once willingly put this guy's dick in my mouth, but according to that test I took in *Psychology Weekly*, I have a thing for assholes with good hair.

His brow lifts and that arrogant smirk tugs at his mouth. "Take it easy. We're not there yet. I just need you to strike up a conversation with some guy at a hotel bar. Easy."

My pulse picks up warily. "And after this 'conversation'? What's the actual catch?"

"You might just end up lifting his car keys and dropping them my way," Deano explains with a sly grin.

I suck in a breath, trying to think straight. So he doesn't want me as a prostitute . . . he wants me as a *thief*?

"Let me get this straight—you want me to seduce some guy and steal his keys, so you can steal his car?" I ask slowly, grappling with the words coming out of my mouth.

"You catch on real fast." He grins, like he's just proposed a harmless round of crazy golf. "Knew you were a smart cookie under all that prickly attitude."

"Absolutely fucking not. Not happening."

He shifts impatiently. "Thought you wanted to help your poor mom." He flicks the envelope against his knee carelessly, like it's not a huge wad of cash that could solve all my problems.

Benjamin Franklin is in there, winking up at me. I need that money. Otherwise, we're screwed— Mom gets evicted without care, I quit work to care for her, Grace abandons school to help. With no income, we'll spiral fast.

"We square away the debt if you do this. Slate wiped completely clean."

I stare at him. "If I do this, the debt magically disappears? Just like that?"

"That's right, sweetheart."

A thrill shoots through me thinking of the breathing room. But my stomach knots up. How did my life unravel like this? I'd almost rather sleep with the sleazeball. "There's got to be another way."

"It's a one-time deal. Take it or leave it." He starts the engine, signaling he's done. "Plenty of girls would jump at this. Time's ticking. Make up your mind."

"Wait," I choke out. "I'm not sure I can pull this off."

Deano gives me a look that's almost kind. "Trust me, the guy won't even notice one car missing from his collection. Just last month, he blew a cool million in Vegas. Your part is minor. Worst case? He'll think he lost his keys during a drunken bender."

"That doesn't make it okay."

My head spins. I'd be an accomplice to grand theft auto, and we ain't talking a beat-up station wagon here.

"Stop stressing that little head," he purrs. "Some of these guys actually pay us to lift their cars for the insurance money. They get bored with last year's model and want the latest thing. You're basically doing the guy a solid."

I let out a strangled laugh. "Yeah, I'm sure he'll be super grateful when he finds his ride missing."

Deano chuckles. At least one of us is getting a kick out of this nightmare.

I let out a frustrated groan, slumping back in my seat. This kind of stuff only happens in movies, not real life. One minute I'm trying to figure out what's for dinner, the next I'm cast in the next *Fast and Furious*.

Looking up at our apartment, I catch Grace twirling around like she's got no cares in the world. Mental note: remind her to shut the curtains.

"Bossman's got his eye on Grace, you know. Thinks she's pretty. He's interested in taking her out."

Fury blazes through me. "You tell *Bossman* he can go to hell. None of you are getting anywhere near my sister, got it?"

In an instant, Deano's demeanor shifts. He grabs my chin, pulling me closer. I try to jerk away but his grip is iron. "Let's not forget—you still owe interest," he says softly, fingers digging in. "My partners aren't as forgiving as I am. We wouldn't want anything bad happening to your sister or mom, especially given her health situation."

His eyes flick meaningfully toward my apartment. The thinly veiled threat paralyzes me.

"I'll try," I whisper through numb lips.

"There's a good girl." He leans back, satisfied with setting the scene for his next thrilling episode of "Let's Fuck Up Lexi's Life."

"When?" I rasp.

"Tonight."

"Are you *insane*?"

He actually has the nerve to chuckle. "I was thinking next week, but you look like you could use a night out right now." His gaze sweeps over me. "Take your time getting cleaned up, if you own anything nice. Those ripped jeans might be a hit with me, but I doubt he'll be into them."

Anger and fear fight inside me. "Who's the

guy?"

"Better you don't know yet. You'll meet him soon enough." He grins, cocky as always. "Relax."

He playfully dangles the envelope in front of me, only to click his tongue and yank it back, like the dick that he is. "Oh, and Lexi?"

I grit my teeth. "What?"

"Try not to look like someone ran over your dog. He's gotta want to fuck you. Get dolled up for your date, Cinderella. Clock's ticking."

I can't help but snarl as I fling the door open. "Guess I missed the part in Cinderella where she swipes the prince's Benz."

Deano cracks up like we're suddenly best buddies. But before I can bail, his hand clamps my wrist in an iron vise.

"You should be thanking me." He winks. "I'm basically your knight in shining armor here."

Yeah, right.

I'm way out of my depth here. But it's not like I have a ton of options.

Guess I'd better go get prettied up for my hot date tonight.

Just my luck that there's no fairy godmother in this twisted tale waiting to pamper and prep me.

Nope, it's all on me, as always.

THREE

Lexi

The air in this upscale hotel bar is so thick with money and ego, I half expect my next exhale to come out as Chanel No. 5.

This, right here, is the scent of *"making it."*

A world away from my reality of unpaid bills, leaky roofs, a toilet that belts out sea shanties, and upstairs neighbors who think my ceiling is a trampoline.

I can't even recall the last time I was in a joint like this just for kicks. It's always work-related, schmoozing clients.

But tonight's different. Tonight, I get the grand honor of feeling wildly out of my league among the Gucci crowd, while becoming an unwitting accessory to grand theft auto.

Girl can't catch a fucking break.

I fidget with my straw, stirring desperately for courage that won't come. My legs uncross-recrossuncross as I scope the room. At this rate the bartender probably thinks I have a raging UTI.

My gaze lands on a guy in a velvet vest. Clearly on a date, yet he has the audacity to throw a wink my way, the filthy bastard. Is it him?

Oh god, I can't do this. I've been here half an hour, eyeing every dude that walks in. Deano said he'll text when the "target" arrives, and that I should expect him here by nine. I've never dreaded a text more. I'm seconds from revisiting that sad noodle salad I choked down earlier.

I adjust the thin strap on my shoulder, cursing the AC blasting my nips. My ancient black satin dress from Target screams cheap against these designer labels. I'm a planner by nature but Deano only gave me thirty minutes to get ready. So here I am, my only strategy being plunging necklines and nipples on full alert.

Because men are programmed to ogle boobs, thanks to some kind of breast voodoo from feeding that forever hooks them through the eyeballs. Vallure PR exploits that weakness constantly—cleavage here, artful sideboob there. Hence my painted-on Little Black Nothing tonight.

Grace nearly choked on her cheesy bites when I strutted out, feeding her some emergency work meeting bullshit for a new client.

I take a deep breath, steadying myself. Ever since I got roped into this madness, normal breathing's been a luxury.

I catch a glimpse of myself in the bar mirror. I've got the whole femme fatale look down— smoky eyes, bold red lips, my dark hair loose and lightly curled, dress clinging like my dignity. But it's only an illusion masking the panicked little girl inside.

I'm not a bad person, I swear. I don't lie, cheat, or steal. That's not me.

I'm trying to convince myself that maybe the target's a grade-A jerk who had it coming. That'll make it easier, right?

To anyone here, I'm just another gal nursing a drink, either because my date's a no-show or I'm unfashionably punctual.

But they don't know about the pair of eyes tracking me from across the lounge. Deano, the Don Corleone wannabe. I feel his gaze like it's licking my spine, sending horrific shivers up and down.

Tick tock.

I can't hear the diamond-encrusted clock on the wall, but I swear it's ticking in sync with my pounding heartbeat. How many times have I snapped my head around to check it, then the door, then back at my drink? A zillion. I must look deranged.

That minute hand just keeps moving, relentless. Deano's mark is late. Apparently, I have sixty minutes once he shows up. Deano seems to have a lot of misplaced faith in my powers of seduction. This entire plan is ludicrous.

I shift uncomfortably on my stool. The bartender catches my eye, lifting a brow. "Another round?"

"I'm good, thanks!" I chirp, taking another tiny sip.

He eyes me a bit too long, especially around the chest area. "Just holler if you change your mind . . ."

Oh, I will, right after I win the lottery. Or get out of prison.

Is anyone else here feeling this crushing weight? I'm surrounded by rich people, all fancy and carefree, clinking glasses to the sound of jazz. And here I am, drowning in anxiety, screaming like a banshee yet somehow producing no sound.

Tick tock. The guy's a no-show. Thanks for nothing, clock.

That pesky strap slips off my shoulder and I fix it quickly. But not before some lecherous old man ogles me with a sleazy grin.

Jesus, is this our guy? Still no text from Deano.

A wardrobe malfunction witnessed by Grandpa Perv is the last thing I need. I sneak another peek back, praying I imagined it.

But nope—there he still is, eye-fucking me hard. A relic easily pushing seventy. Seriously?

Men need to stop guzzling the lies about improving with age.

With equal parts horror and depraved fascination, I'm unable to look away as he locks eyes and fellates that olive in the most vulgar display imaginable.

Well, that's an image seared into my brain forever.

I avert my gaze, trying to compose myself. I'm not sure if I want Olivesucker to be the guy.

Tick. Fucking. Tock.

To my right, a couple is deep in a heated debate about whether to buy or lease a beach house in the Hamptons. Must be nice to have those kinds of problems. I stifle an eye roll and sip my drink. I'm not ashamed to admit I'm an inverted snob.

From behind me, a girl half whispers, half squeals, "Oh my god, guess who just showed up? I knew he'd come."

My heart skips, but I don't dare turn around. Still no word from Deano.

"Are you serious?" her friend breathes. "Okay, here's the plan—we'll create a 'spontaneous' run-in where I fake trip and land face-first on his crotch as an icebreaker."

Giggles dissolve behind me as I casually scope out the bar, my radar on full alert.

Fucking hell, it's Connor Quinn across the bar. The youngest of those notorious Quinn brothers.

Supposedly one of the richest men in the country, with so many hotels the Trade Commission is investigating monopoly practices.

Damn, what a face. I'm temporarily distracted from my horrific plan.

That jawline, rough with just the right amount of stubble; chiseled cheekbones and piercing blue eyes that could make even the toughest women swoon—check, check, check.

You just know he devours girls like me for breakfast, then wipes his mouth and goes back for seconds and thirds with a cocky smirk.

He prowls through like he owns the place. Which he does. Wearing faded jeans and a tight tee clinging to his muscular physique, he stands out from the tailored suits. Guess when you own the place you can break the rules.

I know his type—the kind of dangerous temptation all moms warn their daughters about, while secretly fantasizing themselves. Except my mom, who'd probably be waving her hands in the air and shouting "Hey, mister!" until she got his attention like a crazy lady.

But now's not really the time for eye-banging.

"Hey there, sweetheart."

I swivel and recoil. Fucking hell, it's that decrepit olive-sucking letch from before, now hovering uncomfortably close, bleary eyes fixed squarely chest-level.

"Can I help you?" I ask coldly, angling away and attempting telepathic extermination.

"You look familiar. Have we met?" His hand lands on my arm.

I jerk back. "You probably knew my great-great-grandma before she died. People say we looked alike."

That one lands a solid punch to his ego.

But he shakes it off quick, undeterred. He's like Herbert the fucking Pervert from *Family Guy*, if Herbert was reconsidering his life choices.

"A beautiful woman like yourself shouldn't be sitting here alone. How about some company?"

I muster all the revulsion I can into a glance. It's almost impressive, his confidence. But come on, money or not, the age gap here isn't just a gap, it's the Grand Canyon. "Thanks, but my boyfriend's about to show up. He's probably just wrapping up strangling someone in his MMA class."

Grandpa Olive Sucker plops down anyway, unfazed. "Let's have one drink while you wait."

He snaps his fingers at the bartender. "Another cocktail for the lady here."

I clench my jaw. "I said no thanks."

Unbelievable.

He doesn't catch the hint, eyeing me up and down, practically drooling. "So what does a pretty little thing like you do? You a model? Actress?"

My hands tighten around my drink, imagining

pouring it over his polished head. "Actually, I run bingo nights. You should drop by, it's a blast at the senior center on Tuesdays."

That's the kicker that finally wipes the smug leer off his face. "You little—"

But I'm not listening. My eyes bulge at the flashing message from Deano:

He's here. White shirt. Jeans.

Below it, a picture of Connor Quinn. I nearly choke. This has to be a cruel prank.

"Beat it," I growl at Gramps. I feel sick.

CONNOR QUINN??? My fat fingers can't type fast enough. **THIS A JOKE??**

No way is this real. I'd rather watch *The Texas Chainsaw Massacre* on repeat—and that says a lot considering I've refused Grace for over a year.

Please don't let this end *Chainsaw* style.

I sneak a look across the bar. There's Deano, looking sharp and oblivious, as if he's just a regular Joe waiting for a date. If only the reality weren't so painfully ridiculous.

I shoot him a furious *What the hell?* look.

My phone lights up: **Stop fucking around. It's him.**

A maniac laugh followed by a throaty gurgle burst out of me, making Gramps slide away fast.

Well done, Deano, you've just clinched the title for America's Dumbest and Most Dangerously Delusional.

I whirl around, and there's Connor Quinn, swaggering through the bar. He bumps into some dude hard enough to almost send him flying, but doesn't even pause or look back. The guy's complaint dies on his parted lips the second he realizes who bumped him.

Quinn's heading straight for a stunning blond at the far end of the bar. Every woman in here is laser-focused on him. He dishes out smiles to the prettiest ones, boyfriends be damned.

He slips an arm around the blond and leans in close, saying something that makes her giggle like a schoolgirl.

When she turns around, I can see why he picked her—it's safe to say she doesn't look like the rear-end of a bus.

Fuck.

I finish my drink, grimacing as ice smacks against my teeth. If Deano thinks I can push through Quinn's herd of fangirls and just bat my lashes to get his keys, he's on another planet.

I wish Grandpa was the target now.

My odds are less than zero. Quinn is way out of my league. I'm squinting from the bleachers while Blondie scores touchdowns on the field. I'll have better luck seducing the Moet ice bucket.

The guy grins like he doesn't have a care in the world—probably doesn't—as he hits on Blondie. He slugs back his drink then slams the glass down, missing the bar completely. It shatters on the floor. His new friend startles but Quinn just leans closer, like it never even happened. Charming.

So he's an asshole. It's not entirely unexpected considering the rumors. Apparently he's broken up marriages left and right without so much as batting an eye, putting fools who dare cross him in the hospital, then miraculously making it all disappear. He hardly notices the bartenders sweeping in to clean up after him. Is he drunk?

Our eyes meet for a heart-stopping second before he looks away, dismissing me entirely.

No way this is happening. I don't have the guts to approach Quinn. I'm screwed, well and truly screwed.

But this isn't some silly game. This is nasty real-life business. Deano and his gang don't mess around, and I'm up to my neck in debt to them.

I grab my shawl, bolting for the bathrooms, but *Vogue* cover lookalikes are laughing and blocking the way.

Fuck. I can't deal with people right now.

Then I spot a unisex bathroom tucked away in a less crowded area of the bar. Good enough for me.

I scurry back in the direction I came and swing open the door, finding it empty.

Tucked in a stall, I dial Deano, my hands trembling.

"What?" he barks over the line.

"Are you out of your fucking mind?" I whisper-yell into the phone, glaring at myself in the mirrored walls. "Connor Quinn? Absolutely not!"

"Mind the mouth, honey. He likes classy chicks."

"My mistake, I'll start curtseying immediately. Like seriously, are you stupid? No way. He's too powerful. You looking for the fastest route to jail? 'Cause I'm not tagging along for that ride."

"Calm down," he growls. "Quinn's been off his game, drinking too much. That's why we're doing this now."

"I can't do this. I'm out."

"Not your call anymore, sweetheart."

I'm borderline hyperventilating now. "Can't I swipe someone else's keys? Did you see the old bald guy sucking olives? I bet he has a lovely car."

"Has to be Quinn's ride."

I close my eyes tight.

"Pull this off, or the boss will make you regret it. Got people outside your place ready to visit Grace."

The stall tilts around me. I plant my forehead against the cool mirrored wall, embracing numbness.

Deep breaths, Lexi. You'll find a way through this.

"You sick fuck," I seethe through clenched teeth. "Go rot in hell, you and that stupid goat beard. Prancing around pretending you're Scarface

36

doesn't make you tough."

In my mind, I gleefully dig his grave, eyes wild as I shovel dirt onto his arrogant face. Maybe I'll braid daisies and ribbons into his beard—really doll him up. He'd hate that.

I jab the end call button hard enough to bruise, then release a frustrated groan that echoes off the walls.

Drawing a deep breath, I fling open the bathroom door.

And stop dead.

There, by the sink, stands a formidable figure, veins bulging from clenched fists gripping onto the edges of the porcelain sink. His back muscles ripple beneath his tight T-shirt as he leans over the basin, his strong jaw and full lips set in a silent snarl visible in the mirror.

Oh shit.

Piercing blue eyes slice into me through the reflection.

I drop my phone with a sickening crack.

FOUR

Lexi

For a second, we just stare at each other in the mirror, him looming over the sink, me a deer in headlights barely breathing.

"Might wanna close that mouth before something flies in," he rumbles.

My heart races as I scramble to grab my cracked phone, my hands all shaky. How much did he hear?

"Sorry about that little outburst," I say, trying to sound casual as I move to the sink beside him. I turn on the faucet just for background noise. "How much of it did you have to suffer through?"

Please say none of it. PLEASE SAY NONE OF IT . . .

"I wasn't listening to your boyfriend drama," he mutters, all gruff and dismissive.

Wow, okay, dick. But thank god.

"Still, sorry if I disrupted your peace," I mumble.

"For such a little mouth, you swear like a sailor," he chides with a disapproving scowl. His lip curls in distaste. "Lower the vulgarities. This is a classy establishment, not a damn dockyard."

I bristle at his condescending tone. "Guess you heard more than you let on," I reply breezily. "But hey, swearing is in my job description. How did you know I'm a sailor?"

Idiot. Worst comeback in history.

But since he hasn't dragged me outside to shoot me yet, I'm banking on the fact he didn't hear anything too incriminating.

He spares me a brief dismissive glance, then he's back to staring at the sink. So much for this guy's legendary charisma.

"Sorry us sailors don't live up to the high-class standards around here," I remark, voice tinged with sarcasm. "It's been one of those days."

I risk a longer look at him. Damn. Up close, his intense, almost harsh good looks hit harder. All rugged edges that could cut you open if you got too close. The kind of unfair handsome that likely opens any door he wants, whenever he wants. Legs too. I'd bet Mom's care home fee he's never heard the word no.

The masculine energy coming off him is stifling. And he reeks of top-shelf spirits.

He glowers at the sink like it insulted his mama. Any second now I expect punches to start flying at the poor thing.

I turn off the tap, pulse racing. I hadn't expected to get this close.

Out of nowhere, he emits a deep, pained noise, his hand slipping from the countertop as he fights to maintain his stance.

"You okay?" I ask, real concern in my voice now.

"Leave it," he growls.

"Wow, charming," I snap back. Without his looks and wealth, I doubt he'd be half as charming. The magazines sure do a number on him.

"I'm all charm, little sailor. You caught me at a bad time."

"Same here. I'm charm personified, just having a crap day."

His response is a low, amused chuckle that sends an unexpected shiver down my spine.

I swallow hard, my cheeks warming.

He cranks the tap, twisting it with unnecessary force. Before I can react, he's dousing water on his face with zero regard for the splash zone.

I yelp, jumping back as droplets assault my dress. "Hey, watch it! I didn't come here for a wet T-shirt contest."

"Sorry," he grinds out. Doesn't sound sorry at all.

Just when I think he's going to perform a full-on baptism in the sink, he turns to face me. Those deep blue eyes, a bit unfocused, root me in place.

An awkward eternity passes as we stare at each other.

What's his deal? Is he going to kick me out?

I should fill the silence with something witty, flirty even. But my tongue lies uselessly in my mouth. Besides, the volatility rolling off him in waves means one wrong word likely gets me ejected out of his hotel on my ass.

I contemplate sticking my hands under the dryer, anything to break this tension before I combust.

"Are you an angel?" he asks softly, sounding bewildered.

I blink, wondering if I misheard over the running water. "Sorry, what?"

"You're an angel," he insists, eyes fixed on me. He seems completely serious.

I laugh nervously. He's clearly half-drunk and talking absolute shit. "Angels don't have sailor mouths like mine. Are you high?"

He just keeps staring, lost in thought. "No, I'm pretty damn low," he mutters, more to himself than to me.

He looks it, with that grim expression. Part of me instinctively wants to help somehow. But the guy's giving off some seriously intense, unpredictable vibes that put my nerves on edge.

I gesture toward the sink, where water's still rushing out mindlessly. "Maybe turn that off before we drown here?"

That seems to snap him back to reality. He shuts off the tap, still looking like he's carrying the weight of the world.

Then he steps toward me. Slow and careful, like I'm a skittish deer he's trying not to startle.

His hand glides along the counter, steadying himself as he closes the space between us.

My breath turns choppy and shallow as his expensive shoes bump my cheap Target stilettos.

He's so close.

Too close.

I could count each individual bristly hair along his jawline if I wanted. See every chestnut-brown strand on his head. The small scar cutting through his left eyebrow that somehow makes him look even more rugged. The laugh lines around his eyes, evidence he sometimes smiles.

He smells good. Hot and unapologetically masculine.

"Is it the lights?" he asks, voice low and gravelly.

"What?" I breathe.

"Your eyes." He stares at me like he's witnessing the second coming of Christ, right here in this bathroom.

I feel my cheeks roast. I'm used to the attention

my mismatched peepers bring. One green, the other a brownish color—I used to think I looked like a Cabbage Patch doll that had its eyes swapped in the factory.

But the way he's looking at me now . . . it sends my pulse into overdrive.

I blink hard. The guy must be wasted.

"I thought it was the lights, but they really are different shades," he murmurs, his hand gently lifting my chin so I can't look away. "It's captivating. Never seen anything like it."

Explaining it's a medical thing doesn't feel like sexy banter, so I shelve that fact for now. The moment feels too charged for a biology lesson.

His breath, tinged with whiskey, caresses my skin and sends shivers scattering everywhere.

"You got it right," I play along. "I *am* an angel. The kind with mismatched eyes and . . . wings and all. *Your* angel."

Quinn studies me with hazy intensity, seemingly in agreement.

Before I can react, he drops to his knees before me, wrapping his arms around my waist and pressing his face against my stomach.

I freeze, stunned. Um . . . what is happening?

My hand hovers over his head, unsure and clumsy, as if I'm about to bless him or something.

Yeah, he's definitely high as a kite.

I don't believe in fate, but it's like the universe

just dropped him in my lap.

"I'm really fucking tired," he slurs into my waist.

My pulse spikes. This is new territory.

Suddenly, I'm back in the game—Deano's sick challenge—but with a newfound edge. Now I've got angel eyes and adrenaline pumping through me. Maybe I do have a fighting chance here after all.

Should I go through with this?

Can I even?

Part of me feels bad for the guy, whether he's drunk or high out of his mind.

My thoughts race as I try to form some kind of plan. What exactly am I supposed to do—pretend I'm an actual angel and start belting out "Ave Maria"?

Deciding to freestyle, I run my fingers through his hair. "It's okay," I purr, trying to sound reassuring.

He groans, tightening his grip on my ass, seemingly content to sway in this position forever.

After what feels like an eternity, I manage to haul his deadweight unsteadily upright. He blinks blearily down at me.

My tongue darts out, wetting lips dried by lies and, quite shockingly given my current predicament, lust.

Tick fucking tock. His keys must be in those

jean pockets.

A wave of self-loathing crashes over me. Forgive me for this, Mom and Gracie . . . Dad up above. I wish to god we hadn't hit such desperate straits that I got roped into shady dealings.

No matter—he's got thirty more cars just like it! He won't even notice it's gone!

My inner voice is a dumbass.

Summoning all my bravado, I grab a fistful of Connor Quinn's tee, and yank him against me. In my haste, my nose smashes into his chin painfully.

Shit. That wasn't as seductive as I'd planned.

Pushing past the sting and blinking away stars, I rally my resolve. It's now or never. Without allowing another millisecond for my conscience to intervene, I drag his head down and hungrily press my mouth to his rough, whiskey-soaked lips.

And promptly get a mouthful of 5 o'clock shadow as he jerks back. "The fuck you think you're doing?"

FIVE

Connor

"Taking what I want," she breathes, crushing her soft lips to mine once more.

For a moment, I consider catching that plump lower lip between my teeth.

The five-feet-nothing foul-mouthed pixie with the hypnotic eyes is scaling me like her own personal Everest, grappling for holds. Gotta give her props for being bold despite our size difference.

Before I fully register it, my hands are roughly groping at her flimsy excuse for a dress, desire overriding all coherent thoughts. She might as well be naked, and I just need a good hard fuck to drown out Dr. Caruso's monotonous voice grating nonstop in my skull. Going on and on about his so-called "prognosis."

Tonight, she is exactly what I need—no strings attached, pure, raw fucking. Seems every woman in my bar is circling like a ravenous shark, eyes fixed on the prize—a billionaire's marriage proposal.

They all claim they're just here for fun, but give them a few days and they're hounding me like I owe them something. Some even have the audacity to show up at my apartment, trying to sweet-talk their way past security.

I crush my lips to hers, claiming her mouth in a rough kiss. She claws at my back, fisting my hair, urging me on as our kiss turns desperate and frantic. Like we're trying to fuck away some hollow ache for a while.

A groan rumbles in my chest as I lift her off the ground, wobbling only slightly.

She gasps but wraps her legs around my waist, dress riding up. Her body fits perfectly against mine as I prop her up on the cool marble counter.

My fingers dig into her waist, clutching tight as I grind against her. Fuck, she's scalding hot even through her clothes.

Even with the whiskey haze clouding my mind, I'm aroused.

I pull back just enough to get a good look at her face, our breaths mingling together.

Damn, those eyes are something else. Lethal and haunting all at once. Like nothing I've ever seen before. A wild mix of green and brown, as if nature got into a fight and couldn't pick a side.

I need to silence the voice in my head, if

only for tonight. And this handsy little spitfire promises to be a sweet distraction, my angel of mercy. I don't fuck in my hotel bathrooms, but I'll make an exception tonight.

"So," I say gruffly. "What do I call you?"

She bites her lip, sending electricity straight to my groin. "Rose."

Actually scrap that—no need pretending familiarity exists between us. "You know what, no personal details. But I need to know you're not hotel staff. Because I don't fuck employees. If you lie to me, and I find out after we've fucked, you'll be fired. Are we clear?"

Her eyes narrow. "You're kind of an asshole."

"Just being straightforward." I incline my head. "Well?"

"Well what?"

"Are you currently receiving paychecks signed by me?"

She crosses her arms. *Seriously?* No, I don't work for you. Who are you anyway?"

I chuckle as my hands skim her breasts, feeling her nipples tighten beneath the silky fabric. "Don't play coy, angel. You know damn well who I am."

Then again, maybe she doesn't. She's not a regular here—that much is clear just from looking at her.

"Should I?" she fires back, a tense smirk playing on her lips. "You some kinda hero who cures diseases or saves the rainforest in your spare time?"

If fucking only.

Her sassy words hit a nerve.

I grip her throat, mouth finding her ear as her breath hitches. "I'm no hero, sorry to disappoint you. But you don't want a hero right now, do you?"

In a move that's surprisingly smooth considering the sheer amount of booze flooding my system, I lift her up and carry her into the nearest stall, the door slamming shut behind us.

My hotel bathrooms are a sinner's paradise—muted mood lighting, mirrors to appreciate every angle. Perfect for encounters like this.

I set her down, her heels clicking on the tiles. Her breath catches as I press her to the chilled glass wall, aligning myself to her soft curves. I slap both palms to the wall above her, caging her in place.

She tilts her chin up, almost in challenge. I take a moment to study every detail of those captivating eyes, reading each flicker of fear and excitement.

She's different . . . And different is distracting.

I trail one hand down her tiny waist, silk gliding under my fingers. The other stays braced beside her head.

"You sure about this?" I murmur, a part of me wondering if I've misread the situation.

Something's off.

I can see it in those eyes of hers, they say more than just "let's get busy." There's something else going on. Maybe she's got a man waiting at home. Maybe she thinks this'll make a good kiss-and-tell.

Then again, maybe tonight, with the burn of alcohol dulling the edges, I don't give a damn about her motivation.

In response, she fists my shirt and crushes her soft lips to mine once again.

Maybe all she wants is a good fuck.

Either way, that fiery response is the only green light I need. I kiss her hard and rough, determined to block out anything beyond this moment and these four walls. No tortured thoughts allowed, just skin on skin. Right now, I need to feel good.

And damn, she wants it as bad as I do. Her hands roam urgently, nails raking the muscles of my back before gripping my ass like she's never had a proper man before.

With a low, approving growl I wrench that flimsy black dress up to her hips.

Yeah, reality can fucking wait.

My thumb teases along her soaked panties, feeling how ready she is for me. My cock strains against my jeans, desperate to be set free.

She trembles under my touch, squirming like she wants to climb the damn walls.

I push aside the lace barrier and slide two

fingers into her tight pussy, relishing how wet she is for me.

But then she shoves me back hard, catching me off guard and causing me to stumble against the wall.

"Are you okay?" I rasp, blinking a few times as I try to clear the haze in my head.

"Shit! No!" she blurts out, her eyes widening in shock. "What were you thinking? That I'd sleep with you in a hotel bathroom?"

"What the hell?" I stare at her as she wrenches her dress back into place with frantic tugs.

"I'm out of here."

Before I can process this sudden 180, she's bolting for the door, leaving me standing there clenching my jaw. One minute she's all over me, the next she's running like I'm some kind of predator.

I've never had a woman try to escape from me this fast. Hell, I've never had a woman try to escape from me period.

"Hey, hold up a minute," I call after her too late, the door already swinging shut, heels clicking rapidly into the distance.

I haul myself over to the sink, throwing cold water on my face in an attempt to wash away the stupor. The dim lighting throws back a reflection of my puzzled scowl, amplified in the expansive mirrors.

What the actual hell just happened here?

Did I misread her signals? Was I so focused on getting what I wanted that I turned into some entitled creep crossing boundaries until she felt threatened?

Seriously, what the hell went wrong?

I lean against the sink, self-loathing churning.

My drinking has gotten out of control, no doubt about it. Making moves on random women in the bathroom. I'm missing signals, messing up.

Is this seriously who I've become? Some volatile creep prowling my own bathrooms for random hookups, only to get brutally rejected?

Lexi

Scalding water pounds my face until the bathroom fills with steam and I'm half-boiled. I need the heat to scald away the guilt eating me alive after what I did tonight.

"Why're you hogging the bathroom?" Grace's voice cuts through the steam. "I gotta poop!"

"Hang on," I croak, shutting off the tap before I turn into a human lobster. I wrap a towel around myself, resisting the urge to melt into a sad puddle on the floor and sob hysterically for a week straight. Now I get why Macbeth was so obsessed with washing his hands after offing Duncan.

On the bright side, I've got the cash. I can pay the she-demon tomorrow. Mom's care is covered. For now.

I de-fog the mirror and meet my own bloodshot gaze. I try to take a deep breath, something more substantial than the shallow gasps I've been huffing out all day.

I don't even know if my smooth moves liberating Connor's key fob were enough to have his car stolen. If it is taken, and Mr. Hot Richness calls the cops . . .

There's no proof you had anything to do with it.

I wasn't caught on CCTV taking the keys. It all went down in the bathroom, out of sight.

My pulse pounds a panicked beat. The guy seems like an arrogant jerk. Definitely not the forgive-and-forget type if someone screws him over.

I fling open the door, unleashing a steam bomb like I've been cooking meth instead of marinating in regret.

Grace frowns at me, squinty-eyed. "What were you doing, a spa session in there?" Her eyes go wide. "Holy crap, have you been crying?"

She looks terrified, as if seeing me cry violates the laws of physics.

I wave her off with forced nonchalance. "I had shellfish at the work thingy. I don't react well, that's all."

She's not buying it. "But you had shellfish the other day and you were fine."

I let out a tired sigh, wishing she'd just let it go. "Maybe it was the caviar then."

She bites her lip, unconvinced.

I shrug, the lies flowing easier now. "Really, I'm fine. Just stressed with work stuff. I'm gonna crash."

She still looks skeptical but shrugs. "All right . . . if you say so."

I cut a path for bed, drained. I hear the sink running, along with her off-key humming. Ignorance really is bliss.

Today was screwed up. One minute I'm visiting Mom, the next I'm begging Mr. Faux Mafia for cash, with the grand finale being fingerbanged by a billionaire bon vivant against the bathroom wall before thieving his keys. As one does.

He looked like he was going through some dark shit. Dropping to his knees? What was that about? The guy seems volatile as hell. I feel like I've wounded an already big, wounded bear.

If circumstances were different, would I have gone upstairs with him for a few hours of passion? Abso-fucking-lutely. I have no issues with one-night stands, not that I get the chance often. Or ever, really.

Despite his assholery, no one could look at that ruggedly handsome face and hard body and deny he's hot as hell. He's the type of guy you know is bad news, but you'd sleep with anyway because the sex would be mind-blowing. Then, you'd slink away before sunrise to avoid being kicked out like yesterday's trash.

But as his hands slid into my panties, something clicked in my brain. I realized what I was becoming. Or what I would become if I let him continue. It was like getting zapped by an electric fence.

And yeah, all right, shoving him like that was a dick move too on my part. But even with all that booze flooding his system, his cocky confidence radiated off him.

My feminist side cheered as I left him hanging mid seduction.

But honestly? Some disturbingly estrogen-charged cavewoman part of me wondered what might've gone down if I hadn't fled . . .

The way he had me pinned against that wall with his hard body . . . yeah, I wanted it bad. So bad that I'm disgusted with myself for it.

But it's all irrelevant now anyway. Connor Quinn won't be screwing me anytime soon after the stunt I pulled. He's probably adding my pic to his "psycho chicks to avoid" list for his elite billionaire bro circle.

SIX

Connor

The worst part about crashing in a suite is dragging my sorry ass up before dawn to do the walk of shame in last night's rumpled clothes. No wonder the staff gossip.

This pattern is getting old. Work too hard then drink myself into a stupor, pass out in my private suite, sometimes after a fuck, then wake up feeling exponentially worse than before. Rinse and repeat.

But getting pushed away in the throes of a hookup last night was a new low. That's never happened before, and it's messing with my head. I rake an uneasy hand through my hair. I'm pretty damn sure I didn't overstep, but it's disconcerting. The whole thing leaves me questioning myself in a disturbing light that I don't like. I never want to be *that* guy.

None of this is worth it—the hotels, the cars, the jets, the luxury—if I've become the type of man

I'd be ashamed for my niece to know.

I jab the elevator call button repeatedly as I remember how wasted I was last night. Enough to sink to my knees for that potty-mouthed little pixie like some sad groupie. She better not sell that shit to the tabloids, or I'll destroy her.

No more losing control like this. It ends now.

Sure, she was easy on the eyes. But it's not like there's a shortage of attractive women in New York. She's just another pretty face in the crowd. Except for those unusual eyes . . .

The elevator dings open at the garage, and I make my way to my reserved spot, on autopilot, reaching for the car fob. My hand closes on empty air.

Where's my car fob?

I vaguely remember having it at the bar. Dylan the bartender even reminded me about it before I hit the restroom. Couldn't have left it there. Pretty sure I felt it in my pocket while Rose was all over me.

I stop dead in my tracks, scanning the garage. Because more importantly, where the fuck is my brand new 911?

"You gotta be kidding me," I growl to the empty garage.

I circle the area. No sign of it. Just a gaping hole where a million bucks' worth of sleek German engineering should be.

My ride's been jacked. Son of a bitch.

"No fucking way," I breathe out. Impossible. These cars are supposed to be theft-proof. How the hell did someone manage to crack the facial recognition?

I run a hand through my hair, spewing a string of curses. Yeah, it's not my top choice of wheels, but we're talking about a 911 Carrera Mystique here. One of fifty made, coated in this special Midnight Enigma paint designed to eat light, and with 550 horsepower under the hood.

Could I have dropped the fob? Let some lowlife piece it together and find their way to my spot?

I definitely had it on me going into that restroom. Had it in hand when . . .

Well, fuck. It couldn't have been her, could it?

But damn, her hands were all over my ass, right where I'd stashed that fob. That sudden exit from the bathroom, her shift from seductive to spooked —it reeked of a setup.

I clench my fists behind my head, eyes fixed on the void left by my car.

This can't be a coincidence. Not with a car like that. Had to be someone who knew what they were doing, how to bypass security. People live and breathe for these limited editions—they'd give their firstborn to ride in one.

And there she was, all seductive in that bathroom, disarming me with those captivating eyes and distracting lips . . .

Was I *played*?

No fucking way.

I stride to the security desk, jaw clenched, and find the rent-a-cop with his feet up, chuckling around a mouthful of pizza, oblivious as I approach. Useless idiot. No wonder someone waltzed off with my Porsche.

I slam my hands down on the desk. "Hey."

He jumps so high his giant Pepsi goes flying and drenches his pants.

"M-Mr. Quinn!" he stammers, dripping soda. "Sir, I didn't see you—"

"Clearly," I cut him off. "Maybe if you kept your eyes on the monitors instead of the TV, you'd have seen who rode my Porsche out of here."

His face drains of color. "Y-your Porsche?" He checks the video feed, sees the empty bay.

"Oh god." He looks like he's about to puke or piss himself. Maybe both.

I lean in close, my voice low. "You'll answer for this later."

He stumbles up, soaked in soda, and for a split-second looks like he might protest. But then he sees the look in my eyes and thinks better of it.

I storm back up to reception, interrupting the inane guest chatter. "Someone stole my car. Pull up the security footage. Now."

Sara the receptionist's eyes blow wide, fingers

freezing over the keyboard. "Of course, Mr. Quinn."

They all must think I'm losing it with how agitated I've been lately. But let's be real here, it's hard to joke around with them when this issue is constantly eating away at me, ruining everything I do. Every meeting, every workout, every meal, every fuck—it's all tainted by this nagging feeling that something just ain't right.

Her nails click-clack sluggishly across the keys, and I resist pushing her aside and taking over. Few things piss me off more than having my time wasted. Lately my temper's a lit fuse—doesn't take much to spark an explosion.

"Camera thirty-five. Lobby," I order.

"What are we looking for?"

"Rewind to last night. Between nine and ten."

I lean in close, glaring at the screen. The footage flickers by in a meaningless parade of faces until it's just background noise against my growing irritation. Still no sign of my little hustler.

"Anyone in particular we're looking for?" Sara asks, nervously biting her lip.

"Yeah," I snap, jaw tight with frustration.

The footage stutters forward, and there I am, a mess, hardly the picture of control or dignity. I run a hand over my face in frustration.

"There. Freeze it."

There she is, sitting alone at the bar. The brunette who had me all revved up only to leave me steaming like an enraged bull. She's waiting for someone, but keeps glancing over at me as I stumble through the crowd.

"Fast forward," I command.

I watch as Rose shifts on her bar stool with a hurried, almost skittish energy. None of her movements look practiced, she seems . . . nervous. Wary. Her eyes flick to me briefly before darting back to her phone in a rapid, unsettled motion. She fucking knows who I am. Then she gets up and heads off to the restroom.

Fast forward ten minutes and she is running out of the bathroom.

"Freeze it there."

9:32 p.m.

Now she's hustling through the lobby in her high heels, making a straight shot for the exit.

She did it. The guilt is practically etched into her pretty features.

While I was distracted by her roving hands and sinful mouth, she was stealing something more than just my attention. Clever girl.

I knew something felt off about her. I saw the red flags and still dived in dick-first anyway. In my self-destructive not-giving-a-fuck state I chose to overlook it all.

A fool, that's what I was.

"Camera sixty-seven. The garage."

"Right away, Mr. Quinn." Clickity-clack with

the nails.

"Pick up the pace, Sara," I growl, my patience worn thin.

I fold and take control of the screen myself, fast-forwarding until—jackpot. My sleek black Porsche peeling out well before I'd caught on to her game.

I zoom in on the driver's seat. Not her, but some asshole guy. Can't see his face. Rage builds inside me. Her lover? Partner in crime? Did she go home and fuck him after getting me all fired up?

"Damn," I mutter.

"Sir, we'll call the cops right away," Sara says, voice quivering as she reaches for the phone.

"Wait."

If I let the cops handle this, they'll follow their standard procedures. But handling this internally means I get to deal out my own brand of justice.

Someone had the balls to target me, using a girl in a cheap dress to do their dirty work. Smart play, but they're about to learn they picked the wrong mark.

My nostrils flare. I didn't misread the signals— her indignation, that was all part of the act. Damn, she deserves an award for that performance.

I'm not handing this over to the police.

"I'll take care of it personally," I mutter, scraping my hand over my stubble. "Just get the footage to security. I'll handle the rest."

Sara pauses, uncertainty flickering in her eyes, but then she nods. "Of course, Mr. Quinn."

Fucking joke. That cunning little actress played me good. And here I was, thinking I had the measure of everything that goes down in my hotels.

I must be laughing to myself because Sara's looking at me like I've lost it.

The truth is, the car doesn't matter. A while back, sure, I would've flipped out over a special edition Porsche getting lifted. But right now, with all this medical drama, nothing seems that important.

But I'm damn sure going to track down that little hustler. I know her face now—her scent, her heat, those soft murmurs she makes in the heat of passion.

And when she rushed out of that bathroom, she left something behind—a black silk shawl. And in a moment I can't quite explain, I grabbed it. Probably has her DNA all over it.

She's deluded if she thinks she can just disappear into the night without a trace.

Her first mistake was picking me as her mark. But her second, far graver mistake was pulling it off.

My little rose is going to sorely regret the day she tried to screw me over.

SEVEN

Connor

It used to be that long showers were my go-to for washing away the bullshit of the day. But that was before I got hit with the kind of news that makes you rethink everything. Health is wealth? Yeah, I got schooled on that recently, hard and fast.

I clench my jaw as scalding water pounds over my back, turning my skin a shade of red that screams for mercy. I crank it hotter.

Music pulses from the surround sound, the throbbing bass vibrating the tiles like a heartbeat. That damn doctor's words keep repeating in my head, no matter how loud I turn up the volume.

"Every case is unique," he said. *"We can't predict how it will progress. All we can do is try to manage it."*

I'm usually exceptional at keeping my emotions in check. Like when some snake who's been working with us for years stabs me in the back—yeah, I get pissed, but then I move on. No use dwelling on it. Same goes for bad press—take it in stride and recalibrate.

But this apparent diagnosis . . . this came out of left field. Uncharted territory. I don't handle unknowns too gracefully.

Funny thing is, I always thought my biggest fears were about my business tanking or something happening to my family—Killian, Mom, my niece Teagan. But now, there's a new terror in town—my own body turning against me.

The irony's not lost on me. Spent all those years in my twenties thinking I was invincible, partying nonstop and pushing every limit without a care in the world. Now, it feels like my body's calling in debts, payback for every wild night and reckless decision.

I drag my fingers through my hair, rinsing the last suds. If this diagnosis crap weren't hanging over my head, I would've already hunted down that sneaky little thief.

I have zero tolerance for liars. It wasn't some random hookup. She just got lucky because I was too wasted to see the red flags.

My guys will find her, it's just a matter of time. And when they do . . . well, I haven't decided how I'll handle her yet.

Part of me wants to teach her a hard lesson for that act she pulled. Bend her over my knee and spank that perky ass red until she's screaming apologies. Then call the cops to haul her away.

But she's taken up enough of my time already. Which is why it pisses me off that she's still on my mind.

Especially here in my private office shower.

With a deep, frustrated groan, I grip my throbbing cock. The thought of punishing her makes me so fucking hard.

With one hand braced against the tiled wall, I stroke myself with savage urgency, like a man possessed, my mind consumed by images of her bending over in front of me, taking every inch of me.

I'm an ass guy—always have been. And she has an ass that was built for slapping and bouncing up and down on my cock.

God, the way she'd moan, her voice husky and breathless as I pound into her tight pussy, gripping her hips and leaving marks behind.

With one final grunt I release hard and fast, spilling my load down the drain.

Damn that woman.

I shut off the water with an irritated swipe and roughly towel off.

It's just bruised my ego. I don't really give a damn about the thief or the car. They're both distractions from what really matters.

I'm half-dressed, stepping into my black slacks, when Killian storms in like he owns the place, all polished in his tuxedo and radiating that post-vacation glow only a week in Hawaii can give you. His cheerfulness is almost offensive.

"Ever heard of knocking, man?" I say, not bothering to lift my gaze as I wrestle with my belt. "Could be balls out naked in here for all you know."

Killian sprawls back in the leather armchair. "Tragically, little brother, your balls aren't anything I haven't seen before."

I yank on my dress shirt with enough force to rip it in half.

"I see your sunny mood hasn't improved."

"If I didn't have to attend this thing, I'd be just fine," I grumble, fumbling with the buttons on my shirt.

We're expected at this massive charity gala at our flagship hotel downtown. Kissing ass is not how I want to spend my night, but duty calls. Heads of state, foreign politicians, A-list celebrities, filthy rich tycoons—all crammed into one room. Security's ironclad, with police escorts, metal detectors, and snipers on the roof.

He gives me that trademark Killian look that peels away the bullshit. "So you gonna tell me what's going on with you? And don't feed me that 'nothing' crap, or I'll put you in a headlock. I still have it in me."

"Everything's fine," I dismiss gruffly, avoiding his eyes as I wrestle with my bowtie. Saying my issue out loud makes it more real. Like opening a can of worms with no way to shove them back in.

"You're a shitty liar, Connor. What's going on?"

I scowl. I need a diversion to throw him off.

There was a time in my twenties when Killian forced me to take an extended break from our business. I was off the rails, partying like a madman and letting it mess with my work. And he was right. It took me months to realize that.

But I can't tell him this problem until I've solved it. As much as he is my brother and we've got each other's backs, he's a businessman.

He'll make sure I'm okay but that might mean stepping back. And that ain't fucking happening.

Might as well make the thief useful. "You want to know what's pissing me off? I got hustled by some chick at the hotel bar."

His expression shifts to confusion. "What happened?"

"I was with this knockout brunette in the restroom. Next thing, my new car's gone. She swiped my keys while I was . . . distracted."

"The custom 911?"

"That's the one."

He pauses, looking like he's trying to decide whether to laugh or knock some sense into me. "Christ, Connor. This self-destruct streak you've been on . . . You hit your midlife crisis early or are you just getting too arrogant for your own damn good?"

"Save the lecture," I grumble. "I'm already aggravated enough."

His eyes drift to my open laptop. He lifts it onto his lap, eyebrows rising. "Figured I'd find you neck-deep in some adult entertainment, not . . . What's this? Searching for 'eye conditions one blue one brown'?"

"The woman . . . she had one green eye, one brown. Never seen anything like it."

"Huh. Sounds strange."

"Quite beautiful," I mutter before I can stop myself.

I wonder if her kids would inherit those bewitching eyes. I shake the thought away, repulsed by my own wandering thoughts.

Killian reclines, a knowing smirk playing on his lips as he observes my discomfort. "And you felt inclined to research her rare ocular condition because . . . ?"

"Just drop it." I brush him off, struggling with my cufflinks.

"Seems like she made quite an impression on you."

"Because she stole my damn car," I snap, yanking back my laptop, low-key panicking at him glimpsing my other browser tabs.

Those mismatched eyes—green and brown like a patch of untouched wilderness—invades my thoughts again. For some stupid reason, I still have her shawl. And in a moment of even greater stupidity, I looked up the religious medal pinned inside it. St. Joan of Arc, symbolizing bravery and strength. More like the bravery to con guys like me.

Killian raises his hands in mock surrender but that damn smirk never fades. "No need to get testy."

"Let's just get this over with," I mutter, shrugging on my tuxedo jacket.

"Lose the chip on your shoulder, will you? I need you sharp and on point tonight, not sulking and draining our liquor reserves."

I let out a rough grunt, running my hands through my still-wet hair. "Fine. I'll play nice with Madison, laugh at his pathetic attempts at humor, and lay it on thick. Whatever it takes."

Charles Madison, New York's newest senator, our new knight draped in a power suit and an American flag pin. If we want smooth operations over the next few years, we need to win this guy over. Zoning permissions, development approvals, casino gambling tax laws—he's got it all in his pocket.

So tonight, I'll turn on the charm full throttle, while trying not to get distracted by those horse teeth of his.

"And his daughter's going to be there," Killian throws in. "Try not to rile her up like you usually do."

I roll my eyes. Ah yes, the virtuous daughter running for Miss World. I only know that riveting detail because she's the hot topic among the reception staff.

Okay, maybe I get a kick out of seeing how hard I can make daddy's little girl blush with a few well-placed innuendos and a sprinkle of that infamous Quinn charm. Just a bit of harmless fun to break the monotony.

"Don't worry, I'll try to keep my charm in check around Madison's baby girl," I say with mock sincerity, placing a hand over my heart. "Even though we both know she secretly loves it."

Killian shoots me an irritated glare. "I'm serious, Connor. No playing Casanova."

He's laying it on thick, but the truth is, the idea of another night of empty flirting and putting on a facade is just exhausting. He doesn't have to worry; I'm not in the mood for any of it.

There's a part of me, maybe a hidden, quieter part, that wonders what life would've been like had I taken a different path. Like that electrician apprenticeship I once eyed right out of high school. A life less complicated, just working hard and getting my hands dirty without all this bullshit. But that's not how it played out.

This is my reality.

Tonight's no different. I'll play the role

expected of me, and not a damn thing will veer me off this path I'm on.

I'm not about to let anything or anyone change me.

EIGHT

Connor

Our sedan weaves through Midtown's chaotic traffic, pulling up outside the Quinn & Wolfe flagship hotel.

Every time I lay eyes on it, it stirs a deep, fierce pride in my chest. It's a fucking monument in the Manhattan skyline, a giant tribute to the empire we've built from scratch.

I remember the first time I saw it immortalized on some sidewalk art stand—cost me ten bucks, but I tipped that artist a hundred. Still have it framed in my en suite bathroom.

We're greeted by a media circus—reporters and camera crews roped off behind barricades, celebs and politicians preening for their fifteen minutes of fame before hitting the open bar.

I step out of the car and it's chaos. Mics shoved in my face, reporters shouting over each other like a pack of hyenas. One idiot tries to slip under the rope and nearly ends up eating pavement.

"Killian! Any truth to those bribery allegations on your latest development?"

"Mr. Quinn! What can you tell us about the allegations of financial misconduct with the gambling commission?"

"Connor! Is it true your bedroom is decorated with diamond-encrusted sculptures of your own penis?"

Now that one gives me pause. I can't let such slander stand. "Swarovski crystals, not diamonds," I deadpan, lifting a brow. "Get your facts straight."

We stroll into the lobby, teeming with New York's crème de la narcissistic crème lazily sipping on Veuve like it's water and basking in their own glory. Oblivious, of course, to the diligent staff scurrying around them, refilling their flutes.

Our designers have gone all out with the usual pretentious bling. Servers weave through with champagne and froufrou snacks that wouldn't fill up a bird. Good thing I had a steak earlier.

Off to the side, a string quartet competes with the din of self-important chatter. I pause for a second to appreciate it before straightening up. Showtime.

An hour deep, and I'm cranking out charm

on autopilot—laughing at terrible jokes, stroking egos left and right. The alcohol's doing its thing, loosening everyone up.

Tonight, though, the mask feels suffocating. These events used to be easy. Now the banal small talk grates, my social skills corroding by the day.

If the doctors are right, there might come a time when I can't even play this game anymore.

I grab another whiskey, having lost count somewhere between the mayor's speech and the wasted socialite inviting me back for the best head of my life—her words, not mine. My drinking hand clearly missed the moderation memo tonight.

Can't really fault it, though, not with who's up ahead.

Senator Madison, in all his artificially tanned, bleached-teeth glory. The guy thinks he's the best thing to happen to this state, a self-righteous blowhard with his head jammed firmly up his own asshole.

Killian gives me a low-key nod, both of us *thrilled* about having to suck up to this guy. So I plaster on my most convincing fake smile.

"Senator, it's an honor to have you here," I say, barging into his little circle. "I hope we're giving you the five-star treatment. Anything you need, you come straight to me, all right?"

Our PR squad, the smooth operators they are, gently herds his entourage away. Not a difficult task—the man's a sedative.

"Well, the cuisine is rather lacking," Madison booms, loud enough for everyone to hear over the music. "What's all this fancy French cuisine? Where's the real American food that fills you up? I've seen bigger portions at a kid's party!"

I muster up a laugh, though inside, I'm fantasizing about smothering him under a mountain of foie gras and truffle oil poutine bites. But hey, business is business.

Rule number one when handling political windbags: Keep smiling, keep nodding, and make them believe they're the center of the universe.

"I'll make sure our Michelin-starred chef gets the memo for next time, sir," I reply, my easy smile not faltering for a second. "In the meantime, let me send out a nice rib eye cooked rare enough to remind you that you're still alive and kicking. Sound good?"

Madison's eyes narrow, scanning for sarcasm, before he lets out a hearty laugh. "Now that's what I'm talking about. Forget the fancy stuff; give me good, straightforward American beef."

I subtly nod to one of our team members who overheard the exchange but has mastered the art of blending into the background.

"We've been following your bold policies closely, Senator," Killian chimes in smoothly. "What you're doing for this state is nothing short of extraordinary. Your leadership is ushering in a new era."

Ah, the second rule when dealing with these types: Lay on the flattery thick and fast.

I resist the urge to roll my eyes.

Madison puffs out his suit, preening. "Yes, well, shaking things up is never easy."

"And it hasn't gone unnoticed," I assure, pouring verbal honey despite my irritation. "Your vision for development is groundbreaking. It's what this city's been crying out for. Quinn & Wolfe stands ready to back your initiatives, Senator."

His eyes gleam as he grabs another glass from a passing server. "And perhaps there are other matters you gentlemen wish to discuss."

Translation: show me the money, boys.

"Of course, we'd love to steal some of your valuable time," Killian says smoothly.

Translation: My wallet's open, just slide over a juicy bribe to grease those wheels for our upcoming projects.

Madison gives us a long once-over, then heaves a dramatic sigh. "I'm extraordinarily busy. My secretaries are run ragged trying to keep pace with my schedule."

Busy with bribery appointments, tanning beds, Viagra refills and, if the rumors hold any truth, a squishing mistress in Long Island. It's not something I've tried myself.

The third rule when stroking egos bigger than my own: Appeal to the universal currency of bribery.

"We understand. No one works harder for this state than you." Killian shovels more shit. "You just say the word how we can help. And please, take unlimited worldwide access to all our hotels —a small token of our immense gratitude."

Madison's eyes gleam as he flashes those veneers. "That's mighty kind," he booms. "I suppose I could squeeze you boys in briefly next week. Over steak at your Broadway spot."

His tone makes it clear we'll grovel and thank him for the "honor."

I hightail it before Madison can spew any more of his brand of charm. The guy's a prime example of money swapped for beauty—looking more like a wax figure that's seen too many hours under a UVA light.

But his daughter, now that one hit the jackpot in the genetics department.

Willow Madison gazes at an ice sculpture across the room, looking like she'd rather dive into it headfirst than socialize. Can't say I blame her.

Good thing daddy's little girl takes after her mama. A former Victoria's Secret angel. I remember drooling over those *Sports Illustrated Swimsuit* posters as a hormone-crazed teen, thinking I'd marry her someday.

When I finally met her at twenty, I reverted to a slobbering adolescent. She was—*is*—the epitome of genetic perfection.

Still can't wrap my head around how she ended up with Madison. Bet she's got some hot pool boy or tennis coach on the side.

But here's her daughter, Willow, looking every bit the angel her mother was. She's everything my little thief isn't—delicate, fair, big doe eyes oozing innocence. Speaking of which . . . why the hell did that troublesome minx just pop into my mind? Thief is not my baseline for women.

"Quite the show, huh?" I remark, joining Willow at the bar. A quick gesture, and the bartender's on it, two bourbons making their way to us.

"Connor Quinn in the flesh. The rumors were true. You're actually here tonight."

"Willow. It's always a pleasure," I shoot back, taking her in. She's poured into a modest number meant to please Daddy Dearest. Funny, the material reminds me of the black silk my little cat burglar was wearing the night she played me.

Yet another visceral flash I didn't invite. I force the interloper from my mind, focusing on the woman in front of me.

"Forced to attend as your father's glamorous plus-one again?"

She offers a wry smile, circling her olive in her

glass. "Mother refused duty tonight. I drew the short straw."

"Then I guess I should be grateful for your 'misfortune.' You look stunning, as always."

She glances up at me with a hint of mischief. "You're not too hard on the eyes yourself, Mr. Quinn. But I think you already know that."

"I clean up all right," I reply, the corners of my mouth ticking up.

"I know your game, Connor Quinn," she says, a touch of challenge in her tone.

My brow arches. "Oh yeah? And what's that?"

"Playing nice with the senator's daughter?"

I let out a low chuckle. "I'm not sure the senator wants me playing with his only daughter."

Madison talks a big game about family values. The Madisons aren't just a political clan; they're a squeaky clean, all-American brand. Willow proudly flaunts her purity ring, "saving" herself for some very lucky bastard down the line.

The bartender slides me another whiskey I don't need. I knock it back, the burn failing to take the edge off.

"Rough night already?" Willow eyes me skeptically.

"Something like that." I tap the glass, debating another.

She smiles sympathetically. "I just spent an hour hearing about vacation homes in the

Hamptons and which designer does the best interiors. Believe me, I get it."

She doesn't. If only shallow conversations with the 1 percent were my biggest problem.

I catch a glimpse of an unwelcome face weaving through the crowd, heading straight for us, and mutter a curse. "Think I could pull off hiding behind that ice swan over there?"

Willow follows my gaze and laughs. "That I'd like to see."

I grin at her. "Or maybe you could protect me for a while."

I'm well aware Killian's going to have my head for this later, but dammit, I'm in self-destruct mode after all the shit of the past few weeks.

She nibbles on her lip. "Hiding behind me might not work so well with you standing out in that Armani. It's kind of hard to miss you." Her cheeks flush as her eyes rake over me.

"Well, shit. I don't want to be distracting," I joke. "But hey, here's a better idea. How about I give you a private tour of our brand-new art gallery upstairs? We can escape for a while."

Willow glances uncertainly at Daddy Dearest before meeting my gaze again. "I'm not sure . . ."

I shrug, giving her an out. "No pressure. Another time, maybe."

One Mississippi, two Mississippi . . .

A flash of rebellion lights her eyes. "You know

what? Let's check out that gallery."

Atta girl.

NINE

Lexi

Kayla's text lights up my phone screen: **Where are you? Vicky's on the warpath.**

I groan, shoving my phone away. I overslept and broke my perfect attendance record. Me—Miss Never-Been-Late in my three years at Vallure PR.

I burst through the doors, feeling like I got slammed by a train. Freaking Murphy's Law—after a sleepless night, I finally crashed at six a.m., only to be woken up by Grace yelling at me. I thought SWAT was at our door.

Now I'm LATE late.

This whole mess with Deano and the car heist is throwing me off—can't sleep, can't eat. I didn't even turn on my vibrator at the lowest setting, too stressed. I didn't dare text Deano to see what happened after I fled the hotel a few nights ago. Ignorance is bliss.

But the cops haven't shown up, and I've paid off

my debt. Every day I feel a little more hope that it's going to be okay.

I just have to trust Deano's savvy enough to keep us clear of the cops. These guys have been at this game for years, it seems.

Inside Vallure, *E! News* blares on the giant TV, our biggest concern being celebs in trouble.

Abigail at reception gives me the stink eye that says *You look like shit*.

Thanks, I'm aware.

I'm sweating out the last few nights' anxiety in this silk blouse as I race through the office war zone, phones ringing, papers flying, people yelling. This place is utter chaos 24/7. We scurry around as if brokering Middle East peace accords when really, we're just polishing some teen pop star's image after a DUI.

My younger self would weep at what I've become.

I race down the hall, raking fingers through my tangled hair, before skidding to a stop outside the boardroom. Vicky will scalp me for being late to her passive aggressive Hour of Power meeting. Where she hints she'll fire us all while claiming we're doing "great."

Give me Michael Scott any day.

Inside, Vicky lords over the room from the head of the table, a venti latte cradled in her manicured claw.

"So glad you could schedule us in, Lexi," she drawls. Thigh-high boots and a bandage dress show off her Pilates-and-cigs body.

"Sorry, got held up," I mumble, shuffling to the back of the room so I don't have to smell the cancer sticks' scent.

Vicky smiles, full of ice. "By a gunman?"

I slump into the chair beside Kayla, avoiding Vicky's glare.

"Well, if you're done bringing your personal issues to work, let's continue," Vicky snaps. "Brooke, update on Gina Malone?"

Our top priority right now is managing the PR crisis around influencer Gina and her controversial new fitness app, Butt Buildr.

Brooke tosses her red hair over one shoulder. As the agency's golden girl, she leads most accounts. "It's handled. I secured her an exclusive tell-all with *Fitness Weekly*. She'll cry about being just a girl chasing her dream who got duped by those devious tech devils. It's not her fault the app didn't work."

Butt Buildr claimed to assess the structure of users' buttocks via phone pics, and suggested tailored exercise routines based on their "analysis." You pick your dream butt, it spits out a routine. Total bullshit, experts say.

Vicky gives her seal of approval with a satisfied sip. "Perfect. Make those geeks the bad guys. Turn it into a comeback—technology gone wrong, courageous woman perseveres, yada yada. Announce Butt Buildr 2.0 while you're at it."

She fixes her piercing gaze on me. "Lexi, you'll support Brooke on this. Seems like you've got the bandwidth since you sauntered in twenty minutes late."

Five minutes, max.

"Of course, happy to help," I reply with a tight smile.

One day I'll tell Vicky where to shove it and moonwalk out of this place.

But not today.

Outside the window, the NYU psych building gives me the evil eye. *"Remember your dreams, Lexi?"* it seems to sneer.

I recall, full-on teen angst–style, staring up at it, years ago. I pictured my future self— some badass psychologist striding out those doors, groundbreaking research under her arm, and slightly bigger boobs.

I had dreamed of studying psychology and becoming a therapist one day—maybe a clinical psychologist to help people with mental health issues, a school counselor working with kids, or a health psychologist focusing on wellness. I knew I wasn't brilliant or rich enough to be a psychiatrist. But I was fascinated by human behavior and the complexity of the brain. Science was my best subject. I got accepted into a psych program in North Dakota for almost affordable tuition.

But after Dad died and Mom went into care, life derailed those plans. I deferred school, again and again, until *poof*—dream gone. Instead, I took a PR gig shilling beer in push-up bras to leering frat boys.

I eventually clawed my way into actual PR work.

PR was about as far from my dream career as you could get. Mind you, no one stands up in high school Careers class and declares they want to be a prostitute or drug smuggler either.

At least pitching beer, I was honest about selling my soul. Now my outfits are classier, but let's not kid ourselves—it's still soul-sucking.

Vallure PR does crisis management for celebs caught pants-down in alleys, parks, and restrooms. We're basically a PR firm for morons who never grasped zippers.

There was the boyband member caught in a compromising position with an inflatable doll— that was "artistic exploration."

The family-friendly comedian snapped with a sex worker was just "discussing scripts."

The naked politician found ass-up in a fountain was "researching architecture."

Such is life.

I carefully compose my features into polite

interest as Vicky and Brooke volley tasks about rehabbing Gina's rep. I jot down notes for the rest of the meeting, hoping to redeem myself after this morning's lateness.

Kayla discreetly clears her throat beside me.

Vicky's head whips around, eyes flashing. "Don't interrupt."

Kayla's eyes widen. "Oh, I wasn't! Just had a little tickle in my throat."

Vicky's face is frozen, but a muscle in her jaw ticks. "That's nice. Any other bodily outbursts to share before we proceed?"

"No," Kayla says softly, properly chastised.

I squeeze her arm under the table in solidarity. Vicky's in rare form today, which doesn't bode well for what I'm about to do.

"Coffee," Kayla hisses when the meeting is finally over.

"Give me five," I murmur, then rush ahead and call out, "Vicky, got a minute?" as the others flee.

She narrows her eyes. "Make it quick."

I'm tempted to latch on to her ankles like a whiny toddler until she agrees to my raise. But PR pros have more dignity than that. Maybe.

"I know I was late, and I sincerely apologize," I say, trailing after her. "It's literally the first time since I started here."

She waves dismissively. "Get to the point."

I swallow hard. "Maybe we could sit—"

"Walk." She doesn't even glance back.

"Right." I launch into my rehearsed spiel, hating how grovel-y I sound. "I've been working really hard, early, late, weekends too . . . Hit all my goals, you said so yourself. So I hoped I could get a salary bump to reflect that."

She stops abruptly and I nearly crash into her.

For a long moment she just stares at me in silence, and I worry she'll fire me on the spot. My confidence withers under her gaze.

Finally, she speaks, voice calmly pleasant. "A raise? You think you deserve a raise?" She clucks her tongue in disappointment.

"I hoped—"

"I've invested everything back into this company, you know why?"

I stare at her blankly, panic rising. Where's she going with this? "Um, why?"

"Because I consider you all *family*." She pauses, letting the word sink in for effect. "My blood, sweat, tears, and soul built this place. And I've invested just as much into mentoring each and every one of you."

I nod while imagining pouring rat poison into her morning triple-shot soy latte.

"Knowledge is dollars," she says.

"I appreciate that, but I'm still paid less than—"

"I took a chance hiring you," she interrupts, holding up a hand. "I could've easily found someone more qualified."

"But with Shelly gone, I'm doing her work too —"

"And getting more exposure and experience."

I'm dangerously close to losing it and throwing myself on the floor, thrashing until she caves or calls security.

There's no plan B here. I need this raise.

Sure, I feel temporary relief now that Deano's hustle meant covering this care home installment. But I still have a ticking time bomb. Another massive payment comes due in five months, twenty-eight days and roughly six nerve-shredding hours.

Rumor has it Vicky motorboated a waitress at last year's Christmas party. For a wild moment, I consider ripping open my blouse, shrieking *"Will this help convince you?"*

She fixes me with a stern, disappointed gaze. "You're practically getting one-on-one training with me, Lexi. Girls would commit murder for your job. Think hard about that. I have meetings. We'll discuss this another time."

And she's off, trotting down the hall, leaving me quivering in frustration. Well, that was a complete waste of time and dignity.

I dig my nails into my palms, willing myself not to break down as she disappears around the corner. I think about asking the maintenance guy where the rat poison is kept.

Hot tears prickle as I storm down the hall. Breathe in, breathe out.

I'm monumentally fucked. Vicky just crushed my last shred of hope under her expensive heels.

Fingers suddenly squeeze my ribs and I yelp, whirling around so fast I nearly crash into the giant plant.

Kayla frowns. "I'm guessing the chat with the Supreme Leader didn't go so great?"

I let out a bitter laugh. "Ya think? She shot down my raise fast."

"Crap. Well, there has to be something . . ." Kayla snaps her fingers. "Ooh, what if you pretended to have another job offer? She might counter to keep you."

"I'm applying for millions of other jobs. I just don't know if I can call her bluff."

I dramatically slump against the plant.

Kayla shakes her head, brow furrowed. "There has to be something we can figure out."

"I'm open to creative solutions, short of prostitution," I say. My lips form an upside-down smile and I tilt my head, considering. At this point, even that's not totally off the table. I'm already an accomplice to grand theft auto—it's a slippery slope.

Before Kayla can respond, a cackle from Abigail interrupts. Our gazes dart to where the team is gathered.

"What's got them so riled up?" I ask.

She shrugs. "Let's see."

"What's everyone gawking at?" I ask, sidling up to the herd clustered around the lobby TV.

I crane my neck to see what celeb nonsense has them transfixed.

I suck in a sharp breath, stomach dropping out my ass with a wet splat. Instead of a D-lister, Connor Quinn's handsome, brooding face fills the screen.

Oh, fuck.

Just the sight of those eyes behind aviators makes my knees wobble. Heat floods my veins, followed by icy dread.

His chiseled jaw is hard as granite, full lips pressed thin. The man looks like he's stepped straight out of my filthiest fantasies.

Why the hell is he on CNN? Please, universe, do not say this is about his stolen car. That would take today from dismal to toss-myself-off-a-cliff bad.

Oh god, what if they trace the car back to me via my silk shawl with the lucky St. Joan medal Dad gave me? Maybe the cops will think I'm a saint, not a thief. The patron saint of hotwiring.

You're spiraling. No way a stolen car makes national headlines. *Breathe.*

I spent hours researching car theft insurance, trying to salve my conscience a bit. I looked up

Quinn's net worth, his car collection—he's got a Jay Leno–level stash. So I only kind of feel like human garbage now.

"What's this about?" I ask Abigail casually, despite my pounding heart.

"Mmm, Connor Quinn," she purrs. "So freakin' hot."

"Yeah, but why's he in the news?"

Images flash up and— Oh god, it's the hotel where we . . . met.

My stomach twists as Willow Madison's polished, elegant face appears beside a broody Connor. They make a striking couple.

"Connor and Willow hooked up!" Abigail squeals. "Lucky freaking Willow. Someone caught it on audio. It's bleeped out on TV but you can hear everything online, it's so dirty." She fans herself.

"Willow Madison, the senator's daughter?"

"No, silly! Willow Madison, Miss USA!"

What. The. Actual. Fuck?

Didn't take him long to move on, did it?

Well, that was a stupid thought. Move on from what, exactly?

Be glad he's found a new plaything.

I force my face into cool indifference, like I'm totally unfazed by this "news." Which is ridiculous, since there's no way anyone could guess what happened between me—Lexi Sullivan, lowly PR assistant—and Connor Quinn, billionaire playboy currently plastered across the CNN headlines.

"I better get to work," I murmur to no one in particular.

TEN

Lexi

It's like popping a zit you know will crater yet lacking the willpower to stop.

That sums up me, scrolling the blow-by-blow of Quinn's steamy tryst with Miss America. Their R-rated convo leaked everywhere. Ninety percent too explicit without bleeps.

This is blowing up exponentially. It's like if Mother Teresa, or whoever the popular saint is these days, launched an OnlyFans. America's sweetheart caught with billionaire playboy at a political gala with her senator dad there? Cha-ching, the hits keep coming.

It doesn't help that there's photos of them too, looking cozy.

And me, sadist that I am, just can't look away. I make the conscious decision to put on my headset and seek out the leaked audio. Two clicks and I'm hit with static before Connor's velvet voice slips into my ear.

I wince. Ugh. Well, at least I don't have to feel guilty about leaving him wounded in the bathroom.

"*My angel* my ass," I mutter.

Kayla shoots me a look and I wave her off, irritation simmering.

Clearly he lives up to the playboy reputation, him and that damn husky drawl of his. Churns through women weekly.

I minimize the video to pretend I'm working. But Quinn keeps whispering explicit promises in my ear, along with Willow's breathy giggles.

I know I should click away, but like rubbernecking a highway wreck, I can't seem to stop torturing myself. Imagining his hands on her body, giving her all the top-shelf orgasms.

Two excruciating minutes of audio torture drag by. By the end, I'm numb, mouse clutched in a death grip.

This is great. Quinn's got bigger issues than a stolen car. He's too busy defiling Miss America to care.

He's already forgotten your name, let alone giving a crap enough to hurt you.

I breathe a small sigh of relief and jab my mouse to close the window. Stupid thing is frozen. I need this shit off my screen so I can forget it.

Maybe I'll just bash my head on my desk until

sweet amnesia takes over.

Before I can enact that plan, fingers snap inches from my face, cutting between me and the screen. I jolt back with a yelp.

Vicky looms over me, eyes narrowed.

"When you're done drooling over Connor Quinn, I'd appreciate getting that report before I retire," she snaps, crimson talons tapping my monitor. "Or do you need a couple more minutes to wrap things up?"

Heat creeps up my neck as laughter ripples through nearby desks. "What? No, I wasn't listening to . . . that."

"Really?" She eyes my screen pointedly. "Because your little window box there says, *Connor and Willow: Uncensored Live Audio*."

Crap. No point lying now.

Vicky struts off, her hair bobbing with each step.

I sink lower in my chair as the office buzzes with barely contained amusement. So much for subtlety.

Taking a deep breath, I channel my mortification into work, attacking my keyboard with enough force to dislodge some keys. Why should I care about Connor and Willow's sexy shenanigans? It's none of my business.

I hit send on the report just as Kayla approaches.

"Jeez, you doofus," she teases, perching on my desk.

"Everyone's listened to it," I say defensively. As if to prove my point, a squeal sounds from reception. "See? Abigail's listening to it right now."

Kayla gives a low laugh. "It was pretty hot. Connor Quinn definitely knows how to make a lady sing."

My stomach flips. Did they have sex? Hard to tell from the audio snippet. Maybe they were just . . . playing a very convincing game of Twister.

"Good for Willow," I reply sarcastically, feigning interest in random papers on my desk.

Connor

If there was ever a time to duck out and join a monastery, now's clearly it. Every eyeball is glued to me as I stride for the elevators to the executive floor. Because of course they fucking are.

The reception area's big-screen is broadcasting some news segment about Willow and me. "Did Willow and billionaire hotel magnate Connor Quinn get up to no good at the gala?" some bubbly blond anchor speculates.

I lean in toward the receptionist. "How about we find something worth watching on that screen?" I suggest, barely concealing my irritation.

"Absolutely, Mr. Quinn!" he blurts, his hands shaking as he scrambles for the remote.

The chatter dies instantly, replaced by a tense silence that's been the theme of the day. Everyone's acting like they'd rather jump out a window than make eye contact with me. Try to start a casual conversation, and it's like I'm suggesting they walk across burning coals—pure panic.

Except for the girls in marketing who have been ogling me like I wandered through stark-ass nude just for them. At this rate, I should start charging for the show, considering how many flushed faces I've seen today.

Does a single damn employee have actual revenue-generating work, or has today's main event just become watching me react to the latest tabloid fodder?

As I lock eyes with one of the accountants, her eyes widen like she's seen the Candyman, not her boss. And there goes her giant Smartwater, spilling across the desk. Maybe HR needs to vet for steadier hands during interviews.

I raise an eyebrow at her, and she dives for cover behind her screen.

What a damn mess this morning's turned into. I've had Killian in my ear for a solid hour ranting about "recklessness" and "reputation hemorrhaging."

Sure, the leaked audio mess is on me. The idiot

behind it has been ID'd, and by the end of the day, they're going to deeply regret ever crossing me.

Stepping out onto the executive floor, I spot one of my security guys loitering near my office. "Jim," I acknowledge with a nod.

He shifts from foot to foot, uneasy. "Boss, about the car thief situation."

"You got her?"

"Not quite . . ." He trails off awkwardly.

I stop in my tracks, arms crossed. "'Not quite' is an impotent way of saying you've got jack shit so far. Unless you discovered a severed limb with my car key fob clutched in its cold dead fingers?"

He looks even more sheepish. "She paid her bar tab in cash, so we can't get a lead on a credit card. Our bartender that night mentioned she seemed pretty on edge at the bar. Kept looking around nervously. Facial recognition didn't pull up any criminal history. We're running on the assumption she took the keys, but the only real lead is the timing."

I grunt, my irritation growing. "So, she's a ghost? Vanished into thin air?"

He continues. "CCTV lost her at the street corner. No sign of her meeting anyone else. We'll keep at it, boss, I'm confident we'll find her."

I exhale slowly, trying to keep my cool. Just where the hell are you hiding with my car, you scheming little enigma?

Before I can blow a fuse, my assistant hurries over, looking like she's walking on eggshells. "Sir, I apologize for the intrusion, but Senator Madison insists on seeing you downtown in half an hour."

The fury returns in full force. "He did what now?"

She looks like she's bracing for impact, gripping her MacBook like a shield. "He was rather blunt about it. Made it sound like you don't have a choice in the matter."

Just what I need.

Lexi

"What's with her?" Kayla asks, jerking her chin at Vicky's office.

I glance up from drafting a proposal to rehab some rich brat's image after her fifth DUI this year. Just another productive, wholesome day at the office.

Vicky's grinning at her screen like she won the lottery, Super Bowl, and a date with Idris Elba all at once. She's been acting strange for hours— deliriously happy.

"Has she been doing coke in the bathroom again?" I ask.

Kayla snickers. "Coke or cock, you think?"

After a few years in PR, I've seen truly wild

antics. And 90 percent of them are just Vicky.

The reception phone rings, and Abigail's sudden intake of breath makes my ears prick up. What now?

In a voice rivaling a Disney princess on helium, she chirps, "Send her straight up!" She actually fist-pumps the air after hanging up.

I glance at Kayla.

"So we have a new client then," she muses. "That explains Vicky."

"Seems like it," I reply lightly.

Vicky's door flies open with a bang. She emerges, eyes wild, and charges toward reception. "Hold my calls!" she barks over her shoulder, zooming past.

The elevator dings, and through the blurry divider I glimpse a parade of tailored suits. Maybe Vicky organized a reverse harem of Wall Street guys.

I take a big gulp from my lukewarm soda can, craning my neck for a better look.

Before I can speculate, Brooke strides over. "Drop everything, we have Willow Madison in the boardroom. I need you to assist me."

I choke, spraying Diet Coke across my keyboard. Brooke looks appalled.

"THE Willow Madison, Miss America?" I rasp.

"No, the Willow Madison who runs a sock folding service in Kentucky," Brooke snarks. "*Of course* that Willow! Now come on."

I'm rooted in place, unable to move. The last thing I want is a front row seat to the Willow Madison Reputation Rescue Tour. I don't need the sordid details from the woman herself.

Brooke grabs my arm, propelling me up. I dig my heels in reflexively, still processing this bombshell.

"She's using us for damage control?" I sputter.

Why am I being so weird? It's fine.

"Now's not the time for questions. Grab your laptop and move!"

She drags me away from the safe haven of my desk. I desperately look around for an escape route. I could always just quit on the spot. Or pretend to faint dramatically and hope my acting rivals Scarlett Johansson's.

"What the fuck is wrong with you?" Brooke hisses as I lag behind. "Did you day-drink or something?"

"My stomach's upset suddenly," I lie.

"Suck it up 'til later," she snaps. She whips back around, her dress straining against her backside as she storms on like a woman on a mission—one I desperately want no part of.

I trail, pulse thundering, gripped by irrational dread. This week's been a series of nerve-racking moments, and it doesn't take much to tip me over the edge. Any reminder of my sins sends me spiraling lately. And in a way, Willow is a glaring neon sign.

Brooke pushes open the door. Inside, there are suits everywhere, Senator Madison's weathered face, Willow looking every bit the untouchable beauty . . .

But then my eyes land on someone in the far corner, and my body locks up.

No.

Fucking.

Way.

Connor Quinn.

His brooding gaze lands on me, brows furrowing. Then his eyes blaze with recognition and . . .

Rage.

ELEVEN

Lexi

I stand paralyzed in the doorway, laptop clutched in my white-knuckled grip as I meet Connor's equally stunned expression.

His jaw is clenched, muscle twitching as he grapples for words, opening and closing his mouth in a silent yet terrifying snarl.

He looks utterly mindfucked—a volatile mix of fury, disbelief, and god knows what else swirling across his unfairly handsome features.

What the hell do I do?

Keep staring him down?

Make a run for it?

In this split second, I realize there are only a few ways this could play out, and none look good for me:

Scenario One—Clueless Quinn. He was too trashed to recall our tryst properly. Outcome: Bruised ego that he can't remember my face and vagina, but no jail time. But judging by the flared nostrils and pulsing forehead vein, I'm ruling that one out.

Scenario Two—Pissy Quinn. Remembers me and is resentful I bailed, but his car wasn't part of a crime spree. Outcome: Could tank my job, but no criminal charges.

And last but not least:

Scenario Three—Apocalypse Quinn. Remembers everything and wants my head on a spike for the theft. Goodbye pencil skirts, hello orange jumpsuit.

I nudge my glasses up, praying they'll make me unrecognizable. No such luck. Because the way Quinn is glaring at me across the table, I should start clearing closet space for that prison jumpsuit.

Vicky jumps up, sending my anxiety through the roof. "Senator, Willow, allow me to introduce Brooke Jackson. She'll be spearheading this campaign. You're in excellent hands."

"Senator, Miss Madison." She greets them smoothly, then turns her charm on Quinn and the others. "Mr. Quinn, gentlemen, a pleasure."

I suck in a breath as dread sinks lower. Connor and Willow must be an item if he's here. What a horrible cheating sleaze.

"Pleasure? This is a goddamn circus!" the senator explodes, face tomato-red as he smooths his tie over his belly.

Brooke emits the softest hitch in her breath. Our unflappable Brooke, flapped.

Beside him, Willow looks ready to flee, a startled doe in virginal white. Daddy clearly picked that buttoned-up outfit to really sell the "wholesome daughter led astray" image.

She pats down a stray hair from her severely braided blond 'do. I sympathize with her horrible situation. No one deserves that. The press are assholes. I would say the person who recorded it is too, but maybe they were in a desperate situation like me. In the end, maybe we're all some degree of asshole.

And then there's Connor. He finally shifts his death stare from me to acknowledge Brooke. He leans back in his chair, drumming his fingers impatiently. Clearly Mr. Big Shot, in his sharp navy tailored suit, has better places to be.

"And this is Lexi, Brooke's assistant," Vicky throws in, as an afterthought.

Connor's icy gaze snaps back to me, morphing from suave to downright murderous in an instant.

Oh god. This is really bad. I barely swallow my shriek of alarm.

"Lexi?" he repeats, tone lethally calm.

This is it, isn't it? Scenario Three. The one where I'm found out and possibly murdered in a conference room.

"That's me!" I stammer, feeling like I'm about to regurgitate my grilled cheese sandwich.

Connor's jaw is clenched so tight it might shatter, his eyes drilling into me like shards of ice.

I've never seen a man look so bewildered yet enraged over me. It's not a good experience.

Yeah, he knows exactly who I am. My goose is cooked. Any second now, he'll out me to the room.

I plaster on a tortured smile, bracing for the axe to fall. Fuuuuuck. Will he demand I'm fired? Have me arrested?

Even if he doesn't have enough to go to the cops—and since my front door hasn't been busted down, it seems he doesn't—he can get me booted off this account. And Vicky would fire my ass faster than I could plead wrongful termination.

My only hope is denying everything and pray he lacks evidence.

I slide into a seat as far from Connor as possible, squeezing next to some lawyer looking guy. I open my laptop, but my shaking fingers won't cooperate.

Just blend in, be the invisible assistant, not the girl who played the big bad billionaire then fled.

"My daughter says you're the best for these situations," the senator says, leathery face glistening.

"We are," Vicky assures him with a placating smile. "We deal with these types of hiccups allllll the time."

The senator grunts. "My PR team isn't cut out for this circus. You'll have to coordinate with them." He pauses, his face turning a purplish shade of red I've never seen before. "Sadly, my Willow is too trusting. There are smarmy rakes in this city all too eager to take advantage of such a beautiful girl and tarnish her purity."

The room inhales sharply, collectively bracing itself. I sneak a peek at Connor. His jaw clenches, leashed rage simmering beneath the surface.

"Willow's been under stress," the senator continues. "Her grandmama passed away two years ago, and her charity work's been weighing on her. It leaves her vulnerable." He looks around, clearly expecting everyone to agree with his assessment.

My brows knit together as my fingers hover over the keys, wondering how detailed to get.

"This is very upsetting for us all. My wife is hysterical." He slams his first down, nearly ejecting me from my seat. "I would never have taken my daughter to that event if I'd known some playboy shmuck would set his sights on her!"

I hold my breath, stuck between shock and astonishment. I can't believe he's saying all this with Connor right here in the room.

I keep my eyes glued to my screen, too scared to even sneak a peek at Connor's reaction. In fact, everyone's avoiding eye contact, focusing on anything but the ticking time bomb sitting at the end of the table.

This does not bode well for me. I already poked this bear by playing Connor—the senator is making it exponentially worse.

Down comes the beefy fist again, loaded with extra gusto. "This mess makes my coalition look like we're in cahoots with Hooters!" he roars, spittle raining down. "My opponents are having a field day! I've got Christian delegates withdrawing their support, left and right! My good reputation dragged through the mud! And the same man tries getting in bed with me! Me!"

My eyes snap to the senator, but he seems oblivious to how that sounded.

Awkward tension suffocates the room, dense enough to pass out from. I feel sorry for the two guys stuck between him and Connor.

Then it hits me—Connor's seating at the far end of the table is deliberate. He's been relegated to the naughty corner. I suppose he has been rather naughty.

If I wasn't quaking in fear, this would be downright hilarious.

"Dad." Willow's voice cuts through the tension, sadly ineffectively. "Stop. Please."

But we're past the point of no return.

"I'm keeping my cool out of respect for your

daughter, sir," Connor drawls, his voice eerily calm despite the promise of murder in his eyes. "That's why we're here. Let's get this over with and make a plan. I'll do whatever it takes to clear Willow's name. The accountability stops with me."

I don't miss Willow's grateful smile his way. My hands clench the laptop harder.

"What kind of man preys on a young woman like her?" The senator is working himself into an impressive frenzy now, looking like someone should hook him up to a blood pressure cuff.

Tense silence follows, everyone assuming it's rhetorical. We stay frozen, as if sudden motions might set either of them off.

The guy next to me crosses his arms, and I hear a weird squelching sound from his armpit. I hope to god everyone knows that wasn't me.

Even I have to admit, the man's going overboard. Willow's not exactly a kid—she's what, twenty-four? Two years younger than me. But she just sits there, not moving a muscle.

Vicky opens and closes her mouth wordlessly.

"She's too good for you, Quinn!" He jabs a sausage finger Connor's way, trying to spear him from across the table. "Who do you think you are?" Each word is punctuated with spit flying across the table.

"I don't argue that," Connor grits out. "Your daughter's a much better person than me. My patience is wearing thin here. Can we hurry this up and make a plan? We're all busy people."

He looks equal parts bored and irritated. He's got this dangerous charisma about him that's even more intense than I remember. His bronzed arm sports a flashy Rolex, gold catching the light with each agitated drum of his fingers. As if he's got better places to be than getting scolded like a naughty rake.

Unwanted memories flood my mind. Connor's dilated eyes devouring me, his hard body against mine, the primal sounds of pleasure he made. His dick felt huge.

Heat rises in my cheeks, and I squirm in my seat, trying to push away the image of us fucking. What the hell is wrong with me?

The senator's still not finished roasting Connor. "You with your flashy cars and tacky penthouses, with hot tubs full of champagne and hookers! You young punks have no sense of decency!" he yells, jowls quivering. "I run this city, not you spoiled playboys! Walking around like you own the place, chasing after anyone's backside who gives you a smile!"

Wow. My eyes dart back and forth between the two power players, heart pounding. The two men caught in the middle are frozen, probably holding their breath.

Driven by nervous energy, I start typing the

names of the attendees before realizing this is definitely *not* the time for taking notes.

I freeze mid-type, cringing.

Connor looks calm yet violently enraged. One loafer rests lazily on his knee, suit stretching over those solid thighs that pinned me to the wall just nights ago.

But his breaths are measured, jaw granite. "For the record, I've never had hookers in hot tubs. That was media exaggerated," he says calmly. "I'm quite discerning in my choices." His gaze cuts to me, voice dropping to a menacing tone. "For the most part."

I feel like I've been electrocuted.

"Now, let's focus on solutions so we can get on with our day," Connor directs the table, his deep voice thick with impatience. "But make no mistake, I don't tolerate betrayals of trust."

I don't miss the dagger-sharp edge when he says *trust*. Aimed right at my face. I slink lower, wishing the chair would swallow me.

"I'd prefer my own team handle this, but Willow insisted on your firm. So tell me—how exactly do you verify integrity?" Even as he speaks to Vicky, his glare is fixed on me. Probably picturing one billion ways to end me. "Why should I trust your people?"

I swallow hard, my bobbing throat surely visible to all.

"We have a very thorough screening process," Vicky lies smoothly. Our "rigorous" process meaning hiring any warm body, like stoner Jess. "Only the best make it through. We'll share it with your legal team."

Connor snorts derisively. "I'm sure you're very selective." His husky drawl drips with sarcasm.

A shiver skitters down my spine at his menacing tone. He's toying with me, a big cat playing lazily with his trapped mouse.

I'm *so* getting fired after this. But he wants me to sweat first.

Brooke smooths her skirt. "You've come to the right place, Mr. Quinn."

Connor barely acknowledges her, his eyes coolly critiquing a Butt Buildr ad on the wall. "I can see that. What a comforting indication I've found the right agency to spearhead my reputation turnaround."

Despite everything else going on, I shrink in my seat in shame.

But Brooke is unfazed by his sarcasm and dives right into her pitch. "Let me outline some strategies for immediate image repair," she continues bullishly. "I recommend issuing a heartfelt public apology, complemented by a significant gesture—like donations to a charity that's topical right now. Give the public something positive to focus on right away."

The senator grunts. "It'll need to be the apology of the century!"

Connor's handsome face remains carved in hard, unforgiving lines.

I keep my eyes glued to my laptop, pretending to work but really just hitting random keys.

Get through this now. Panic later.

Brooke concludes her pitch. "Then, we strategically rehabilitate both your images— spotlight your leadership, philanthropy ..." As she talks, the details swim out of focus.

Connor responds with yet another one of his signature grunts as Brooke finishes.

"And you." He pins me with a look so intense it feels like a physical force. "What's your take, Linda?"

I choke on thin air. Who the fuck is Linda? Do we have a Linda? "Uh, it's Lexi. And I agree with Brooke's strategy, Mr. Quinn."

"*Lexi*. Right." His tone oozes disgust. "No original thoughts in that head of yours then? Just gonna nod along?"

Before I can respond, Vicky interjects. "Brooke and I will handle the strategy. Lexi is one of our junior team members."

But Connor's not having it. "You included her in this meeting. I want to hear her perspective. Let's have it then—how would you fix up this PR mess?"

Vicky pales at his abrasiveness, but nods for me to speak up. I swallow down my nerves. What's his game here?

I'm about to parrot Brooke's scripted apology-plus-donations tactic when defiance grips me. Maybe it's the steel in Connor's glare, like he's daring me to challenge him.

I shut my laptop and clasp my hands together, trying to project calm.

"Sure, throwing money at the problem might help optics," I say evenly. "But people see through publicity stunts these days. We need a game plan that's more about rewriting the story than just hiding the messy parts."

With a fake smile, I float my next idea to the group. "Now, we all know Connor's got this . . . reputation. Why not use that to our advantage?"

Vicky gasps, looking ready to pass out. But Connor silences her, laser-focused on me. I feel sweat pooling in my pits, but I keep my chin raised.

"Let's leverage the extremes of their public images," I say, smiling at Willow. "The public sees you as a wholesome role model—Harvard grad, Miss America, human rights advocate. A paragon of virtue."

"Now I'm a bad meme," Willow whimpers.

I smile sympathetically at Willow while ignoring Connor's death glare. "But tabloids paint Connor in a . . . less flattering light."

I don't dare look at Vicky.

"And how exactly am I painted?" Connor asks, his tone dangerously soft, like velvet wrapped around a knife.

I force an innocent expression even as my knees shake under the table. What am I doing, poking the beast?

"Well, the media loves spinning stories of your champagne-fueled hot tub orgies and revolving door of lingerie models," I say breezily. "The tabloids speculating about your threesomes probably gets you more press than your *Forbes* achievements. Terrible rumors, of course."

Loaded silence follows. Even the suits fight grins. Vicky looks one shade shy of a stroke.

Connor's face remains stone, but his jaw feathers.

Brooke tries to jump in, "Maybe we should—"

"No, I want to hear this plan," Connor sneers. "Tell me, *Lexi*. I'm on the edge of my seat here."

Refusing to squirm, I continue. "We put a spin on it. Play up the angle of Willow, the symbol of morality, transforming the notorious playboy Connor into a reformed man." I even spread my hands as if envisioning the headline. "Through love."

"It could work," Willow chimes in bubbly agreement. At least someone appreciates my creativity, even if it involves whoring out her love life.

"How?" her father bellows.

"Is that all you've got?" Connor growls, eyes blazing blistering contempt.

Heat floods my cheeks. Asshole.

Vicky moves to intervene, but Connor silences her with a raised palm.

I straighten my spine. "The facts remain, Mr. Quinn. You got caught with your Armani trousers down, quite literally, at an important event."

Vicky makes a strangled sound.

"So, we spin it. Make it a love story, not just some fling."

"Willow rescues me from fast cars and casual sex, we skip off into the sunset, and what? I'm a saved man?" Connor surveys me calmly, cocking one arrogant brow. "Is that the fairy tale?"

My pulse leaps at the car reference.

I hold firm. "That's the idea. Paint it as true love conquering all."

He smirks. "Who's to say it isn't true love?"

My breath stalls. Well damn. Wasn't expecting him to lean into it.

"In fact," he drawls, "no other woman has even come close lately. They've all been entirely forgettable." His wolfish smile widens.

Jerk.

The senator makes another noise of deep displeasure while Willow smirks.

"That's great!" Vicky chirps.

I ignore them and meet Connor's gaze coolly, staring him down like we're the only two people in the room. "Perfect. Then I suggest going very public with your new relationship. Declare your undying love from the rooftops. We can even stage a loved-up photoshoot on the Empire State Building or somewhere fabulously romantic. Really sell the love story."

All eyes turn to Connor, waiting for Mount Quinn to blow.

"How strategic of you." I can't tell if he's being sarcastic. His jaw tightens up, solid as rock. "Willow, is this really what you want?"

"I think it'll work," she says softly, gazing at him adoringly. "We fake being in love."

Yeah, no faking required there.

He lets out a heavy sigh, the sound loaded with frustration, and turns to her dad. "Senator?"

"The last thing I want is my daughter associated with the likes of you!" A bit rich considering Willow's smitten gaze.

Connor levels him with a dangerous glare, almost making me feel bad for the old guy.

"This better work," the senator blusters. "Or you'll find yourself in a lot of hot water, my boy. I need these ridiculous headlines about my Willow off the internet!"

A charged look passes between them, rife with

unspoken threats. I wonder if Connor's playing along just for Willow's sake or if the Senator has some leverage over him.

"We're done here," Connor declares abruptly, standing.

"Mr. Quinn, wait!" Vicky blurts, leaping up.

My eyes widen. What does that mean?

"My legal team will handle the contract. If Willow wants your services, I'll finance it." He nods curtly at Vicky.

Holy shit, am I off the hook here?

"We'll get right on it, sir," Brooke assures him.

Connor flashes her a wolfish grin. Does he reflexively flirt with every woman?

Then his eyes spear me again, pinning me in place. "Lexi, stay back. I need a word."

My pulse kicks wildly. Spoke too soon. The beast still wants a bite.

The senator stands, puffing out his chest. "Any meetings need me there." His gut peeks out, trousers riding low.

Connor's not having any of it, though. His eyes flash dangerously. "With respect, Senator, I don't answer to you. I'll do what it takes to restore your daughter's reputation, but you don't dictate my actions."

Testosterone thickens the air, the older man spluttering while Connor remains unmoved. An unstoppable asshole meets an immovable dick.

"Now see here—"

"Enough." Connor's arctic tone brokers no room for argument. "This discussion is over. Lexi, stay behind."

Vicky's voice is barely a whisper. "Should I stay too?" I've never heard her so meek before.

"No one else is required," Connor states with finality.

The room seems to shrink away from him in fear.

My mouth goes bone dry as his eyes fix on me. The trapped little mouse under the predator's glare.

TWELVE

Connor

"Dad, let's give them some privacy, shall we?" Willow guides her father out, shooting me a sweet smile.

"Appreciate it, Willow," I say, my gratitude genuine.

Vicky and Brooke look ready to piss themselves as I shut the door, leaving me alone with Little Miss Thief. She's clearly not trotted out for major clients often.

"Sit."

She bristles. "I'm not a dog."

"No, you're more of a sneaky little honey badger stealing what isn't yours."

Panic flashes in those expressive eyes before she quickly masks it. "I've got no idea what you're talking about."

"I think you do. Sit down."

Reluctantly, she perches on the edge of her

chair, laptop balanced precariously on her lap.

I position myself between her and any possible escape route, casually leaning against the table.

Is this all part of some setup? The car, the leaked audio, her sudden appearance on Willow's team . . . What the hell is really going on here? Is one of our competitors trying to screw me over in some elaborate scheme?

"Aren't you going to sit?" she asks, trying to sound brave, but I can hear the fear in her voice.

My gaze travels over her slowly, deliberately. Savoring each flicker of discomfort in those doe-like eyes.

No, she clearly had no idea the man she hustled would be staring her down now. If I weren't so enraged by the audacity, I'd be laughing. My security team couldn't track her down, yet here she is, delivered right into my lap like a pretty gift begging to be unwrapped.

There's a twisted kind of pleasure in seeing her again.

"I'll stand. Gives me a better view. What a lovely surprise this is."

Her voice trembles, breathy and nervous. "Y-yeah. Big surprise."

"I haven't stopped thinking about you since our intimate encounter."

She coughs, then clears her throat. "Uh-huh."

"Wanna know what I've been thinking about?"

I lean in close.

She swallows hard. "You'll tell me either way."

"Oh, definitely." My hand braces the chair arm, breath fanning her ear. "Mostly I've been thinking about how satisfying it would be to punish you."

"What? There's nothing to punish me for."

"Isn't there?" I tilt her chin up, forcing her to meet my gaze. "How does the agency feel about your side hustle robbing clueless men for fun, hm?"

She moistens her lips, throat bobbing with another hard swallow. "You've got the wrong girl."

I chuckle. "Ah, that must be it. You've got this cute nerd vibe with those glasses. But take them off and your disguise crumbles."

She shoves her glasses up her nose even though they're already as high as they can go. "Ridiculous. I just don't wear my glasses when I'm out at bars, that's all."

I'd imagined this showdown going a few ways. She'd bat those Bambi eyes, all sweet and innocent, feigning ignorance. Or she'd go full *Kill Bill*, hissing and clawing at me.

I prefer the latter. I like a girl with fight.

She was the only interesting thing about that ridiculous meeting.

The facts remain, Mr. Quinn. You got caught with your Armani trousers down.

Trash-talking me so boldly to my face. Brave

girl.

But sadly, she's going the denial route now. She'll whimper out some lies about what a good girl she is, how she'd never dream of robbing a man blind.

"Tell me, why target rich guys like me? Just for cash, or do you need some cheap thrills in your sad life?"

Her nostrils flare. "If this is about me bailing the other night, I apologize."

I shrug. "I'd have gotten bored after a quick fuck in the bathroom anyway. But you know damn well it's got fuck-all to do with that."

Her hand twitches as if fighting the urge to slap me. "I'd never have done that."

I chuckle. "Don't worry, angel, I understand why you throw yourself at men like me. I saw your scumbag boyfriend on the security footage driving off with my car."

Satisfaction fills me as her face loses color. She clutches her laptop like a shield from my interrogation.

She might as well have *Guilty* stamped on her cute forehead. Was it relationship drama with the deadbeat boyfriend that caused her to mouth off that night? Is he forcing her to run these scams to fund his weed and Xbox addictions?

Doesn't quite add up. She's clearly got a real job, seems smart enough to thrive on her own. This petty grifting seems more like a twisted thrill ride, padding her savings with easy cash for kicks.

I loathe women like her, expecting handouts and taking shortcuts. I came from nothing, clawed my way up to build this empire with Killian, all through sheer grit and sleepless nights.

And here she is, batting those eyelashes, thinking she can play me for a fool and take what's mine.

It reminds me too much of my old man —Mr. Charming himself, duping everyone while he drained my mom's bank account and dreams. I still remember coming home to no lights or heat because he was out buying drinks for some random woman. People like her hit too close to home.

She worries her lip between her teeth, leg bouncing with nervous energy. Her incessant heel tapping grates on me. I fight the urge to free that lip with my thumb.

I lean in real slow, deliberately invading her space. My hands press down hard on the armrests, boxing her in the chair. "Nowhere left to run now."

Her chest pumps fast between us, quick, nervous breaths warming my skin. Those wide eyes track me.

Instinct takes over and I let my eyes roam down her body before forcing them back up, disgusted with myself. I won't give her that satisfaction.

"I have no intention of running," she breathes, lifting her chin in challenge even as her pulse visibly flutters.

Her gaze flicks to my arms barricading any escape. I have to grudgingly admire her boldness, holding her ground against me.

"I want to know," I say in a low voice, "did you swipe the key fob before or after I slid my fingers into your tight little pussy?"

Her eyes widen at my crude words.

"I didn't take any keys," she splutters unconvincingly, eyes glued to my chest.

"Cut the bullshit, angel. Where's my damn car?"

"I don't know anything about it, I swear." She's lying, right to my face.

Those spellbinding eyes won't work on me again. I hate being so brazenly deceived.

"I can't stand sly women like you. At least hookers are honest about screwing men. But you? You're worse."

She bristles, looking ready to brain me with that laptop. "You have no right speaking to me that way. You don't know the first thing about me," she fires back defiantly.

I skim my finger down her jawline, relishing her racing pulse under my touch. Her lips part but nothing comes out.

"All I know is you're a liar," I say in a low voice.

"If you really believe I stole your car, why don't you call the cops?" she snaps.

"I prefer to handle things myself. And I want the truth from those pouty lying lips of yours." My thumb traces over her trembling bottom lip. "But honesty isn't your strong suit, is it?"

We glare at each other in charged silence, broken only by her shallow breaths.

"You've got no proof," she finally says.

I smirk. "I have cameras all over my hotels." Except in the right fucking spots.

Her face pales as she weighs my potential bluff.

I release her chin and stand tall. "Maybe I'll just enjoy the show of you groveling before I turn you in."

My fingers slide lazily along my zipper, a mixture of disgust and undeniable arousal coursing through me.

Lexi. When I fantasized about her, she was always Rose in my mind.

Can't believe I'm half-hard over this conniving woman.

Her eyes follow my movements, like they're about to pop out of her skull.

"Let's see if you'll get down on your knees and suck my cock in exchange for your freedom. Finish what we started off that night," I taunt with a smirk. "I'll even let you enjoy it."

"Go to hell!" She jumps up, eyes shining with angry tears. "You're an asshole. If someone took your precious car, then good for them!"

I brace against the pull of her tears, reminding myself who she is. I despise a woman's tears as much as any man. I clench my jaw, clinging to my anger by a fraying thread.

Yeah, maybe I am being an asshole. But she had the nerve to fuck with me at my lowest, too wasted to tell which way was up.

Fuzzy memories taunt me—grabbing her hips for support in the bathroom, words slurring together. Kneeling before this deceitful siren. Humiliating details made hazy by booze, yet that shame still burns relentless.

But she brought this on herself by stealing my keys. I didn't force her hand. We all face the fallout from our choices—I'm dealing with the circus now that my personal life is splashed across the rags. Wasn't my finest moment, but we all have our vices.

"If you breathe a word of what happened in that bathroom, I'll come down on you so hard you'll wish you didn't have a tongue," I warn.

"Nice visual," she huffs. "Worried being seen with a regular girl like me will ruin your reputation?"

I stare at her. "That's not what I'm talking about."

A silent understanding passes between us, the air thick with unspoken words. The fact that I knelt before a stranger in a bathroom like a pathetic, emasculated boy. Now that would make page six, much more than any orgy. My downfall on lurid display in a public bathroom.

"I wouldn't have said anything, no matter who you are," she says softly. "Honestly, I just thought you were high."

"Don't make out you're a fucking good girl. You helped yourself to what wasn't offered regardless," I snap.

She meets my accusation with a look bordering on hurt, clutching her laptop tightly. "The world isn't so black and white for everyone, Connor. Your reality is far different from the rest of us."

Her words fall short of the confession I want.

"It's Mr. Quinn to you."

"Mr. Quinn," she corrects quickly.

"Just admit you took my car, and maybe I'll consider lenience."

"I don't know anything about your car," she whispers.

Dammit.

"You're going to regret playing it this way," I warn, turning to leave.

"Wait." Her hand shoots out, latching onto my forearm. Every muscle in me tenses instinctively.

"Please." She blinks up at me, lower lip

trembling as tears cling to her lashes. Something tugs in my chest at the sight, even as I fight the unwelcome swell of sympathy.

"Give me a chance. I'm begging you. I can't get fired. I'll do anything, work any hour, night and day, to keep your account."

I roll my gaze over her, taking in those features. Heart-shaped face framed by dark waves. Full lips parted in a desperate ploy for sympathy. Those mismatched eyes shimmering with crocodile tears meant to manipulate me. So deceptively innocent. Can I even trust her around Willow?

She's not the most stunning woman I've laid eyes on, but maybe the most striking. Can't quite put my finger on it.

I peel her grasping fingers off my arm, grazing her knuckles with my thumb. Her breath catches before I release her. Good—let her squirm.

She's lying through her teeth, but I don't have any proof. Yet. However, it just so happens I'm a big believer in keeping your friends close . . . and enemies closer.

Real close.

And since we sure as hell aren't friends, I'll be keeping this sneaky little nemesis very close. Perhaps I'll take more satisfaction in making her professional life a special kind of hell.

Part of me wants to toy with her until she breaks. A small monkey-brain part of me also wants to take her hard against the wall. Right here. Right now.

The toying side is winning by a landslide.

"Looks like you just can't stay away from me, *Lexi*. Guess I'll have to keep you real close from now on. This should be all kinds of fun."

THIRTEEN

Lexi

Connor strides out of the boardroom ahead of me, leaving me feeling like I've just been run over by a steamroller of rage. I've met the devil himself—and he's dressed in navy Armani, no less.

I know what I did was wrong on every level. I justified it by telling myself he wouldn't miss one car from his massive collection, that he's filthy rich while I'm filthy desperate.

But that's bullshit, and I know it. A crime is a crime, regardless of how much money you have or don't have. Dad would be ashamed. I'm a failure and a fraud. But I literally do feel like a cornered rat.

I can't tell Connor or the cops. Deano's thugs would come for Grace and Mom. So I'll be the villain here, live with the guilt gnawing at me.

But I'm still stunned by Connor's cruelty. He made me feel lower than dirt—something foul scraped off his expensive shoes. I've never felt such complete contempt from someone before. Regardless of the car, that man harbors a monster's capacity for cruelty.

And now I have to slap on a smile and masquerade as an emotionally stable adult when all I want is to run to the bathroom and break down in tears.

Vicky and Brooke loiter nearby, pretending to chat over coffee.

The whole office has their eyes on me, doing a lousy job of pretending otherwise. It's like a scene from *The Office*, if it were directed by Hitchcock. Trapped in my own living nightmare, right in the middle of my day job.

Across the cubicles, Kayla mouths a *WTF* while Abigail practically mounts the reception desk to hear better.

"Connor." Vicky steps in front of him, blocking his escape. "Everything okay?"

Without missing a beat, Connor's face breaks into the kind of grin worn by attractive psychopaths.

"Couldn't be better," he replies, smooth as silk.

He turns to me, eyes locking on mine, his grin morphing into something cruel. Before I can flee, he clasps my hand in an iron grip, fingers grazing my wrist with goose bumps.

"Good to see you again, Lexi," he drawls, his

mellow tone belying the predatory glint in his eyes.

No, Connor. Nothing about this is good. Because I see the volatile, dangerous man behind the charm.

I force out a reply, voice rough as a smoker's. "You too, Mr. Quinn."

Connor saunters to the elevator with his pack of suits in tow. Vicky scurries after, shooting me a death glare first.

"What was that about?" Brooke hisses.

I watch Connor disappear, feeling a cold dread unrelated to the busted AC.

Think fast.

I blurt out the first thing that comes to mind. "Funnily enough, he went to school with my cousin way back when," I mumble. I attempt an unbothered sashay away, suddenly very busy.

"So what? Why the private meeting?" Brooke demands, storming after me. "What did he want with you?"

Yikes.

"He was just being friendly, asking about my cousin," I say, trying to sound bored. There, that should sound sufficiently dull and uninteresting.

She squints suspiciously. "But he called you Linda."

"Oh, he just messed up names. It's been forever . . ." I trail off, grasping for plausible details as panic constricts my windpipe. Is this my life now, tangled in lies?

"Who's your cousin?"

I glance desperately at the poster of Gina Malone mid–squat thrust. "Cousin . . . Gigi! Yeah, Georgina."

Brooke scrunches her nose, clearly not sold.

I plop down at my desk forcefully.

Please fuck off, Brooke.

But of course, Abigail materializes at my other elbow. "Spill! What was that about?"

"He knows her cousin apparently," Brooke answers, eyes narrowed.

I flash my most innocent smile. If they buy this, I deserve an Oscar.

They exchange doubtful looks.

"Well, I must get back to that super urgent report," I say, tapping away at my laptop. What I wouldn't give for a meltdown in the ladies' room right now.

"That report's for me," Brooke points out, unamused.

"Right! Can't keep you waiting." I give an enthusiastic thumbs-up.

She huffs in irritation. Silently, I'm begging for any kind of distraction—a fire drill, a sudden tremor, you name it. Anything to avoid continuing this charade about my mythical friendly chat with Connor fucking Quinn.

When she finally storms off, I let out a huge sigh of relief. Crisis dodged, at least for the moment. I was half convinced I'd have to dramatically faint.

Alone, I stare at my computer screen. It's as if the universe took a good look at my life and decided "Yep, let's crank up the misery to the max for this one."

Connor's cruel words echo through my mind on a torturous loop. *"At least hookers are honest about screwing men. You're worse."* Just what every girl wants to hear.

What a monumental jerk. I get he's upset about his car, but nothing justifies that cruelty.

Standing there smirking, like he's the center of the universe. As if he's so far above me that I should be grateful just for the chance to drop and suck him off right there.

I swallow hard, blinking back tears to see my screen.

Deep breath.

So, Connor's a grade-A ass. And Deano definitely swiped his car. But the fact is that Connor hasn't called the cops on me. He must not have solid evidence against me. And even with all his anger, he's letting me stick around on the account.

He seemed more ticked off about being "played" than the actual car theft. Maybe he's not going to the cops to avoid more embarrassment after the whole Willow mess? Maybe I'm not totally done for.

"You gonna spill what that was all about?" Kayla props herself against my desk, arms folded. "Come on. Coffee time."

I just nod, trailing her to the break room.

She spins around, jabbing an accusatory finger at me. "You're the worst liar! He does NOT know your cousin."

"Fine." I sigh, thoroughly depressed. I run a hand through my tangled hair, wondering if it's too late to escape to a nunnery and take a vow of silence. I can't even tell Kayla the truth without spinning it. It's too dangerous with Deano involved.

"Okay, we met recently under less-than-ideal circumstances," I say carefully. "I was at his hotel bar . . . with Gracie."

Kayla's eyes bug out before narrowing. "What? I ask you out all the time and you say no!" She's clearly wounded.

Now I feel even worse. I force a smile, wondering how much more of my soul this web of lies will cost me. Pretty soon there won't be anything left but a shriveled black lump.

"I'm really sorry. I promise to make it up to you," I say, taking a deep breath. "Anyway, I got into a bit of a spat with Connor."

"What?!" Kayla screeches, managing to spray my face in the process.

I laugh despite the pit in my stomach, dabbing the droplets now decorating my face. Why is everyone spitting today? "Thanks for the free facial, Kayla. My pores needed a good misting."

"Sorry. It's just—I could tell something was off with you. What happened?"

Man, I didn't plan this far ahead.

A bunch more nonsense spills out. "It was dumb. He took my drink and wouldn't give it back."

Kayla's mouth drops. "Connor Quinn nabbed your *drink*? But he owns the place!"

"I know, right?" I scoff, doubling down on my bullshit. "What a jerk." I rub my neck, Pinocchio nose growing by the second. "Drinks thief."

The lies just keep piling up. And the crazy thing is, I'm no fan of lying.

"Rich people do some crazy shit. Like shoplifting from Target." She shakes her head, disbelief written all over her face as she leans against the fridge. "But let's be honest, he's insanely hot. He could pretty much get away with murder." She snickers. "He's definitely not lacking in the whole package department."

No, he's not. In fact, the man is packing some serious heat. I felt him hard against me in the hotel bathroom. Even when he was giving me the third degree in the boardroom, I couldn't help but notice the bulge in his pants. The same one he wanted me to suck off.

I keep that little detail to myself.

I give a noncommittal grunt. "If that's your thing."

She barks out a laugh. "Oh, you're such an ass. So, what'd you two talk about in the boardroom?"

I look at her blankly. "He wanted to clear things up."

Yeah, right.

She makes a surprised face. "Wow, I can't believe he'd bother."

"Yeah, it must be part of his billionaire 12-step plan for recovering drink thieves," I joke weakly.

"Even hot rich dudes need to learn manners." She nudges my arm playfully. "Anyway . . ."

She gives me that look that says whatever comes out of her mouth next, I'm not going to like. "To make up for going out without me, you owe me one. And I'm not taking no for an answer."

"What?" I ask warily.

"You're going on a double date with me."

"No way."

"Yes way."

I try to object, but she bulldozes right over me. "Don't even start! You need to get out, Lexi. When's the last time you got laid or did anything besides work and worry?" She grins mischievously. "Just look at the guy's pic, you'll change your mind."

"Ugh, all right, show me this hunk." I sigh, knowing resistance is futile when Kayla gets an idea.

She pulls up her phone to show me this Brad guy. Sure, he's a looker, but I'm not exactly in the mood for the dating game right now.

"I dunno."

"Come on, remember our New Year's resolution? We're in our twenties, not eighties, Lexi. We're supposed to be living it up and trying new things."

Kayla's always on my case about getting out more. I'm a boring grump. I've never even had a guy motorboat me, while *Vicky*'s doing it at the Christmas party to the servers.

Kayla's doing her puppy-dog eyes again. "One night out won't kill you. You've been so tense. And with all the stuff going on with your mom . . ." She softens her tone. "You've gotta take some time for yourself too. Cut loose and enjoy life for a change."

To my horror, tears prick at my eyes. I turn away quickly, pretending to be very interested in making coffee.

"Fine," I sigh, too exhausted to resist Hurricane Kayla. She's got a point—I've been nothing but a bundle of nerves and worry. Maybe I do need a night off. My vibrator can only do so much. I need real warm male skin. The throbbing, veiny kind.

There was a time my life had balance—thought-provoking psych talks, happy hours that led to happier nights, hobbies not involving penny-pinching. Remember eating, sleeping, and sex for the fun of it? Good times.

Lately, it feels like my whole life's been one big grind, just trying to keep us above water financially. These last few years, with credit cards hitting their limits and debt stacking higher and higher, feel like a never-ending series of IOUs.

A night to cut loose, to feel more like a woman —or even just a human—might actually do me some good. It's been ages since I was properly laid. What harm could there be in seeing if Brad can help scratch that itch?

"Conference room, now!" Vicky's shrill voice slices through the office. She snaps her fingers at us.

Kayla and I shoot each other an *Oh boy, here we go* glance and hurry into the meeting, sliding into our chairs.

Vicky paces at the head of the table, heels striking the floor like she's summoning a demon—or becoming one.

"Listen up," she barks. "In case your over-caffeinated and under-worked brains haven't picked up on it from the blast across social media, the Madisons' good name is tanking because of Willow's drama. How we navigate this PR nightmare in the next few days is critical."

She slams her hands down on the table, making the plant on it jump. "Operation 'Make Connor and Willow America's Sweethearts' starts now. Forget your social life. Friends, family, pets, sex—consider them all dead."

"So, Connor liked Lexi's idea to portray him as a slimeball," Brooke says tightly.

Vicky whips to me. "You still have a job because Quinn didn't lose his shit. Pull a stunt like that again, and you're out. But good job."

I nod like my life depends on it. "Understood."

She resumes pacing. "Brooke, update on Willow's public apology?"

"Draft's ready, just needs the legal green light," Brooke answers without missing a beat, her eyes glued to her MacBook. "We're setting up more press as we speak."

"Good." Vicky nods. "Willow will have wings and a fucking halo by the time we're done. Saint Willow, Savior of Horny Billionaires."

"Think he'll keep it in his pants?" Brooke asks wryly.

Vicky lets out a derisive snort. "Fat chance. Let's just hope he's discreet about it."

Brooke's brows lift. "I wouldn't like to be the person who recorded the audio. Quinn's not a guy you want to mess with."

My throat tightens.

Vicky barks out orders as we frantically scribble notes on Operation Redeem Willow. For once, I pray my role is limited to admin and coffee runs.

"We spin this as the greatest love story since *Twilight*. Sweet, innocent deer meets dark, mysterious wolf. An irresistible love."

Clearly, Vicky hasn't read *Twilight*.

Spin, spin, spin. We're human centrifuges.

Vicky's focus lands on me. "Lexi, you'll interview Connor first thing tomorrow."

Excuse me? This has to be a joke.

If Willow's the deer and Connor's the wolf, what does that make me? The sly fox about to lose her tail.

"Me?" I choke out.

Vicky's brow arches. "Is there another Lexi I'm unaware of on my payroll? He asked for you specifically. Brooke said he knows your cousin?"

This has bad news written all over it.

She side-eyes me but shrugs. "Maybe he wants to sleep with you." Then she has the audacity to laugh and add, "Odd, but hey, stranger things have happened. Let's roll with it. Hell, do a threesome with the cousin if that sweetens the deal any."

I'm too busy panicking to be offended.

Vicky clicks her tongue in annoyance. "Honestly, Lexi, close that gaping mouth. Rise to the challenge."

I clamp my jaw shut, force a thumbs-up. The universe really has it out for me. "You got it, boss! I'll handle it."

Brooke glares daggers, her go-to look for me these days. "He must realllly like your cousin."

I plaster on a pained smile, wondering if I can sneak off and drown myself in the toilet to avoid this meeting.

Connor Quinn isn't done with me, not by a long shot. And that chilling realization makes my knees quake.

FOURTEEN

Lexi

The elevator doors slide open to the penthouse floor of the imposing Quinn & Wolfe HQ and my dread deepens exponentially.

I can't stop a whispered "Oh damn" from slipping out. The Empire State Building looms right there through the floor-to-ceiling windows, its spire piercing the clouds. I half expect King Kong to come swinging by. This place screams money and power—and I've screwed over the guy at the top.

I feel sick to my stomach. I had not a single hour of sleep last night, all thanks to worrying about this showdown. I'm here to work, but also to gauge his next move. Now being surrounded by Connor's empire reminds me even more of the formidable enemy I've made.

He's on to me because of a gut feeling, surely. There's no way he has CCTV footage of the bathroom.

The big question now is, how far is he willing to push his hunch?

In all my (albeit) few years in PR, I've never played at stakes as high as this.

The receptionist throws me a look that's equal parts bored and judgmental as I stand there taking it all in. Her gaze basically says "Yeah, it's impressive, get over it."

"Can I help you?" she asks, in a tone that suggests she's hoping she can't.

I muster the most composed smile I can. "Lexi Sullivan. I'm here for a seven a.m. with Connor Quinn."

She glances at her computer and gives a nod. "Mr. Quinn's not in yet. Feel free to take a seat." She flicks her eyes at the leather chairs dismissively.

"Great, thanks." I drop myself into one of the chairs, picking one that gives me a clear line of sight to the elevators, and try to look relaxed. The executive floor is pretty quiet, only a few folks around.

I've spent all night trying to work out what his game plan is. The uncertainty is killing me. Maybe he plans to "accidentally" push me out a window.

Each ding of the elevator sends my heart into a leap, only for it to plummet when he's nowhere to be seen.

The time creeps by. Seven . . . seven thirty . . .

eight o'clock.

Where the hell is he? Connor demanded we meet on his terms, citing his "packed schedule."

By eight fifteen, I've chewed my nails to bits. Every little noise has me jumping. Even the receptionist shoots me pitying glances. At this rate, I'll be starting on my toenails next.

At long last, the elevator doors slide open and out strides Connor. My stomach swoops violently with nerves. I think the bastard got better looking overnight just to torment me.

He looks fresh from the shower, hair still damp and tousled. His top buttons are undone, just enough to reveal a tantalizing glimpse of chest hair. Not an Austin Powers rug situation, but enough dark fuzz to spark the imagination about what else is hiding under that perfectly tailored shirt.

He flings a tie around his neck but leaves it hanging. He looks like he just sauntered off a *GQ* cover, and I hate that I'm not immune.

"Morning, Mary," he purrs at the receptionist, who instantly melts. Seems he reserves that charm for everyone but me.

I stand up, all stiff and awkward. Just when I think he'll breeze past, he stops dead. Those piercing eyes rake over every inch of me in a slow, invasive appraisal.

My stomach doesn't just swoop—it plummets

eighty floors and is sprinting for the lobby exit.

"I couldn't decide which Lexi I'd get today," he muses, full lips curving patronizingly. "The sex kitten hustler in fuck-me heels and a dress barely fit for the public, or the prim librarian in her granny glasses and orthopedic shoes."

Granny glasses?

Jerk.

His gaze sweeps me again, deliberate and violating. "I see we've landed somewhere in between. Love the color, by the way. Brings out your eyes."

At least he's smirking rather than emitting icy rage. Maybe it's a trap to lure me into complacency.

I glance down at my carefully chosen dress, noting the unintentional color coordination with him in navy. Fucking brilliant. I agonized over this outfit knowing I'd be at fancy Quinn & Wolfe HQ.

"Good morning to you too," I reply breezily, refusing his bait. "I thought you wanted to see me at seven?"

"Is there a problem with when I choose to arrive?" His tone drops several artic degrees.

"No, no problem at all!" I chirp with my best customer service smile. "Gave me a chance to admire the lovely view up here. The feng shui is just *chef's kiss*. Shall we begin then, Mr. Quinn? I know your time is precious."

He tsks under his breath, the sound raising

tingles across my skin. "So formal, Lexi. I thought we were on much more intimate terms now." He steps closer. Too close. His expensive cologne and freshly showered scent envelop me, tightening things low in my belly against my will.

I step back sharply, death-gripping my bag. In my heels, I reached his nose, but today in my sensible pumps, I'm hobbit-sized next to his towering frame, barely grazing his chin.

"You *asked* me to call you Mr. Quinn," I grit out.

He smirks. "You can call me Connor . . . if you behave. Come along then." He turns abruptly, clearly expecting me to scurry after him like a smitten lackey.

I hurry to match his long strides, anxiety churning my gut. I feel exposed for a million reasons. Not just our horrific first encounter. And second. But also because I'm out of my depth here —I've never met with an exec at his level before, solo.

I follow him into his lavish office, taking in the imposing space. Sprawling views of the city skyline, of course.

The office reflects its owner—masculine, intimidating, arrogant. Every piece of furniture and decor screams expensive, carefully curated to intimidate. No crap flowers like at Sunnyhill. All the brooding art looks like it's from a pretentious gentlemen's club. I bet that other door leads to a sex dungeon.

The only hint of personality in here is a framed photo of a smiling redhead; probably Killian's teenage daughter. It almost makes Connor seem human.

"Take a seat." He gestures lazily to a chair facing his imposing desk. At least he didn't snarl *sit* this time. "And try not to steal anything."

I cautiously sit down on the edge of the sleek leather chair, which immediately betrays me with a sound so embarrassingly close to a fart it resonates through the office.

I freeze, mortified, as his eyes dart to mine. So much for cool professionalism.

I shift and another squeal rips out, as if the damn chair is mocking me. Fuck's sake.

"You, uh . . . might want to get someone to check this chair," I manage to say, cheeks burning.

The corners of his lips twitch. The jerk looks amused by my mortification.

I clear my throat, trying to salvage some dignity, and pull out my laptop. "Okay, so, let's get down to—"

Before another syllable leaves my lips, Connor storms over and fires a stack of documents onto my knees. I glance down confused, then the blood drains from my face.

It's pictures—at least twenty crystal clear images of me at his bar. God, I feel sick. There's me sitting at the bar. Staring into my drink. Looking pained. Running for the exit. I look ready to shit myself in one shot.

Jesus, what has he found?

"Pretty intriguing, huh?" he drawls, reclining lazily in his throne-like leather chair that doesn't dare squeak under his arrogant ass.

I flick through the photos, heart pounding but trying to keep my cool on the surface. Nothing jumps out as a smoking gun. I force down the panic that's threatening to choke me.

I have only one option here. Time to call his bluff.

I beam at him, all teeth. "You're into making a photo album of me? That's sweet. You want me to sign a few of those for you?"

His face lights up with anger, but I can tell he's also a bit thrown off. Didn't see that coming, did he?

"Smartass," he growls, the word rumbling from deep in his chest that could either be taken as a backhanded compliment or an insult.

As he knots his tie with unnecessary force, his gaze locked on me is so intense I half expect him to vault over the desk. I wonder if he's imagining choking me out with it.

"It's interesting how you're looking at me so much in these shots. My team is using tech to decipher what you were reading on your phone that night. We'll uncover the truth."

Shit. I let out a fake scoff, ignoring my galloping pulse. "That's a real violation of privacy you've got going on. I hope I wasn't sexting anything too scandalous. Well, enjoy the read."

Connor sizes me up with that signature icy stare of his, but there's a brief twitch in his expression, so quick I almost miss it. "Does everyone look like they're at a crime scene when they're sexting? I know a guilty face when I see one. And those . . ." He glances at the pictures burning holes in my lap. "Those are the face of a hustler, plain as day. The footage is rather damning as well, *Alexa.*"

Call. His. Bluff. Don't let him see you sweat.

He said they were *interesting.* Interesting doesn't equal *evidence.*

Despite the intensity of his stare sending shivers down my spine, I hang on to my sass for dear life. And damn, despite everything, I can't help but notice he's got the longest, most beautiful eyelashes I've ever seen. Lashes a giraffe would envy. It's not really fair given his ruthless personality.

Time to double down.

"Connor, they're just pics of me unwinding at a bar," I say evenly. "I'm pretty appalled you'd jump to absurd conclusions based on that. Is it really such a crime for a woman to enjoy a night out

153

solo?" I force a breezy laugh. "You should hang some of these shots up. They'd give your macho office a bit of flair."

I catch his jaw tightening, but I press on. "And it's Lexi, not Alexa. I wouldn't want your digital Alexa getting the wrong idea and ordering 'How not to be a naughty rake' during our meeting."

He actually *growls* at that, a sound straight out of the wild.

Too far—I've crossed the line, no going back now.

I give him a defiant smile. "Now, is there anything else substantive you'd like to discuss, or can we get down to the real reason I'm here—your PR campaign?"

I'm the mouse roaring back at the lion.

"You're on thin ice now," he murmurs, his voice a dangerous purr. "Lexi . . ." The way he draws out my name as he leans closer, like it's both a caress and a threat, makes me shiver.

Our volatile stare remains locked, the space between us thick with enough tension to choke on.

I'll need a cold shower if I survive this.

Then, out of nowhere, Connor chuckles, a rough sound that slices through the tension. "All right then, impress me with this PR genius of yours," he drawls.

I'm thrown off for a second, blinking in confusion. Wait, does this mean I've won this round?

I straighten up, trying to get my head back in the game. "Let's dive into the proposal. The idea is sculpting a redemption arc for you—from playboy to devoted partner, with Willow as your inspiration for change."

"Enlighten me," he sneers. "How does a man like me 'redeem' himself exactly?"

I sigh, seeing this isn't being taken seriously. "I'll cut to the chase then. Step one: No more scandalous behavior. The rake is dead, you're a changed man. Two: You're now the poster child for Senator Madison's political campaign. Three: You and Willow become this era's great romance, maybe with you lingering wistfully outside engagement ring displays."

He pulls a face like I force-fed him vinegar. "I intensely dislike all those options."

"But you made a commitment to Willow," I remind him. "You owe it to her to at least try."

"Firstly, I don't give a damn about the tabloids or public scrutiny of me. Spin my image however you want to shield Willow." His voice hardens. "Second, I won't blindly support any campaign. I disagree with most of his stances. And third— absolutely no engagement stunts. I don't do rings. End of discussion."

"But the public needs to buy into your transformation," I push back.

He locks eyes with me, his expression ice-cold. "I'm not going to be the senator's puppet, and you can forget any grand proposal schemes. Those are off-limits."

"Got it. We'll scrap those ideas." Clenching my teeth, I throw out, "But if you're serious about shedding your unsavory rep, how about we play up a struggle with sex addiction? You know, a stint in rehab, with Willow as the loyal lady waiting for a tearful reunion?"

Internally, I'm cursing Vicky for making me pitch this.

"Are you fucking kidding me?"

"So that's a hard no on rehab then," I say tightly. "We'll find another angle."

Leaning back, he regards me with an infuriating smirk. "Now it makes sense."

"What does?" I'm on edge now.

"Your penchant for wild schemes like key theft. This whole PR thing's a farce," he says, waving me off like I'm ridiculous. "Surely this can't be what you want to do with your life?"

My temper snaps and I tamp down the hurt. "No, it's not what I want." I didn't even mean to admit that.

He seems amused by my irritation. "Then why stick with it?"

I roll my jaw. "I have responsibilities, okay? Can we get back on topic please? It's your image being worked here, not my career plans."

He hit a raw nerve, but I'm not about to lay out my life story for him.

He watches me for a beat, trying to read me, then finally gestures for me to continue. "What's your next brilliant idea?"

I take a moment to regroup. "Rehab might be out, but we need to show the world a different side of Connor. Willow has to be front and center. No more random hookups."

Something dangerous flickers in his expression, eyes dropping briefly to my mouth. My skin prickles.

"Why would I look elsewhere when I've got her?" he says softly, almost challengingly.

My face burns as unwanted images flash through my mind—his hands sliding over my body, his mouth claiming mine, finishing what we started in that hotel bathroom . . .

I wet my dry lips, pulse kicking. "I just needed to clarify expectations moving forward."

"Rest assured, I wouldn't disrespect Willow by sleeping around." Then he smirks. "But tell me, am I allowed to fuck my own fake *girlfriend*? Or are you sanctioning my entire sex life here?"

Heat coils traitorously in my core as his words spark illicit images in my mind. I force it down, keeping my tone even. "Whatever you and Willow have going on behind closed doors is your business, not mine."

"I thought being good at PR meant you had to be a pro at lying," he muses, smirking at me infuriatingly. "Is that why they keep you hidden away from us important clients?"

I bristle, stung. "You don't know a thing about me," I snap. "I work hard and do my job well."

"Oh, I don't doubt your capabilities, Lexi. But I do know how to get under that prickly exterior of yours." His eyes gleam knowingly as he reclines, manspreading his thick thighs. *No need to remind me you have a penis. I remember. But please, continue lounging there, airing out the family jewels.*

I tense, trying to regain some control here. "Let's focus on the campaign for now, shall we?" I tap my pen on my notebook. "Why don't we find some common ground between your interests and the senator's campaigns. Tell me about the community work you do with NexiHubs. We could link that to his push for tax breaks for businesses investing in local talent training."

His piercing eyes size me up disdainfully. "If you did an ounce of research, you'd already know all this. But by all means, make me repeat myself."

Grrrrr. I force a polite smile, though I'd love to wipe that smug grin off his infuriatingly handsome face. Or sit on it. Both options seem appealing in their own right.

"I'm already familiar with your public

endeavors, but I'm interested in hearing about them from you, firsthand."

"It's a project I started, funding trade schools throughout the state, in fields like plumbing, electrical work, carpentry. It's about giving kids who might not go to college a shot at a solid career. Plus, it keeps them out of trouble."

I nod, though I was already familiar with NexiHubs long before I sat down to do my research last night. What I didn't know was that Connor personally funds them, a fact that isn't widely publicized. Reading about how he used his own substantial wealth to establish centers in underprivileged neighborhoods felt strangely disarming.

Almost dangerously close to seeming like he cares.

In a way, Connor is like the Batman of community education centers.

He scrubs a hand over his jaw, like he's erasing the momentary openness along with his stubble. Or just his irritation with me. "Sometimes I go over to give talks at the local ones. Or shoot hoops and mess around with them," he mutters.

That I didn't know. Unwanted warmth spreads through me at the mental image.

Before I can stop myself, I blurt out, "My sister Grace is in your IT program. We couldn't afford college, so thank you. It's given her real opportunity."

There's a brief moment where his impassive facade cracks, revealing a glimpse of something more beneath. But it's quickly hidden behind a grunt of indifference.

I shouldn't have told him about Grace. The less he knows about my personal life, the better. I cough slightly, trying to move past my overshare.

"Anyway, the work you're doing with the NexiHubs is impressive. We should set up some visits to the schools, get some shots of you engaging with the students. Highlight your involvement."

"Fine." He dismisses with a wave, like I'm an annoying fly. "Are we done here?"

I tighten my grip on my notepad. "Not just yet."

He leans back, cockiness pouring off him. "Well come on then, do you have any hard-hitting questions in that pretty head of yours? Starting to feel like I'm being interviewed by an awestruck intern here."

Condescending prick. I clasp my hands and gaze at him sweetly. "Oh it's just *so* hard to think of probing questions for the guy caught with his pants down at a public event."

I actually make his jaw drop a fraction.

"You've got some mouth on you," he growls.

"You bring out the worst in me."

A hint of both amusement and frustration

dances across his face.

"Unless you make better headlines, we're stuck managing this mess," I say breezily. "So back to business—do you think you and Willow can convincingly fake a relationship?"

He smirks. "Oh, I can be very convincing. Willow has all the right qualities—elegance, grace, beauty. Everything I want." His gaze sweeps over me, loaded with implication. "I have no doubts we can make it believable, whether we're out in public or not."

"Fabulous," I grit out.

"The real question is, can you handle this without your obvious jealousy showing?" he taunts.

I take a deep breath, visions of throttling him dancing in my head. "My only concern is selling this convincingly. I don't care who warms your bed, as long as you both play your parts."

I inject breezy nonchalance into my tone. "I'm sure you'll put on quite the performance. Just try to keep it tasteful in public this time. I know restraint is difficult for you."

Vicky would murder me for sassing a client like this. But Connor brings out a defiant side I can't seem to control.

He chuckles, clearly enjoying our verbal sparring. Then he leans back casually, arms behind his head, showing off his sculpted biceps. I hate that I notice.

"What constitutes 'tasteful' in your view then, Lexi?" His eyes glitter with humor, like he's laughing at me.

"You're a grown man. I'd have thought you learned this lesson already." I glance pointedly at the photo of his young niece. "Don't you even care that the recording's out there for the world to hear? For your family to hear?"

His amusement vanishes, face hardening. I've hit a sore spot.

"Of course I care about my family hearing that. They're important to me. As for everyone else . . ." He gives a dismissive shrug. "If they want a show that badly, let them feast."

I still, a twinge in my chest. It sounds like they did have sex.

"Did you listen to it, Lexi?"

His question makes me tense up. "I—yeah, had to . . . for work reasons . . ."

He lets out a low chuckle. "For work, huh?"

I give an awkward laugh, looking away. "Yeah, really wish I could scrub that audio from my brain. Made me want to go temporarily deaf after."

My attempt at humor falls flat as his expression turns to stone.

"We're done here. Leave," he orders coldly.

I stare at him, bewildered by the sudden ferocity. We've traded far worse barbs before.

Why's he so pissed all of a sudden?

When I stay frozen, he snaps, "Did you understand the command?"

"Loud and clear, Connor."

"It's Mr. Quinn if you can't fucking behave yourself," he bites out sharply, raking a hand through his hair in agitation.

What the hell? I quickly gather my things, pulse racing.

I lift my chin, keeping my voice steady. "With pleasure, *Mr. Quinn.*" *You big jerk.* "I'm leaving."

At the door, I risk a quick glance back at his brooding form. His stormy eyes meet mine, simmering with emotions I'd need a psych degree to decode.

What triggered that explosive reaction?

FIFTEEN

Connor

Visiting Killian's Fifth Avenue brownstone is like entering a different world from mine.

Here he is, living out the white picket fence fantasy with Clodagh and my sweet niece Teagan. Meanwhile, I'm still the eternal bachelor, enjoying the perks of variety that come with the unattached lifestyle, in my penthouse in the sky.

I'm not throwing shade at Killian's picture-perfect life. Far from it. He and Clodagh, they've got something real, something solid, especially since he got down on one knee a few months back.

They met when Clodagh started working as a nanny for Teagan a few years back. He's not the easiest man to share a roof with and she's a fiery Irish lass who refused to be intimidated by him. Those two constantly butting heads provided no shortage of amusement in the early days. But Killian just couldn't keep his hands off her, and now here they are.

But I've never been sold on the whole "happily ever after" fairy tale. Call me cynical, but believing one person can continually satisfy all your needs for fifty years straight without turning into either a source of uncontrollable rage or a human sedative . . . yeah, I'm calling bullshit. People change, desires evolve. My longest relationship capped out around a year before the novelty wore off.

Still, seeing Killian thrive as a dad makes me proud as hell considering our unstable childhood.

The moment he opens the door, his expression is a clear giveaway—he's pissed.

"Hey man, *Incredibles 3* is starting soon," I greet. "Teagan ready for our movie night?"

Teagan and I, we've got this tradition. Every other week, just us, we have an uncle-niece date at the movie theatre.

She even circles them on her calendar with *Uncle C* scribbled in glitter pen. Not gonna lie, it hits me right in the feels whenever I see it. Maybe it's the closest I'll come to fatherhood.

After the week I've had, I'll gladly take some fun time with my niece.

But Killian blocks the doorway, jaw set. "That's not happening this week."

I frown, confused. I didn't get the date wrong—my memory's rock solid when it comes to Teagan.

"What's going on? She sick?"

He sighs, running a hand through his hair. "I can't have her seen with you right now. She's embarrassed enough as it is."

What the hell? I stare at him as dread settles in my gut. "What's that supposed to mean? Come on, Killian, you gonna let me in at least?"

He seems to check himself and opens the door. "Of course, come in."

I follow him to the kitchen in tense silence. Clodagh's there and comes over to give me a kiss and hug, but her smile doesn't reach her eyes.

"What's this about?" I ask as I slump onto a barstool, though I'm not sure I want the answer.

Killian's face hardens. "Teagan's catching heat at school because of that damn recording of yours."

Jesus Christ. It hits me like a sledgehammer to the chest. This is my worst nightmare come to life. Lexi's pointed questions about family echo in my mind, now feeling like a direct call-out on my recklessness. "Are you serious?"

"Yeah," he replies wearily. "I've tried to shield her but . . . you know how kids are. They've heard it and are using it to taunt her." His eyes meet mine, simmering with anger and disappointment. "You've gotta think about Teagan when you pull this shit, Connor."

Shame slashes through me, sharper than

any blade. After everything that's happened—the senator, the ravenous tabloids, the doctor visits—this cuts deepest.

"Jesus Christ. I'm so sorry," I mutter, my head sinking into my hands.

My niece shouldn't suffer because of my bullshit. What kind of uncle am I? My depraved actions have now spilled over to hurt Teagan, who's more precious to me than anyone.

Killian's always been paranoid about screwing up this dad thing. No wonder he's pissed at me over this.

I stare at the granite countertop, unable to meet his eyes. "I really messed up. Teagan doesn't deserve this."

Killian's quiet for a long moment before Clodagh slides a glass of wine over to me.

"It'll blow over soon, Connor," she says in her lovely Irish lilt. "Kids'll find something new to talk about next week."

Killian just grunts. "Think first next time."

My jaw tightens. "There won't be a next time." Not if it means Teagan dealing with the fallout because of me. From now on I'll be a celibate monk. I have to be a better man for her.

"You don't want me around her anymore?" I ask, throat tightening.

He sighs. "I might've sounded harsh before. I want you around, but just hang here for a while.

No more big outings until this blows over."

I nod, relief flooding through me. "Is she in her room? I want to apologize to her."

Clodagh gives me a sympathetic look. "She already left to catch the new Tarantino flick with friends. She'll be back soon."

My shoulders slump. Not only am I the world's biggest fuckup of an uncle, now I'm the disconnected old guy completely clueless about her life too. Of course she bailed to hang with actual peers instead of her embarrassing uncle.

"You know, if Willow were just some celeb," Clodagh muses, "this would play so differently rather than blowing up. You've done waaay worse than this."

"Thanks, Clodagh." I roll my eyes. "The press always dramatizes stuff—I'm hardly the first guy to hook up."

Killian shoots me an irritated look. "Maybe not, but the senator's daughter?"

Fair point.

"All right, I really screwed up. But some of those headlines are just abusive."

Clodagh tilts her head pensively. "I think it's jealousy. Men hate you because they ain't you. And women hate you because they want you but can't have you."

I blink in surprise. "Damn, Clodagh, that's dark for you."

She just shrugs. "I've been around your world a while now. It's not all glam. I hate the tabloids—feels like they're waiting to snap me falling on my ass if I go out."

Killian's expression sours. "I'll kill any of them that do that." His eyes meet mine grimly. "Heads-up . . . Mom listened to the recording too."

"What?" I choke on my wine, balls shriveling. "Why the hell would Mom listen to that?"

"Her friends were all talking about it. Guess curiosity got the best of her," he says, leafing through a cookbook nonchalantly while dropping this bombshell on me.

"What the hell," I mutter. "I'm going to need a shrink after this. It's like Mom catching me with Kirsty Davies post-graduation."

I thunk my head into my hands. "I had Mom fooled into thinking I was some sort of gentleman. That ship's sailed now."

"Pretty sure that ship sank with Kirsty Davies," he retorts.

I lift my head to glare at him. "Not helping, man. Just the thought of Mom hearing . . . stuff . . ." I shudder.

"You'll survive," he says with a hint of a smirk. "Stay for dinner? I'm tackling that lamb curry again. My 'signature dish,' remember?"

I return a weak smile, gladly taking the olive branch. "The one that tastes different every time?

Sure, I'll risk it."

Anything for some normalcy. I half considered telling Killian about my health issue earlier, but scrapped that once he laid into me. Made me realize what an asshole I've been lately.

For now, I've gotta focus on fixing things with Teagan. That's priority number one. I'll handle the rest on my own quietly.

◆ ◆ ◆

Teagan comes through the door an hour later as we sit down to dinner.

"Teagan," I say seriously, deciding to rip off the Band-Aid. "I'm sorry you had to deal with this audio nonsense, sweetheart. I never meant for my stupid choices to hurt you. But I promise I'll do better from now on."

She's grown so much lately, looking less like a girl and more like a young woman at fourteen, going on twenty. It scares the hell out of me. Her long red hair flows down her back in soft waves. I still vividly remember the day I held her tiny newborn self, becoming her godfather. I made so many promises then.

She shrugs, scooping up some rice. "I just thought it was super gross hearing my old uncle make out. Like, totally ew."

She shudders dramatically, her face twisting up as if she's in agony. Then she sticks her fingers down her throat, making loud, exaggerated gagging sounds like she's trying to hack up a giant hairball.

Under different circumstances, I'd laugh, maybe even remind her that at thirty-five, I'm far from old. But guilt tempers my amusement.

Killian frowns disapprovingly. "Teagan, that's enough. You're being obnoxious, not entertaining."

She just flashes a cheeky smile, totally unapologetic. "What? I'm totally scarred from Uncle Connor's nasty make-out session!"

I let out a deep groan, dragging a hand down my face.

"She's aiming to be an actress, so the drama comes with the territory," Clodagh says with a smirk. "She landed the role in *Macbeth*. Our girl's gonna play Lady Macbeth."

Pride swells in my chest. "That's incredible, kiddo. I can't wait to see you kill it on stage."

Her eyes pop wide, panic setting in, and she nearly spits out her rice. "What? No! You can't come, everyone will totally freak out!"

I recoil, suckerpunched by her rejection. Jesus, Teagan's never openly refused to be seen with me before. Some naive part of me hoped Killian was just being overprotective. But now she's genuinely mortified by me. Having my own niece view me as an embarrassment stings like hell.

Can't say I blame her though. Why would she want her manwhore uncle there, causing a scene and humiliating her in front of her friends? She deserves way better than that.

I clear my tight throat. "All right, sure—you just focus on nailing your big moment, superstar."

"It's still months away," Clodagh says gently. "We'll revisit who attends closer to the time."

I nod vaguely, appetite gone.

In a few months' time you might not be able to enjoy it anyway.

Fuck. I take a too-large gulp of wine as the doctor's words echo through my skull.

After dinner, Teagan disappears to the TV room.

"For what it's worth," I start. "I'm trying to support Willow through this PR nightmare. I feel like shit for putting her through it."

Clodagh nods sympathetically, refilling our glasses. "It's not totally your fault. When you hook up publicly, there's always a risk." She shrugs. "But that poor girl . . . This happening is just awful."

"Yeah, it's a mess," I mutter. "My goal now is protecting her as best I can. Hence this whole bogus dating scheme."

"Does she know about you and the hustler chick?" Killian asks. I'd already told him about the

172

surprising run-in with Lexi.

I stiffen. "Of course not. And there is no 'me and Lexi.'"

"So she's *Lexi* now instead of 'Little Thief'? Interesting evolution there."

I roll my eyes. "I can hardly call her 'Little Thief' with Willow around, can I?"

Killian frowns. "I don't get why you don't just fire her. You can investigate without her on the campaign."

I grunt, scraping a hand over my stubble. Christ, I wish they'd let this Lexi thing go already. It's not as if I haven't endlessly debated my own motives. I don't need her that close—my team will uncover who stole the car eventually, it's just a matter of time.

If any of my employees backtalked me like she did, they'd be gone already. Or promoted. Maybe I'm enjoying the sparring a bit too much because I know she'll pay in the end.

Clodagh makes a face. "Willow won't be happy when she finds out."

"She's got no reason to be upset. This is a charade for the media, we're not baring our souls to each other. I'm not making real promises here."

She lifts a brow. "You sure Willow sees it that way?"

"Of course. I never explicitly offered her anything real."

"Willow's a catch," Killian chides. "Ivy educated, stunning, refined. You'd be lucky if she gave your shady ass a real chance outside this sham."

"I'm well aware."

"Seriously, maybe it's time to plant some roots, huh?" Killian says, tone half teasing. "Settling down could keep you out of trouble."

I scoff. "Don't start with me just because you've gone and done it."

He winks at Clodagh. "And I wouldn't change it for the world." Back to me. "What's stopping you from giving it a real shot?"

I knock back my wine. "Simply put, I have no interest in commitment right now."

Killian frowns. "Now's as good a time as any. Having a partner helps in tough times."

I imagine telling Willow about my health issue. Yeah right.

Clodagh slides into his lap. If only they knew my problems can't be solved with a sympathetic ear.

"When you vent about work, I just nod along dumbly," Clodagh tells him with a smile. "I know for a fact it doesn't help you in the slightest."

Killian grins. "You don't need to. Seeing your pretty face gives me perspective on what matters. That's all I need."

"Wow, romantic," she laughs, fixing his hair.

Watching their domestic bliss makes me feel hollow tonight. I force an easy smile to mask it.

◆ ◆ ◆

I click open Grace Sullivan's NexiHub application from two years back, even though I've got a mountain of more pressing shit demanding my attention. Just the latest in a series of irrational choices lately.

Her smiling face stares up at me from the screen. A dead ringer for her sister—same olive complexion and tumbling dark waves. It's the eyes that set her apart; Lexi's are a stormy, unmatched pair that pierce right through you.

I skim the standard fluff—career goals, hobbies, community work. But my eyes snag on her answer for "biggest influence."

My sister Lexi. She's always been my rock. Lexi pushed me to chase this dream and apply, even when I doubted myself. My sister has been my fiercest supporter and believer. Her resilience and tireless work ethic is something I hope I've gained. She's sacrificed so much for me without hesitation or complaint. I wouldn't be where I am without her.

I lean back with a slow exhale. Christ, it could

just as easily be me writing that about Killian years ago.

I've got a shareholders' meeting that needs my head clear, new hotel blueprints screaming for my attention. And here I am, sifting through some girl's history, hunting for . . . what? Redemption? A scrap of understanding?

I click back to Lexi's file. Straight As. Partial academic scholarship. Psychology major. Then she dropped out halfway through freshman year.

She was a driven overachiever once. So what the hell happened to send her from star student to hustling me in my hotel bathroom that night?

Her dad was successful, they would've had family money—why resort to stealing cars? Did she think stealing cars was more thrilling than reading Freud? And why waste that sharp mind now on babysitting braindead celebs?

And more importantly, why do I give a damn about her motivations or wasted potential?

My desk phone buzzes over the sounds of Beethoven filtering through the speakers. Can I hear it as clearly as yesterday? I keep the volume on the same notch now, monitoring it daily like an obsessive freak. According to Killian I already have it cranked too loud. But I need to know.

Mary's voice filters through. "Doctor Caruso is on the line for you, sir."

The hell's he doing calling my office?

"Put him through."

The moment Caruso's voice hits the air, I'm on him. "You got some nerve calling me here," I snarl into the receiver. "What the hell were you thinking?"

He stammers, "Mr. Quinn, you didn't return my calls. I wanted to make sure you were okay."

"I'll tell you what's wrong—your blatant disrespect for my privacy. You remember that NDA you signed? Or should I refresh your memory?"

"Sir, I just asked to be transferred, I'd never break confidentiality—"

"Save it. Consider your services terminated, Doctor."

I slam the phone down hard enough to shake my desk. I told him only to use my personal cell. I told him five times. Did he think I was kidding?

I wheel around to face the city skyline. His voice grated on my nerves anyway. I'm seeing a new specialist in a few weeks. Someone better.

I don't give a damn what fancy degrees these hack MDs have. I'm thirty-five and in the best shape of my life, for Christ's sake, not on the brink of a midlife breakdown. I eat clean. Max out my protein, eat enough greens to shame a vegan bunny. My regular bloodwork is flawless.

Okay, so I've been hitting the bottle too hard for reasons I'll rectify. But I still run five miles daily and crush the gym before work. I'm up at five a.m.

no matter what. I don't do long dates because I try to be in bed by eleven on weeknights, believe it or not.

So I'll keep training and eating whatever Captain America eats. And this new doc better have solutions, or he's gone too. They all seem to have the same doom and gloom script. Like they enjoy it.

Well, screw that. I just need the right specialist to tackle this head-on. And I'm sick of driving to East Fucksville in the sticks so I'm not papped outside some Manhattan clinic.

Even if I have to move heaven and earth, I will find a way to fix this.

I'm not giving up control. Period.

The only stress relief I get these days is getting my ass thoroughly kicked in the executive gym downstairs by Vik, my sadistic trainer. It's a rare sight, seeing anyone from the board down there —they're mostly a bunch of soft-bellied suits too cozy in their corner offices. So it's just me, Killian, and a handful of others who dare to brave Vik's brutal regimen.

After an hour as Vik's human punching bag, I

can think straight. Usually.

It doesn't help that I can't even blow off steam right either. Willow's the only one I can fuck, and that ain't happening despite what Lexi thinks. Never has.

So on top of dealing with my annoying medical issue, I'm also walking around horny as hell. Talk about a short fuse.

A sharp knock at the door cuts through the rhythm of my fists hammering the pads.

"What?" I bark. I'm pissed at the interruption barely twenty minutes into my session.

Jim from security sticks his head in hesitantly. "Sorry, sir. But you wanted an immediate update on the background check..."

"Yeah, let's have it."

I stop short, hit by dizziness. Must've halted too fast. Fucking perfect timing.

Bent double, hands clamped over my knees, I try to catch my breath, my heart pounding against my ribcage.

"You all right, boss?" Vik asks.

"Just a head rush," I manage through gritted teeth, straightening up and making my way to the corner, using the ropes for support as I fight to steady my breathing. "Go ahead, Jim. Spit it out."

"We're confident it's that east coast carjacking ring, run by this guy." He shows me a photo. "Yours was likely the highest profile mark yet. They use 'bait bunnies' to lure guys in, get access to the cars."

"And Sullivan?" I ask tightly, gripping the ropes. "She's one of these bunnies?"

Jim nods grimly. "We think so. Still piecing it together, but there's gang members near where she lives."

I exhale harshly, swiping sweat off my brow.

"Sometimes they work marks for months," Jim says. "Very persistent."

My jaw clenches. She worked me over in thirty minutes. Some wariness around pretty hustlers I've got.

"She's run this scam before then?"

He hesitates. "They use the same girls multiple times."

A cold fury settles in my gut. She's as deceitful as they come. How many others guys has she done this to?

"She targeted me on purpose that night?"

"We think so, sir."

I grip the ropes, knuckles white. Played for a goddamn fool.

"We'll get the proof to locate your car," Jim assures me.

The car. Fucking laughable now. I'd forgotten all about it. This is personal.

She's found my big red rage button and she's not just tapping it, she's slam dancing on the damn thing trying to smash it apart.

She's got a talent for getting under my skin like no one else.

And I fucking despise her for it.

SIXTEEN

Lexi

Vicky and Brooke zero in on me like assassins.

"He wants you." Vicky shakes her head. "I don't like this one bit."

My pulse goes wild. I thought I had the all-clear. I thought my involvement could stay behind the scenes now. The guy kicked me out of his office for god's sake, and now he wants me back?

"He asked for me specifically?" I wheeze, wondering if this is what a panic stroke feels like.

"Yes," Brooke hisses, her usual cool facade gone. "What's the deal with you two? And don't feed me that cousin crap."

Vicky's eyes bore into me as she aggressively crunches on a carrot stick like it's a dick that's wronged her. Cocaine, champagne, carrots—the holy trinity of the Vicky Diet.

"Maybe he's into Lexi?" Kayla pipes up from her desk.

Vicky and Brooke burst out laughing so loud, it fills the office. Seriously?

"Did he say why he wants me specifically?" I ask carefully.

"No."

I shrug, playing it cool. "Well, then it's anybody's guess."

"You have to do the school shoot with him. Get your little butt over to his office." Vicky jabs her half-mangled carrot at me. "And make sure he's photographed with some really pitiful, broke-looking college kids. The kind that look like they've been living off cheap noodles for a year."

I wonder, not for the first time, whether there's a special place reserved in hell for this woman.

She fixes me with an icy glare when I don't immediately move. "Well? Make it snappy."

And just like that, she's clicking away, with Brooke shooting me one last suspicious look before following.

Kayla leans across her desk, lowering her voice. "Maybe you should just tell them the truth?" She frowns. "Although it doesn't really add up. He's pissed at you but still wants you close?"

"Beats me," I say honestly, feeling ill.

I don't have a clue what Connor's playing at. But my stomach's currently hosting a butterfly rave, and all I know is—this can't end well for me.

She gives me a sympathetic look. "On a more

fun note, send me dates you can make for the double date."

Ah shit, I'd forgotten about that.

"Fine. Just don't make it somewhere too expensive. I'm broker than broke right now."

"Great." She beams.

I should've known Connor making me wait an hour would become standard operating procedure. The receptionist looks almost sympathetic as I shift in the sleek leather chair, thumbing through back issues of *Grand Hotels*, now an expert on their spa reviews.

Executive types in fancy suits strut past, off to important meetings. And here I sit, still cooling my heels.

It's not like I don't have a heaving pile of work waiting back at my desk, what with all those D-listers out there in dire need of PR help. Brooke is busy coordinating Willow's re-rise to grace with a million photoshoots and interviews; meanwhile I get to babysit the billionaire.

When the elevator doors open, for a second I think it's the Prodigal Timekeeper himself. Similar mesmerizing eyes, but slightly older and just as striking—his brother Killian. Behind him is their business partner JP Wolfe who I recognize from news articles. Killian's got a fine ass, clearly runs in the family.

I immediately sit up straighter, a new spark of nerves hitting me as Killian turns like he just realized something. Oh shit. JP walks off.

"You must be Lexi," he says, voice frosty.

"Guilty as charged," I reply, my attempt at casual landing closer to strangled. "Lovely to meet you, Mr. Quinn. Did Connor mention me or . . . ?"

"In passing."

Oh god. I force out an awkward laugh despite my knees literally knocking together now.

"I'm sure it was all terrible," I joke weakly, freaking the fuck out inside. Maybe I'm the punchline at Quinn family dinners.

Killian just smiles slowly, more like a shark baring teeth. "What a coincidence, you and Connor meeting again. Small city, New York, isn't it?"

"Very small." I swallow hard under his penetrating gaze, feeling two inches tall. He looks almost intrigued now, and that terrifies me more.

"You're not quite what I pictured," he muses after an endless excruciating moment.

I chew my lip. "Oh? What were you expecting?"

A balaclava and a few jacks for stealing cars, no doubt. Or some trashy gold-digger.

The bastard just smirks conspiratorially and

185

saunters off, leaving me hanging like the world's most horrific high-five.

That was horrendous, I feel thoroughly unnerved. He must think I have some devious scheme going on. Great, now both notorious Quinn brothers see me as the enemy. This just keeps getting better and better. I'm gonna end up behind bars. Grace will lose her scholarship. And Mom . . . she won't get the care she needs.

Stop spiraling, you idiot.

The elevator door slides open and my stomach drops yet again. You have got to be fucking kidding me. Again, somehow, overnight the bastard has gotten even sexier. Now his hard, angular features are strikingly accentuated by his new buzzed haircut.

"Morning, Mary," he purrs, grinning at her in a way that could soak panties at fifty paces.

I shift in my seat, smoothing my figure-hugging black dress. After his orthopedic shoes dig, I was determined to land firmly on the "sex kitten" side today rather than "frumpy librarian."

I stand to greet him, but he launches into a full conversation with Mary without so much as glancing my way. I hover awkwardly, debating whether to sit back down. Bastard's ignoring me on purpose, I'm sure of it.

Finally, he deigns to acknowledge me, striding over with an infuriating smug grin. My pulse skyrockets traitorously.

"Hello, Lexi," he drawls, vivid blue eyes even more intense against his shaved head. As if they needed any more focus.

I crane my neck to meet his gaze, even in my tallest heels. Damn him and his sky-scraping height. And damn him for that intoxicating scent wafting off him, unfairly delicious.

"You shaved your head," I blurt, stating the obvious.

"Thank you for that brilliant insight. I was concerned it might go tragically unnoticed," he says, deadpan. He invades my space, and I'm hyper-aware of every molecule of air between us. "Do you like it then?" One brow lifts in challenge.

"You look like a convict," are the words that tumble out before I can stop them. "Actually, you look like that guy with the blue eyes whose mugshot went viral. He became a model after."

His eyes blaze like he might commit a felony right now. "I'm sure you're quite cozy around convicts these days. Considering your own extracurricular activities..."

My fingers clench around my laptop bag. He got under my skin in under a minute.

We head for his office, me trying to match his long strides in my stilettos.

"Guess I should get used to waiting around, huh?" I say lightly. "Since that seems to be my role here—tortured with brochures for company."

He throws a scorching look over his shoulder that makes me stumble back a step. He seems extra volatile this morning, like I managed to piss him off in his sleep.

"I'm an extremely busy man," he bites out. "Consider yourself lucky I'm even considering this farce your agency pitched."

I bite back a sharp retort, reminding myself to play nice. But his arrogant dismissal shreds my composure like nothing else. I've never dealt with a client like this before. Connor seems to relish getting under my skin.

He holds the office door open with a mocking undertone. "After you."

I step in, expecting him to plant himself behind that gigantic desk of his. But nope, today's power play is the sofa. He sprawls across the black leather, legs spread wide in unapologetic dominance.

Then he crooks a finger to summon me. I perch warily on the edge, nerves humming this close to him. I felt safer across that desk.

"So what's today's grand redemption scheme?" he asks silkily. "Rescuing kittens? Helping old ladies cross the street?"

I stiffen, trying not to show how much he irks me. He knows damn well what's scheduled. "You know, helping old ladies should be your default, not a scheduled event," I shoot back. "As for today, you're speaking at a NexiHub. It'll take about two hours or so."

His smile drips mockery. "It'll take one hour. You seem to forget I run an international empire, Miss Sullivan. I don't exist solely for photo opportunities at your whim."

I press my nails into the leather. "Maybe you should've thought about that before that rousing game of hide-and-seek with the senator's daughter."

"Jealousy doesn't suit you, Lexi. Keep it in check."

"Don't flatter yourself," I snap, forcing indifference even as my nails dig in so hard I'm probably leaving a fossil record for future generations. "You're not even my type."

Connor's eyes glint as his lips curve into a smirk. "Could've fooled me, judging by how hot and bothered you get around me."

"You got one of those right. Now, if you're done trying to provoke me, we need to be at NexiHub shortly."

I snap open my folder briskly and hand him the outline.

He gives it a cursory glance, grunting noncommittally as he drapes his muscular arm along the sofa back. Clearly this is the absolute highlight of his day.

How the man is fine winging a speech to hundreds of college kids is beyond me. I'd need a month at a silent meditation retreat to even think about it without hyperventilating.

"It's a Q&A and meet-and-greet," I explain. "You'll get to check out their projects. I'll have press there, get it trending on social."

He grunts again, not giving a single shit about my digital domination plans. "This fluff makes news now?"

"The influence of the younger demographic can't be underestimated." Then because my filter's gone MIA, I add, "Plus the hot older man angle doesn't hurt."

His gaze snaps to me, brow cocked. "Less of the older. I'm thirty-five, just nine years your senior."

I shift uncomfortably as heat flushes my neck, forcing myself back on track. It's unsettling he knows my age off the top of his head. "Right, well . . . I switched venues to the campus in Queens —that okay with you?"

A shadow of something unreadable passes over his face. "That's where your sister goes to school."

How the hell does he know that? I edge closer to the armrest, putting precious inches between us as unease swirls within me.

"Yes, that's her campus," I reply evenly. "I figured it's a good look for you, speaking at your hometown. Adds a nice touch to the narrative."

"Of course," he replies, his voice dripping with disdain. "It's all about the optics."

"In PR strategy, yes. How did you know about my sister's campus?"

"I took the liberty of running a background check on you."

My stomach lurches. "You run checks on all your PR people?"

"No, angel. Just you." He leans closer, eyes spearing mine. "You're special."

My pulse kicks as I shrink against the armrest. Being "special" sounds a lot like a threat. The predatory gleam in his eyes confirms it.

Everything about Connor seems heightened today—his imposing frame dominating the space, his burning stare, the rigid set of his jaw. He's radiating barely leashed aggression that warns me to tread carefully.

What happened to set him off?

Did he roll out of his Egyptian cotton sheets on the wrong side of his California King this morning? Trip over his Gucci slippers and faceplant his marble floors? Or is he just extra irritated with me today? I didn't think it was possible for me to annoy him more than I already do.

His hand grazes my shoulders and I stiffen, skin prickling. He's throwing me off-balance on purpose.

The last thing I need is him digging into my personal life. Thank Christ there shouldn't be anything linking me back to Deano.

I think.

I pray.

I clear my throat, aiming for casual and missing spectacularly based on his smirk. "What exactly did you find in this investigation?"

He holds my gaze for a long moment. "How does a girl like you get into so much debt, I wonder? I'm trying to figure out your vice, Lexi." His eyes travel over me deliberately. "Clearly it's not designer clothes."

I bristle, defensive anger churning. "My *vice*?" I spit. Trust a guy like Connor to assume I'm in debt from some crazy shopping spree. "You think I'm in debt because of a rampant shopping addiction? That I've got a secret Jimmy Choo stash? This may come as a shock, but us normal people have real problems."

His eyes narrow. "Enlighten me."

"Yeah, no. My finances aren't your business," I say sharply. "Now can we redirect this back to the matter at hand?"

His gaze sweeps my face. For an instant conflict flickers across his face and I think he'll back down. But then his expression shutters, jaw tightening stubbornly. Clearly not yet done dragging this wound open wider.

"That daily commute from Yonkers must be a real drag for your sister."

I cross and uncross my legs, a little freaked out that he's done his homework on where I live. The hairs on my neck stand straight up in warning. He must have studied that background check hard. "I'd move closer if I could just snap my fingers and magic it done. But sadly my letter to magic school got lost in the mail." I force brightness into my tone. "Now, shall we get going?"

Later I'm stress-drinking an entire bottle of wine over Connor knowing where I live. Probably my bra size too. But for now, time to work.

But he's not done needling me yet. Connor's fingers drum a slow, deliberate rhythm on the sofa's back, each knock of his knuckles ratcheting up my shot nerves. His icy stare spears me and I brace for fresh trauma.

"Tell me, Lexi . . ." His voice drops lethally. "Would you come clean about my car if your sister's future was on the line?"

His words slam into me. I freeze, stunned. "What?"

"You wonder if I worry about my family finding out about my mistakes," he continues, his tone deceptively calm. "Shouldn't you worry about yours finding out about your sins?"

I don't like where this is heading. At all.

"I fund her tuition," he says casually, purposely inflicting maximum hurt. "What if I said that all goes away unless you come clean about my car?"

The room spins around me. This can't be fucking happening. He did not just . . .

"Leave her out of this," I snap, red rage crashing through my shock. I stand on shaky legs, feeling caged and suffocated. He can't threaten Grace's future as leverage against me. He just can't.

Connor rises to his full height, looming over me. "Why should I finance her education when you're lying to me?" His glacier stare holds no empathy. Only ruthless calculation.

"Do what you will with me but leave Grace alone. She's innocent and doesn't deserve to have her dreams shattered."

Hot tears prick my eyes, but I furiously blink them back. This is Connor's MO—charm before the slash and burn.

"Congratulations, you've made me cry," I say bitterly. "Is that what you wanted?"

He's treating this like a twisted game, callously dangling Grace's future as a power play. I know what I did was wrong, but I'd like to think overall I'm a decent person who was in a desperate situation. Connor is just cruel.

His jaw sets firm. "You're right. Your sister shouldn't have to pay for your screw-ups," he says after a paralyzing moment. "Seems there's a shred of integrity in you after all, Lexi."

And that's the breaking point. Something primal in me detonates. "And you, you've got even less decency than I thought possible," I snarl, heat coursing through my veins. "Grace is off the table, understand? Your beef is with me, not her. Are we clear?"

Connor's handsome features transform into a hardened mask as my daring words slice the tension. The weight of what I've just done crashes down on me.

Oh man. I really did it now. Stepped way over the line.

But when someone threatens Grace, this protectiveness overtakes all sense. Just like years back when she was tormented in middle school by that little sociopath Margo Lexington.

The office temperature plunges to arctic levels. Time stops in strangling silence. I can hear my own heart racing.

There's this tiny sane part of my brain observing the pending train wreck, thinking I'm absolutely going to hurl on his wildly overpriced shoes.

I should be groveling, swearing I'll be his slave or whatever it takes to pacify him.

But that defiant streak woven into my DNA snarls in protest. Some reckless impulse refuses to cower. If I'm going down anyway, I may as well go down in flames.

After what feels like an eternity locked in this lethal standoff, I detect a subtle shift in his demeanor. The chill in his eyes thaws just a fraction. Unexpectedly, the corner of his mouth twitches upward into a smirk.

"Loud and clear, Miss Sullivan," he responds, his voice eerily composed.

I'm so floored I nearly topple over.

"But get one thing straight," he continues, voice smooth as silk. "Disrespect me like that again, and it'll be the last time you do."

Message received.

"Understood," I say, hoisting my bag strap up with as much backbone as I can summon. "We should head out now. Time to put that media charm of yours to use, Mr. Quinn." My voice surprises me by not wavering.

His eyes glitter with dark amusement. My misery clearly entertains him.

Good to know where we stand. But hey, at least I'm still standing.

"Just so you know," I feel compelled to add, even though I know I shouldn't push my luck. "Everything I do is for my family. Even my mistakes. That's the difference between me and you."

Our eyes lock, and for a split second, I think I spot a glimmer of something different in his—

perhaps respect.

SEVENTEEN

Connor

I'll admit it—I might have crossed a line by bringing up Grace's sponsorship.

But damn, Sullivan's reaction was something else. Clearly her sister is a sore spot that I jabbed at like an asshole. At least she proved she has some scrappy unyielding morals though, and that's . . . mildly interesting, as much as she grinds my gears. She has lines she won't cross, things she fiercely protects. I can't help but grudgingly respect that.

The car ride over was tense as hell. Miraculously she agreed to let me drive her instead of taking public transit. Though she fought me hard there. Clearly wanted to avoid extended alone time. Can't imagine why.

Are we clear?

I should have bent Little Miss Mouthy over my desk and tanned that sassy ass right then and there. Teach my insolent girl a lesson in respect.

Who the hell does this hellcat think she is, mouthing off to me like that?

And why in god's name am I letting her get under my skin, challenging me without facing any blowback? To say Lexi Sullivan has been tearing through my peace of mind is the understatement of the fucking century.

There's something about her defiance that's . . . paradoxically captivating. She's got some serious lady balls standing up to me like that. I'll give her that—marks in her favor for sheer audacity if nothing else. And I guess I'm faintly impressed she didn't crack and confess under the heat.

But now the little criminal has the gall to fume at me instead? Un-fucking-believable.

The talk at the campus was even more awkward than the car ride, if that's possible. I spent the entire time trying to focus while Lexi's silent rage scorched the side of my face, not to mention the growing ache in my ear.

Didn't help having a hundred glazed-eyed college kids gawking back, half of them looking stoned out of their minds.

And I gotta wonder—how am I the villain here?

"You gonna sulk all damn day?" I challenge as we make our way off campus.

Lexi spears me with a fierce glare that either means she's imagining me naked and entangled between her sheets, or picturing my severed head and dick in her freezer nestled next to a tub of Häagen-Dazs.

With her, it's hard to tell, could go either way.

She halts, planting herself firmly on the sidewalk, hands defiantly on her hips. "Why the hell did you ask for me today if I piss you off so much?"

I run a hand over my shaved head, stifling a groan. I should've kept my mouth shut. The last thing I need is another confrontation, especially with the pressure in my ears building to a near-debilitating level. The entire Q&A session was a struggle. It took everything in me not to walk out.

Students openly rubberneck as they pass by. It's not an ideal spot for a personal chat.

"The rest of your team bores me senseless. You make things slightly less tedious at least." And I need as many distractions as I can get these days.

She narrows her eyes at me. "I don't get you, Connor. I can't figure out your angle here."

You and me both, angel.

More students snap pics not-so-subtly. Still Lexi remains oblivious, eyes locked on me. "For what it's worth, you were impressive on stage. You had every student hanging on your every word. Leadership suits you."

I lift a brow, not expecting that 180. "What's this, a play for my good graces, Lexi?"

"No. We're way past that point," she retorts, but her tone softens just a tad. "Just calling it as I see it. It was refreshing to witness some genuine charisma from you. I was beginning to think it was all just a hoax."

A wry grin tugs my lips. "Would you look at that. A backhanded compliment, but I'll take it."

Lexi sighs. "I guess I just bring out your worst." There's a flicker of something in her eyes. "Everything okay with you, though?"

I frown, confused. "What do you mean?"

"You keep fidgeting. Do you have a headache or something?"

I shove my hands into my pockets, not liking one bit that she's picked up on it. "Yeah, just a headache. It'll pass."

"I could grab you something from the pharmacy here," she offers, those eyes of hers full of concern.

"I'm good." The last thing I need is her playing nurse. "Don't need anything, thanks."

"Okay," she says softly. "Sorry to make you do this with a headache." She pauses. "You must really care about Willow to go through with it."

My first instinct is a flippant remark, but I pause, holding her gaze. "I want to do right by her. Contrary to what you believe, Lexi, I'm a gentleman."

Her eyes spark. "I can see that. To everyone but

me, it seems."

We stare at each other, the air suddenly charged between us.

"I'm not a soft touch," I say finally, voice low. "You shouldn't expect otherwise."

The longer I stare into those big doll eyes of hers, framed by a heart-shaped face and those pouty lips, the more I realize how she managed to entrap me that night. I was too wasted then to notice her obvious beauty.

But after the stunt Lexi pulled, there's no way in hell I'm letting her one-up me again. Being played for a fool isn't something I take lightly. She may have some redeeming qualities, but they pale in comparison to the huge, ugly lie that stands between us.

Maybe I'll fuck her once the guys have gathered enough evidence. Revel in telling her when I'm balls-deep that she's busted.

Just as long as those doe eyes don't stare into mine at the same time and make me question everything.

Not that it's relevant right now anyway—I can't do a damn thing with anyone while this charade with Willow is ongoing.

The standoff between us stretches, thick with tension, until her stomach decides to join the conversation with a roar loud enough to break the spell.

I debate poking fun but decide against riling her up more.

"How about lunch with me?" I find myself asking, the words out before I can think better of it.

"No, but thank you," comes her immediate tight reply. It annoys me more than it should.

I'm about to push the issue when a cheery voice interrupts us from behind.

"Lexi!"

Lexi whirls around, her expression flipping to one of sheer panic. "I thought you were staying home this afternoon. We'll catch up later, okay? I'm in the middle of something."

Lexi shoots the younger girl, unmistakably Lexi's sister, a desperate *Get lost* stare.

I can't help but smirk; this is going to be good.

"Hey there, Grace," I say. "Nice to meet you. I'm Connor."

Grace's eyes light up with recognition. "Oh my god. I can't believe I missed your talk. Are you, like, one of Lexi's clients or something?" Her gaze darts back and forth between us, suspicion written all over her face.

Lexi forces out a nervous laugh.

"In a manner of speaking," I reply smoothly. "I hear you're studying IT? Impressive choice."

Lexi lets out an almost strangled sound, but Grace remains blissfully unaware. "Yeah. Actually, one of your people, Lucy, came to talk to our class. I'm really interested in graphic design."

I nod approvingly. "Graphic design is a solid choice. You must have a creative streak."

Grace's excitement spills over like a dam burst. "I'd love an internship at Quinn & Wolfe actually! I'll work super hard, I swear."

"Grace!" Lexi looks like she's about to explode.

I tsk, enjoying her barely concealed panic. "No need to be shy, Lexi. I'm happy to pull some strings." Leaning into Grace, I drop my voice, conspiratorial. "Got a bit of pull in IT. Toss your resume my way, and I'll see it gets to where it needs to."

Grace's eyes widen like saucers. Lexi seems to be silently losing her mind, a throbbing vein on her lovely throat serving as a telltale sign.

If looks could castrate, I'd be bleeding out on the pavement right now.

My grin just widens.

"But there's one condition, Grace." I let my gaze wander down Lexi's tense form. "You give me some dirt on your darling sister here." Like how many nights she secretly spends baiting rich idiots. I wink at the younger Sullivan.

Grace scoffs, seemingly unfazed by the tension in the air. "I'd have to get creative to find any dirt. Lexi's all work, no play."

"Is that so?" I drawl.

"Listen, we need to go," Lexi pleads. Fucking priceless.

"There's time," I say easily. "Relax, Lexi. The reporter got what he needed."

Lexi's frown deepens as I turn my attention back to Grace. "Grace wants to tell me more."

"There's zero dirt. Lexi is a workaholic," Grace insists, a bit too enthusiastically. "Her social life is basically just work events."

I let my gaze linger on Lexi. "All work, huh? Wonder how her guy feels, competing with a job for attention."

"She's not dating anyone," Grace blurts out, and Lexi lets out an audible groan, her face reddening.

"Though Mom's been playing matchmaker with this good-looking nurse from the care home," Grace adds cheerfully.

"Care home?" I inquire, noticing Lexi's sudden stillness.

"Our mom's in Assisted Living," Lexi says tightly.

"Three years now," Grace throws in. "So go easy on sis, she's basically my stand-in mom."

I nod, keeping my expression neutral. This little detail hadn't made its way into my meticulous background check. Dead dad yes, but this . . .

"Must be a heavy load. What's the reason, if

you don't mind me asking?"

"We manage," Lexi's voice barely conceals her strain. "COPD. It's a lung condition that makes it difficult to breathe. Years of smoking finally caught up with her."

I take a moment to digest this newfound information. Does it cast her in a different light? Explain the financial issues and exhaustion? Her old man had money, though . . . Something isn't adding up.

"My condolences," I offer sincerely. "That's a lot on your shoulders."

"It's fine." She bristles, her defenses snapping back into place. She checks the time, then nudges her sister. "I'll catch you at home, Grace."

"Don't overwork her!" Grace playfully warns as she walks off.

"Don't you dare mess with my sister's future," Lexi fires at me once Grace is out of earshot. She stands there glaring at me, arms crossed like an angry mama bear protecting her cub.

My spine stiffens, caught off guard by this unexpected verbal attack.

"I was just being nice to the girl," I snap, glaring back. "How's that make me the bad guy?"

Lexi narrows her eyes, looking ready to breathe fire back. "That stuff about her résumé—did you mean it or were you just jerking us around?"

My jaw clenches in frustration at her

insolence. Does she want me to rescind the offer? "I don't say things I don't mean. Send me the damn thing."

She studies me, finally seeming to buy my integrity. "Okay."

I keep my glare locked on her. I'm itching to put this infuriating woman in her place. Teach her some manners. Maybe hate-fuck the hell out of her right now for sassing me like that.

"I'm sorry," she says softly. "I overreacted."

I give a curt nod, reining in my temper. Her protectiveness, however misguided, comes from a good place.

"Your sister's spot is secure, I give you my word," I assure her, tearing my gaze away before it pulls me in again. "No need to stress over that."

"Okay." She offers a small, appreciative smile. "Grace means the world to me, so I genuinely appreciate it. Thank you."

There's an unexpected vulnerability in her voice now that's disturbingly disarming.

I clear my throat brusquely. "Come on, let me take you to lunch. A temporary cease-fire," I hear myself say. "Before your stomach starts snarling again."

But she's biting that lip, hesitating. "Thanks, though I better not. I'll find my own way, but I'll see you tomorrow for the couple's photoshoot with Willow. Don't forget it."

Her refusal hits an indignant note somewhere, plucking a nerve. An uncomfortable blend bubbles up inside me. Annoyance. Wounded ego? Affronted pride?

Rejection isn't something I'm used to dealing with. Lexi Sullivan turning me down twice? That doesn't sit right with me, not one bit.

EIGHTEEN

Lexi

"She's late," Connor snaps, eyes narrowing as his jaw clenches. "You think I have nothing better to do?"

I plaster on a strained smile as he resumes his aggravated pacing, finding it a bit rich considering he's perpetually late himself—at least for me. But pointing that out now would be like tossing gasoline on a bonfire.

"I'm sure Willow's just caught up. She'll be here." I hit redial on Willow's number for what feels like the hundredth time. No answer.

Willow and Connor's romantic photo shoot was supposed to kick off thirty minutes ago. We're all set up in a picturesque, secluded—well, as secluded as you can get in New York—spot by the Hudson River, ready to capture their "epic love." To immortalize their undying passion for the glossy magazine pages.

Yet, the star of the show is MIA, and Connor, usually the king of lateness, is uncharacteristically on time and not handling the role reversal well. I suspect that when other people are counting on him, he's punctual.

Jacob, our photographer, throws me looks that scream *Do something* as Connor's irritation fills the air, his glare practically burning holes in the both of us.

"If she's not here in sixty seconds, I'm out. This charade can go on without me." He exhales forcefully, checking his ostentatious watch in a deliberate gesture before stalking several feet away.

I wonder who pissed in his protein shake today.

I'm not thrilled about this situation either. I rushed all the way here from visiting Mom at Sunnyhell just to make sure everything was perfect. Now I'm wondering if it would've been better to bring a cardboard cutout of Willow instead of relying on the unpredictable real thing.

Finally, a sleek black SUV with ominously tinted windows pulls up. The driver hops out and hurries around to open the rear passenger door.

Cue the grand entrance.

First a spindly heel pokes out of the SUV. It's attached to a leg that seems to have borrowed extra length from a baby giraffe.

Then, in a scene so slow-mo it could be ripped from a hair commercial, Willow emerges, accepting the driver's hand with the grace of a Disney princess stepping off her pumpkin carriage.

Two others exit the vehicle after her. One dressed in jeans hauls what looks to be lighting equipment while the other, also in casual wear, wrestles with a large suitcase.

Willow tosses back her hair in a dramatic cascade of waves and flashes us a megawatt smile paired with a dainty flick of her wrist. She's clad in a tailored skirt and silk blouse ensemble worthy of a First Lady. She looks beautiful. Meanwhile I'm a sweaty mess after sprinting here from the subway.

Beside me, Connor makes a low sound in his throat, maybe somewhere between an annoyed growl and a primal grunt of attraction. Likely both.

Willow sashays toward us, laughing with her entourage. She seems oblivious to our waiting. Or is pretending exceptionally well.

The murderous waves rolling off Connor are palpable as Willow takes an eternity to cover ten feet in her stiletto hooves.

"You're late," he grits out as she finally reaches us.

Her surprise at his anger is comical. "Oh, just by a few minutes! Got held up," she titters, going in to wrap her arms around him.

"I'll make it up to you," she purrs, whispering god knows what into his ear. Then she plants a lingering kiss on his cheek, leaving behind a lipstick stamp as if to visibly stake her claim.

I tamp down a flare of annoyance. I don't have time for her to bat her lashes and wrap Connor around her French manicure. We have a shoot to do.

She turns my way and gives my cheek an air-kiss, surrounding me with a whiff of her rose-scented perfume.

"Why don't we get started with the shoot?" I suggest loudly, forcing cheerfulness. Inside, I'm imagining a world where it's socially acceptable to throttle her for swanning in late without a hint of apology. But she's the client, so she gets to be the diva, and I get to pretend like I'm totally cool with it.

I wonder how much they "talk" outside of these staged events.

Sure, there's some spark there, if their little rendezvous at the charity event is anything to go by.

No doubt they're both insanely hot creatures. But there's also an obvious vibe mismatch. She's twenty-four going on sixteen, all whimsical princess vibes, while Connor's got that "been there, done that, bought the company" air of a mid-thirties man who's seen a thing or two and shoved his cock in the various holes of many attractive women. There isn't a massive age gap numerically but with these two, it feels like it's stretching wider.

Maybe that's the appeal—he likes the notion of settling down with the virginal type. I can totally see him following the *Screw then marry the never screwed* playbook. Cliché.

There was this one psych class I took—it talked about why powerful alpha dudes are into the whole damsel in distress act. Supposedly it relates to recapturing a sense of innocence and purity they lack. Or ensuring their spawn don't turn out equally sociopathic.

Best find a type like Willow who can whip up a nurturing palace for mini Connors complete with ass-kissing staff, a white picket fence, and some swans in the pond.

I have to wonder what common ground they share, though. Do they dive into deep discussions on politics, philosophy, the meaning of life? Or just bask silently in each other's flawless aesthetics?

Maybe their main "conversation" happens between the sheets.

One of Willow's assistants begins setting up what looks like a full-fledged Hollywood set, complete with fancy ring lights. The other pops open a suitcase overflowing with makeup and dusts Willow's already perfect face.

I stare in confusion. "Willow, our photographer Jacob already has professional equipment set up. You didn't need to bring anything extra."

She laughs it off, like I just suggested using a flip phone to snap her pictures. "All my Insta shoots require these lights. I wouldn't dream of posting without my team!"

Hold up.

Are these two always on standby to light and powder every "spontaneous" moment in her life?

Her feed's full of those "oh, just whipped up this little smoothie" posts, but who knew it was an honest-to-god production?

Actually, why am I surprised?

"Your face is perfect, Willow," Connor says sternly, like a father scolding his child. "As is the rest of you. Now let's get this damn shoot over with."

Jacob takes charge, positioning them for their first pose. He molds Willow into Connor's arms, fitting her curves against him as if he's a sexy mannequin. He adjusts Connor's strong arms around her waist, just short of indecent.

"Great!" I chime, overly bright. And they do look great. How amazing. This couldn't be going better.

Jacob "subtly" takes advantage of the moment

to cop a lusty feel of Connor's imposing bicep, pretending to fix his shirt. I bite my lip to stifle a laugh at Connor's warning snarl.

Jacob's camera clicks away frantically as he nudges them closer—Connor's arms wrapping more snugly around Willow's striking figure, her chin gently tilted for the perfect angle, her thigh pressed intimately against Connor's.

They look unfairly hot together, two annoyingly beautiful people. Connor is dressed even sharper than usual in a tailored vest that clings to his muscles in a way that should be illegal. Yeah, he's looking devastatingly hot, and I'm not thrilled about admitting that—even in the privacy of my own head.

Is this effort all for Willow's benefit?

Apparently, Willow and I aren't the only ones doing a double-take. Female joggers running along the river are now inventing reasons to stop—suddenly afflicted by phantom stitches or mysteriously unlaced shoes. Can't blame them really.

Connor catches on to the sudden interest, and if anything, that sulky, broody scowl deepens further.

Willow leans back, head on his heart, hair cascading everywhere, pushing her breasts up like they're vying for a spot in the skyline. Any man with even a hint of a pulse would need to rearrange his slacks.

Connor meanwhile stays iceman statuesque.

Willow presses her rear suggestively against Connor's groin. His jaw tightens, but he doesn't pull back.

A flash of irritation hits as I watch Willow play supermodel. Okay, so she's hit a rough patch with the whole audio leak fiasco, but let's be real—life's handed her a pretty good deck. Born with a silver spoon and supermodel genes, while the rest of us mere mortals are trying not to faceplant on our way to work.

And here *I* am, sweating in my Target shirt after sprinting like a madwoman to get here.

I bury my cattiness quick.

Jealousy is not a good look on you, Lexi Sullivan.

It's not her fault she's an heiress with legs for days while I look like I get dressed eyes closed. And she's the client—I'm here to do a job, not envy her lavish lifestyle.

"Smile, Mr. Quinn!" Jacob yells.

Connor grimaces like he's passing a kidney stone.

"No, no, no, this won't work!" Jacob laments dramatically. "Mr. Quinn, you've got to loosen up! I'm looking for the radiance, the fire of a man deeply, passionately in love!"

"I am loose," Connor grinds out, looking anything but.

Willow writhes against him. Connor's hands clamp her waist to stop her overeager undulating. Jesus, is she trying to get him hard right here?

"No, no, no!" Jacob pulls at his hair tragically. "Mr. Quinn, you're holding her like she's your little sister! Where's the passion? The hunger?"

He manhandles Connor's tense hand onto Willow's waist. "Forget I'm here! Touch her like you're alone and just got out of prison!"

Connor's eye twitches. His stony expression isn't cracking.

"Give me intimacy! Passion!" Jacob gesticulates wildly, snapping with the camera.

My stomach twists with anxiety. I need these shots to turn out right for the project's sake, yet part of me wishes we could just get this torturous shoot over with before I claw my eyes out. I feel weird watching the "lovebirds." That's the only way I can describe it. I feel *off*. Probably because of all the drama with Connor. I mean, how am I expected to relax around the man?

Willow lets out this huge sigh, leaning into Connor like she's trying to become one with him.

I quickly turn my gaze elsewhere, pretending to be utterly fascinated by Jacob's artistic process, which mostly consists of him snapping pictures and cursing.

The whole scene drags on for what feels like an eternity. Jacob is moaning and wailing with his hand on his head while pleading with Connor to "give me passion!"

Connor moves stiffly, like rigor mortis set in and no one told him. In his defense I think he is actually trying, through what looks like immense internal pain. He might have the chiseled looks, but his modeling skills are giving off strong "CPR dummy" energy.

Yeah, he looks like an older version of that hot felon, but his stiff moves aren't about to land him any modeling gigs. Which is really weird because anytime I've seen him in interviews or in photos with attractive women, he's all grins, practically dripping with charm.

I bite down hard on my cheek trying not to crack up.

Connor narrows his eyes. "Something funny?"

"Nope, nothing at all," I reply innocently. Christ. I didn't even know he was paying attention to me.

"Connor, come on!" Willow explodes, losing her patience. "This needs to be perfect."

Mid-tirade, she lets out a sneeze—this delicate, pixie-like sneeze that appears to rock her entire existence. Her eyes bulge like she's been shot.

"Oh my god!" she shrieks, patting her face as though it's on fire. "Do I look okay? Be honest with me!"

I can't help but think, if a sneeze gets her

this riled up, seeing her react to a fart would be something else.

"You look flawless as always, Willow," I say smoothly, hoping to avoid a meltdown. "No issues whatsoever."

She's having none of it. "No. I need my team to check me."

Cue the entourage descending like a NASCAR pit crew to triage this code red situation. They blot her already immaculate complexion and slather on more products.

Connor looks like he's about to blow a fuse as the shoot screeches to another halt.

Jacob shoots me a desperate look. "Lexi, this isn't working. Talk to him. I need fire! He's giving me nothing. He's as emotive as a pile of bricks."

I let out a heavy sigh and head over to Connor. "A little enthusiasm wouldn't kill you," I suggest with a light tone.

Connor's reply is a low grumble. "Don't test me, Lexi. I'm here, aren't I? If that photographer lays one more finger on me, his camera's going for a swim."

"I know you're not big on taking orders, especially from me, but please—"

"I don't take orders from anyone."

I clamp down on my rising frustration. "Right, I get it. First rule of the Billionaire's Playbook, answer to no one," I toss back, trying to lighten the mood and maybe crack that tough exterior of his.

His lips twitch, a hint of amusement breaking through.

"Look, the faster he nails these photos, the faster we can hit the road. How about trying not to look like you're scheming someone's downfall? Preferably not the photographer's or, heaven forbid, mine."

"I'm pretending just fine," Connor snaps. "Guy says smile, I smile. What's he expecting, a Broadway performance?"

I can't suppress a laugh. "Baring your teeth isn't smiling, Connor. Where's that famous charm of yours?"

He narrows his eyes. "It died along with my patience about an hour ago."

"Oh, come on, it's not that bad," I say, rolling my eyes. "Some people have to clean the subways. You get to cuddle with a supermodel. I bet you're still making a small fortune standing here, with hotel guests checking in all over the country. What, a million bucks for a half hour of flashing those pearly whites?"

He arches a brow, amused. "Let's not get carried away. Good thing you're not in charge of payroll."

Jacob's shrill voice cuts in. "Lexi!"

I turn to see him violently snapping his fingers at me. "Stand in for Willow. I need to test the lighting and angles. Something's off."

I freeze. "Sorry, run that by me again?"

"Take Willow's spot." Jacob charges toward us.

I barely have a second to brace myself before he's shoving me straight into Connor's rock-hard chest.

The impact forces a gasp from my lips, my hands instinctively spreading over the hard, sculpted surface beneath my fingers. Connor's response is immediate, a deep growl rumbling from his chest, vibrating against my palms.

"What the hell do you think you're doing?" he snaps, glaring at Jacob.

"I need to check angles," Jacob says, completely ignorant to the electric discomfort sparking between us. "I think it'll work best if you're facing each other. Lexi, wrap your arms around his neck."

I go rigid. "Can't we just—wait for Willow?"

"No time!" Jacob shrieks.

Connor's eyes blaze with irritation. "Just do it. Let's get this over with."

Dammit, this is so not in my job description. I turn to see what the hell Willow thinks of this, but she's still in the midst of post-sneeze beauty triage.

Heart pounding, I wrap my arms around Connor's thick neck.

Our eyes lock, and suddenly it's like someone's flipped a switch, cranking up the voltage in the air. His stern expression doesn't soften, though the muscles of his neck flex and tense under my tentative fingertips. Tension radiates off him in savage waves.

Then, with torturous slowness, Connor's hands find my waist. His grip tightens, pulling me in close until there's no space left between us and I'm right up against him.

My stomach flips madly as the space between us heats to scorching, charged enough to power Manhattan. Zero to nuclear intensity in a heartbeat.

"Chin up," Jacob commands.

I do as I'm told, lifting my chin and locking eyes with Connor again.

Oh god. This is dangerous territory. Chest to chest, thigh to thigh.

His heated exhalation makes my chest move along with his and my nipples respond. My heart thumps so wildly I'm afraid they can hear it all the way in New Jersey.

Fucking hell. Who knew angry, powerful men were my weakness. Especially tall, broad-shouldered, muscly ones with hard bodies pressed against mine.

"Here we are again," Connor murmurs, granite expression giving nothing away about how this close contact is affecting him.

His grip on my waist tightens, his fingers brushing against the bare skin where my top has crept up. "Brings back memories. I better keep an eye on my belongings this time."

"Hilarious," I manage tightly.

"No witty comeback, Lexi?" he breathes out. "You disappoint me."

Tell me about it. I can't use my tongue.

I have to look away as heat scorches my cheeks. I'm hyperaware of every inch of hard muscle against me through that shirt. I try to focus on something, *anything* else—like how Connor's throat moves when he swallows. It's a safer choice than meeting those stormy eyes.

Jacob buzzes around, oblivious to what's brewing between Connor and me. "That's perfect, hold it right there."

I awkwardly shift my leg, needing some space before I spontaneously combust.

Connor's eyes flash dangerously. "Don't," he says, his voice coming out all gravelly.

"Don't what?" I breathe.

"Don't move like that."

And then I feel it—his hard cock pressing against me. Oh holy hell.

His jaw clenches as he meets my gaze.

"You're hard!" I shriek-whisper.

"You're pressed against me," he grits out. "And as much as you irritate the hell out of me, you're not exactly hideous."

"Now who's the one giving backhanded

compliments."

"Yes, this is what I'm talking about!" Jacob says, buzzing around us with excitement. "This is exactly the kind of chemistry you need with Willow."

I let out a shaky breath, attempting to play off the tension as a laugh. But it's hard to ignore the fact that there's a raging erection pressing into my stomach. "Jesus, I feel like a professional fluffer getting you ready for the big show."

"Keep moving like that against me and you might just become the star of the show," Connor growls in my ear, sending shivers down my spine that have nothing to do with the cool breeze from the river.

"I'm ready now," Willow announces sharply from behind us. Whiplashed, I jerk back from Connor as her tone slices through the haze. "That's enough *testing*."

Oh boy. I'm stumbling over my own feet trying to create some space between Connor and me, my face burning up.

He doesn't seem thrilled either, jamming his hands in his pockets and grumbling under his breath with words that definitely wouldn't fly in polite conversation.

"Great," I shriek, sounding like I've taken a leaf out of Jacob's book of hysteria. "Let's resume the shoot."

Connor coughs, and now he's the one looking all embarrassed. My eyes widen as I catch a glimpse of the bulge outlined in his slacks. Surely Willow and Jacob have noticed too.

"Give me a minute," Connor mutters. He turns toward the Hudson and pretends to text while my pulse stays at unhealthy levels.

He finally returns to Willow's side, who gives him a suspicious glance before taking her place against him.

I can't escape fast enough, ducking behind Jacob, my heart pounding. Christ, what just happened?

Jacob dives back into photographer mode, snapping away.

Click click click.

The question lingers in my mind: does he still have a massive hard-on?

"No, no, no!" Hands fly up in exasperation. "You had it before. Mr. Quinn, be like you were with Lexi."

Connor's jaw is so tight I'm bracing myself to hear it crack. He shoots me a foul glare, like this is all my doing.

I watch him and Willow striking their perfect couple poses and feel about as comfortable as the time Deano texted saying Connor was the target.

I don't know why it's so unsettling seeing them mimic the exact poses I did with Connor just moments ago. That's the whole point of the shoot, for god's sake.

But internally, I'm throwing every curse I know, desperate for it to end so I can escape and clear my messed-up head. Maybe a freezing shower will help me forget how it felt with his hands on me. If I stand under that cold water long enough, maybe it'll wash away this . . . thing . . . I definitely shouldn't be feeling.

My prayers are answered. As if choreographed by the gods themselves, the skies open up with a torrential downpour just as Willow unleashes a piercing shriek. So much for a smooth photoshoot.

"It's all good," Jacob shouts above the din of raindrops. "Rain's romantic. Think *The Notebook*."

Miraculously, Willow seems to buy into the idea. Her crew jumps to action, keeping her dry with umbrellas and wrapping her in a big coat.

Connor and I, though, we're getting drenched. I hug myself, shivering from the cold.

Connor's sharp eyes scan my drenched state with evident annoyance. "Where the hell is your coat?" he demands.

"I didn't have time to grab it," I call back defensively.

Before I can react, he's striding over, peeling off his suit jacket and firmly wrapping it around my shoulders.

"Hold on, I can't take your jacket!" I try to

argue, but it's weak.

The rain's now a downpour, and I yelp as more cold water hits me.

"It's not up for debate," Connor says, his strong hands maintaining a firm grip on the jacket until I relent and slip my arms into the oversized sleeves.

"I feel like a kid playing dress-up," I joke lamely.

His eyes trail down my rain-soaked figure, his mouth set in a hard line. "That's not how I'd describe you in my clothes," he mutters, a gravelly edge to his voice that does strange things to my heart rate.

His nostrils flare as he takes in my soaked appearance, now draped in his fancy, tailor-made suit jacket.

Then he walks off, leaving me there, trying to sort through my tangled thoughts.

"Let's finish this," he barks out, his commanding voice getting Jacob moving.

I pull his jacket tighter around me, catching the subtle scent of his cologne.

He's unfazed by the rain, with water streaming down his defined face and his shirt sticking to him.

God. His shirt's all but transparent now, revealing the outline of a dark tattoo across his chest. Damn, he looks good all wet.

I huff with annoyance.

I see what this is—a silly little crush, probably

because I'm not used to being around guys like Connor much. Or ever.

He's throwing me seriously off-kilter, and I don't like it one bit.

I need to get a grip, fast.

NINETEEN

Lexi

I collapse onto the couch, laptop on my knees, totally spent, while Grace is next to me, noisily sucking down noodles.

It's nine thirty and my eyes are screaming for mercy after being glued to this screen all night. Between work and checking in on Mom, all I'm dreaming of is bed. And if I'm honest, getting myself off fantasizing about that steamy photoshoot with Connor days back. Welcome to the tragic saga of my lady blue balls.

He. Was. Hard. The man was fucking hard. Over me. I haven't been up close and personal with a cock in so long. No wonder I went to pieces.

We've kept a wide berth ever since that photoshoot, only interacting for more of Willow's annoying photo ops. Being dragged by Willow to her upscale charity luncheon almost did him in. And then there's been a steady stream of those "bad boy turned good" college gigs and other PR stunts, even including, by some miracle, an event thrown by a senator for a cause Connor doesn't completely despise.

All the while I lurk in the background like a nanny, making sure he behaves himself. Not that he tosses anything more than the occasional scowl my way. He seems eternally angry that he got hard.

I've watched him turn on the high-voltage charm for the crowds—flirty smiles, swagger galore. Students, professors, whoever. Some of these women were swooning so hard we needed a mop to clean up after them.

But when it comes to me, he's all dark looks and underhanded comments, like acting normal is beyond him. It's tiring, this push and pull.

And to be totally honest, seeing him lay it on thick with everyone else stirs up this weird concoction in me—not exactly jealousy, more like a blend of annoyance and relief. Relief because, thankfully, he's not aiming that suffocating charm at me.

Not that I'd want him to. Obviously.

I just grit my teeth and hang tight until it's time to escort him out.

Grace slurps her noodles in a manner that's just inexcusable.

"Grace!" I snap, massaging the angry red mark where my glasses have been gouging my poor nose.

She widens her eyes, all faux innocence. "Jeez, someone's grouchy," she mumbles, mouth full of food.

I huff out a breath, rereading Connor's scripted love proclamation for the umpteenth time, my focus shot.

After countless rewrites, Vicky finally approved my draft. Now we anxiously await the verdict from our lord and master, Mr. Connor Quinn. The stills came out decent, all thanks to Jacob's magic touch-ups.

And so begins phase two of our grand PR scheme—the Love Declaration.

The gossip columns have been on fire with tales of the billionaire playboy and his pristine princess getting snapped in a steamy situation. But, thanks to a few well-placed stories on NexiHub, we've managed to sprinkle a bit of romance into the scandal.

I give the letter one last read-through. Trying to predict Connor's reaction is like trying to stick Jell-O to a wall.

I'd like to sincerely apologize for my reckless behavior recently. I allowed myself to get swept up in the moment . . .
blah blah blah
Willow handled the situation with complete grace

and class. She is an amazing woman who brings out the best in me. I'm truly grateful to have her in my life. Our relationship is still new and finding its footing. We kindly ask the press to respect our privacy during this time. We both value the special connection we're building together.

This experience has been a wake-up call for me to grow and better myself. Willow inspires me to become the man I want to be,

More blah.

We appreciate the public's understanding and support moving forward.

Final blah.

So much bullshit blah. I hit send before tossing off my glasses with a groan. What I really ought to publicize is more like:

"Dear America, please accept my sincere apologies for acting like a straight-up dog at the event. Had one too many fizzy drinks and my cock did the thinking for me. The end."

Something along those lines anyway.

"You gonna send my resume to *Connor*?" Grace pipes up.

She loves that she's on first name terms.

I sigh. "I'll get to it tomorrow, okay?" At her fallen face, I gently add, "Don't get your hopes up too high. He may have just been mouthing off with that offer."

Never mind Grace's resume. I've been busting my ass sending out my own, trying to secure a salary hike. I've got some interviews lined up but nothing's concrete yet, while that looming installment bomb ticks ever closer, fraying my last nerves.

I close the pyramid scheme tab giving me false hope. Desperation drives people to illogical shit, as I discovered after falling down an MLM rabbit hole.

"Want to earn thousands extra a month?"

Yes, I do, Scammer! Tell me more!

The only feasible option so far was a niche squishing fetish site. Crushing tiny toy cars for quick cash and I wouldn't even have to show my face. Tempting. Might have to revisit that idea.

I shut down all the job sites tabs on my laptop —the ones with legit PR job listings, and the ones where I fantasize about being a psychologist. A girl's allowed her dreams.

Then my phone lights up with an unknown number. I answer with a hesitant "Hello?"

"That message you crafted is rather emotionally charged," comes Connor's unmistakable voice.

Instantly, I'm on edge, heart racing. Speak of the arrogant devil. He must've got my number from my email or that damn background check.

"We're aiming for 'madly in love' here. The message fits," I fire back, trying to sound unfazed that he's calling me at home.

Connor lets out a sigh that I can practically see turning his frustratingly handsome face into a frown. "Please tell me we're fucking done for now."

I slip into my bedroom for privacy. "Not yet. You've got that big, lovey-dovey public date with Willow next. When can you make that happen?"

In the background, there's a burst of female yelling, and my heart does a quick panic dance. He's not supposed to have women over during this campaign. Unless it's Willow?

"Who's that?" I rush out, way sharper than intended.

Another female voice chimes in, rocketing my stress levels through the roof.

He chuckles. "Relax, it's just my niece and her pal. They've commandeered my home theater for a *Fortnite* marathon."

Oh. Relief washes over me, and I guess he can tell because he chuckles again. I brace for some snarky jab about my reaction, but it never arrives.

"So, you're playing babysitter?" I ask, picturing Connor in the midst of teenage chaos. It's a strangely endearing image.

"Not exactly. She's nearly fifteen—thinks she's all grown up. But I give them free rein of the home theater for their game wars. It's the only way she'll hang around me these days. Apparently I'm the most embarrassing part of her teenage years and she refuses to be seen with me in public."

Another shriek sounds in the background. Someone just won a round.

"I'm sorry she's embarrassed," I say, a smile creeping in despite myself.

"Yeah, well, so am I."

"You sound like a pretty cool uncle, scandalous reputation aside. My uncles never spent time with me. Actually they're all dead now so that's good. But when they were alive, I only saw them at each other's funerals . . ." I ramble on. "But that was okay, their nostril hair situation was a bit of a deterrent."

His laughter rumbles through the phone, a deep, sexy sound that hits me right in the girly bits. I like how I can make him laugh like that. "If only I could convince my niece I'm a cool uncle. She remains unimpressed. And my nose hairs are under control."

"I just figured you'd spend your nights living up to the media image—guzzling champagne off supermodels' ass cheeks and rolling around naked on piles of money."

"Not every night, Lexi," he replies with a hint of sarcasm. "Sometimes I'm just a regular guy trying to connect with his family."

My stomach does a little flip at his sincerity.

"A regular guy, huh? I'm beginning to think you might actually be a nice guy."

In fact, I'm starting to think there's a side of Connor that only a lucky few get to see. Those either handpicked by him or connected by family ties.

There's a pause on the line before he says, "I am —to the people I care about."

For some reason, his words sting a little. Logically, it makes sense. Yet, it feels like he's caught himself being too genuine, too open—with me, of all people. So he had to remind us both who I really am to him.

I push down the growing annoyance and pivot back to business. "Can we meet to sort out the details of your big date? I need to line up the right media to capture your love-struck performance. America needs to buy into this fairy tale. See you do romance."

He makes a derisive sound. "I know how to romance a woman, Lexi."

I roll my eyes even though he can't see. "Yes, I gathered from your trail of jilted supermodel exes that you're quite the romancing expert. But this performance needs to convince all of America, not just the ladies."

"All right. Drop by my office first thing tomorrow."

I try to sound breezy. "I'm starting to think you set these dawn meetings just to torture me."

His laugh gets my heart racing—a fact that

annoys me more than I'd like to admit. "I prefer to clear the annoyances off my plate bright and early. Makes the rest of my day brighter."

"Charming as always," I reply drily. "Good thing no one else gets to experience this delightful side of you."

His voice drops a register. "Only those foolish enough to try to fuck me over, angel."

Just like that, the brief glimpse of "regular guy" Connor is gone. He's back to reminding me exactly who he is.

"All right, then, good night," I say, cutting the call short before my mouth runs away with me. My phone lands on the table harder than I meant to throw it.

Connor's never going to let my "betrayal" go. We seem to take one step forward, two steps back in this exhausting dance.

And the truth is, I did fuck him over. My reasons came from a pretty desperate place, sure, but they don't erase what I did. No matter how I spin it, I know I lost a piece of myself that night that I'll never get back.

He thinks he can't forgive me, but I can't forgive myself either.

Sometimes I think I should come clean to him. Yet, the more sensible side of me sees the mountain of debt, the bills stacking up, and Mom and Grace depending on me. It's too big a gamble, no matter how much the lie gnaws at me.

I wish I could make him understand the impossible corner I was shoved into. Though I suppose it hardly matters anymore.

The damage between us is already done.

TWENTY

Lexi

The next morning, I'm bracing myself for the usual long haul camped outside Connor's office, but to my surprise, his assistant gives me the green light to head on in. That's a first.

As I get closer, I hear music seeping out from under his slightly open office door.

I knock hard. "Connor?"

Silence.

I push the door open and step in cautiously. "Hello? It's Lex—"

My voice trails off when the bathroom door flies open, and a freshly showered Connor strides into view, wearing nothing but a towel slung criminally low on his carved hips.

I freeze as we lock eyes, my gaze involuntarily sweeping down his bare torso to that precarious towel line hinting at dark hair below.

Damn.

Now that's a man right there. Six feet something of raw, muscular male in the flesh. He may work out, but those muscles are all natural, like he's spent his entire life chopping wood in the wilderness and wrestling bears for fun.

A mix of desire and embarrassment crashes over me, and we stand in charged silence.

I can practically hear his arrogant amusement in my head. *See something you like?* His lifted brow taunts me.

Oh, absolutely.

I want to lick the water droplets off those abs like a dirty horny hoe.

I can't be trapped in here with *that* barely clothed. I haven't even had my coffee yet.

I do my best not to ogle the eye-catching tattoo sprawled across his chest. The design is a maze of bold, dark lines forming knots and curves, centered around a fierce-looking wolf. Definitely has some tribal or maybe Celtic vibes going on, probably because of his Irish American heritage.

"I can come back," I stammer, already inching backward even as every hormone in my body screams otherwise. "I knocked pretty loud, but you probably didn't catch it over the music."

"It's fine, come in," he says, voice sounding oddly rough. "I'm running late."

Could it be that Connor Quinn, Mr. Always-In-Control, is actually thrown off by me walking in on him like this?

Something thrills wildly inside at seeing his breath coming just a little too fast, color creeping up that strong neck.

I wet my dry lips, willing sensible speech to return before I do something truly reckless. Like grabbing that flimsy towel and giving it a firm yank southward. I bet he's big everywhere. I felt it at the photo shoot. Proportional to the rest of his hulking frame. It makes sense. The man is built like a giant oak tree, so of course he has a massive trunk to match.

Thankfully before I can execute that plan and get myself fired (or possibly arrested for sexual assault), Connor strides over to the stereo and kills the music, leaving the room filled with the sound of my awkwardly loud breathing. Smooth, Lexi.

"Is this another ploy to torture me?" I try to joke, fighting the urge to let my gaze wander. Eyes. Up.

He laughs, a bit huskier than usual. "Not this time. You're the one who waltzed in here unannounced."

"Your assistant told me to come right in!"

One brow arches. "I doubt that."

Damn, did she set me up?

"But you're here now," he says, voice dipping lower. "Give me a minute," he informs me, disappearing into the steamy bathroom. I can't help staring at his sculpted back muscles. And yeah, that towel does wonders for his backside.

He leaves the door cracked open. Of course he does.

I'm supposed to play it cool while this Greek god incarnate gets dressed a couple feet away, the door wide open? Come on now.

I stand there, hyperaware of every little sound. The rustling of clothes. Faint jingle of a belt buckle. Don't picture those bare thighs sliding into slacks . . . If he weren't already a billionaire, he could make real money on OnlyFans, even just crushing watermelons between his thighs.

"So, about the big date. How's tomorrow night sound?" I call out, purposely fixing my eyes on the breathtaking city view outside the window, trying hard not to think about the guy getting dressed in the bathroom. I mentally list every unsexy thing I can think of. Clogged toilets. Mistaking wasabi for guacamole. Taxes. My dead uncles' nose hairs. Vicky motorboating waitresses.

It's useless.

Cock.

That's all I can think of. His cock.

"Didn't catch that," comes his voice from the bathroom. Moments later, he steps out, smoothly pulling on a crisp white shirt over those broad shoulders. Of course it's still unbuttoned. At least he's in black slacks now, though they're tailored to leave little to imagination.

I yank my attention back up. "I was talking about setting up tomorrow night for the big date. I need to finalize some spots to ensure we get that ideal 'candid' photo op."

He reaches for a cufflink on his desk. "Fine. Let's do dinner at the Orchid Room. I'll tell my assistant to sort out some jewelry."

It takes everything in me not to roll my eyes. "Letting your assistant pick out jewelry? You sure know how to sweep a girl off her feet."

He freezes, cufflink paused in midair, and fixes me with a sharp look.

Uh-oh. I may have poked the bear a bit too hard. I'm finding it increasingly difficult to understand where the line is.

Connor closes the gap between us in a few strides. For a second, I consider stepping back, but nope, I'm standing my ground.

My pulse quickens as irritation ripples off him. Stretch out my hand, and I'd touch the tanned skin peeking through his partially buttoned shirt.

"Forgive my oversight, I wasn't aware you were the leading expert on romancing women," Connor says bitingly. "Why don't you share some of your vast knowledge then? What am I missing here?"

"Hey, I'm no Dr. Ruth, but come on—having your assistant buy gifts? Why not try actually getting to know Willow first? Her dreams, what she's passionate about, not just daddy's press releases . . ."

I trail off at his thunderous expression.

His reply is deadpan. "That would require actual conversation."

I can't help myself this time—I roll my eyes. "The brain's the sexiest organ in the body so it's nice to see a guy use his, not just flash his wallet and . . . other large assets."

Shut up, you fool.

A flash of anger sparks in his eyes. Connor shifts even closer, his scent—hot, masculine— wrapping around me. His open shirt grazes my arm, raising goose bumps.

His voice turns to a dangerously soft murmur. "You think it's smart to sass your clients, Miss Sullivan? I run a multibillion-dollar empire, yet you imply I lack brains."

I force down a hard swallow, clinging to my cool. "I wouldn't dream of insinuating such a thing. You're obviously a powerhouse in business. I'm just pointing out the cliché of outsourcing your romantic gestures to a PA."

Grabbing his belt, he slides it on slowly, the movement loaded with an unintended sensuality. "I've got a schedule that's packed 24/7. I don't have time to go traipsing around Tiffany's debating bracelets. Whatever I give her, she'll love it."

I scoff at the arrogance. "That perfectly

demonstrates the classic difference between men and women."

He smirks as he casually loops his belt. "This ought to be good. Go on, enlighten me."

"Simple. Men overplay their charm and talent, while women downplay theirs." I smile. "Classic case of men overselling, women underselling. Broad generalization, sure, but it holds up. Just look at any dating app profile ever."

He smiles. "You could be on to something there."

"It's not just me talking, there's actual research backing this."

Connor just chuckles patronizingly. "Ah yes, my mistake. I forgot your extensive psych background from not quite a year of academic psych study."

His low blow about my derailed career ambitions hurts more than I want to admit. Trust him to use the information from my file as ammo.

I cross my arms, partly in defense, partly as a challenge. "I learned enough to recognize an overinflated ego when I see one. But I'm sure a successful businessman like you has at least one skill to back up all that arrogance and swagger."

"Come on, Lexi, you know I've got skills." His eyes scan my flushed cheeks, pleased with himself. "And you're dying to experience them firsthand. You think I don't know what you want? It's been written all over that pretty face since you walked in here."

I lick my abruptly parched lips. He watches the gesture, his gaze darkening.

"Hate to break it to you and your ego, but you're way off what I want," I rasp, sounding more like a phone sex operator than the poised professional I'm aiming for.

Those intense blue eyes bore into mine, cutting through my weak attempts at indifference.

"Is that so?" he hedges, a half-smile forming. He reaches out, lightly pushing a stray hair behind my ear, his fingers just grazing my skin. I suppress a shiver.

I force my shaky legs to stay firm, my heart racing like crazy. "You're really confident, and I can't for the life of me figure out why."

Objectively, the guy's a sensory overload —undeniably handsome. Pair that with my weakness for arrogant jerks, and this situation gets complicated fast.

So when Connor starts dipping his head closer, alarms blare that he's actually going to kiss me.

My brain short-circuits. Is this really happening?

Instead, he takes my trembling hands, placing them firmly on his chest, chuckling softly at my startled intake of breath.

Fresh heat scorches my nerve endings feeling

those firm, sculpted pecs that I can now confirm are indeed rock-fucking-hard.

His voice gets all low and gravelly, right in my ear. "Indulge me a moment here. You're questioning my ability to dial up the romance? Imagine this: I turn up at your doorstep holding flowers, the exact shade of your eyes. I've been all over town for hours, tracking down a scent that's unmistakably you—bold, a tad untamed, yet unmistakably vibrant. And then, I whisk you off to a place so magical, so steeped in romance, it feels like it was made just for you . . ."

I have to catch my breath. Damn, this guy knows how to lay it on thick.

He's still holding my hands against his chest as if it's the most natural thing. I feel my palms start to sweat.

"Would I tempt you then, Lexi?" His voice takes on a dangerous tone. "If I pulled out all the stops for one night just for you, paid attention to every little thing to show how damn incredible I find you . . . would it get that sexy brain fired up?"

For a moment I'm caught up in the fantasy, pulse racing. Part of me wants to surrender to his intense sensuality.

Maybe he's actually serious.

"But hey, just so you know, I'm with you—the brain is without a doubt the sexiest thing about a woman."

Oh god. My sexy brain is moments from meltdown.

Now I get it. It's not just his looks. The way he's gazing at me, saying these things like I'm the most captivating woman alive . . . it works. It's a neat seduction technique.

Holding my gaze hostage, Connor drags my trembling hands down his chiseled chest, brushing over his hardened nipples.

My heart pounds like it's trying to break free.

"What's the story with your tattoo?" I ask breathily, tracing the intricate pattern inked across his chest, feeling his warmth.

He glances down. "It's Celtic, an old Irish symbol for protection and loyalty to family. Marks my commitment to those I care about."

His eyes lock with mine again and my mouth goes dry. Sweet mother of god, if I survive this without melting into a puddle of my own arousal, it'll be a miracle.

"It's beautiful. I've always wanted to go to Ireland."

He lets out a low chuckle, probably picking up on my nervous chatter.

Then my hands are on the move. South over that hot tattoo, over those delicious ridges of his criminally sexy abs. I feel his stomach muscles contract under my fingers, right on the line of scandalous.

A totally embarrassing sound slips out of me—half gasp, half *holy fuck* arousal that I can't even try to hide.

Inhibitions fraying by the second, I let him guide my hands closer to where his belt buckle rests, fingers just brushing the tempting trail of hair leading downward . . .

As I glance down, my breath catches in my throat at the sight of a very blatant, very prominent bulge in his trousers. He's rock hard and ready to go.

This is actually happening. And I sure as hell don't want to stop it.

What would it be like to have Connor fuck me? Just one round of angry sex. That's not too much to ask for, is it? It's been forever since I've been fucked, and if I'm being honest, I've been fantasizing about this ever since that disastrous hotel incident.

My hands tremble as I greedily grab on to his thick, hard cock through the fabric of his slacks. Connor is all fucking man. God, it feels good—it's been too long since I had a solid decent dick in my hand to play with, and his is thick, throbbing, and primed for some serious action.

Damn, he's huge.

I could do so much with this. Arousal pulses through my body at the image of him filling me up.

Just let me at it. Let him ravage me like there's no

tomorrow.

Our eyes lock in a heated stare as I grip his cock tighter. And fuck, I can already feel my panties soaking.

"How many nights have you lain in bed, fantasizing about me, Lexi?" he murmurs. "How many nights have you made yourself come, imagining it was my touch?"

"As if," I lie, still rubbing his length.

He clasps my chin in his grip. "Don't lie to me."

"Once or twice," I admit shamelessly. Once or twice a night, more like, but who's counting?

He grins, enjoying this power over me. His finger traces lightly over my bottom lip before catching it possessively.

Lost in lust, I fumble with the button on his pants and try to push my hand inside. But he catches my wrist before I can explore further, a smirk playing on his lips as he traps my fingers against his belt buckle.

"Easy there," he growls in a husky voice. "It's not gonna happen. You had your chance and you blew it."

My eyes go wide. "What? You're playing with me?"

Christ, what am I doing here? Horror floods me, snuffing out any leftover flickers of desire. I'm meant to be selling this guy as Monogamy Poster Boy of the Year, not trying to manhandle the goods behind closed doors.

His infuriating smirk deepens as he removes my overeager hands from his belt. "Those privileges are reserved for Willow," he chides with a tut. "Weren't those your rules? But I gotta say, it's pretty interesting to see how quick you can stray from the company script." His eyes light up with a mix of amusement and a touch of mockery at my embarrassment.

I snap my hands back as if scalded. "You're a jerk. And if it's only for Willow, why are you so aroused?"

"Your little hand was all over my dick, Lexi. That'll generally get its attention. I don't see what's so surprising about that."

Ugh. I could use ten deep breaths in the bathroom right about now.

Finally taking a solid inhale, I get a grip on myself. "Fine, let's do the date your way then," I say evenly, smoothing my tone. "Extravagant dinner at your five-star place. Have your assistant fetch an obnoxiously huge bouquet and half of Tiffany's best sellers. Willow's a lucky girl."

The sarcasm spills out of me as Connor casually finishes buttoning his shirt, that signature crooked smirk plastered across his face.

I have to get out of here before I completely lose my cool. I make a beeline for the door and am almost there when—

"Lexi." His voice freezes me in place.

I pivot around. "Yeah?"

He stares at me. "What does this elusive 'perfect date' of yours look like, huh?"

His directness throws me.

"Well?" he prompts when I'm slow to respond.

Do I even have a clue?

I look at him, taking in his sharp suit and those intense blue eyes.

"It's not about the upscale places or the flashy gifts," I begin tentatively. "It's about feeling truly understood. Finding out who she really is—her dreams, her fears, her secrets." I pause, carefully picking my next words. "You know, regardless of how rich or poor you are, what women really want is for men who are genuinely interested in knowing them. Not just as a conquest, but as a real person. To feel we're more than just a game, a notch in the bedpost. A man who's excited to learn all the parts of you, not just the surface stuff."

I shrug, my vulnerability making me squirm. "I want that immediate spark, but also the slow burn that lasts past the first night."

My rambling confession lingers in the air between us.

I brace for some cutting remark from him, but instead, he surprises me with a genuinely warm smile. Totally didn't see that coming.

So, I gather all the courage I've got left and

say quietly, "For what it's worth, I believe you're capable of everything I just described. I think you've got the whole romance thing in you, when you actually want to."

And with that mic drop, I spin on my heel and walk out.

TWENTY-ONE

Lexi

"We're on Quinn & Wolfe's dime for this, right?" Kayla asks, eyeing a cocktail that's literally on fire on the bar.

"Yep," I reply. We're "casually" hanging out in the Orchid Room, yet another pretentious establishment under Connor's hotel empire. The place where he plans to very publicly woo Willow, and I'm here to ensure the bloggers and paparazzi don't miss a second.

I'm jittery as hell, but I'm also feeling kind of fierce in my outfit. I unzip my NSFW bodycon leather dress even further down my front. The front zipper goes all the way from my tits to my bits with no stops in between. Decided to go braless tonight—nothing's cramping my style. Although, gotta admit, this dress is a bit snugger than I remember. Wrestling the zipper up felt like a workout. I'm pretty sure if I sneeze, my bust will pop out.

"So, what's our spending cap?" Kayla asks eagerly, scanning the menu.

I shrug. "Connor didn't give me one."

Her eyes gleam. "We can order *anything*? Even their top-shelf champagne?"

"Hmm, testing Connor with a hefty tab might not be the best idea. But then, his idea of 'expensive' probably doesn't match ours." Glancing around the plush bar, I muse, "If I owned a place like this, I'd probably spend my days making snow angels in cash and swinging from the chandeliers."

"Can you imagine." Kayla sighs dreamily.

No, I cannot. My dreams are more down-to-earth—a place of my own, taking care of Mom. That's about the size of it.

I watch the other crowds of girls in the bar—with their friends, with guys, on good dates, some on bad dates. It dawns on me. I used to be like them, out just for the laughs.

What I'm doing isn't working.

Never allowing myself to have fun has turned me into a massive grump. I'm trying so hard, sacrificing everything—for what? I'm spending all this money to keep Mom nearby in New York, but I'm not actually living. It's a sad epiphany to have in this upmarket bar.

We go for a couple of glasses of champagne that won't break the bank. I take a big swig of mine, maybe too enthusiastically.

"You okay?" Kayla asks, brow furrowed.

"Oh yeah, just this dress is squeezing the life out of me," I joke.

It's partly true but not the whole story. Still, she grins and accepts it. "You look really sexy tonight. Why didn't you warn me you were going full bombshell? I look like I'm about to chair a board meeting next to you."

Kayla's in her office attire while I'm looking like a rockstar's questionable date in this dress. I paired it with my trusty Doc Martens, aiming for that *Trying but not trying too hard* look. Even my hair got a special twirl today, a rare event in the history of my hairstyling.

"Sorry, I guess I went a bit overboard. It's not like I have many excuses to dress up these days."

And let's not even mention Connor's imminent appearance. As if my outfit choice had anything to do with him. Yeah, right.

Who knows, tonight I might stumble upon . . . someone. Anyone. I'm so sexually deprived I may start humping a bar stool leg if I don't get some action soon. The thirst is real.

I've already signaled the paparazzi around the bar, ready with their cameras. Willow's social media stars are here too, to craft those "spontaneous" couple videos.

"Did you figure out why he wants you on this

campaign? Maybe he's got a thing for you?" Kayla asks, wiggling her eyebrows suggestively.

I shift in my seat, the leather squeaking under the strain. Leather's pretty sweaty.

"As if." I take a deep breath, feeling the confession brewing. "But um ... actually ..."

I spill about Connor's office striptease, barely able to meet her wide eyes.

She looks at me like I'm delusional. "Are you sure?"

"I didn't hallucinate it, if that's what you're asking."

Kayla practically bounces in her seat. "Can you imagine the headlines? 'Connor's Steamy Moment with PR Gal Amid Love Saga with Willow.' It's practically on par with the original Willow scandal!" She seems more thrilled than concerned.

"You cannot breathe a word of this," I warn sharply.

She mimics zipping her lips and throwing away the key, a little too theatrically.

I take another big sip of my champagne, immediately thinking it might've been a mistake. The fizz is starting to make me feel like a balloon. Which isn't the greatest look in a zip-up bodycon dress.

"Anyway, he didn't exactly make a move, more like a tease before shutting it down."

"What a jerk." She eyes me with a mix of

shock and intrigue. "But if he had made an actual move . . . would you have . . . ?"

"I'd like to think not." I chuckle, though it's weak. "Though the man's not lacking in the looks department. And it's not like I'm drowning in offers these days."

She grins, nudging me. "Don't forget about the double date we've got lined up."

"Oh, yeah." I try to muster enthusiasm, but it comes out more like a grimace. "Everything's still good with Justin, then?"

I glance at Kayla, secretly hoping she's grown tired of her new guy. I know, it's not the award-winning friend move, but the idea of ducking out of our planned double date suddenly feels tempting.

Kayla swipes on every guy like he could be her Prince Charming. I'm more skeptical. How are you supposed to find a real connection through a few pics and texts? It's like trying to start a meaningful conversation with a store mannequin.

We need to use *all* our senses. Literally sniff out that primal chemistry, like werewolves in those sexy romance novels. Get the full pheromone picture before leaping into anything. Men sniffing around for fertility, women sniffing for testosterone and a good hairline. I learned that in a really cool sex physiology talk.

Kayla beams. "Things are great. We've hit date

number ten . . . or maybe eleven. I've lost count. And get this—I snored in front of him and he's still around!"

That's how you know it's true love.

I raise an eyebrow, impressed. Double figure dates in the online dating world? They might as well be picking out nursing homes together.

I'm the queen of the three-date curse. Either they disappear into thin air, or I get the too-much-too-soon guys. Like that one guy who blurted out "I love you" right when he came. Talk about jumping the gun. I mean, I know I'm good, but I'm not that good. Apparently later, he agreed because after that grand declaration of love, he vanished. Maybe he was too mortified to face me again. Or maybe he realized he didn't actually love me, he just loved my vagina. Sad to say, he's the only one to drop the L-bomb on me in my twenties.

"Have you guys had the 'let's delete our apps' chat yet?" I ask her.

Kayla squirms. "Not yet. Feels too soon."

"But it would bug you if he was still scrolling through other girls, right?"

"Well, duh," she huffs.

"Ah, the delicate steps of modern romance," I muse. "First, stop swiping. Then have the 'let's delete our accounts' talk. That's the big one."

"Do people actually ever fully delete them though? Feels like a lifetime subscription. Like, 'till death do us part, or until I get bored and reactivate my account.'"

I can't tell if she's joking. It's depressing.

"Anyway, now that we've done anal, I assume we're exclusive, right?" She turns to me, giving me a serious look. "I'd be disgusted if he was still trying to hook up with other girls."

I almost spit out my drink as she gazes at me with innocent eyes, like she didn't just drop a bomb on us. "No, I'd expect you have rite of passage now."

"Justin's definitely more daring than my usual type," she muses. "Makes me feel like such a prude in comparison. Have you ever tried anal?"

"Not unless you count that one time with an enema," I quip weakly. A prude? My sex life is dead compared to Kayla's.

Curiosity getting the best of me, I add, "What's it like?"

"Intense. A little painful. Uncomfortable at first. Feels like you gotta take a dump, but you don't."

I suck in a sharp breath, clenching my cheeks instinctively. "But do you actually enjoy it?"

"Yeah." She shrugs. "I think so."

Mom's living precariously through me and I'm living precariously through Kayla, it seems.

Having no experience with anal to share, I decide to be productive and signal the bartender.

The bar's buzzing with the energy of office people celebrating their temporary freedom from spreadsheet purgatory.

And I must admit, it feels good blowing off steam. Even if it means playing an extra in Connor and Willow's made-for-TV romance.

I'm mid–drink order when a Wall Street Ken type shoulders me aside. "Four Macallan, neat." Oblivious as his chunky Rolex smacks my bag on the counter.

My bag spills its guts—lip gloss, tampons, you name it, now decorating the floor. Great.

Fucking moron.

I bend down, fuming, to pick up my things, and the dress tightens around my chest, squeezing my lungs. Suddenly desperate for air, I inhale deeply into my stomach and hear the sound no one in a zipper dress wants to hear. *Rrrrrippppp.*

This can't be happening.

Oh, but it fucking is.

Full-on full frontal wardrobe malfunction.

I jerk upright.

"Shit! My dress!" I shriek in dismay.

The tiny teeth are mangled out of alignment, never to reunite again. Half the dress splits dramatically down the middle, exposing way more torso than appropriate, barely held together over my breasts by a flimsy zip, holding on for dear life.

I frantically try to hold it together but it's too

late. The damage is done. This isn't just a wardrobe malfunction, it's a wardrobe apocalypse.

Kayla's eyes are saucers of horror as she takes in the scene.

"I can see everything!" she squeals. She's got that look, like the kid from *The Sixth Sense*, except she's seeing way more than dead people.

"A little help here?" I hiss through clenched teeth, fumbling to bring the rebellious zipper ends together.

"You'll have to go to the bathroom and put the dress on the other way or something."

"I can't walk to the bathroom like this!"

Wall Street Ken swivels around, leering openly. "Damn baby, look at you."

I unleash my inner feral cat, hissing at him as I desperately try to push my dress back together. I'm showing way too much underboob, as well as torso.

Kayla tries to push the two parts of the dress together. "It's very stiff, I can't!"

Wall Street Ken, now the comedian, fires back with a "That's what she said!" line, earning a high-five from his buddy. Really original, pal.

His crew's loving it, hooting like a pack of hyenas as they feast their eyes on my fashion fiasco. More Toms, Dicks, and Harrys turn to gawk too. Lovely.

As if perfectly timed to maximize my

humiliation, in come Willow and Connor, making their grand entrance fashionably late. Because of course they fucking do.

What's left of my shriveled soul after becoming an accomplice to grand theft auto officially dies from shame.

Connor's hand rests casually on Willow's back, like they just stepped out of a Ralph Lauren ad, all glamorous and put-together.

Connor cuts through the crowd, his stare landing straight on me.

Kill me now.

He actually stops dead, jaw dropping open as he takes in the spectacle.

To my blistering dismay, he charges toward me, dragging Willow behind him. They were supposed to go right to their table. This wasn't in the script.

Kayla winces sympathetically. "I can't watch this trainwreck."

"Thanks, Kayla. I don't know what I'd do without you."

I reluctantly meet Connor's blistering stare as he stops directly in front of me, eyes homed in on my futile attempts to hold my dress together.

"What the hell are you wearing?" he snaps by way of greeting, raking a hand over where his hair would be, had he not been sporting that ruggedly shaven look.

"It's not a style choice, my zipper exploded!" I shoot back indignantly. Painfully aware of Connor's heavy gaze sweeping my exposed skin before snapping back to my surely crimson face.

He looks momentarily thrown, muscle feathering his tight jaw. "Jesus, Lexi . . . you're practically indecent." His gravelly reprimand sends more heat flaming my burning cheeks.

I grunt in a very unladylike manner. "Thanks, I hadn't noticed!"

Willow's attempt to hide her giggle behind her clutch does nothing to ease the tension.

Connor curses under his breath. Then shockingly, starts unbuckling his belt. Um, what's happening right now? Is he going to spank me for my fashion faux pas?

As he slides the belt from his waist, I can't resist a quip. "You don't have to go all Magic Mike on me in solidarity."

That earns me a withering glare.

"Hold still," he orders gruffly. Before I can protest, he wraps the warm leather firmly around my exposed waist. Rough hands take control—forcefully pressing the two halves of the dress together and cinching it tightly to keep the ragged fabric in place.

I gasp involuntarily—whether it's from the scrape of his knuckles leaving trails of heat across my sensitive stomach or the commanding dominance as he fixes his belt on me, I'm not entirely sure anymore. It's like he's claiming ownership over my body with each tug of the belt.

"There, you're not flashing the entire bar anymore," he rumbles low near my ear.

"Oh thank god," I breathe unevenly, even though I look ridiculous wearing a bodycon dress with a broken zip up the middle and a man's belt securing me in place. It's not exactly runway material, but at least it's not rated R anymore.

My hand moves unconsciously to loosen his makeshift belt corset strangling oxygen from my lungs. Only for Connor to clamp my wrist midair before I make contact, danger smoldering in his sudden warning stare. "Don't . . ."

Pulse galloping, I let my hand drop obediently.

Willow looks murderous now, her smile dried up. Oh yeah, we've gone off-script big time. Again.

"I hope the press didn't catch that little show," she snaps, blinking aggressively enough to sprain something. Her insanely long lashes have to be fake. I've never managed to successfully glue a strip of falsies onto my stubborn lids.

Connor, meanwhile, looks like he's swallowing glass, his gaze burning a hole into me before he abruptly looks away. He shoves his hands in his pocket with a gruff cough.

"You guys should head to your table," I say, wanting them away.

Far, far away.

Connor just grunts, shaking his head as he steers Willow off, hand on her back.

Little prickles of awareness I don't want to acknowledge dance down my spine as I watch him attentively settle her into her seat, his big hand lingering almost possessively on her bare shoulder. Willow preens under the PDA.

"Well, fuck me sideways," I hiss to Kayla. "That was . . ." I trail off, no words sufficient.

"At least Vicky's done way worse in public," Kayla offers.

She's not wrong. But talk about an HR nightmare.

I sneak a few glances over at their table, where Connor's sprawled back in his chair looking sinfully attractive. His shoulders stretch the seams of that shirt almost illegally.

Meanwhile, Willow's fawning all over him, letting her nails dance up his thick forearm.

Connor catches her hand, bringing those red tips to his mouth for a brush of a kiss without breaking his stare. Smooth operator.

He leans in, murmuring something that makes Willow melt against him with a dreamy sigh.

And damn it all, their display sparks an unwelcome flicker of envy in my gut.

Willow looks stunning. That hair of hers—it's like it has its own entourage of tiny hair fairies primping it. I'd kill to wake up looking half that good.

"They sure look hot together, don't they?" Kayla remarks.

I grunt something noncommittal, trying to squash the envy bug. Hormones make asses of us all, I remind myself.

I'm supposed to be polishing Willow's image, not making eyes at her guy. Or letting him get handsy with my dress. Guilt hits me.

Poor thing's had her share of drama lately. Though I suppose being crowned Miss USA takes the sting off a bit.

I watch Connor order champagne, sending a bottle to us and one to his table.

Kayla bounces in her seat. "Dom Pérignon! Oh yeah, I'll have some of that."

I quickly calculate in my head—that single vintage bottle likely costs a full week of care hours for Mom. I debate trying to sneakily return ours for the cash instead.

I paste on a smile for the server who's making a big show of presenting our bottle to us. "Super generous of him. Do send our thanks," I say, voice dripping with forced cheer.

"Cheers to us!" Kayla sings out, lifting her glass.

I clink glasses with her, my mind still stuck on what a waste of money this is. I'd rather have a week's wages. But I guess to him, it's petty change. He probably uses champagne as mouthwash, and then spits it out because it's not fancy enough.

Now my sexy leather dress feels exactly what it is—cheap pleather I snagged during a Black Friday blowout sale.

These people were born wrapped in silks and gold. Christ, the diamonds dripping from Willow's earlobes alone could fund Mom's care for the next five years.

I stomp on the green-eyed monster threatening to rear its ugly head. It's not a good look, and it sure isn't helping anyone.

"I wonder if he'll be stealing drinks tonight," Kayla says, giving me a knowing look.

I wince, the memory of my made-up "meet cute" crashing back. "Uh, yeah, maybe," I mutter, not meeting her eyes.

Willow throws her head back, laughing obnoxiously loud at something Connor said, or didn't say—it's hard to tell. All her actions seem carefully staged for social media. Watching her is like seeing a reality show unfold live. I half expect her to turn to the nearest camera and start giving a confessional.

Now she's hand-feeding Connor a bite of food, giggling loudly as he nips at her fingers. It's so cliché it's painful. I think I just threw up in my mouth a little.

I spot a blogger angling greedily for the money shot.

I take a cautious sip of my champagne, scared in case the dress decides to pop further. Expensive bubbles or not, I'm going to need it. This is going to be a long, tortuous, excruciatingly well-documented night.

TWENTY-TWO

Lexi

An hour later, after I've ninja'd my way through the bloggers and press hounds, I return to find a champagne-trashed Kayla, blissfully oblivious to the world around her.

"Mistake," I mutter to myself, snagging her abandoned water glass and taking a hefty swig. "Hey, party animal, maybe try matching that with some water?" I suggest, throwing her a *Get your shit together* look.

She just gives me a sloppy shrug. "What do you expect? I was bored out of my mind. Had to make my own fun."

"Hey there," an unfamiliar male voice asks from over my shoulder.

I turn and nearly choke as I take in Michelangelo's blond David statue come to life behind me, all chiseled muscle and tousled hair. His eyes glint with amusement. I wonder if it's at my bug-eyed reaction to him or the fact I'm wearing a man's belt holding my dress disaster together.

I eloquently reply, "Are you talking to me?" Smooth. Nailing the first impression as always.

He chuckles. "Yeah, I was talking to you, Lexi."

My eyebrows shoot up. Wait, he knows my name?

He catches the look of utter confusion on my face and nods to the happy couple. "Relax, I'm a buddy of Connor's. I know about your PR stunt tonight."

"Oh." Act cool. Don't drool.

Easier said than done.

"Mind if I join you?"

"Please do." A smile slinks onto my lips. Don't mind if I do. Let's hope he didn't catch the Great Zipper Incident earlier. Or maybe that's why he's here?

"So, how do you know Connor?" I ask.

"We're old drinking buddies. I produce *Hello, New York*," he says casually.

Oh, just the producer of one of the biggest talk shows in the city, no big deal.

Connor's all set for his charade on New York's sensationalist gossip show in a few days' time, ready to play up his "reformed bad boy" image for the cameras. Meanwhile, Willow's been laying it on thick on social media, dubbing Connor as *the one* and *her soulmate*—much to the delight of her followers who lap up this overly sweet narrative. He has to keep his side of the bargain.

Hot Producer settles in beside me and Kayla. Suddenly, Connor's interview just got way more interesting.

"I'm a huge fan," I lie with a poker face. Truth is, his show is gossip TV's version of Vallure PR, showcasing celebrities who are famous for being famous.

The last episode featured the Butt Buildr queen herself, Gina Malone. No need to burst Hot Producer's bubble, though.

Connor wasn't exactly thrilled about headlining the show, but it's pure gold for Willow. Her demographic devours this kind of shit.

Hot Producer chuckles. "Don't think I'm buying the flattery, but thanks for the ego boost. I'm Mason, by the way."

"Hello, Mason," I purr, ignoring Kayla's impatient demand for another round in the background. I'll make it up to her.

"You're handling PR for Connor's latest drama?" Mason asks, a teasing glint in those chestnut eyes. "That must be a true test of wills."

"You have no idea," I reply, sipping my drink with a smirk.

"Must be fun, chaperoning his dates." He nods at the cozying pair. "No surprise he's after Willow though. Considering his thing for her mom and all."

My eyes widen slightly at that tidbit. Ugh, I wouldn't put a twisted threesome past Connor and his insatiable libido.

"They sure look close," I say breezily, steering my gaze away from infuriatingly photogenic couple. "And Willow's stunning."

"Like yourself," Mason returns, dragging his gaze down my body appreciatively. He is so full of shit, I'm nowhere near Willow's league. "I like your dress. Bold choice."

My smile stays delighted at the attention from this hot guy, but inside, I'm on alert. Did he catch the nipslip show earlier? This dress is still sweltering, so I may have unzipped a tad bit more . . .

Right as I'm about to dazzle Mason with some witty repartee, I'm aware of a presence looming behind me. A scent that's all kinds of sexy wafts over, derailing my train of thought.

In other words, it's Connor.

"Mason," his rough voice cuts in. We swivel around to find him standing at the bar. His smile is tight, not quite reaching his eyes as he sizes Mason up.

Kayla shields her drink protectively. No way she's letting him swipe this one.

His steely gaze then lands on me. "Remember

why you're here, Lexi," he says, his tone dripping with condescension.

My temper flares. "Actually, there's nothing needing my attention right now. I might as well leave."

"You'll leave when I give the word."

My stomach swoops traitorously as I gape at him. Who the hell does he think he is?

Mason's warm chuckle cuts through the crackling tension. "No worries, I'll let Lexi be. Got someone else to catch up with anyway." He takes my hand, kissing it gently as Connor looks on, his annoyance barely contained.

I can't believe Connor's cock-blocking me. The nerve. If I didn't know better, I'd think it was jealousy instead of him just trying to ruin my happiness because he hates me.

Red-hot rage blazes through me, and any scrap of professionalism flies out the bar. "Do you get your rocks off on these power trips?"

"Try to restrain yourself," Connor growls. He seems to think my question was rhetorical. "I know Mason's got a Beamer, but no need to throw yourself at him."

"Oh fuck off," I snap, my fists clenching involuntarily. "If I sleep with Mr. Hotshot Producer, it'll be for that glorious body and mind-blowing sex. Not his car!"

Beside me, Kayla sits very still, not breathing.

Bracing for the impending explosion.

I watch with bated breath as he ever-so-slowly palms the polished wood on either side of me, effectively caging me in. He takes full advantage of those extra inches, looming over me intimidatingly. When he speaks, his voice is lethal. "Is that what you need then? To be fucked senseless? If you wanted my undivided attention tonight, there were easier ways than wearing that dress."

"As if," I huff, but my body betrays me as a coil of forbidden heat uncurls. I clench my thighs against the throb there, pulse kicking. Oh god, I do just need to be fucked. Otherwise, I might never find my senses again.

"Maybe I should give Mason a heads-up about you," he murmurs in my ear, making sure Kayla can't hear. "He's quite attached to that fancy car of his."

My jaw drops in indignation, a fire burning inside me at his arrogance. He'll only ever see me as gutter trash, someone beneath his standing. He thinks he can treat me like garbage and I'll just smile and take it. And the messed-up part is, I kind of have to. Because he pays the bills and I need the money. A nasty power play.

I force my lips into a bright, artificial smile, like the good little actress I am. "Don't you worry about my love life, Connor. Just concentrate on your own. Enjoying your little performance tonight?" My tone drips syrupy sarcasm. "It's nice to see you on your best behavior for the cameras for once."

He cocks one arrogant eyebrow. "Me? As I recall, you were the one putting on quite the performance earlier."

His gaze pointedly coasts down my body, lingering briefly before meeting my eyes again. I flush, squirming at the memory of his hands on my bare skin, securing me in his belt.

"That was a wardrobe malfunction," I snap. "Drop it."

"If you say so." Amusement glints in his eyes. "I hope you're getting my best side in all those paparazzi shots, Lexi."

"The view of your back as you leave, right?" I shoot back. "Got it covered. Seems you and Willow are having a right cozy time."

I try to keep the bitterness from seeping into that last part.

He leans in, voice pitched low. "Oh, I'm enjoying myself thoroughly. All this gazing and hand-feeding for the cameras before I have my way with Miss USA in the coat check later . . ."

My eyes blow wide in shock.

Connor chuckles.

"Just messing with you, Lexi." He winks and saunters off, leaving me standing there, my face burning. The nerve of him.

I let out a long breath, watching him return to Willow. Screw professionalism, I can't cope with much more of these verbal spars without losing my head completely.

I lean against the bar, needing support. "Hit me with another one," I tell the bartender.

"Damn," Kayla says, exhaling. "That dress with the zipper definitely did the trick. He looked like he wanted to rip it right off your body with his teeth."

◆ ◆ ◆

Connor and Willow's choreographed date from hell drags on for hours. I've done my part, but it seems like Captain Ego's enjoying keeping me here as his own personal entertainment.

Enough's enough. I stand to go to the restrooms, then decide to hell with it—I'm bailing.

I spot Willow sans her obnoxious other half and stride over. "Heya, do you know where Connor is?"

Willow smiles thinly at me, obviously still salty about the whole wardrobe malfunction. "He went to take a call that way." She fidgets with her diamond bracelet. "And did you manage to snap some pics of me hand-feeding Connor earlier?" she asks excitedly. "It was such a cute moment between us."

I'm doing my best not to let my eyes roll out of my head. "Yep, we caught that adorable moment," I say, trying not to choke on my words.

Willow peers at me, slight panic in her eyes. "You didn't actually catch me eating in any of those shots, did you?"

Oh, for god's sake.

"You looked amazing, as always. Now, excuse me, I need to have a quick word with Connor."

As I head toward the restrooms, I overhear Connor's unmistakable velvety voice just around the corner, freezing me in my tracks. "Lexi's team is handling this PR shitstorm, yeah."

My ears instantly perk up, pulse fluttering nervously.

"Vallure PR is a joke company." His voice drips with so much contempt I actually flinch. "They're like the dollar store of PR firms. Perfect for those 'It girls' slinging fake designer gear who need someone to clean up their mess."

I bristle instinctively, stung. Sure, Vallure isn't the top PR firm in town, but hearing it said so brutally is a gut punch. Just once, I'd like to be part of a firm that gets real respect, not just sneers. I'm sick of feeling that sting of embarrassment every time I hand out my business card.

"I know them. Vicky and I run in the same circles." Mason's casual tone holds a hint of amusement from around the corner. "She's a handful. Your PR girl tonight, Lexi, she seems all right."

A knot of unease twists in my belly. Please don't say anything demeaning, Connor.

"Her? Wouldn't waste your time, man. She's probably already eyeing your black AmEx and loosening that dress zipper on cue."

His ugly words land like an open-palmed slap. So, after everything, Connor still sees me as nothing more than a gold-digger? That's his takeaway from our interactions?

Pain and outrage flood me. I pivot back toward the bar, blinking furious tears, refusing to shed them over this jerk. For a second, I want to go full-on *Braveheart* and let out a primal scream of rage.

So I'm just a walking punchline to him. A joke PR girl, from a joke firm, who jokes her way into men's wallets.

I glance down at my cheap pleather dress and even cheaper shoes and fly past Willow who looks like Blake freaking Lively, except with bigger boobs. Blond, beautiful, sophisticated Willow who seems to embody everything I lack.

Fine, I'll give Connor his glossy, airbrushed photos of him and Willow, looking like Ken and Barbie if they were less plastic and more cunning —it's my job after all. But after tonight? He can take his millions and his smug grins and cruel assumptions and shove them right up his—

"Kayla, get your coat," I say, charging toward her as fast as the zipper dress will let me.

She blinks up at me, her tipsy haze momentarily lifting.

"We're out of here. It's late, we've got work tomorrow. Plus Connor Quinn is an absolute bastard, and I can't stand another minute in the same room as him."

Kayla pouts dramatically but slides off her stool, unsteady on her feet.

"A bastard, am I?" I stiffen as Connor's voice drifts from behind me.

Slowly I turn to face his towering, perfectly tailored frame, hands casually in his pockets. Like he doesn't have a care in the world.

"How will I ever get over such a harsh critique, Lexi?"

My face heats up, but I stand my ground. "Sometimes the truth stings, doesn't it?"

He lets out a low, amused chuckle. "It's fine, you're free to go. Willow and I will be heading upstairs soon . . ." His words hang in the air, heavy with implication.

Jealousy stabs at me, unwanted and sharp.

Don't do this in front of me, I want to plead. *Don't rub your perfect little romance in my face when you just got done tearing me to shreds.*

"Great. I'm so glad your fake romance is real," I

say, my voice strained with forced indifference.

He lazily digs into his pocket and pulls out a wad of bills. "Here, take this for the cab ride home," he murmurs, pressing the cash into my numb hand.

How charming. I wouldn't be surprised if he patted me on the head and called me a good girl. It's beyond humiliating. His taunts hit me again and again, like a cruel boxer, for maximum humility. For reminding me of my station in his life, of what I am.

If I knew I was winning the Mega Millions later tonight, I'd cram the bills down his throat. Watch him choke on them like he's choking on his own ego.

My chest tightens as I watch him saunter off toward the elevator without a care in the world, presumably to dislocate something in bedroom Olympics with perfect Willow.

I look down at the thick wad of cash crumpled in my sweaty palm. Enough to get me to the next state, never mind over the bridge. To travel far away from here. From him.

And I hate myself for slipping it into my purse anyway as I watch his arrogant back recede.

TWENTY-THREE

Lexi

"Morning, Willow!" I chirp when she answers, my tone all slick professionalism. Inside though, I'm ashamed to admit I lay awake imagining her and Connor's hotel porn shoot in vivid detail. Because I'm a masochistic loser. "Did you see the press coverage from yesterday? It's great!"

I wonder if her eyelashes survived the night.

"Yeah, I had a quick look at the shots," comes her breezy tone. But there's this little uptick in her voice, a tiny crack in the veneer. It's broadcasting loud and clear that Willow's been deep-diving into the social media abyss, leaving no blog unturned, no reel unwatched. "They're good, though they made my knee look weird in one. Can you fix that?"

"Sure." Lying flows like Connor's expensive champagne for me these days.

I hear the swish of sheets and her footsteps echoing on floor. No doubt meandering some presidential suite wrapped in a teeny silk sheet, with a naked Connor lounging on Egyptian cotton.

It's 10 a.m. and they're still in fucking bed?

I grind my teeth, envisioning myself on a beach with a Jason Momoa cabana boy massaging me while Connor and Willow are conveniently lost at sea. Happy thoughts. On a different beach to Mom and her Sean Connery cabana boy, obviously.

"I'm certain it's just the lighting. You look flawless as always." Casually I probe, "How's Connor feeling about the photos this morning?"

"I'll ask him," she hums distractedly.

He's still there then.

Against my will, I picture her raking her nails on that sculpted torso like I did in his office that day, making him shudder. My gut twists, simmering with resentment. Why the hell do I even care?

"Oh, hey, this is a little awkward," Willow says, lowering her voice conspiratorially like she doesn't want Connor to hear. "Last night with Connor was magical, but he needs to step it up publicly, you know? For the press narrative."

She pauses before hitting me with, "Could you suggest to him that he buy me that new Tiffany choker that *Vogue* is raving about? The super exclusive one with only a few in existence? I just think a symbolic gesture like that could really showcase our devotion."

I nearly gag at her brazen move, but I keep my cool. "Yeah sure, I can pass along the request. I can't guarantee it, though."

I know full well she could buy a diamond choker for every day of the week herself. This is about Connor kneeling publicly in front of her. An Instagrammable romance ritual.

"Great. Thanks, Lexi."

I say bye and toss my phone down in disgust as a hungover-as-fuck Kayla blinks at me.

The absolute last place *on earth* I want to be today is Quinn & Wolfe headquarters. And the absolute last man I want to lay eyes on is Connor bloody Quinn.

But, for the sake of this upcoming *Hello, New York* interview that's supposed to paint him as boyfriend of the year, I have to grit my teeth and handle a strategy session with Prince Charming himself.

He grunts a greeting when I enter his office, looking exhausted from his all-night romp with Miss Wholesome America. His shirt's undone, displaying his tanned chest because he's physically incapable of buttoning above the fourth hole apparently. Annoyingly, my pulse kicks up despite still simmering over his nasty comments last night.

Vallure PR is a joke company.

Boom.

She's probably already eyeing your black AmEx and loosening that dress zipper.

Boom.

The first one I don't care about so much. The second one, I definitely fucking do. That one has replayed in an infuriating mental loop since. How dare he.

"Are you satisfied with the press coverage?" I ask crisply, taking a seat. I plan to keep this quick and professional. In and out.

He grunts again, not tearing his eyes away from his screen. "Long as Willow's not complaining, I don't care."

Charming as ever.

I call upon my last scraps of professionalism. "Speaking of your lady love, she has a suggestion. She wants you to buy her a diamond Tiffany choker so she can showcase it on her Instagram and show how devoted you are."

That gets his attention. His gaze locks on mine, intense and piercing. "And how's a piece of jewelry supposed to prove I'm devoted?" His tone is laced with skepticism. And possibly a hint of disdain.

I brace myself. "It's not just any piece. It's going to set you back a quarter mil."

A shadow of irritation flickers across his face. "Fine. Just handle it."

Just handle it. Sure, no problem. I'll just pop on over to Tiffany's and plunk down a quarter of a million dollars like it's chump change.

His dismissive tone sets my nerves on edge. Not even a raised eyebrow? A jaw clench? Nothing? "That's your take? Dropping hundreds of thousands on a trinket merits no reaction?"

He rolls his eyes as if I'm wasting his precious time. "What do you want from me?"

What do I want from him? A dozen reckless thoughts skitter through my mind, each more inappropriate than the last, before I tamp them down.

I want to strangle you with the stupid choker. I want to take that money and run.

"Seriously? You're okay with shelling out for a two-hundred-and-fifty-grand necklace that means nothing to you?" I ask incredulously, my voice rising with each word.

"Unless you'd rather explain to Willow why her 'devoted' boyfriend can't be bothered with 'symbolic gestures.'" He lays on the sarcasm thick.

Taking a deep breath, trying to collect myself, I watch as he runs a hand over his shaved head. He lounges back, the action causing his loosely buttoned shirt to gape ever further, revealing a swath of his bronzed chest. I drag my gaze away.

"Come on, out with it," he goads, eyes glinting. "Let's hear what you've really got on your mind."

I meet his gaze evenly. "Connor, your attitude is shocking. Yes, it's your money. And you do so much good with it. But can you appreciate how life-changing that sum is for most people?"

I think of my tiny shit apartment. La Maison du Leak. That necklace could buy me a nice home for Mom and Grace. A better life.

"You're sending me to buy some jewelry that costs a house," I continue, unable to shut up now. "It'd just be nice if you acknowledged the impact. That kind of money changes people's lives."

My life.

I think again of my crappy apartment with its leaky ceilings and peeling linoleum. Then picture Mom and Grace happily making dinner in a cozy, warm kitchen.

Mom's life.

Grace's life.

Anyone's really, apart from the mighty Connors of the world swanning about in bespoke Armani suits without a care.

His eyes flash with anger. "Perhaps I shouldn't trust you with the task since you'll probably end up spending it on a Lamborghini Huracán. The new model's just out with diamond-studded rims."

He just doesn't get it. Never will.

"Maybe I will," I snap. "I deserve a treat

for putting up with patronizing clients. I'll grab Willow some piece of junk from a pawn shop since you clearly won't notice. May as well buy her affection from the lost and found bin. Then I'll splurge on a hot new car for myself, like the lowly gold-digging thief that I am."

"Just get the damn necklace," he growls, pressing a hand to his ear as if my words are physically paining him. Maybe it's just the sound of my voice getting on his nerves. "Sort it with my finance team."

"With pleasure," I spit back, already imagining him choking on that quarter-mil receipt. This is what my career's come to—playing errand girl for overbearing tycoons.

"There's a good girl," he sneers, adding insult to injury.

I resist grabbing that ridiculous crystal paperweight off his desk and smashing it over his arrogant head. If he calls me a "good girl" in that condescending tone one more time, I'll show him exactly where he can shove that crystal blob instead. And it won't be pleasant for either of us.

I exhale slowly, willing the shreds of my patience not to detonate completely, and pull out my laptop alongside his belt from my bag. "Here's your belt back. Thank you."

He smirks. "You could've kept it. I wasn't expecting it back."

"And why exactly would I want to keep your belt?" I sneer. "What, is it studded with diamonds I can pawn off?"

He cocks an eyebrow, clearly entertained by my snark. "Gotta say, it looks better on you."

I make a noise between a scoff and grunt. Connor throwing compliments, no matter how half-baked, instead of his usual barbs throws me. He doesn't get to do that after spending all night with Willow.

"Irrelevant," I snap. "Can we discuss prepping for the interview now?" I need to get us back on safer ground. The fact that Connor can still knock me off-balance so easily is an irritation I'd rather not examine too closely.

I'm just escaping Connor's office when Nurse Ratched calls. My stomach drops, knowing it's never happy news from Brenda.

"Your mom's had a nasty flare," she barks, skipping any kind of hello. "Needs you here straight away."

I jab the elevator button as my gut swoops. "Is she okay? What's going on?"

"She's had increased breathing struggles, chest tightness. We re-stabilized her oxygen, but she's back on supplementary gas flow."

Ah, the oxygen tank, Mom's most hated accessory.

Brenda should never pen a *COPD for Dummies* guide. Too personality-deficient to use normal words for us clueless civilians. Thank god for my late-night internet deep dives into COPD.

"And now? How's she doing?" I push, heart in my throat.

"Resting finally, but anxious and asking for you repeatedly. So hurry along."

She cuts the call with her usual warmth.

As the elevator drops, so does my heart. Please let it be just a blip. Mom's condition has been like a ticking time bomb lately, and this sounds like a big, bad boom.

Dammit, Vicky will flip. But work will just have to wait.

My feet barely touch the ground as I race to the care home through three subway rides. Mom's exhausted but breathing easier. I hold her hand, providing whatever comfort I can until she drifts off. The doctor says it was temporary. Still, leaving her guts me.

I'm starting to wonder how many more heart-stopping, panic-inducing, rush-to-the-care-home episodes I can handle. Life is so damn hard sometimes. While an absurdly priced diamond necklace is being delivered to Willow as we speak,

I'm over here trying to scrape together enough cash just to keep us afloat.

The difference in our lives blows my mind. I know I shouldn't compare, but it's tough when their world of extreme wealth is thrown in my face every day. A world I'll never experience, no matter how hard I work.

I slip back into the office quietly, praying to avoid Vicky.

No such luck. She clicks her fingers an inch from my face. "Where the hell have you been?"

"I had a family emergency," I say evenly. "Sorry."

"We don't pause business hours for personal shit," she snaps. "You don't see me running off when my mother fakes another shower slip for attention."

My eyes widen. Kayla's jaw hits the floor behind Vicky. Mental note: remind Mom to time her lung disease flare-ups outside of Vicky's business hours.

"Of course, won't happen again," I force out, biting my tongue.

Vicky scans me critically with her shark eyes. "Willow wants you off the project. What the hell did you do to piss her off?"

"What? Nothing!" My confusion is genuine, as is my dismay. "I positioned Willow flawlessly in the press. They painted her as an angel. I don't get it. I'm really off the campaign?"

"Nope, Connor insisted you stay. Said he can't be bothered with someone new now." She shrugs. "His words: 'She's less irritating than the rest.'"

What?

That makes zero sense. If anything, I annoy him more than everyone else in the world. The man must be a secret masochist, wanting to drag out our mutual misery.

Or he still has a game plan with you.

Vicky claps loudly, making everyone jump. "Listen up, people, we're going to the Quinn & Wolfe drinks tonight."

Kayla gasps. "Lexi and I have plans already."

We do? This is news to me.

"Yes, you do," Vicky snaps, eyes flashing. "I just spelled it out for you. Tonight, your one and only mission is to be the face of this company, ladies."

Kayla's face crumples. "But we have a double date planned."

Shit, it's all coming back to me now. I forgot that I promised Kayla about the damn double date.

"Raincheck 'em," Vicky sneers. "If the guys are interested, they'll come begging later."

With that, she whirls around and storms off to her office.

Kayla slumps back, defeated. "Justin's gonna kill me if I bail last minute."

I wince in sympathy. "Hey, we'll go for a quick

drink then sneak out. Vicky won't even notice."

I force a bright smile despite feeling dead on my feet. After the day I've had, all I'm craving is a steaming bath and the soothing sound of murder podcasts. I don't want fake small talk at Connor's office bar or flirting with Kayla's new boyfriend's buddy.

I can never focus after Mom's health scares. And I'm still monumentally pissed over Connor's cruel jabs this morning. And having to manage his stupid fake dates. I hate everything about being on their ridiculous look-at-our-bullshit-love-story campaign. Watching them play kissy face last night was fucking awful.

Maybe I should ask one of those "Am I The Asshole?" forums. This is a complex situation with a number of potential victims and assholes. Sounds like a job for the wisdom of the internet.

But Kayla's counting on me. So I'll suck it up, play social butterfly for an hour. I can smile through anything for an hour or two.

Here's hoping.

TWENTY-FOUR

Connor

"Slider, sir?" the server asks, rolling over with a tray of mini-burgers toward me.

I grab a couple, my patience wearing thin.

Normally, these shindigs are my bread and butter—an opportunity to mingle with the team, to catch what's on their minds when they clock out. Let them let loose a little, spill their guts.

But tonight, I'm not feeling it. A throbbing pain hammers away in my ear, dragging my mood down to an all-time low. The headaches have been more frequent, more relentless. Luckily, I've got that session with the new doc booked.

And as if the pounding in my skull wasn't enough, I've got Ethan, our Food and Beverage Director yapping my ear off about his honeymoon. Something about private pools and hula dancers. Lately, having anyone talk on my left feels like nails on a chalkboard to my sanity.

I muster a half-assed grunt as Ethan pauses to take a breath.

I down another hefty swig of Macallan, the burn the only thing taking the edge off this bitch of a headache. Then I slam another slider into my mouth as if it's to blame for my foul mood.

Ethan keeps prattling on, oblivious. Volcanoes or snorkeling or some other tropical crap. Who gives a fuck. If I wanted a riveting tale of tropical escapades tonight, I'd have sat in with a *Lonely Planet*.

That image of Lexi in the lethal zipper dress from last night is seared into my brain on a damn loop. That kind of outfit could stop a man's heart. Stepping into the bar and catching her looking like she forgot half her wardrobe, I thought I might have to call a doctor for an entirely different reason. Did she wear it to get a rise out of me? Both figuratively and literally? Wouldn't put it past her.

I tear into another slider, this one getting a double dose of my pent-up frustration.

And despite deliberately goading Lexi all night, I let Willow stay in our most expensive available suite then went home alone. Willow tried her best to pull me upstairs, but there's zero happening there.

I haven't jerked off as much in years. I couldn't keep my hands off my cock, the need for release consuming me until I lost count of how many times I came last night.

All I could think about was taking Sullivan by her ridiculous zipper and ravishing her in the hotel elevator, pressing the button for the penthouse while we banged against the mirrored walls on our way up to the 70th floor.

I'd finally finish what we started weeks ago in that damn hotel bathroom. Since she first walked into that meeting with the senator and Willow, the sexual tension between us has been building like a wildfire.

We could bang it out and put us both out of our misery. I'd slide every thick inch into her, claiming what I'd been craving ever since she wrapped those creamy thighs around me. And this time, I won't stop until Lexi is a quivering, moaning mess under me.

One and done. One intense, hate-fueled session to get her out of my system once and for all. Life could continue on its course, and maybe the flames would die.

No wonder Mason was salivating over her like a starved mutt. My inner caveman couldn't help but take over. It was like a jolt to my competitive edge, like she's my plaything and I didn't want Mason having a turn with her. I didn't get to finish what we started that night, and I'll be damned if he gets his shot.

"Connor?" Ethan's voice cuts through my

thoughts, his expectant look suggesting I've missed a part of his riveting monologue.

"Huh?" I respond, caught off guard. Damn, I must've spaced out while he droned on. Trying to pay attention is exhausting lately.

Salvation comes in the form of Jim from security showing up at my side. "Sir, can I have a word?"

I clap Ethan on the back, maybe a bit too hard. Just my way of saying thanks for nearly putting me to sleep. "Ethan, gotta handle this."

I turn to Jim.

"We found a lead on your car," he informs. "Identified a guy potentially connected to the theft ring."

He drops a name that doesn't ring any bells. "And is he tied to Lexi Sullivan?"

Jim looks uncertain. "We're not sure yet. But the guy knew his way around the garage cams."

"Good work. Stay on it."

And speak of the little devil herself—there's Sullivan, thankfully not in a dress that's a walking heart attack waiting to happen.

Her boss, Vicky, muscles her way through the crowd with her Vallure squad in tow, setting her sights on me. That woman gets under my skin like nobody's business.

Sullivan's hot on her heels, looking like a million bucks in some simple blue number. Damn, why does she have to be so easy on the eyes?

Wonder if she's gonna hit me with the cold shoulder act again, like she did this morning.

Vicky flashes me her phony smile. "Connor, thank you so much for extending an invitation to us tonight."

"You can thank my events team for that," I reply drily. "The team invited all our vendors."

Unfazed, she steamrolls on. "The campaign is going swimmingly, don't you think? You and Willow are trending as New York's hottest couple!"

"Thrilling," I deadpan. "Trending's always been a dream of mine."

"We've even got cutesy monikers for you lovebirds making the rounds!" She's all grins.

Are we even speaking the same language here?

"Come again?" I ask, completely thrown.

"Monikers, like Bennifer. Yours is Cillow! How adorable is that?"

Lexi makes this tiny, irritated sound. Like a kitten with a hairball.

"I'm perfectly content remaining blissfully ignorant about my nicknames," I say, brushing off the topic.

I turn my attention to Lexi, giving her my undivided focus. "Lexi's been my trusty sidekick, keeping me on a short leash, making sure I don't misbehave." My voice drops, a playful lilt creeping in. "Haven't you, Lexi? I'd be lost without my guardian PR angel."

She bares her teeth back at me. It's a smile in name only. "It's just a pleasure working with such a professional and successful man like Connor. Watching your 'love' story unfold has been the highlight of my career."

She angrily snatches an hors d'oeuvre off a passing tray. Well, well. Seems like someone's still got her panties in a twist from last night. I decide to fan the flames a bit more.

"I can see it," I say, cracking a smile. "Your happiness just explodes around you whenever we're in the same space. It's like working with a ray of sunshine."

"That's incredible," Vicky gushes. "At Vallure, we pride ourselves on the deep, meaningful connections we forge with our clients. You're practically part of the family."

Lexi's expression suggests she'd rather demonstrate our deep and meaningful connection by introducing her fist to my face.

Vicky's no fool; she spots the tension crackling between us. But as long as my checks keep clearing, she's all smiles.

Brooke, the red-head, leans in, intrigued. "Small world, isn't it? You guys knew each other before this?"

Lexi freezes, an appetizer suspended in midair. Oh, this is just too good. I'm dying to hear what fairy tale she's spun for her crew.

I smirk. "We go way back. Lexi told you the story of how we met, right?"

She chokes on a shrimp, mayo smearing her cheek. "Oh, well, uh, Connor knew my cousin Gigi from way back . . . Not much to tell, really."

"Gigi," I drawl, laying it on thick. "What a story there. Such a tragic turn of events."

All eyes glue to me, hooked. I lean in, milking it. "Ten years behind bars for luxury car theft. Tough break." I tsk, shaking my head. "She was quite the firecracker. Shame, really. She had so much potential."

Vicky looks at Lexi accusingly. "You never mentioned any of this, Lexi!"

Lexi's smile is strained to snapping point. "Just didn't think it was relevant."

I raise my glass, a sly grin playing on my lips. "Ah, Gigi. We were quite the item back in the day. Hot and intense, until she ditched me for that loser . . ." I snap my fingers, pretending to rack my brain. "Damn, what was that fool's name again? You remember, don't you, Lexi?"

She looks at me weird. "Mike?"

"Nah," I draw it out, "Oh, that's right. Wait, I remember now. Deano."

The instant the name leaves my lips, Lexi goes rigid, eyes wide with dawning horror.

Bullseye.

"Deano Johnson, right?" I keep on, twisting the knife a little more. "Tore me up, watching her run off with that no-good. But you remember Deano real well, don't you, Lexi?"

The look on her face is fucking priceless. Like I lit her hair on fire then handed her a mirror to watch herself burn. Never seen anything quite like it.

For a split second I almost feel a twinge of remorse.

Almost.

Maybe I played my hand too soon, without concrete proof to back it up. The strategic move would have been to bide my time, gather more evidence.

But the chance to see her squirm was too tempting to pass up.

And now, I have all the intel I need.

Lexi stands paralyzed. Those hypnotic eyes blink rapidly, her usually quick comebacks nowhere to be found.

Check and mate, angel.

I study her, my pulse quickening. There it is, the confirmation I've been chasing, laid bare before me in flushed cheeks and expressive eyes.

Yet I'm not quite sure how to feel about this damning revelation.

A part of me relishes finally catching my little hustler red-handed. But there's this unexpected, unwelcome twinge of . . . what? Concern? Protectiveness? It's a vexing sensation, especially when it's directed at her.

"This shrimp . . . not sitting right," she mutters, her complexion drained of all color. "Excuse me." Her entire demeanor is on the verge of collapse. She looks dangerously close to retching on her shoes. "I just need to . . . restroom."

As she makes a beeline for the exit, her friend calls, "You need someone with you?"

"No!" Lexi snaps.

I watch her dash off, a mix of irritation and something else brewing inside me. Something that's really grinding my gears.

"Excuse me," I mutter, shouldering my way through the crowd, hot on her heels.

"Lexi," I shout, but she's already dodging toward the elevator, pretending she doesn't hear me.

I make it just in time to jam my foot in the closing doors. "Hold up," I demand, my stare clearing the elevator. "Everybody out. Now."

They don't need to be told twice.

Lexi tries to slip past me, but I block her way with my arm. "I said wait."

She refuses to meet my gaze, and I notice the telltale shimmer of unshed tears in her eyes. My annoyance flares—she doesn't get to play the victim card here, just because she's been caught.

But then a single tear escapes, rolling down her cheek, and something in my chest constricts painfully. Dammit, this isn't part of the plan.

She shrinks back against the wall, every muscle coiled tight, body tensed for fight or flight.

"Hey, look at me." I hammer the button for the executive floor as if it's somehow responsible for this mess.

"I told you to look at me," I say with a bit of an edge when she doesn't look up. "The game's up."

Something seems to shift and snap in her. She lifts her head, bracing for a fight. "Fine. You know what? I did it. I had my reasons, not that you'd get it."

I'm momentarily stunned by her brazen admission.

"I did it," she repeats, louder this time, almost challenging me to explode.

"You did it," I echo, still processing. I didn't expect her to cave so easily.

Her chin sets in defiance. "If you want to call the cops, go right ahead. If you want to get me fired, be my guest." Her voice trembles, but she presses on. "If you're determined to destroy me, then just do it already. But I refuse to live like this anymore! I won't be a victim of your whims, always at your mercy!"

"You really think you had good reasons to steal? That's your angle?" I throw back at her, arms crossed. "There's always another way out. Ever heard of asking for help instead of resorting to car theft?"

She has the audacity to laugh right in my face. "Get real, Connor. Ask for help?" She shakes her head. "I get it, you built this empire from the ground up, and that's commendable. But did it ever cross your mind that maybe, just maybe, you had a bit of luck on your side too?"

"Irrelevant. We're not talking about me. This is about you, your mess-ups."

But she stands her ground, her eyes blazing. "Oh, is it so irrelevant? Imagine this: back in your early days, you and Killian struggling to make ends meet, and suddenly you're hit with a sick family member. Medical bills piling up, treatments you can't afford. Would you still be sitting pretty in your fancy office if life had thrown you that curveball?"

She's practically vibrating with intensity, her words coming fast and sharp. "Yes, you've worked hard. But everyone faces different obstacles. It's not just about working hard and being a good person." She jabs her finger into my chest, punctuating each word. "Spare me the holier-than-thou bullshit about 'finding other ways.'"

She's right in my face now, pushing against me, sparking for a reaction.

I start connecting the dots of her defiance.

"You pulled this stunt to cover your mom's medical bills?"

Her lips press into a thin line. "Yeah, I did it. And even with all the fallout, I know in my heart it was for the right reasons. It was a mistake, sure, but if I had to go back . . ." Her voice quivers, but she's solid as a rock. "I'm not sure I'd change a damn thing."

She jabs her finger at my chest again. "But this isn't really about the theft, is it, Connor? It's about you and your need to control."

Her gaze is fierce. "Wouldn't have mattered if I'd taken a toy car key. You'd still have lost your shit. Well, I refuse to grovel for your understanding or forgiveness."

"Enough," I growl, catching her accusing hand in mine, feeling her pulse hammer wildly against my skin. "Can you prove that the money went toward her care?"

Hurt flashes across her face. "Really, Connor? Even now, after everything, you still think I'm just some gold-digger?"

She tries to pull her hand back, but I'm not letting go, our eyes locked in a showdown.

"I don't see you like that," I grit out. "But dammit, you could've hit me up for help instead of pulling that stunt."

Her laugh is full of scorn. "Yeah, right. You were all heart, weren't you? You'd have told me to fuck right off."

"You're wrong," I counter. "I know I was messed up that night, but I would've helped if you'd told me you were in trouble."

I hesitate, a flicker of self-doubt gnawing at me. Was I even capable of helping that night?

Her tears are flowing now, and on impulse, I reach out, awkwardly trying to wipe her tears.

As we reach the executive floor, I jam the elevator on hold. Can't have her running off now.

"We could've skipped all this drama if you'd just been upfront with me," I say, my voice heavy with irritation. "Remember that first sit-down with Willow and the senator? I gave you plenty of shots to be straight with me."

Through her tears, she bites back with sarcasm. "Right. Just spill my guts to Connor Quinn. 'Hey, I snagged your keys for a quick scam. Cool, yeah?'"

"If you had been honest, things might've gone differently. But you never gave me that chance, did you?"

She breaks down, covering her face, her words barely audible through her sobs. "I'm so screwed. They'll come after me . . . after Grace . . . my mom . . ."

I clench my teeth, trying to rein in my conflicting emotions. "Listen, nobody's coming after you or your family. I'll be damned if I let anything happen to you."

This isn't how I envisioned this confrontation going. I thought I'd be basking in catching my thief red-handed.

How the hell did I end up the bad guy again?

"No, you'll go after Deano, and then he'll know it was me," she panics.

I let out a sharp breath. "I promise, I'll keep you and your family safe. You have my word."

Her frantic eyes search my face, looking for some hidden agenda. "Are you playing me? Acting nice just to draw me in and rat me out?"

"For fuck's sake, no," I snap, the accusation striking a raw nerve.

Suddenly, she's right up in my face, fury blazing in those mesmerizing eyes. "I know what you think of me, Connor. I heard every nasty word you said to Mason. That I'm just some thief chasing credit cards and Porsches. In the almighty Connor Quinn's eyes, I'm just another gold-digging whore, right?"

Fuck. I'm a colossal asshole.

"Lexi, that was all a load of crap. I didn't mean a single word of it."

"Sure you didn't," she fires back, disbelief written all over her face.

"I swear, I meant none of it," I stress, desperate for her to believe me.

"So why the hell say it?"

I lock eyes with her. "I ran my mouth to Mason to make him back off. It was a dumbass move, completely out of line."

At her bewildered look, I add gruffly, "Couldn't stomach the thought of him getting his hands on you."

Her "Why?" is barely a whisper.

Why indeed?

Because you're fucking mine.

Mine to fight with, to taunt, to hate.

I don't share what's mine.

And I sure as hell won't share you with anyone.

"Do I really have to spell it out for you?" I give a cynical laugh. "For the same idiotic reason I let you believe I spent the night with Willow, just to watch you spit fire at me. Believe it or not, Lexi, you've become the sole bright spot in my bleak fucking days lately. Our fiery little arguments are what I look forward to."

It's not even the Macallan talking. This nonsense is spewing out of my mouth like it's god's honest truth. Raw and real.

She gears up to sling another sharp retort, but I'm done with the back-and-forth.

Without hesitating, I grab her face and crush my lips against hers, pouring every ounce of frustration, desire, and all the things I can't say into that red-hot kiss.

TWENTY-FIVE

Connor

Our lips collide with an intense heat, enough to make the whole damn building catch fire. Her nails dig into my shirt, tearing at it like she's trying to strip me bare.

In this moment, it's just us. No bullshit, no lies, no hidden agendas.

Just pure, unadulterated lust for each other. And damn, she's responding to me with everything she's got.

I press her against the elevator wall, kissing her hard and rough.

But abruptly, she pulls away. "Wait," she says sharply, her grip on my shirt now more angry than aroused. "This doesn't change anything between us. It's just a one-time thing to get this tension out of our systems."

She clenches her fists around my shirt as if daring me to argue. "We finish what we started the first night. That's it. We never speak of this again or even acknowledge it happened."

"Works for me. Glad we're on the same page."

But she's still not done laying down the law apparently. "And just so we're clear—this has zero impact on my job or the campaign."

I can't help but let out a low, mocking laugh. "You really don't think too highly of me, do you?"

Her eyes flash. "I have a hell of a lot more to lose here than you, Quinn."

"Fair enough," I reply, lifting both hands in surrender.

My eyebrow shoots up, waiting to see if she has any other stipulations for me. But apparently she's said her piece, because she wraps her arms around my neck and rises up on tiptoes, mouth seeking mine again.

"You sure about this?" I ask, pulling back just a fraction, giving her another out.

"Yeah," she pants, chest heaving with every breath. Those mesmerizing eyes of hers lock on to mine with a challenge.

I tangle my fingers in her hair, tilting her head back as I kiss her again.

Fuck, her lips feel like pure sin—just like that first explosive night. And the way she matches my every move with a ferocity that borders on feral . . . It's like a shot of pure adrenaline straight to my veins.

For the first time in longer than I care to admit, I feel a glimmer of my old self resurfacing.

And it's all thanks to this infuriating, intoxicating woman I've got wrapped up in my arms.

My hand roams up her thigh, hitching her leg over my hip. I grip her hips tightly as I press my hard length against her.

Fuck. I need to feel her skin against mine, to hear her heart pounding against my chest. I've been craving this since she ran out on me that first night at the hotel.

I have to have her. Right fucking now. I have to see those kaleidoscope eyes roll back in pleasure and hear my name spill from those plump, kissable lips as I bury my big angry cock punishingly inside of her.

Take it easy, man. Don't scare the girl.

I pull back just enough to get a good look at her. Lips all puffy and swollen, thanks to me.

I try to speak, but all that comes out is a hoarse "*Lexi.*"

"*Fuck me,*" she groans. "I need you inside me. Now." She looks up at me, her eyes burning with raw need. There's nothing sexier than a woman looking at me like she can't fucking live without me.

"I'll give you everything you need, baby," I murmur as I lift her up. She wraps her legs around my waist, her body fitting perfectly against mine. She's so small compared to me that I barely feel her weight. "I'm gonna make you scream so loud the whole damn building will know who's giving it to you."

She moans in response, already trembling under my touch. "Yeah . . . oh god."

I stroll us out of the elevator with Lexi tightly in my grip. I kick open the office door, long strides carrying us to my desk.

I'm way too desperate to take this slow—I need to be buried inside her five minutes ago. I've imagined this every fucking angle and position there is available.

I set her on top of the desk, hiking up her dress to reveal those smooth thighs that could make a monk rethink his celibacy.

Trying to be as slow as I can, I lower her lace panties down her thighs and let out a low groan at the sight of her perfectly smooth pussy. Been craving it since our first fight.

"Fuck, you're stunning," I growl, my need driving me almost feral. "You need me, baby? Tell me you fucking need me."

She moans in response, arching her back. "Yes."

"Yes, what?"

"Yes. I need you. Connor, *please*."

Our eyes lock as I swiftly undo my belt,

practically ripping it off. I jerk my pants down below my hips, too impatient to take them off properly.

I pull out my throbbing cock and give it a few rough strokes, every nerve electrified with the anticipation of finally having her.

She stares at me wide-eyed, taking in every inch of my cock. "Damn," she breathes, biting down on her lip.

"Spread those legs for me. For once, just do as you're told and don't sass me."

She eagerly obeys, offering up every inch of her delicious pussy to me. Fuck, she's begging for me.

"That's it. There's my good girl."

I have to taste her. I drop to my knees, gripping her thighs as I dive my tongue into her wetness.

She moans and grinds against me, driving me wild. Her mouth hangs open as she curls her back, dying for attention. Christ, my self-control is already hanging on by a thread. My angel tastes like pure fucking heaven, and I can't get enough of her.

I love how responsive she is to me. Every touch, every word, makes her squirm, and damn if it isn't the most erotic thing I've ever experienced.

I stand up, trying not to lose my mind. By some miracle, I find a condom in my wallet and swiftly sheath my hard cock.

She grabs at it greedily and presses it against

her wet pussy like she's been waiting for this moment forever.

"God. I haven't had sex in so long," she whimpers, her voice thick with need.

"Good," I growl, my inner caveman reveling in the thought of being her first in a while.

I grip her hips and slowly slide into her tight heat, groaning at how wet she is already.

She gasps and I force myself to pause, letting her adjust to my size. As she exhales, I withdraw and then thrust back inside her deeply.

A deep rumble erupts from my throat as every nerve in my cock comes alive with pleasure.

Damn.

She melts against me, moaning and gasping with every touch. God, she's so damn responsive. It's been too long since I've felt this good. My body knows exactly what to do, rather than rebelling and fucking up on me. I know exactly how to make her vibrate and hum.

"Fuck," I growl through gritted teeth. "You feel incredible."

"So do you," she whimpers.

I can't get enough of her tugging at my fresh buzz cut and tearing at my shirt. Like she can't keep her hands off me.

I fuck her with everything I have, like my life depends on it. "Say my name, Lexi. Moan it out with that fiery anger you have for me."

"Connor," she gasps out. "Oh, god, it's too much." Her nails scrape against my back through my shirt, but I barely register it. All I can focus on is the overwhelming pleasure.

I thrust harder, feeling her body start to tremble as her soft moans turn into desperate pleas.

Fuck, this is almost too much. I'm drunk with desire. Being inside her is like reaching a whole new level.

"Connor . . . shit . . . oh my god . . ."

I suck in a sharp breath. I ain't gonna last much longer.

I pump in and out of her sweet tightness, grunting against her lips. Feeling every quiver of her muscles tightening around me.

Owning my cock.

"Fuck . . . Connor . . . oh . . . god . . ." Her words mix with my own grunts and panting as we both approach the edge of pure carnal release. "Yes, yes, keep going. Don't stop."

As if I could.

I'm losing my mind, seeing stars with every thrust.

I lean down and whisper in her ear, my voice dripping with lust. "You can hate me all you want, but you can't deny how fucking amazing this feels."

Even if the whole damn office barged in right

now, nothing could stop me from claiming what's mine.

I just about hold on as she comes hard on my cock.

With a tortured groan, I hold on to her hips tight to keep her still as I release myself into her wet heat.

But then the euphoria quickly turns to . . . disorientation.

Jesus, what the fuck? I can barely stay upright, the whole room spinning like crazy.

I pull out of Lexi, my cock drenched in her arousal. My hands drop from her as I stumble back, wondering if I'm about to pass out cold.

I grasp the desk for support as everything spins nauseatingly. Shit, it's like the whole world just went sideways.

"Connor?" Lexi's voice cuts through my dizziness, soft with concern.

I force my eyes open to see her staring at me, her brows pulled together with worry. She blinks, confused, and hastily smooths her dress down over her hips.

The last thing I need is her pity.

Teeth clenched, I steady myself on the desk, letting out a pissed-off growl. Fucking vertigo has to hit now of all times . . .

She reaches for me cautiously. "What's wrong, tell me?"

I shrug away from her touch. What the hell, this issue is impacting me even when I'm with a woman now? "I need a minute. See you back at the bar."

Her hand hesitates in the air. "What's going on, Connor?"

I grit my teeth, trying to keep it together. I don't want her fussing over me. Seeing me like this.

So this is how it's gonna be now? Everyone walking on eggshells around me, giving me those pitiful looks, treating me like I'm about to shatter into a million pieces?

"Just leave, Lexi," I order in a low voice.

She flinches at the sudden change in my tone. "What the hell? Are you serious?"

"I said go. We'll hash this out later." I glare at my desk, trying to keep the room from spinning. Moving right now would only make it worse. "Get out. Please."

But she just stands there staring. And that's when I feel my patience slipping away. "Are you fucking deaf? Get the hell out of here."

Her sharp intake of breath tells me I've gone way too far. "Is this your messed-up way of getting back at me for the car?"

"No," I manage to grunt out, each word a battle against the dizziness.

"Whatever, asshole. It's done. Forget this ever

happened."

As the door slams violently behind her, I sag against the desk with a muttered "*Fuck*."

I screwed this up. She didn't deserve that rough treatment. But better she thinks I'm an asshole than me having to explain the truth.

It's ironic. A few weeks ago, this was the ideal scenario—get her admission of theft, use her, then discard her.

But now, as I slump against my desk, I feel nothing but emptiness.

◆ ◆ ◆

After what feels like an endless dizzy spell, I finally pull my shit together and go looking for Lexi. But turns out she already stormed off on me. Great.

I call her number. No answer. I try again. And again. And yet again.

By the eighth unanswered ring, the reality sinks in that she has zero intention of picking up.

I really crossed the line this time, pissed her off to a point that feels irreparable. I'm not sure if we can come back from the damage this time around.

TWENTY-SIX

Lexi

Enough. No more getting pushed around. I'm done being everyone's punching bag. No more Miss Nice Girl.

Having sex with Connor was a special kind of mistake, a monumental screw-up in my otherwise bland existence of professionalism. Even though it was frustratingly incredible.

What was I thinking? Oh wait, I wasn't. I was too busy letting my lust bulldoze over every rational thought. Willow, the campaign, my career . . . all casualties in the great hormone war.

I don't know if I'm more disgusted with Connor or myself. Bravo, Connor, you really outdid yourself by showing me the door post-coitus. Chivalry's not dead.

"Hey, slow down, sweetie!" Mom's voice cuts through. "I haven't gotten a chest upgrade since you last saw me."

I whip around, realizing I've left Mom and Gracie in my dust. My bad. I usually dial it down to a snail's pace to stick with Mom. But now I'm trying to speed walk my way to better life decisions, it seems.

We're walking through Sunnyhell Gardens in the beautiful New York sunshine. Too bad I'm still too busy riding the fury from the showdown with Connor last night to smell the roses.

"Oops, sorry, Mom."

"You're looking kind of pale," Mom observes, her brow creased with worry as she pushes her walker. "Are you working too hard?"

"Just a crappy night's sleep," I deflect with a shrug. Hope she lets it go.

"Looks more like a hangover to me!" Grace snorts. "She was out partying."

"Just mingling with some clients," I smooth over, picking the least scandalous part of the night.

No way I'm diving into what's actually bringing me out in rage hives. After the disastrous romp with Connor, I had to follow through on my promise to Kayla for that dreaded double date. My date Brad was a smokeshow, sure, but my turbulent emotional state made it impossible to be present. We had drinks and I managed to smile through it, wondering if they could smell Connor on me.

"Well isn't that lovely you're getting out there

and mingling," Mom gushes, completely oblivious. "What did you get up to?"

"She was at Quinn and Wolfe," Grace jumps in before I can sidestep the question. "You know, the one with those iconic spiky towers?"

Mom looks pleased. "Sounds swanky."

"And guess who her client is? Connor Quinn—one of the actual brothers," Grace blurts out, barely containing herself.

I just grunt, studying the pavement as if it holds the secret to life.

"And get *this*! He passed my CV to his tech team," she squeals. "I'm this close to snagging an internship there."

"Grace, cool it. It's a long shot," I urge, trying to inject a dose of reality into her dream world. She's been harping on this internship fantasy for days, and it's got to stop, especially with the way things went down last night.

"Hey, I met the top dog himself. I think my chances are solid," Grace counters, all sunshine and positivity.

If she only knew.

Mom jumps aboard the happy train too. "That's incredible, Gracie! What are those Quinn guys like? They as shark-like as everyone says? I've been glued to *Suits* and I imagine them as a pair of Harvey Specters in the wild."

I can't help but snort. "Try Patrick Bateman

in *American Psycho*," I say, my voice tight. "All the more reason to steer clear."

But Grace is undeterred. "Come on, it's a great opportunity. Plus, think of the money. We could even move to a bigger place."

I lose it. "Grace, just cut it out!" I snap, louder than I intend. "It's not happening. Drop it, okay?"

They both freeze, staring at me like I've sprouted twin horn-like spires myself.

Mom's face creases with worry. "Lexi, you sure everything's okay?"

I burst into tears right there in the middle of the path.

The big, angry kind that feel like they've been stewing for ages. These aren't your gentle sniffles. Oh no, this is the big league, the I've-had-it-up-to-here-with-this-crap waterworks.

I gave him the power to make me feel worthless. I should have known better than to expect any decency from that arrogant prick. He hadn't even pulled off the condom when he shoved me out the door like I was nothing. And now I feel like a piece of trash, used and tossed aside after his massive dick had its fun with me.

Thanks for the memories, asshole.

◆ ◆ ◆

Strutting into the flashy *Hello, New York* studio for Connor and Willow's interview, I'm weirdly upbeat about Friday's catastrophe. It's Monday and I've had time to chill since then.

The debris of Friday has settled because I realized something important—my worst fear manifested. Connor knows all the dirty details.

And you know what? The world didn't end. Here I am, still standing, breathing, and surprisingly not in handcuffs. He's not dialing 9-1-1 on me.

Connor rejecting me so brutally after fucking me puts us on equal ground in my book. He doesn't have power over me anymore. I'm not going to jump or tense up every time he enters the room.

Grace tippy-toed around me post-meltdown, brewing tea and tidying up like she's auditioning for the role of the next Florence Nightingale.

This weekend marked a rare moment of vulnerability in front of Mom and Grace, a scene not witnessed since Dad's passing. Both of them looked seriously freaked. You'd think they caught me shifting into werewolf form. They love to poke fun at my usual hard shell. Grace is the softie.

I mumbled something about work stress, and off we went on a merry-go-round of advice—new job prospects, the magical healing powers of yoga, kombucha, and whatever the hell pressure point tapping is.

And I'm sure as hell not going to cry anymore.

A new Lexi is stepping onto the scene today.

My hands squeeze around the weird ginger concoction that Butt Buildr's Gina Malone recommended for Willow. Despite my new attitude, I need to ready myself for the *Cillow* interview—a prospect that makes my skin crawl. Willow and Connor, same room, with me right smack in the middle.

While Willow's been primping in the studio dressing room for what feels like an eternity, I'm relegated to drinks runner. Connor is late, per usual. Probably got waylaid hiding a dead hooker's body or something.

I can't help but feel a bit paranoid. I had sex with a *client*. Not just any client—*Connor Quinn*. What if this gets out? If Willow gets even a whiff of suspicion, I can already picture her sweet, angelic demeanor doing a 180 into full-blown Godzilla mode. She'll get me fired for sure.

But Connor, he wouldn't go shooting his mouth off . . . right? And there's no worry about me opening my lips.

The *Hello, New York* studio is like a beehive on a caffeine buzz. Everyone's in a state of organized panic, shouting and darting around. I've been bombarded with at least ten questions about

Connor's ETA, each laced with more expletives than the last.

Sound checks, tweaking the lights, running camera drills—the pre-show chaos is a thrill to be part of. It'd be an even bigger rush if Connor had the decency to show up. If he bails, Vicky's going to have my head on a platter, and I'll be ready to serve Connor's right next to it.

My phone goes off, nearly giving me a heart attack. I'm bracing for it to be Connor bailing out. Instead, it's a text from Kayla.

I met her for a coffee and spilled everything about Connor. Had to vent to someone. Watching her face as I unloaded the story was priceless—her jaw hit the floor. It felt great to get it all off my chest and have someone to rant to.

Kayla: **Double date tonight with Brad and Justin! They got exclusive tix to some hot show.**
X

Hell no. I text back a firm no and chuck my phone back in my bag. All I'm craving is to collapse under my duvet.

Naturally, my phone rings straight after.

I cut Kayla off before she gets rolling. "Not happening, Kayla. I need a quiet, drama-free night."

She powers through. "But you're gonna love it!

It's one of those immersive movie experiences."

I raise an eyebrow, though she can't see it. "Immersive, as in, we're part of the movie?"

"Exactly! I've been dying to try one. It's supposed to be so cool." I can practically hear the grin in her voice. "It might just distract you from a certain tycoon we're not naming."

I exhale, long and hard. Maybe getting lost in some fantasy world isn't the worst idea. "Okay, what's the movie?"

"I dunno yet," she says down the line.

"If it's some gruesome shit, I swear to God, Kayla . . ."

Her giggle trickles through the phone, yet she offers no reassurance. Hmmm. Maybe I'll get lucky and score the part of the chick who dies in scene one.

My skin prickles as the energy subtly shifts in the room. I don't even need to turn around to know the cause, to feel his presence.

In walks Connor, flanked by some blond assistant toting a clipboard. Just the sight of him is enough to reignite my inner volcano of rage. *So much for being upbeat.*

My heart trips over itself seeing him decked out in that exquisitely tailored suit.

The dark scruff peppering his hard jaw probably means he spent the entire weekend lost in some hedonistic binge, drowning himself in booze and women, not giving a damn about anything. Or anyone.

"I have to go," I say quickly, hanging up.

His gaze sweeps the room, landing on me with a nod so brief it's almost dismissive. Really? Now I don't even warrant basic professional courtesy? He's probably fuming I didn't answer his calls on Friday.

I bite back a curse, irritation flaring. This guy has some nerve.

He heads straight for Mason, surrounded by a fan club of women. But I'm set on showing him I'm oh-so-unaffected, even if it's the last thing I do.

I march up to them, clearing my throat loudly. "Hey there."

"Lexi, great to see you," Mason says, but his smile doesn't quite reach his eyes, and I can almost bet it's because of Connor bad-mouthing me. He's likely already checking his pockets to make sure I haven't swiped his wallet.

"Lexi," Connor grumbles, giving me the briefest look before dismissing me again.

"We're on in fifteen," I remind him, trying to keep the edge out of my voice. "You're late."

Assistants bustle around us, the air charged with pre-interview tension.

Connor finally looks at me, annoyance clear in his tone. "I'm here now, aren't I?"

No shit, Sherlock. What do you want, a gold

star?

Mason chuckles. "Rough weekend, Connor?"

"Something like that."

Ugh, what an ass.

Then his cologne hits me, throwing me straight back to Friday night, the scratch of stubble against my skin . . .

Shake it off.

Still facing his shoulder, because apparently I'm not worthy of eye contact, I try again, attempting to be the bigger person. Metaphorically, at least. "You look tired. Everything okay?" My tone's casual, but the annoyance is there, just under the surface.

He might as well be alone in the room for all the attention he gives me. He scans the set looking thoroughly pissed. Not even a sideways glance in my direction. It's as if I no longer exist in his world.

I crank up the volume. "Connor?" I bark out, frustration edging into my voice.

Without a glance in my direction, he turns to Mason, his expression taut with annoyance. "How long is this gonna take?"

Embarrassment washes over me, cheeks burning. Mason shoots me a sympathetic look, clearly thrown off by Connor's cold dismissal. "Uh, Lexi was actually talking to you, man."

Finally, Connor deigns to acknowledge me, his gaze sharp as if seeing me for the first time. "Yeah?

What's up, Lexi?"

"Nothing," I snap, seeing red. Unbelievable. I hope his dick falls off.

A production assistant waves a sign—ten minutes to go.

"Connor, we need you on set," Mason says. The two walk away, leaving me standing there alone. My cheeks blaze as I imagine the whole studio watching him flat-out ignore me.

I watch him saunter toward the set, memories of that night flooding back. God, I gripped those broad shoulders so hard. I hope I left permanent bruises.

It was proper no-holds-barred animal-style fucking, consequences be damned. And now I can't get the images out of my head. How can he act so casual and indifferent today after *that*?

Because that's just an average Friday night for the jerk, the nagging voice in my head sneers. Probably a dull one at that. His office desk must be worn from all the action it's seen.

I bristle and pretend to focus on my notes on the pad.

Willow glides out, her squad in tow, all mic'd up and camera-ready. She gives me a little wave, and I reluctantly wave back, feeling even more disgusted with myself.

Connor, on the other hand, drops into his chair like he's on death row and it's his time, all grim face and gritted teeth. He's clearly in a foul mood about something.

"Connor, Willow, welcome," purrs Lucia, the host, in her signature sweet voice.

I'm only half-tuned in as she hammers Willow with questions about her charity work and, of course, her wardrobe. Willow's all smiles, in her element.

And honestly, credit where it's due—the woman's done some incredible stuff, supporting education for women in conflict zones, volunteering her time to various causes. Kudos to Willow.

Compare that to me and my work with the D-list celebs. If I had some extra cash right now, I'd love to sponsor someone in her charity. Maybe someday.

As Willow gushes about her charity work, irritation prickles under my skin. Something's shifted in Connor. They've got this connection—a shared drive for making a difference in education. It's their common ground. His eyes stay fixed on her, like he's discovering a whole new side of her. If they weren't fucking before, they certainly will be now.

The dream team. How heartwarming.

Keep it together, Lexi. Focus on the job.

Connor knows about the car hustle but isn't pressing charges. And with the campaign ending,

I'll never see him again anyway.

I should be feeling relieved. Ecstatic, even.

I guess I am. Sort of.

Lucia turns to Connor, eyes glinting. "New York's most eligible bachelor taken off the market. Connor, you've been the city's leading ladies' man for what feels like forever. So, what made you switch to a one-woman man?"

I feel a weird twist in my gut. Of relief. Definitely, definitely relief.

Connor looks like he's just bitten into a lemon. "Hadn't met the right one."

"So, you've found her? The elusive Miss Right?"

His jaw tightens, muscles working overtime. "Yes," he says, almost snarling, "I've found her." He rubs his stubble, clearly wishing he were anywhere but here.

Oh god. Every time I look at him, all I can think about is sex. And I *hate* it.

Remembering his grunts and moans, the look of ecstasy on his face when he comes. The feel of that big, hard cock—all wrapped up in his fancy suit now—driving me wild with each and every thrust. How those muscular thighs felt. The feel of his taut back muscles as I ran my hands over them.

I snap myself out of my dirty thoughts with a mental slap. He's not worth it.

"We're all absolutely enchanted by this fairy-tale romance," she gushes. "But let's get real, shall we? There are some not-so-pleasant whispers going around that this whole love story is just a PR stunt after the, hmm, incident. Care to comment on those rumors?"

My grip on my coffee cup tightens, the temptation to hurl it at the stage real.

Connor looks like he's on the verge of storming off the set. "Rumors are just that—rumors."

My chest constricts. Come on, Connor. You've been media trained. Stop acting like a sulking teenager.

He's meant to be charming, not brooding. Is he trying to tank the interview on purpose?

Lucia, unfazed by his moodiness, leans in even closer. "Tell us, is Willow your one true love?"

He scowls. "Could you repeat that?"

Is this his attempt at humor?

She laughs it off. "You said in a previous interview that you thought the concept of soulmates was ridiculous. How about now? Is Willow your forever girl?"

Cue the most cringeworthy silence in television history. Connor looks like he's in a mental tug-of-war. What the hell is he waiting for, phone a friend?

Beside him, Willow squeezes his hand and forces a tight smile. This isn't exactly Connor's finest hour.

"Willow is one of a kind. Her charity work has left us all in awe. But I don't believe in 'soulmates.' If we all had just one perfect match, humanity wouldn't stand a chance," Connor states.

Willow and Lucia respond with laughter, but Willow's eyes scream *Wrong answer, buddy*.

"So, what's in store for the lovebirds? Any wedding bells on the horizon?"

He just stares at her blankly, the silence stretching uncomfortably.

"Umm," Willow stammers, shooting Connor a look that could easily set the set on fire, though her smile stays mannequin-frozen.

Connor's brow furrows. "Run that by me again?" he asks slowly, confusion and irritation evident in his tone.

This is getting awkward. My heart beats faster.

"Is he high?" someone mutters behind me.

Lucia obliges with her trademark broad smile, over-enunciating like she's talking to a child.

Connor's face shifts to anger, his grip on the chair arms so tight that I can see every tendon and vein. He looks like he's in agony, or maybe just grappling with the idea of a future filled with wedding planning and honeymoon destinations. This image of domestic bliss that the public expects from him now.

I hold my breath, watching him. Something is definitely off—he's been unusually moody and volatile, even for him.

"Let's move on," he says tensely, his body rigid.

The studio's atmosphere thickens with unease, everyone exchanging perplexed looks at Connor's unexpected reaction. This is definitely not following the script.

"Oh, we're just enjoying living in the moment," Willow says with a nervous laugh, attempting to gloss over the awkwardness.

"Let's talk about that rock weighing down your neck, Willow," Lucia smoothly transitions, her smile aimed at a camera. "Can I get a 'wow' for that diamond?"

Willow caresses it lovingly, nearly a quarter-million dollars sparkling against her skin. "Connor's so considerate," she swoons.

My heart skips a beat as Connor's eyes meet mine.

"It's like Rose's jewel in *Titanic*," Lucia trills. "How does this grand gesture make you feel, Willow?"

"I love it," Willow gushes breathlessly.

"Connor clearly believes you're his diamond of the sea," Lucia coos. She turns her attention to Connor. "Come on, don't be shy. When are you putting a ring on it?"

He stares at her as if she's speaking Klingon. A hush falls over the room. I was expecting a smooth comeback from him, like in every other interview

I've seen him in.

"Connor?" Lucia prompts, her smile turning razor-sharp.

Still nothing. Connor wipes at his brow, confusion etched across his rugged face.

My heart remains lodged in my throat.

All of a sudden, his body jerks forward, his chair screeching like nails on a chalkboard. His knuckles grip the armrests like a vise, tendons standing out. There's a caged, almost panicked intensity in his eyes that contradicts his usually cool demeanor.

My stomach drops. Something's way off. The Connor Quinn we all thought was unflappable looks like he's on the edge of a cliff.

Lucia tosses another fluffy question into the mix. Connor's face turns to stone, and then he's on his feet as if he's just touched a live wire. "We're done here," he declares, his tone leaving no room for argument.

The studio descends into mute chaos.

With a violent yank, he tears off his microphone, cables snapping in the tense silence.

Then he's out, marching off the set, leaving behind a wake of stunned confusion.

Lucia's smile wavers for a moment. "Well, folks, looks like our city's most eligible bachelor didn't come to chat about love today!"

The studio feels ready to rupture with tension.

Everyone trades freaked looks, like their charming prince morphed into the Hulk before their eyes.

Whispers explode all around me. Some outright label him as an asshole as he strides away. It's not the most catastrophic thing to happen on live TV, but it's far from ideal.

Willow makes a feeble attempt to salvage the situation with a nervous, forced laugh. "Oh, Connor, always so grumpy on Mondays!" But the train already derailed.

I feel horrified for Willow, left to deal with the fallout. Lucia does her best to pivot, cracking a joke about "men leaving us to pick up the pieces," then shifts the spotlight to Willow's fashion ambassador gig.

But this meltdown isn't about Connor hating Mondays. His reaction is too extreme, too visceral. Storming off like that goes against everything he puts out for the world to see. It makes absolutely no sense why those questions triggered such a strong reaction.

On impulse, I dash after him. "Connor, hold up!"

He's barreling through the studio, not bothering to look back.

My heels click furiously as I try to catch up. "Slow down, will you?"

When I finally catch his arm, forcing him to face me, he looks like he's ready to breathe fire.

336

"Just go back to Willow."

I scowl right back, hands on hips. "You don't have to be a raging jerk just because you're in a pissy mood. What the hell is your problem?"

His eyes narrow dangerously. "You're pushing it. I did their bullshit interview. I'm done."

"You just made things worse back there!" I shoot back, exasperated.

He rubs the bridge of his nose, eyes shut tight like I'm giving him a headache.

I stare at him in disbelief. "What is going on with you? I know you can be a jerk, but this is extreme."

For a moment his mask slips, a glimmer of vulnerability in his eyes. But then the walls slam down again.

Hearing footsteps coming, I grab him on impulse and shove him into the supply closet.

He slams back into the shelves, sending bottles rattling around us. Considering his Viking-esque stature, it's no small feat, but I guess the element of surprise was on my side.

He looms over me, disbelieving. "*Now* you want to hash things out? You should've picked up your phone on Friday, Lexi."

I close the distance, meeting his gaze with a fierce one of my own. "We don't mention Friday again, I'm over that. Now cut the crap. This isn't about me. Why'd you really storm off set?"

"I told you. I had enough of their damn questions."

"That's crap, and we both know it." My tone softens. "Come on, you can talk to me. What's going on?"

I need something real, some shred of evidence that he's not just a total jerk. That there was a legitimate reason he pushed me away so cruelly on Friday. Some glimpse behind the cold mask.

His eyes turn to ice. "I had a headache and needed some fresh air. That's all there is to it."

I'm not buying it. I grip his arm. "You don't cause a scene over a headache. I know you can put on a show for the cameras." My voice takes on a growl. "I'm not backing down until you're straight with me."

He steps closer, using his size to crowd me. "Back off, Lexi. Just because we fucked once doesn't mean you know a damn thing about me. Stay the hell out of my business, understand?"

I recoil as if he's slapped me, his harshness stinging more than I'd like to admit. Seriously, why am I even surprised?

"Why are you being such a jerk?" My voice wavers pathetically. "You were Mr. Nice Guy before we hooked up. You even promised to keep me safe when I told you about the car theft—"

"I meant what I said," he cuts in, suddenly serious. His eyes soften faintly. "I'll keep you safe.

Now more than ever."

I let out a bitter laugh. "Yeah, only after we screwed around though, right? I bought your protection with sex."

Connor's face hardens to stone, nostrils flaring at my accusation. "That's bullshit and you goddamn know it. I would've protected you either way if you'd just trusted me with the truth from the start instead of hiding things."

"Whatever." I wrap my arms around myself, feeling exposed. "I can't figure you out, Connor. On Friday, when you pushed me away, I brushed it off as just another episode of your asshole behavior. But then today, you were even more erratic. There's obviously something deeper going on you're not saying."

"Let me simplify things for you so there's nothing left to figure out. Yeah, I'm an asshole, and I'd really appreciate it if you'd stop sticking your pretty little nose in my business. Clear enough?"

I snap my glare up to his infuriatingly handsome face as rage boils over inside me. "You know what? I don't care about your issues anymore. Because deep down, you're just a horrible man."

My words don't even scratch the surface. He gives me this condescending eyebrow raise. "Yeah, you've made your hatred for me pretty clear."

The air between us crackles, like the heavy

stillness before a violent storm erupts. One of us might not make it out of this supply closet alive.

My voice shakes with emotion. "I mean it. I hate you, Connor."

His gaze rakes over me, voice low and rough. "Then start acting like it, angel."

Before I can even react, Connor grabs me by the waist and pulls me in tight. My hands instinctively grip his solid chest, feeling the heat of his skin through his shirt, wanting to feel his bare skin.

He crashes his mouth to mine, angry and fierce like he's punishing me for daring to speak against him.

I lean into the kiss for about five seconds, my traitorous body melting into his.

But then reality comes crashing back, and I remember how he treated me so coldly.

With all the willpower in the world, I shove him back, hard. He stumbles, caught off guard.

He blinks, looking genuinely stunned. "Sorry," he mutters. "That was out of line."

"You think I'm just going to go there after how you rejected me Friday?" I ask incredulously. "You think you can just kiss me and make me forget?"

"You didn't answer my calls. I tried to apologize."

I narrow my eyes, temper rising. "Yeah, well, sorry doesn't magically fix everything. Sort your issues out before using me as an emotional punching bag."

His eyes narrow. "Give me a break. You're the one who hauled me into this closet. I'm not in the mood for this drama. Whatever happened between us was obviously a mistake."

"Believe me, I regret it even more," I fire back. "Let's just get through this campaign, make Willow happy, and then never see each other again. Deal?"

Connor's face hardens. "Works for me."

I shake my head. "I really hope you find what you're looking for so you can drop the whole angry, bitter act. Because this charade of playing charming prince while nursing a heart full of nails must be exhausting."

I give myself a mental high-five for not face-planting into a mop bucket on my way out. That would ruin my dramatic exit.

As I storm off, leaving him in the closet, I pray my eyes only show anger. Not the hurt I'm too stubborn to admit, even to myself.

TWENTY-SEVEN

Connor

I stride into my office and dry swallow another useless painkiller.

I try Lexi's cell. Voicemail. I tap out an inadequate **I'm sorry** text instead, well aware she deserves far more after my behavior.

She pushed my buttons at the worst possible time, coming after me. She should have just left me the hell alone, not kept prodding the raging bull.

Her reply comes quick: **Thanks. Vicky's blaming me.**

Hell. None of this falls on her. She's not my goddamn handler. Vicky has even less sense than I credited if she expects Lexi to somehow control my actions.

And now thanks to my fuckup, Lexi is unfairly catching heat.

I can fix the Vicky situation easily enough, at

least smooth that over.

I slump into my desk chair and press my palms into my eyes until I see stars. I've never felt as out of control as I did in that interview. Completely fucking powerless.

Lucia was sitting on my bad side, and my left ear might as well have been dead to the world. It was like I was dipping in and out of water. Her words just swirled around me, distorted and muffled. "Soulmate" turned into "date." "Date" turned into "hate."

By the time my brain caught up, the interview was already a smoldering wreck.

And it was just some dumb gossip interview. I should be able to shake that off. But what if this happens at the World Economic Forum in Davos? Or at the Fortune Brainstorm Tech conference? Or even at the Quinn & Wolfe annual all-staff meeting? Hard to say which would be worse.

This hearing issue is stripping away everything that defines me. Now, I can't even get through a simple interview without making a fool of myself. I make a mental note to move up the appointment with the new specialist—I delayed it, thinking the issue would resolve on its own, and besides, the company's swamped right now. All my hopes are riding on this new specialist—he's not just the best in the industry; he's the best in the world.

There's a sharp rap at the door before Killian barges in, looking revved up to tear me a new one.

"Jesus Christ, were you hammered during that absolute shitshow?" he demands.

"No, I damn well wasn't," I fire back.

Killian shakes his head. "This is getting out of hand, Connor. Getting drunk in your own bar—we agreed not to do that. We keep our personal lives away from the staff. And now, you're mixed with this woman with a shady past, making a mess of media appearances, stirring up scandal again. We've been down this road before, and I don't want to revisit it."

"Jesus, Killian, lay off. So I screwed up a few times. It's not like you're a saint just because you've settled down."

"Fine, but can you at least tell me why you stormed off set? Did someone insult you?"

I grit my teeth and offer a half truth. "I couldn't hear her questions clearly. Had a killer headache."

He pauses, concern softening his hard gaze as he takes a good look at me.

"Just bad timing," I mutter dismissively.

"Maybe you should lay low until these scandals blow over. Take a vacation."

"I'm not getting shipped off to dry out, Killian. This isn't like last time."

He exhales heavily. "I didn't mean it like that. I was thinking more along the lines of an actual vacation. Maybe even take Willow with you and try to make something real with her. Forget about Vegas or any wild spots. Go do some yoga and find some inner peace." He grins like he's just invented the concept of relaxation. "What about one of JP's wellness retreats?"

JP, our third business partner, used to head up our casinos. But he got tired of the game and decided to jump on the wellness bandwagon by opening up Quinn & Wolfe retreats. Apparently downward dogs hold more appeal than blackjack for him these days.

And it's working. Those retreats are raking in the dough. Turns out, wealthy burnouts are a lucrative market.

"Yeah. Maybe." I force a smile, the muscles in my face straining with the effort. "I'll think about it."

I can't be completely outraged that Killian is suspicious. Back in my twenties I was that guy who snorted coke off a supermodel's butt. Your classic playboy asshole. I overindulged in every vice imaginable, consequences be damned.

It was all fun and games until Quinn & Wolfe really took off and suddenly, people were relying on me. I couldn't afford to be a hungover mess when an empire was on the line.

When the money started pouring in, I could've gotten coached on anything—public speaking, business acumen, finance, racing million-dollar cars.

But there's no training for being filthy rich and having people crawling out of the woodwork to love you. Unless you were born with a silver spoon up your ass, it's a mindfuck.

Thank Christ for Killian keeping it straight, even when I fought him kicking and screaming.

He served up the tough love I desperately needed, threatening to boot me from the board if I didn't get my shit together. He wasn't about to watch our hard-earned success go down the toilet with my reckless behavior. I got serious, thanks to him. A real come-to-Jesus moment behind closed doors, courtesy of my big brother.

Now of course, everyone thinks this is round two. Killian, the staff, the media . . . they all think I'm back to my old party ways.

Murphy's Law at its finest.

I'm doing daily two-hour workouts, saunas, ice baths—you name it, I do it. My metrics are off the charts, my diet is as strict as ever. Is there even a point to all this hard work if I'm still going to be damned in the end?

TWENTY-EIGHT

Lexi

Tonight, I'm in dire need of some liquid courage and a hottie on my arm. I've said yes to Kayla's double-date plan for an immersive cinema experience with her beau, Justin, and Brad—the guy I previously grabbed a couple of drinks with.

It's a hell of a lot better than brooding at home about Connor's crap—how he screwed me over, not once but twice. I'm done renting him space in my mind free of charge. It's been a few days since that interview went south, and thankfully, there's been zero reason for us to cross paths—fine by me. I did the professional thing and smoothed it over with Willow after he stormed off—probably to sulk or put his fist through something. Who knows with that guy.

And if he thinks a lame "I'm sorry" text is going to fix things, he's sorely mistaken.

Brad slings his muscular arm around me as we

weave our way to the immersive theater, laughing like idiots.   He's a doctor, and you don't get much sexier than that. The guy's straight out of a prime-time medical show—tall, built, dripping with charm. A real head-turner, and he's got the gift of the gab too.

I'm out to have a good time tonight, feel appreciated, not discarded like trash. A night of drinks and laughs is just what the doctor ordered . . . and maybe a little groping, depending on how things go.

Though, in hindsight, chugging wine on an empty stomach might not have been my brightest idea.

"What's with all the mystery around this immersive theater thing?" I ask Brad. Up ahead, Kayla glances back at us, clearly buzzed. "Is it that *Back to the Future* show? I've been seeing ads for it all over." Honestly, I'd rather just hole up in some dive bar with a bottle of bottom-shelf bourbon, but hey, I'm game for whatever.

Brad stops dead in his tracks, giving me a look like I just grew a second head. "You're kidding, right?"

"Nooo?" It comes out sounding more like I'm double-checking with him. We're heading to some horror show, aren't we? Kayla's been too giddy. Too weird.

"Jesus Christ," Brad stutters, looking horrified.

"I thought Kayla told you. Lexi, we're going to a *kink* club. This is it."

My mouth hangs open in shock.

We come to a stop outside a club called the Velvet Whip, the neon sign giving us all a nice pink hue.

"Softness and sting," I mumble, reading the tagline. Huh.

I whip around to Kayla. "What the hell, Kayla? When you said 'immersive theater,' I thought you meant audience participation. Not audience fornication!"

But before she can answer, Brad jumps in with a disapproving frown. "Nope, not happening. Kayla, this is not cool. You should've given Lexi a heads-up." He shakes his head like a disappointed parent. "Lexi and I will find a normal bar."

I grab Kayla's arm and hiss, "You brought me to some BDSM club?!"

She winces and starts twirling her hair nervously. "So, surprise?" she squeaks out. "Sorry, I figured you'd bail if you knew, since you were already hard to convince for a normal girls' night out."

"Give us a sec," I say to Brad, dragging her away from the guys.

She attempts what I guess is supposed to be an innocent grin. "But come on, it could be fun, right? A fresh experience to distract you from . . . well, you know."

I cross my arms, unimpressed. "Ah yes, nothing like an unprepared wander through a sex club to get over the mistake I made with a client," I reply flatly.

"Please don't be mad," she pleads, her hands clasped like she's about to pray. "I just thought, maybe this would help pull you out of your slump. But we can leave if you're really uncomfortable."

I want to strangle her. I'm no prude, but a warning would have been nice before walking blindly into an apparent sex club. This is why you can never trust Kayla's planning skills.

"I was expecting an immersive cinema experience," I choke out. "Something more PG."

Kayla bites her lip, eyes looking anywhere but at me. "Yeah, uh, this is clearly a misfire. I just wanted us to do something exciting for once. Remember our motto—be more adventurous?"

Brad comes over hesitatingly to break up our little feud. "Hey, Lexi, there's a nice wine bar just around the corner we can hit up instead."

I nod instinctively. "Yeah, okay that sounds . . ." But then something makes me pause. Some wild impulse fueled by tequila and maybe one too many clashes with Connor Quinn recently. It's like a little devil pops up on my shoulder, whispering in my ear, *"You're such a bore. Live a little."*

"Actually, you know what?" I say, eyeing the

club again. "Let's do this. I'm in."

Kayla, Justin, and Brad exchange wary looks. They spend the next five minutes trying to convince me out of it, but their disbelief only cements my decision. New Lexi tries new things. New Lexi is bold and daring.

I shrug. We're already here. And honestly, some fun new memories would be awesome instead of replaying *that* office moment on loop.

We step into a hallway decked out in hot-pink velvet. It's like stumbling into Barbie's dream dungeon. A hostess wearing a leather bikini and collar greets us enthusiastically.

My jaw drops as I see some girl strutting by with a dude on a leash. And he's wearing a diaper. Like, what the actual fuck? I am beyond confused.

Brad leans in, still looking wary. "Hey, there's no pressure to participate in anything you're not comfortable with."

"I know. Have you been here before?"

"A few times," he says casually. "You cool with this?"

Honestly, I have no clue how I feel right now. Intrigued? Curious? Completely overwhelmed? "I'll give it a go."

"Welcome to the Velvet Whip, ladies," the hostess announces with a seductive smirk. "First time here?"

"Yeah, first time," Kayla pipes up with an

anxious laugh. She darts her eyes my way, trying to gauge if I'm about to go nuclear on her.

"I take it you ladies are new to exploring daddy dynamics then?" our hostess asks brightly, leading us into a vivid pink room. There are things in here that I wouldn't even know where to begin guessing their use. Holy hell.

I make a strangled noise. "I'm sorry—daddy dynamics?" I choke out. My eyes bug out taking in leather paddles, feathers, handcuffs dangling from the velvet walls. The air is thick with the smells of leather, heavy perfumes, and god knows what else. People of all genders and orientations are scattered throughout the lounge, some in nothing but artfully arranged leather harnesses and chains.

I gape at the sight of a grown man sucking on a pacifier while getting spanked by a woman in leather.

"It's the elite club for all your daddy kink needs in the city," the hostess coos as a lady in latex cracks a whip over her partner's ass. He seems into it.

I glance around anxiously, feeling completely out of my depth. Note to self—avoid eye contact with anyone currently sucking on an adult soother.

I mutter a curse under my breath.

"Come onnn," Kayla begs, hitting me with her best puppy dog eyes. "It'll be an experience!"

Experience. Ha. That's the phrase people use to describe something they never intend to do again.

I glance around, half curious and half shitting bricks. Everywhere you look, there are people in leather or lace, getting their freak on in all sorts of ways. It's overwhelming and a little intimidating. We pass a woman cradling a grown-ass businessman in latex underwear like he's a giant baby.

"Are you pissed at me?" Kayla whispers, biting her lip.

"Are you kidding me right now?" I hiss, rolling my eyes theatrically. "Did you really expect me not to be? I know my social life has been boring of late, but you dragged me to a BDSM club. What did you think was going to happen?"

Her face falls. She looks like a scolded puppy. "Oh geez, you're really mad then? Should we just leave?"

"No, we're here now. Might as well see what happens I guess."

An escape from my boring life for a few hours.

"Ladies, have you chosen which type of daddy you'll be for the evening?" The hostess looks straight at me and Kayla with her piercing gaze.

I sputter, caught off guard. "Wait, *I'm* the daddy?"

"Most of our daddies are women." She smiles enthusiastically. "We encourage female empowerment here."

Huh. Well, I should check my unconscious biases.

"What exactly are the different types of daddies?" I ask, my wariness making way for intrigue.

The hostess smiles. "We've got all sorts of flavors here, sweetie. Some like to coddle and nurture, while others prefer a firm hand and strict rules. Some like to be called 'daddy' or 'mommy,' while others prefer 'sir' or 'ma'am.'" She winks. "It all depends on what kind of dynamic you're looking for."

I shift nervously as Brad chuckles softly near my ear, his breath tickling my neck. "And you'll make a damn sexy daddy for me."

My eyes widen and I spin around to stare at him. "I'm sorry, you actually want *me* to be *your* daddy here?"

"Mm-hmm," he murmurs, gazing at me with bedroom eyes.

I'm not sure how to feel about this. This is definitely not what I envisioned when I rolled out of bed this morning. But this seems to be the theme lately—my life taking wild, unpredictable turns I never see coming.

I clear my throat delicately. "I'm not . . . you don't expect me to walk you around on like, a dog collar and leash or anything though . . . right?" I ask weakly, trying to wrap my head around this new development.

Brad just laughs. "That's not really my thing. But I do enjoy a good spanking now and then."

I nearly choke as Kayla mouths, *Go with it! Are you okay if I leave you for ten minutes?*

"What?!" I squeak in alarm. Okay, I've had three tequilas and a few glasses of wine with this guy, but I never signed up for this level of intimacy. It seems more intimate than anal.

The hostess sizes me up. "Shall we fit you with some dominatrix attire? A leather harness maybe, or thigh-high boots?"

"*What?*" I screech again, sure I'm being Punk'd.

"We'll just take a whip for now," Brad suggests. Like he's picking out toppings for a pizza. This situation is spiraling so fast, I can barely keep up.

"How about we start with something a bit more vanilla? Like a drink at the bar?" I ask. "No need to bust out the whips and diapers just yet."

Thankfully, Brad takes mercy on me. But not before grabbing a freaking giant pink whip from Mistress Hostess on our way to grab drinks. This is not your typical second date.

Kayla scuttles off to a secluded booth with Justin, shooting me a dramatic thumbs-up.

I shake my head at her like a judgmental nun.

My kink experience is limited to fuzzy handcuffs from the clearance bin at Target. But here I am, about to star in my own version of Fifty Shades of WTF.

Perching up awkwardly on some stools in our own private booth, I take a much-needed gulp of my cocktail.

Brad gently squeezes my knee in reassurance. "Let's take it easy, all right? No rush. Sip your drink, get a vibe of this place, and see if it clicks. And hey, if you're not feeling it, just say the word, and we're out."

His laid-back vibe helps ease my jitters a bit. After a few more generous swigs, I grab his hand, ready to dive in.

I'm already here, might as well go all in. If he wants to be spanked, I'll just imagine his cute butt is Connor's punchable face, although that's probably against the code of conduct.

Normally, I wouldn't even consider something this wild. But with all the drama lately, something in me snaps. I'm done with the same old grind, just scraping by. Time for a change.

My heart races as I blurt out, "Okay, fine. Let's do it." I take a deep breath to steady myself, but it feels like I've swallowed a mouthful of sand. "What exactly does this whole thing entail?"

Brad grins, thrilled that I'm on board. "We'll start nice and easy—maybe some light spanking to warm up. Establish safe words too so we know each other's limits. We go at your pace, Lexi. As the daddy, you're in charge. You get to punish me when I'm naughty. And reward me when I'm obedient." His eyes smolder as he says, "Think you can handle that role for me . . . Daddy?"

WHOA there. I try not to choke on my drink as he talks about floggers and safe words.

I eye him. "So which one are you right now? Naughty or nice?"

Tipsy me can't tell if I'm intrigued or totally bewildered by this proposed power dynamic. But I'm not completely turned off either.

He gazes back at me through hooded eyes. "I'm *definitely* being very naughty right now, Daddy." He seems dangerously turned on just saying that. Oh boy.

I shift on the plush velvet, skin flushing. "Then I guess you need to be punished? For misbehaving?" I manage to get out.

Brad grins in satisfaction and begins to remove his pants. Down come his briefs. He's hard already. A second dick for me to see in the space of a few days. Lucky me. It may not be as impressive as Connor's, but it'll do the job just fine.

Brad gets on all fours, shaking with anticipation as if he's about to present me with the holy grail of asses.

And here I go, diving into this kinky rabbit hole.

God, am I really doing this?

I stand and awkwardly grab on to Brad's ass cheeks, trying to channel my inner spa masseuse before giving him a satisfying slap that echoes throughout the room.

"God, yes!" His moans confirm that my spanking skills are on point.

I feel like I've gotten to know a decent amount about Brad despite it being only our second date. He works at a hospital downtown, hails from Ohio, rides a motorbike, and his grandma is ninety-seven. Oh, and he loves chana masala.

But I definitely didn't expect to find out the color of his asshole so soon.

I take a quick breather, unsure of what to do next. Rinse and repeat seems like a good strategy.

Each time my hand connects with his skin he moans, and I can't help but think *Damn, I'm really good at this.* I pause for a moment, basking in my glory and wondering if there's a medal for this kind of talent.

I continue slapping away, each one eliciting a satisfying groan from Brad. Looks like we'll be at this for a while and he's not complaining one bit.

"So, uh . . . are you having a good time down there?" I ask awkwardly.

Brad looks back at me, his eyes glazed over with pleasure. "Hell yeah, Daddy. You've got one damn strong hand."

I feel guilty for imagining it's Connor's ass

under my hand. I want him to feel pain. Connor, not Brad. Although Brad wants to feel pain too.

I know Connor loved the sex just as much as me. It was rough and wild, almost savage how he pounded into me. And when we came . . . it was like nothing else mattered except for that moment of pure bliss between us.

So why did he freak out afterward? Is he really that much of a one-and-done player that he couldn't even stand *looking* at me afterward? He just wanted to screw me out of his system, that's clearly what that was about.

"Am I being too rough?" I ask, trying to catch my breath. This is turning out to be a workout. Like a CrossFit class.

"Use the whip," he grunts in between thrusts. "And tell me off! I want you to scold me."

I grab the pink whip. Tell him off? What the fuck do I say? "You've been a bad boy," I say, channeling my inner dominatrix. "And . . . Daddy's home," I add for extra effect, feeling ridiculous.

"LOUDER," he barks.

"All right, all right. You need a good spanking for being such a naughty little fucker!" I declare with newfound confidence.

"What the hell, Lexi?"

That criminally sinful voice cuts through the room, freezing me mid-swing. I look up in horror to find a very tense Connor filling the doorway.

I go still, pink leather whip poised in hand like some sort of demented dominatrix Barbie doll.

Oh shit.

TWENTY-NINE

Lexi

"Hey! Get your own booth, man," Brad shouts, still bent over obediently in front of me.

I scramble to find my footing, my jaw almost hitting Brad's backside.

"Connor?" I choke out, half convinced the tequila's messing with me. But no, there he is, fuming, even after I blink.

"How did you—have you been *tracking* me?" My voice hits a new high.

Connor's expression is downright murderous as he takes in the scene before him. His glare shifts over my date, who's still loyally at my feet.

"Yeah, I've had someone on you," he growls. "I promised to keep you safe. With an international cartel that's potentially a threat to you, what did you expect, Lexi? You and Grace have been under constant watch."

"That doesn't mean you can just storm in

here!"

"I thought something happened to you when my guys reported you were here," he retorts, frustration clear. "I called you ten times. No answer. I thought someone might be forcing you into something against your will."

"I came here of my own free will, Connor."

I stand there dumbly, dominatrix whip dangling uselessly.

Connor shoots Brad a death stare. "Time to go, buddy" he says sharply.

I bristle, snapping back to life. "Excuse me? You're the one who should fuck off! I'm trying to enjoy a date here, not put on a peep show for you."

Connor's eyes flash dangerously. "Not anymore you're not."

"You're Connor Quinn," Brad mutters, obviously thrown by the situation.

I march right up to Connor, temper flaring. "Get out. You have no right to be here. This is a private party, and you weren't invited."

"I was worried. I broke speed limits to get here. I might as well hand over all the keys to my cars to you now, since I'll probably be banned from driving after tonight."

"Thanks for the overkill concern and for the cartel watch, but this is goodbye. Adios. Auf Wiedersehen."

"We've got to talk, Lexi."

"We're way past talking." I stand chest to chest with him, glaring up defiantly. Even in heels, he towers over me. "I told you to leave. I can't stand looking at you right now!"

His jaw sets hard. "I don't like how we ended things the other night."

"How *you* ended things, you mean? I was perfectly polite."

"Yeah, how I ended things," he grits out through clenched teeth, like the words physically pain him.

"That's your idea of an apology?" I fire back.

He runs a hand through his hair. "I just ... Let's just talk, okay? Hear me out."

Our eyes clash in a heated staring match. My heart is betraying me, beating faster at the sight of him. Damn him for still affecting me after everything.

I try to mask my feelings, but the pain leaks through. "You made your stance pretty clear."

Poor Brad hovers awkwardly behind us. Probably rethinking his Dominatrix Barbie Dream House adventure thanks to Connor's dramatic entrance.

Connor's gaze flickers to Brad then back to me, disbelief in his eyes. "Really, Lexi?"

Rage spikes through me at his judgmental audacity. "You lost any say in what I do when you kicked me out of your office." I jab at his infuriatingly hard chest for emphasis, ignoring how good touching him feels.

I grab the whip again, aiming it at him in a defiant gesture. I feel like a woman on the brink. "And now I'm imagining each scorching lash is across your ball bag or better yet—that massively inflated ego!"

To my surprise, Connor looks genuinely remorseful. "I didn't mean to lash out at you like that. It was a shitty overreaction," he says quietly.

I squint at him. "Then what's your excuse?"

He shoves his hands in his pockets, shifting his weight. What, is he here because I didn't go chasing after him, begging for scraps of attention? Guys like Connor only want what they can't have— which, with their mountains of cash, isn't much.

The awkward silence stretches, and my impatience spikes. I tap my foot, waiting for him to justify himself. "Well? You've got nothing?"

"Let's talk somewhere more private."

"Hello?" Brad's irritated voice slices through our standoff. I turn to find him now dressed, glaring daggers at Connor. "We're kind of on a date here."

Connor barely spares him a glance. "Not anymore, you're not."

I grimace apologetically at Brad "I'm really sorry. This thing with us . . . it's done." I exhale heavily. "At least it was memorable, right?"

He shakes his head and mutters, "Unbelievable," as he shoves past us.

"I was playing daddy for him tonight." I shrug at Connor, a hint of defiance in my tone.

Connor visibly flinches, raising a hand as if to block the mental image. "I don't need the play-by-play," he growls.

He lets out a deep sigh. "Look, I was out of line at the studio. Let's talk this out back at my hotel suite."

I narrow my eyes at him. He can't seriously think I'll sleep with him after everything. "You want me to come back to your hotel room to 'talk'? Yeah right." I scoff.

Annoyance mars his handsome features. "I mean a real conversation, nothing else."

I'm skeptical, still gripping my whip. "So why a hotel and not your place?"

"My personal space is off-limits," he states flatly. "I don't bring anyone there."

"Real charming," I retort, laying the sarcasm on thick. "What, am I not classy enough to get past your upscale doorman?"

He breathes out hard, frustration evident. "It's not about you. I just value my privacy, that's all."

His arrogance is off the charts. God forbid I contaminate his bachelor pad by setting foot inside.

I snatch up my bag with finality. "Thanks but

no thanks on your 'conversation.'"

He pauses, a muscle in his jaw ticking. Clearly, he expected me to melt gratefully into his arms at the mere suggestion.

As I turn to leave, he catches my wrist. "At least let me drive you home. Consider it a peace offering. My car's right outside."

Part of me actually wants to grab this infuriating man and kiss him senseless. But that would make me an idiot.

We crossed a line, he kicked me out without even an Uber, and now Mr. Tall, Dark, and Sorry is back with apologies? Yeah, no.

What's next? We gallop out of here on a white horse and ride off into the sunset while I'm still clutching this whip?

I give him a sharp nod, my voice laced with edge. "All right, you can give me a lift. But let's get one thing straight—it's on my terms, not yours."

◆ ◆ ◆

The ride in Connor's high-end sports car is filled with a tense silence, only broken by the low purr of the engine.

He grips the steering wheel like he's trying to strangle it.

I gaze out the window, the city lights blending

into a stream of neon, wondering why he bothered tracking me down if he was just going to act like I'm invisible.

"First time at that club?" he finally says, not taking his eyes off the road.

"Yeah, decided to try something new. You probably have a dedicated VIP booth on retainer there."

That cracks a small laugh out of him. "Been there a few times over the years. But I didn't expect it to be your thing."

I arch a brow. "What, you thought I'd be moping at home after you left me hanging last weekend?" My words come out more bitter than intended.

"Of course not," he grumbles.

We drive on in loaded silence for a few blocks until he speaks up again, his voice deeper, tinged with something I can't quite place. "Seeing you with that guy tonight . . . didn't sit right with me. Couldn't handle it."

Hope thrums traitorously in my chest. I turn to fully face him. "So why push me away if it kills you to see me with someone else?"

Dead silence. Connor's jaw works, the only sign he's even listening.

"I don't like the idea of sharing you," he admits, his voice gravelly. "I know I shouldn't say that. I don't have any claim."

My heart skips a beat at his raw admission. I lick my lips, suddenly dry. "What are you saying, Connor? What do you actually want from me?"

"Nothing," he answers, voice flat, his expression closed off. "I don't have any right to feel possessive."

"You don't want anything, but you don't like seeing me with other guys?" I shoot back, my words sharp with resentment. "We said it was just a one-time thing. You see me out and suddenly you're busting in like some jealous boyfriend?"

His jaw sets tight. "It's not that simple."

"Isn't it?" I can't help but scoff. "Then enlighten me, because this all looks pretty damn selfish from where I'm sitting."

He stiffens, hands tightening on the steering wheel. "Look, I have some things going on with me," he grinds out cryptically.

I wait, but nothing more comes. ". . . that's it?"

"That's it. That's all I can give you right now."

I grip the seat belt tight, feeling its edge bite into my palm. "So, you brand me as a mistake, barge into my date, and think a lukewarm apology is gonna cut it?" I shake my head. "I should've known. You're Connor Quinn—use and discard is your formula. Because you can, right? There's always someone else willing to take the spot, no matter how you treat them."

I lock eyes with him. "But I actually thought

you'd be decent enough to show me some respect after. Looks like I was fooling myself."

He turns, his face serious, almost tormented. "It's not like that, Lexi. If you're hunting for love and a fairy-tale ending, I'm not the guy." He stops, struggling with his next words. "But I am sorry for acting like a jerk after we had sex. I've got some issues that are messing with my head."

His apology barely registers as I stare blankly out the window. Connor speeds toward my apartment, halving the time in this beast of a car.

I chew on my lip. "Do you seriously have protection on me?"

"Yes." He frowns. "I didn't want to worry you, so I didn't tell you, and maybe that was the wrong call. But that crowd you got mixed up with aren't friendly."

My stomach does a nosedive, feeling all kinds of queasy.

"It's okay," he says softly. "Nothing will happen to you. I won't let it."

"Thanks," I say quietly.

He throws the car into park outside my apartment and faces me. "Can I come up for a bit?"

"Why the hell would you?" I ask, stunned.

"I'm not ready to say goodbye yet."

I chew on the inside of my cheek, holding back a sharp comeback. Great, NOW Mr. Moody decides he's not done with me. How utterly convenient.

There's this tiny, toxic part of me that's thrilled. He's not ready to say goodbye. He wants to spend more time with me.

Then there's the other part itching to knock him down a peg.

A plan for a little payback starts forming in my head.

"Fine. You can come in for five minutes," I state coldly. "Don't expect the Ritz though."

❖ ❖ ❖

"Keep it down," I whisper, easing open the door to my dingy apartment. "Grace is asleep."

Connor steps in, and it's almost comical how out of place he looks here—an Armani ad come to life in the middle of a thrift shop. He practically takes up the whole room. He's the largest human to ever grace my apartment.

I notice his gaze sweeping over my less-than-luxurious setup, and I instantly go on the defensive.

"Welcome to my palace," I declare with mock grandeur, arms wide. "I know it's a real step down from your swanky pads I'm apparently not good enough to see."

"Don't, Lexi."

I imagine the shabby interior through a

billionaire's eyes. Great, my laundry's on display in the living room.

"It's got charm," he offers.

"Charm is what you say when you're being kind." I stand taller, refusing to be embarrassed. "You know, once I would have died of embarrassment having you see this. Now? I couldn't care less."

Connor faces me, the usual arrogance wiped from his face.

"Lexi, I don't care about your decor," he says, his voice low. "But you, on the other hand, I'm starting to realize I do care about, annoyingly enough. And just so we're clear"—his tone gets firmer—"this place needs work."

I scoff lightly but feel a weird twist inside.

He shoots a quick glance at the kitchen, then back at me, his frown deepening. "You've got some serious dampness issues here. The floor's all warped."

I roll my eyes dramatically. "Tell me something I don't know. The kitchen's a ski slope. Fancy a drink?"

He declines with a shake of his head. "No, I'm good. I'll have someone come look at this."

"Save it," I snap back, maybe a bit too fiercely. "I don't want your pity fixes or your crew of Mr. Fix-Its. I can handle my own mess."

Connor's voice drops an octave. "Don't be

stubborn, Lexi. Just accept the damn help."

"I don't *want it*," I fire back. "And watch your step, that floorboard's loose."

He exhales audibly. "Why are you fighting me on this? I'm trying to do something decent for you."

I grab his hand, pulling him toward the bedroom with determination. "Oh please. This is just you trying to clear your conscience, trying to play the good guy." I toss him a challenging look. "I don't need your pity renovations."

Connor closes the gap between us, eyes blazing fiercely. "Is this why you let me in here? To fight?"

No, I did-fucking-not. I yank him into the bedroom and slam the door shut. I dragged him back here to give him a taste of his own medicine.

THIRTY

Lexi

"All right, listen up," I announce, poking a finger into his sturdy chest. "This is my place, so it's my rules. You wanted to spend time with me? You're gonna do it on my terms. That means I'm in charge here. Understand?"

Watching his stunned expression is like hitting a small, deliciously petty jackpot. No way he's used to women standing up to him instead of melting at his presence.

But this is the same guy who slept with me only to reject me seconds later. Who tanked our interview. Ruined my date. And now he expects to call the shots?

Not anymore.

I step closer, my head tilted up defiantly.

Connor's eyes flash with heat. He grips my hand tight against his chest. "Is that it? You want to control me for once?"

I hear the stress on "for once," as if he thinks this is just a temporary revolt against his dominance.

"Don't like it?" I point to the door for dramatic effect. "The door's right there."

He moves in until my legs hit the bed, smirking. "Never said I had a problem with it."

His other hand grips my hair, tugging just enough to make me gasp as he leans in for a kiss.

But I push him back with force, my hands flat against his chest, then toe his leather shoes meaningfully. "How about you get on your knees instead, pretty boy?"

Connor raises an eyebrow, amusement glinting in his blue eyes. "*Pretty boy*?"

"Did you not hear me? By all means, make me repeat myself," I sass, throwing his own words back at him from our first meeting in his office.

He chuckles low and dirty. Still smirking, he sinks to his knees before me, never breaking eye contact.

Holy crap, this is wild. And hot as hell. I didn't think he'd actually go through with it after what happened in the hotel bathroom.

"All right, Lexi," he drawls in a husky voice laced with playful mockery. Like he's humoring me. "What's the plan now?"

My eyes drop to the obvious bulge in his pants, sending a rush of heat through my veins.

I smirk down at Connor's hungry gaze, euphoric rushes of power and dominance pulsing through me. But secretly, my heart pounds wildly with nerves.

With deliberate slowness, I trail my fingers over his handsome face—the strong jaw, those sensuous lips—teasing him with featherlight caresses.

Hmm, look at that.

The Connor Quinn, on his knees, eyeing me like a starving dog awaiting a juicy bone. In this moment, I feel like a goddess—confident and completely in control.

Maybe I *should* clip a leash on this arrogant man. The thought sends a wicked thrill through me.

"You look good down there." I tilt his chin up with one un-manicured nail. "On your knees for me."

He tightens his hold on me, a low growl rumbling in his chest, as if fighting for control.

In what I hope is a seductive move, I shrug off my dress and let it drop to the floor. His eyes never leave my body as I unhook my bra and let it fall to join the dress.

"Fuck," he mutters under his breath as I shimmy out of my panties, standing there completely naked in front of him. Trying my best to exude confidence, even though I'm feeling anything but. This guy's used to supermodels, but damn if he isn't devouring me with his gaze. Seems like he likes what he sees.

"You trying to make me lose my mind? I knew it from the moment I laid eyes on you—you're an angel."

My chest pangs. I wish he wouldn't say shit like that. It stirs up all sorts of unwanted feelings. And the worst part is, he doesn't even mean it.

Gripping his shoulders tight, I lean in close and whisper, "All right Connor, let's see what you've got."

I try to hide the fluttering feeling in my stomach as I spread my legs wider.

His hungry gaze lingers on my exposed pussy. He glances up, flashing that cocky grin of his. "The pleasure's all mine."

With ease, he lifts my leg over his shoulder and puts me in a dominant hold that makes me weak in the knees.

"I'm going to take you to heaven, angel," he growls playfully, trailing kisses down my inner thigh.

His skilled tongue finds its way to my slick heat, making me gasp and squirm. A slow, pulsing heat builds between my legs as he expertly teases my swollen clit.

I think this guy must have an instruction manual on how to make a woman lose her mind with just his tongue. Clever bastard. And it's rough and fast and dirty in all the best ways. So much better than using my vibrator and watching OnlyFans Dan sweat it out on camera.

Holy shit, I've had guys go down on me before, but this? This is next level. Connor is devouring me like I'm the last pussy on earth.

There's something so heady about having a man like him between my legs, completely focused on making me feel good. A man who's used to taking charge and getting what he wants. But for now, he only cares about getting me off. And let me say, he knows exactly what the hell he's doing.

I grip his shaven head, moaning his name desperately as his mouth works magic on my throbbing clit.

The neighbors must think there's an animal being slaughtered in here, but I couldn't care less. All that matters is this intense pleasure he's unleashing upon me.

I cling to him for dear life, nails digging into his muscular shoulders. I'm beyond begging for release, arousal coursing through me like a drug.

The intensity builds until I can no longer support myself standing. As he eats me out, his forearms hold my shaking legs up. If he wasn't holding me upright, I'd have collapsed onto the floor long ago.

Holy hell, the view from up here is insane. I'm

practically drooling as I watch his head between my thighs, his back muscles flexing as he goes to town with that talented tongue.

His eyes never leave mine as he eats me out. It's almost too much for me to handle. Watching him fuck me with his mouth feels a million times more intimate than even sex.

And just when I think I can't take anymore, he pulls out this new trick with his mouth that sends me crashing over the edge. My eyes roll back, my legs jerk, and I'm done for.

"Yeah, Connor," I moan. It's a delicious kind of pain that I can't resist. "Oh god, I can't hold it any longer. I'm . . ."

My body trembles, a tsunami of tingles washing over me. Every nerve, every muscle, every cell bursts with intense, raw pleasure.

My leg slips off his shoulder as I let out a satisfied sigh, feeling like jelly. I need to catch my breath, feeling a little weak in the knees. But my mind's already racing ahead to what I'm going do next.

He tries to pull me close as he stands, but I smoothly sidestep him.

"Well, that was a blast," I say, quickly slipping into my dress. "But it's time for you to head out, Connor."

"What?" He gives me a look as if he's not sure he heard right.

"I'd like you to leave now."

The smile on his face disappears in an instant. "Seriously?"

"Yup. Thanks for the orgasm. I'm done now. You can leave. We'll hash this out later," I retort, tossing his own lines back at him.

I swing open the bedroom door and turn to face him.

He stands there, looking confused as hell, as if he's taken a direct hit to the gut. "Lexi, dammit, I've already said I'm sorry. Whatever you want tonight, it's yours. Hell, I was into it as much as you were. It's been too damn long since I've felt anything remotely good."

"Aw, that's sweet, but we don't always get what we want."

When he keeps standing there confused, I tighten my grip on the door handle. "Are you suddenly hard of hearing?" I throw his own words back at him yet again. "I said leave. Now."

His eyes sharpen, turning into cold blue slits, jaw set like he's chewing on gravel. Man, he looks pissed.

"You've never been told to leave anywhere in your life, have you?" I force myself to stay firm. "Should I fetch a megaphone to make it crystal clear?"

He glares at me, anger etched on his face as he heads for the door. "Fucking whiplash is what you give me, Lexi Sullivan.

"Me? That's rich," I scoff after him.

"This is exactly why I don't fuck the same woman twice," he mutters.

"Finally, something we can agree on." Although that didn't come out right.

He stops in the doorway, giving me one last hard look. I half expect him to start up again, but he just turns and leaves, thankfully not slamming the door behind him. Thank god Grace sleeps like the dead.

I lean back against the now-closed door, letting out a slow breath.

Doesn't feel too great being shown the door, does it, Connor? Now you get it.

I don't know why he's so pissy. It's not like he'd have stayed over at Maison du Leak anyway. Not unless he's starring in some "secret billionaire slumming it" show.

I wait for the rush of victorious smugness to hit me. I landed the final punch—outplayed Casanova at his own game. Tonight, I was the one in charge. Point for team Lexi.

But the victory doesn't feel sweet. Instead, it feels like I've lost something valuable.

THIRTY-ONE

Connor

"It's time we pay the cunt a visit," I say to Jim. The file on Deano Johnson is spread out on my desk. Jim, being ex Special Forces, doesn't bat an eye at my choice of words. Nothing shakes him.

Jim gives a nod. "How nice do you want us to be, boss?"

"Friendly enough to ensure he enjoys a vacation in the hospital. Then we can hand him over to the cops," I answer. "Let's not go overboard, no need to kick off a full-fledged conflict. Just a clear message about the boundaries concerning my assets from here on out."

We have enough dirt to bury Deano. He may not be the top guy, but he made off with my car. Now, he's going to serve as the warning. The message is clear—stay away from my stuff.

That includes my cars. And Lexi.

"Consider it done. Anything else, boss?"

I lean back, my gaze sweeping over the cityscape. Somewhere below is Vallure PR, too small to see from this height. Insignificant.

"We still got eyes on Miss Sullivan's place? No gaps in coverage?"

"Yes, boss. Around the clock, just like you wanted. Nobody gets close without us knowing," Jim assures me.

I exhale slightly. One less weight on my mind.

I've got to make sure she's safe. It's been a week since she kicked me out of her apartment. A week since that sassy mouth got under my skin. Feels like forever since someone's got to me like that. I mentally salute her audacity for daring to put me in my place. I had to physically restrain myself from tossing her onto that tiny bed and taking her right then and there when she threw my own words back at me.

Now, we have no business crossing paths.

And that pisses me off more than it should.

I wasn't lying when I said I enjoyed myself too. Making her come was the first time in days I could get out of my own head. Finally feel free for a moment. The only break from the endless worrying gnawing at me.

I scrap the email I'm halfheartedly banging out because I can't focus worth a damn. I switch over to the bunch of photos Vallure sent over from that over-the-top couple's photoshoot. I breeze past most of them but pause at the only candid shot that made it through.

It's a picture of Lexi and me, my arms around her from behind. A mistake, not meant to be included. But there it is.

As much as you get under my skin, Lexi, you're the only one who's made me feel good these past few weeks.

Almost worth all the trouble.

Almost.

I close the photo, my finger lingering over the delete button.

Lexi

My phone buzzes right as I'm sorting through notes on my latest "high-profile client"—some Real Housewife from Ohio with a shoplifting scandal.

It's Grace on the line. I take a deep breath and pick up, always half expecting it to be something about Mom's health.

But no, she's buzzing with excitement. "Lexi. You won't believe this. Three seriously hot dudes just showed up saying Mr. Quinn sent them? To fix up our place? One looks like freaking Magic Mike!"

I freeze, my heart skipping a beat. You've got to be kidding me. I shot down his charity offer, and now he sends a squad of muscled fixer-uppers to my place?

I don't want his sympathy gestures. It's been a full week since I gave him the boot, and the only thing tying us together—the campaign—is cruising along just fine with Brooke at the helm.

He didn't bother to reach out, not that I had any delusions about it. Guys like him don't grovel or mope. They just keep on living in their perfect little world, doors flying open wherever they go.

And honestly, I'm glad it's playing out like this. It's a break from being yanked around by his hot-and-cold antics.

Plus, Willow and Connor's not-so-secret steamy audio mishap is old news now, overshadowed by some pop star deciding to reenact a wildlife documentary with his bandmate on live TV. Though Connor's recent interview disaster did stir the gossip pot a bit more.

"Grace, listen. Send them away, okay?"

She makes a noise of extreme protest. "What? But they're here to fix everything—the floor, the toilet, even that nightmare of a radiator."

I breathe in, aiming for some zen-level calm. "No, Grace."

"Lexi, our toilet's still on the fritz. Can't we get that fixed at least before we boot them? Magic Mike over there says it's a quick fix. Imagine, a toilet that actually flushes!"

Damn. The thought of a fully functioning

bathroom does have its appeal.

"All right, fine," I sigh, already regretting this. "Fix the toilet. But that's it, then they're gone. And tell them thanks a ton."

It's not the repair guys' fault they're chess pieces in Mr. Deep Pockets' game.

Grace's voice drops conspiratorially. "Did we win some competition or something? This is nuts."

"No, Grace, we didn't win anything."

Then she hits me with more news. "Oh, guess what, I got an interview with Quinn & Wolfe for that internship! How cool is that? Maybe our luck's finally changing."

I tense up. This isn't our luck changing. We're just pawns in Connor's power play.

But how do I rain on her parade?

"That's awesome about the interview," I force out, trying to sound stoked. "You'll knock it out of the park."

I just hope Connor doesn't use this as a move in his "manipulate Lexi through her sister" strategy. That'd be a new kind of low, even for him.

◆ ◆ ◆

Walking into Sunnyhell with Grace, I slap on a bland smile.

Lately my life's been almost creepily stress-free.

I'm immersed in new PR campaigns, working with clients who don't leave me perpetually upset. Got a functioning toilet thanks to Connor's unrequested handyman services. No follow-up date with Brad the Doc, but hey, at least I'm out there again. And I've still got time to figure out how I can pay for the next care home bill. It's fast-approaching, but I have an interview for a new job coming up soon.

Honestly, things could be much worse. I should feel relieved, maybe even happy.

I just feel a bit numb.

"Hey, Mom." I greet her with a quick cheek kiss.

"Lexi, I've got something to show you," she says, her voice raspy as she clears her throat. Oh no, is this going to be another one of her "hobby projects"? The last one was that horrendous sweater with the craziest looking flowers on it —I was convinced she must have been on psychedelics or something when she knitted that monstrosity. And yes, I had to model it on every visit for a good few weeks after that gift.

She fumbles with some file on the table before passing it over to me. "I was never good with the business stuff. Your dad was the numbers guy." She smiles wistfully. "But handsome Josh helped me out. He's quite the heartbreaker that one. I think he's keen on you, Lexi."

I look down at the spreadsheet, its rows and columns just a blur. "What's this supposed to be?"

Mom squeezes my hand. "It's a financial plan for moving me to a more affordable care place close by. So you don't have to stretch yourself too thin."

I take a closer look at the plan, my frown getting deeper. Sure, the numbers might add up, but only because it's for a place outside Baltimore. "Mom? That's hardly nearby! Come on, that won't work."

Her smile doesn't waver. "It's doable, honey. You and Grace can hop on a plane, visit me once a month or something."

"Baltimore is hundreds of miles away!"

She's unfazed. "It's practically next door by plane."

"This is ridiculous."

Grace lets out a little choked sob beside me. "But . . . my interview . . . with Quinn & Wolfe," she manages through her tears. "I could be making some real money soon."

Mom pats her hand. "That's great, Gracie, but it's not a fix for this."

Then she turns to me, sitting up straighter. "Listen, Lexi," she says, her voice quivering. "Even if I were in perfect health, we wouldn't be joined at the hip all the time. You'd be out exploring, hanging with your friends, maybe even meeting a guy. Josh, even." Her attempt at a smile is clouded by sorrow. "It breaks my heart to see you put your life on hold for me."

Tears blur my vision. I want to shout that she's my top priority. That I'll work it out. That leaving her is not an option. "Mom, New York is your home. I've got interviews lined up too. I'm gonna land a better job, with real money. There's even one with a signing bonus."

She gently touches my face. "Shush now. It'll be okay. We can do this."

I shake my head, a tear escaping. "I can't do that. I can't just send you to Baltimore."

"You have to. In all these years I haven't seen you cry until a few days ago. I can't be the reason for your tears, sweetie. I'm supposed to be your rock, not your anchor."

"Those tears weren't about you! It was . . . something else."

"Carrying this burden will make everything else hit harder. You being happy, that's what makes me happy. This is a good thing for both of us."

I shove the papers back to her, my voice breaking. "No, Mom. We're not going through with this. Let's just drop it. Can we talk about something else?"

"The toilet's fixed," Grace chimes in weakly.

◆ ◆ ◆

We skirt around the big issue for the next hour, talking instead about the now wonderfully quiet and efficient toilet. Then we shift to Grace's exciting internship interview and the latest questionable food choices at Sunnyvale.

Mom senses I'm not in the mood for heavy conversation, not risking a repeat of the last emotional outburst, especially with Nurse Ratched lurking nearby.

Right on cue, Ratched signals me with that *Come here* finger gesture.

What now? Just weeks ago I dropped a payment that could finance a mini space exploration.

"Hello, Lexi," she says briskly.

"Hi," I reply stiffly, wondering what I did to deserve a rare greeting.

"I need to confirm authorization for the next payments," she states impatiently.

"Next payments?" I blurt, starting to panic. "I just paid up for this term."

Did the transaction not process correctly?

She sighs heavily, showing her impatience. "The next three years. They're ready for your approval."

I'm bewildered. "I can't cover three years

upfront."

Where does she think I can pull that kind of money from? Is this her twisted idea of a joke?

"Well, it looks like someone can. Should I go ahead and process it?"

My pulse skyrockets. Paid in full? This can't be real. Can it?

My mouth goes dry. My stomach is flipping. My guts are flopping.

I struggle to suck air into my constricted lungs. "I-I'm sorry, you're saying . . . three years' worth has been paid already?"

Ratched looks at me as if I'm slow on the uptake. "Yes, that's correct. I just need your signature."

I take a small step back, head spinning. Three years. Three whole years of debt just *poof*! Gone. Thousands of dollars. Enough cash in one-dollar notes to fill a small pool.

There's only one person with deep enough pockets to wipe out such a massive amount without blinking. Only one guy who could afford to throw money around like it's nothing. And I won't be indebted again, especially not to him.

"No," I whisper, even as everything in me screams to just take it and run.

THIRTY-TWO

Lexi

"Meeting, now," Vicky barks, eyeing me and Brooke sharply. "Connor and Willow just arrived."

Shit. My gut plummets like a sack of bricks.

I trudge into the boardroom, trailing behind Brooke's assertive march.

Willow's planted at the head of the table, looking so tense she might be secretly doing Kegel exercises.

Connor's pacing like a predator in a trap, every movement radiating tension and barely contained energy. His hands are hidden in his pockets, sleeves pushed up to reveal those distracting forearms. He's making our tiny office feel even more cramped.

Same damn shirt from the night we hooked up in his office. Probably has an endless supply, like there's a "Dress for Success: Brooding CEO Edition" subscription service.

For god's sake, I thought this nightmare was over. There's nothing left for me to do. Brooke's handling the rest of the campaign, so why am I even here?

His brooding gaze lands on me instantly, and my traitorous heartbeat stutters. Does he practice that smoldering stare in the mirror every morning?

I slump into a chair, wishing I could up and vanish.

"We need to fix this mess," Willow snaps, with more backbone than she usually shows. "The pictures make us look all lovey-dovey, but the interview paints us as a trainwreck of a couple. It's a total disaster."

She gives Connor a scathing glare that would make a weaker guy cower.

"I've done everything you wanted, Willow," Connor retorts, stopping his restless movement to lean against the wall, his muscular arms tensed. "From those staged photos to that absurd interview and all your charity events."

"I didn't tell you to storm out mid-interview!" she screeches back, throat flushed.

"I've apologized for that. Enough is enough. We're done playing this game."

He turns to Vicky, his voice heavy with irritation. "Tell the world Willow called it off. Spin it however she wants."

"No way," Willow explodes. "I'm not ready for that."

"It's not open for debate," Connor states coldly, his voice as firm as a brick wall.

"My dad is going to lose it when he finds out," she warns, playing the daddy card. Classic move, Willow.

"Well, I'm grown enough to handle your dad."

Willow's eyes blaze my way with scorned fury, like I'm the wicked witch who stole her designer ruby slippers.

She spears an accusing finger at me, and I instinctively recoil. Panic swells in my chest as I try to predict what she's going to throw at me.

"It's because of her, isn't it?" she spits out, her voice dripping with venom. "You have a thing for her. I've seen the way you look at her."

Connor's jaw locks up tight. The accusation looms heavy in the air.

My throat tightens. *Fuck.*

Vicky lets out a nervous chuckle, trying to ease the tension emanating from Willow. "I doubt that's the problem. Connor isn't into Lexi, believe me."

"No, it was Gigi he was into," Brooke chimes in. "That's his reason for talking to Lexi."

Willow looks utterly appalled. "Gina Malone? Butt Buildr?"

"No, no. Lexi's cousin, the one caught stealing

cars," Brooke explains matter-of-factly,

Willow recoils. "A criminal?"

"A young woman in a difficult situation," Connor retorts, his tone dripping with annoyance. "A beautiful girl who couldn't ask for help. But that's beside the point. This conversation is absurd and a waste of my time."

Willow's lips twist. "I want Lexi fired."

The words hit me like a sledgehammer to the stomach, knocking the wind right out of me. "You *what*?"

There's a quick flash of regret on Willow's face, but she steels herself again. "I'm sorry, but I want you gone."

My heart plummets to new depths.

Losing this job is not an option, no matter how much I dislike it, no matter how many times I've fantasized about telling Vicky where to shove her campaigns. Everything will go off the rails if I lose it. I don't have a big enough safety net to catch me.

"I've put so much work into your campaign, Willow," I say, my voice tinged with desperation.

"No one's getting fired," Connor interjects. "Vicky, Quinn & Wolfe have some opportunities that might interest you." He glares at the poster of Gina Malone. "We'll have her promote one of our new hotels in . . ." He mutters a curse under his breath. "Alaska. My team will work out details."

Obviously bullshit, but his tone brokers no

argument.

I know he's just trying to save me from Willow's wrath, but it feels like a slap in the face.

And Willow isn't backing down either.

"He's just trying to cover for her," she fires back, jumping to her feet. "He's protecting her because he wants her!"

"I don't have time for this." Connor's stare is cold and commanding. "Vicky, you and Willow can agree on your own business relationship after this. If it's business you want, it's business you'll get. But nobody's getting fired over this nonsense. Are we clear?"

"Absolutely," Vicky agrees, all smiles and nods.

"All right, that's enough," Connor says firmly, waving his hand to signal the end of the discussion. "Everyone out. Except for Lexi."

Now I have déjà vu.

The others begin to leave, with Vicky attempting to soothe an enraged Willow. Brooke lasers me with a probing look before the door shuts.

Now that it's just Connor and me, I brace myself.

Oh god, what now?

I clear my throat, trying to keep it light and breezy. "Thanks for not completely throwing me under the bus with Willow's accusations about, you know, us."

"It was my actions that put you in that situation."

"Willow has every reason to be mad at me."

"No, she doesn't. Look, I'm not heartless, Lexi. I didn't sleep with you and make promises to her. I was upfront that the campaign was all for show."

"You don't need to justify yourself. You were single. You *are* single."

He looks at me stone-faced. "Why did you refuse my help with the medical bills?" Straight to the point, no beating around the bush.

I cross my arms, defensive. "That's my responsibility, not yours." But then I relent a little, because I'm not a total ungrateful bitch. "Still, thanks for offering."

His jaw sets in that all-too-familiar stubborn line. "I can easily cover it, Lexi. Stop being so damn headstrong."

Talk about the pot calling the kettle black.

"I don't need rescuing, Connor. I'm not sure if this is you trying to do the right thing or just feeling guilty about our situation, but I can't take your money. It would cost me too much, in ways that aren't financial. I'd end up bearing the cost with my own soul."

But as I shut down his astronomical offer, there's a flicker of doubt, a tiny voice whispering in the back of my mind.

What if I caved and let this powerful man work

his magic money wand, making all my problems vanish into thin air? To him, it's like picking up the tab for a round of drinks. Pocket change.

But to me? It's everything.

I could finally breathe, *really* breathe. I could focus on Grace, on my career, on building a better life for us after years of treading water.

My mind betrays me, conjuring up hazy visions of carefree laughter, maybe going back to school, a better apartment, wild nights out with Kayla . . . and, of course, more time for . . . well, other enjoyable activities. Maybe even the Velvet Whip, minus the money woes breathing down our necks.

But I meant what I said. I'd pay the price for that with my soul.

Connor seems baffled by my refusal, his brow furrowing deeper, his voice rougher. "You could've at least accepted the apartment improvements," he insists, his tone laced with frustration. "Beyond the toilet."

Clearly his work crew ratted out every detail.

My lips quirk reluctantly. "Well, Gracie has IBS, so fixing that toilet was an absolute must."

"You're something else, Lexi Sullivan." His tough exterior softens just faintly. "You're a good girl, you know that?"

His compliment catches me off guard, sending an unexpected flutter through me that I quickly cover with sarcasm. "I know. You were pretty vocal about it when you were pounding into me."

"I didn't mean like that. I meant you're pure through and through. You've got integrity flowing in your veins."

I try not to let his rare, sweet compliment go to my head. Experience has taught me that Connor's moods can change on a dime—now he's all charm, but who knows when he'll switch gears. I've learned that lesson the hard way.

"I just try to do the right thing when I can. It's only in desperate times that I resort to extreme measures, like, you know, 'borrowing' keys to a luxury car." I clear my throat awkwardly. "So, uh, what happened with Deano in the end?"

"Nothing for you to lose sleep over anymore. You're safe. He's taken care off."

My eyes widen in horror.

He chuckles. "He's not dead, Lexi."

My shoulders slacken in relief.

"But he might as well be if he ever thinks of crossing your path again."

His protective tone sends shivers down my spine.

"Thanks. Seriously. You could've easily ratted me out to the cops."

He looks away sharply. "Then neither of us would be sleeping too soundly," he mutters.

We're wrapped in awkward silence until he

speaks again. "I still think you should accept the money for the care home. You were right. If my mom had gotten sick when Killian and I were just starting out, it could have derailed us completely. Set us back years."

I smile weakly. "You and Killian would have powered through anyway. You both have that 'never say die' attitude."

One side of his mouth quirks up slightly. "You've got that same drive, Lexi. You're smart, hardworking. That attitude of yours could open doors—or get you in trouble," he says, a hint of amusement in his voice. "I'd hate to see it go to waste. To see you settle for less than you deserve."

To my dismay, my eyes start to mist up.

"You hate this PR grind, I can tell," he continues, an unfamiliar gentleness softening his tone. "Getting the care home costs handled would give you the freedom to chase what you really want."

I shake my head with a sad smile. "I can't, Connor. Not like this. Plus I've got this other agency interview lined up already—better pay at least."

His irritation seeps through, his jaw clenching tight as he gives me a stern look. "Screw that, Lexi. You can't stand PR. Don't waste your life mastering something you hate. Finish your psych course, dammit. It's better to be a rookie in something you love than a pro at something that drains you."

"I get that. But it's easy to say when money's no issue. I need some security. I need to know that Grace and I will be okay."

His eyes harden. "I'm offering you financial security right here. No strings attached, no ulterior motives. Just take it. Let me help you."

I stare at his handsome but guarded face, my heart somersaulting.

I'm not sure when things shifted.

For all our clashes, when did I start seeing him differently?

Maybe it was when I saw him talking to the college kids at the NexiHub, his resilience shining through as he inspired them to chase their own dreams.

Or when he forgave me for swiping his car fob.

Or seeing little traces of the fun, caring uncle underneath the billionaire exterior.

Or how he went out of his way for Grace, getting her résumé to his IT team.

Or perhaps it was during those seven-and-a-half minutes (or however long it was) when he rocked my world, making me feel alive in a way I hadn't in ages.

Or maybe it's happening right now, as he's saying all these sweet things about me, as if he truly gives a damn. As if he truly sees me. Truly believes in me.

And there it is. The truth I've been relentlessly burying, trying desperately to ignore.

"But that's it, right? You're not offering anything else, are you, Connor?"

A small, foolish part of me sparks with dangerous hope.

He freezes, his eyes cautious, guarded. "Like what?"

I drop my gaze, hating this weakness, this neediness, but unable to stop the words from tumbling out, from laying my heart at his feet.

"More," I whisper.

I want fucking more. More intimacy. More trust. More layers of this complex guy to discover and unravel.

More of Connor Quinn in every possible way.

I'd even take the mood swings if it meant getting past those walls he's built so high.

When I find the courage to meet his eyes again, the silence is excruciating. So thick, I swear you'd need a hacksaw to cut through it.

When Connor speaks again, his voice is cold, sharp like shards of ice—a brutal contrast to the gentle warmth of just moments ago. "I can't give you anything more, Lexi."

That rejection cuts deep, but I manage to keep my expression neutral, hiding the sting. Now, all that's left is to swallow the hurt and maintain whatever shred of dignity I still have.

His phone interrupts the heavy silence, buzzing insistently from his suit pocket.

Muttering a curse, he checks the caller ID and grumbles about being late for something.

He strides past me toward the door, his shoulders tense, and just when I think he's out for good, he stops short.

Before I can react, his fingers gently grasp my chin, tipping my face up to meet his gaze.

"Take the care home payment," he murmurs in that gravelly voice. "You're one of a kind, you know that? Too proud and selfless for your own good. But so damn special, Lexi. You deserve a break for once."

With a nod, he's gone, leaving me frozen, staring numbly at Gina Malone's perfect ass on that awful poster. A brutal reminder of how much I loathe this job.

THIRTY-THREE

Connor

Striding into Dr. Hayes's office, tucked away in some forgotten corner of Staten Island, I'm already questioning this journey. But if this guy has the power to fix me, then it's worth enduring the headache of getting here.

My lawyer's slapped non-disclosures on Hayes and his team, making it clear what happens if details leak. Good thing this medical team is highly vetted for discretion.

I've moaned about pointless meetings, torturous charity gigs, and rubbing elbows with slimy politicians. Even the laughable PR stunt with Willow. But that's just surface level. This thing I'm dealing with now? It's a whole different kind of hell.

It's completely foreign, this feeling of helplessness, of being at the mercy of something beyond my control, and I fucking despise it.

I'm not interested in adapting to a "new normal." I want—no, I *need* everything to go back to the way it was before.

I need a solution, and fast.

"Got an appointment with Hayes," I mutter to the receptionist, feeling like a fugitive in my shades and ballcap.

"I apologize for the wait, sir. He's running about five minutes late. Would you mind waiting?"

Yes, I bloody well mind, I want to snap. I don't want anyone spotting me in this place. I eye the others in the waiting room warily.

"Sure." I force a strained smile and choose the most isolated seat far away from the rest of the crowd.

I take out my phone, looking for any sort of distraction. It's useless.

The waiting room is filled with a middle-aged guy, a mother with her daughter, and a couple deep in their own world of sign language.

The woman giggles and playfully smacks his hands while sharing a private joke. Their moment of genuine connection tightens something in my chest, stirring emotions I can't quite name.

He laughs when she whispers in his ear, but it's a little offbeat. The lump in my throat grows bigger.

Will that be my future if I can't fix this problem? Laughing a bit out of sync? I feel like a jerk for even worrying about it. Who cares if my laugh isn't perfectly synchronized with everyone else's?

I picture myself trying to communicate and charm someone with just my hands. Would they still find me interesting? Would my sarcasm still hit its mark? Would my jokes still land if they had to be told in a language I had to learn from scratch?

Out of the corner of my eye, I catch the girl kissing her guy. And her hair, god, her hair . . . it's just like Lexi's. I'm suddenly thinking about how it would feel to run my fingers through Lexi's hair, right here, right now.

But imagining her here, seeing me struggle, would kill me. Lexi's the caring type, always looking out for others, always putting their needs before her own.

In my less-than-sober epiphany that night, I nailed it—she's an angel in her own right. But I don't need her looking at me like some project to fix. Goes against everything I am.

I refuse to be that guy, the one who needs rescuing.

In a different life, with a different career, maybe I could have given her everything she deserves—and even found joy in doing so, in being the man she needs.

But right now, I can't deal with any more curveballs, can't juggle any more wild cards in a game that's already far too complicated.

Caught staring, the couple smiles at me. I manage a grimace that barely passes for a smile and quickly look away. With these oversized sunglasses, I must look like a paranoid celebrity. The last thing I need is a touching moment with strangers in a waiting room.

Over in the other corner, the little girl says something to her mom, but the words come out muffled. My heart starts hammering in my chest.

Fuck me, the inane things I used to get annoyed over seem so inconsequential now. I don't give two shits if the senator throws a fit over me bailing on the fake dating scheme. And I'd trade a million cars to avoid this. I've been such a self-centered asshole . . .

I take a deep breath, feeling my T-shirt cling to my skin. I discreetly lift it to catch a breeze. Shifting uncomfortably, I take slow, deep breaths.

Damn, is this what a panic attack feels like?

That little girl, though, she's got more guts than me. Dealing with something like this at her age?

Maybe it's easier when you're younger. How the hell could I learn a new way to communicate at my age? I've spent thirty-five years relying on my ears. Now what? Enroll in sign language classes at night and continue as normal? Who am I kidding?

It all began with what I thought was an

ear infection a few months ago. Took antibiotics, assumed it would clear up fast. But the muffling and blockage came back, worse than before.

Doctor Nasal Voice, with his irritating tone, broke the news to me that I have what's called "Autoimmune Inner Ear Disease." My own body's turned traitor, attacking my hearing like it's got a personal vendetta. Seems my cells didn't get the memo that we're all supposed to be on the same side.

He pushed steroids on me—not the good gains kind, the inflammation blockers. He couldn't even give me a straight answer on how much hearing I'd lose, or when. Useless.

Fear, real fear, is something I thought I understood. Like the kind of fear when Teagan lost her mom. That deep, gnawing sense that you're not in control. That's what this is—amplified.

If Hayes can stop this, I swear to god almighty I'll never take things for granted again. I'll start appreciating the little things. No more moaning about boring meetings or pointless galas. I'll quit fussing over the temperature of my coffee or flipping out when my staff don't get things perfect on the first try.

No more griping about trivial shit—like water pressure in my marble bathroom. Or in-flight Wi-Fi reliability in my sixty-million-dollar jet en route to Vegas. All those ludicrously petty concerns that felt important now seem laughable through this lens.

I just have to hold it the fuck together a while longer. I'm not beaten yet. Solutions are on the horizon. And once I've got a plan, I'll fill Killian in.

Finally, the receptionist calls my name. I'm out of my seat and through the door before she finishes speaking.

"Connor, take a seat." The doc greets me, that forced smile saying he's heard a thing or two about me. "I've looked over your files from Dr. Caruso. How are you holding up with the steroids?"

I settle into the chair, shrugging irritably. "All right, I guess. The muffling still comes and goes. It's worse in my left ear."

I think back to the disaster interview, with Lucia seated on that bad side. The pressure had been building all day, then it just blew up right there. Terrible timing.

"And the steroids, noticing any side effects?"

"Some moodiness, but that's nothing new for me," I joke dryly.

Doc forces a strained chuckle then continues. "The tests confirm Dr. Caruso's diagnosis. You're dealing with Autoimmune Inner Ear Disease."

I swallow hard, feeling like I've been sucker-punched. Caruso, with his lousy bedside manner, wasn't supposed to be right. The guy is everything I can't stand in a doctor.

But this doctor, he's supposed to be the top of the line, the guru of ear health. If anyone's going to pull me through this, it's him.

"So what's the game plan? Is there some kind of surgery that can fix this?"

"There's no surgical fix, I'm afraid. We'll keep going with the steroids, keep an eye on the inflammation, and then see where we stand. If we need to, we might consider Immunosuppressive Therapy." He clears his throat. "Connor, it has gotten worse since Dr. Caruso ran his tests. More aggressive than we would like."

Fuck.

"Is there a chance I'll end up completely deaf?" I ask straight up.

"There's a possibility, yes. But complete deafness in both ears isn't typical for most folks with AIED. With the right treatment—meds, hearing aids, implants if we need to go that route—many of my patients lead rich, fulfilling lives."

My jaw tightens. "Why now when I'm as disciplined as a damn Spartan warrior? Is it because I didn't take care of myself in my twenties? My diet's clean now, my workout routine's solid. Sure, sometimes I indulge in a few too many drinks but overall, I'm pretty regimented."

"Autoimmune diseases are complex. They could be kicked off by infections, environmental factors. Without a full family medical history, it's hard to say if you were more at risk for AIED. Stress, though—we've long suspected it aggravates autoimmune conditions. And the latest research backs that up, showing how chronic stress really can fan the flames."

"So, what's my move? What do I do now?"

He raises an eyebrow. "Lower those stress levels. I get it, easier said than done, especially for someone in your position. But Connor, you've got the means. You're a billionaire. Take a year off. Hit the brakes, travel, find something that chills you out."

I shake my head, almost laughing at the suggestion. "Taking a year off isn't in the cards for me."

"Okay, let's talk about what's realistic for you to start. What activities help you de-stress? When was the last time you felt truly at ease?" he presses on.

I have to think for a moment, but damn if the answer doesn't hit me fast.

The night I fucked Lexi.

It was like everything else just evaporated, and we were left in this intense, raw bubble. We stripped life down to its bare essentials—heat, touch, focusing solely on making each other feel incredible.

Lexi is apparently my answer to "de-stressing" these days. Maybe the tough-talking, car-stealing, spirited angel was sent for me, crashing into my life right there in my hotel bathroom.

I almost give a rough laugh at the realization, and Doc arches a brow, smiling and clearly waiting for me to dish on my magical peace-inducing secret.

But where does that leave me? Lexi doesn't seem like she's in the market for just a brief fling. And I'm not going to fill her head with lies and false expectations just to get close.

"Stress less" is a damn hard task to execute. Deceptively hard.

If the business plan for the year demands we open a new hotel in the frozen wilderness of Alaska, the deserts of Nevada, or the heart of Detroit, I've got it mapped out. I can execute. But this so-called small ask to 'reduce your stress levels'? It's ironically stressful.

I feel fucking blindsided. Whiplashed. Like the reliable ground I've always walked on has suddenly turned into quicksand.

I'm leashed to meds that could fail, and I could still lose my hearing. Yeah, reassuring.

Could get worse fast, or not much at all. Maybe it'll hit me when I'm an old man, or maybe it'll sneak up on me sooner.

Anything could happen and I'm simply along for the chaotic ride with no control.

I can't stand the uncertainty, the endless what-ifs that hang in the air. I need to know what's going to happen. I can't function in a silent world.

How do I run a boardroom if I can't pick up on the cues, the tension?

Or call out the bull when someone tries to pull a fast one on me?

Argue with Lexi when I can no longer hear each subtle nuance and emotion underlying her words? Miss making her breath catch when I lean in close . . . Her laughs, her vexation, her sass, her moans . . .

It changes the entire game.

Adapting to this doesn't sit right. Sure, people are born with hearing problems and lead great lives—I respect that. But this feels like it's tearing away part of me.

My whole persona—my success, my charm, my authority—it's all tied to how I communicate. If my hearing goes and I have to relearn how to connect with people, then what? Who am I without those tools?

Right now, I hear everything. The doctor's voice, a car backing up outside, someone coughing in the hallway. All these sounds I've always just ignored, and now they hit differently. Hanging out with Killian, cracking up at stupid movies with Teagan, blasting music. Even the everyday stuff— the delivery guy, office chatter, the toaster.

The background audio of normal life I never

appreciated before.

All those daily sounds I never truly heard until now.

If I can keep hearing them just as they are, I'll be grateful every damn day going forward. No amount of money in the world can buy back something so vital once it's taken away.

THIRTY-FOUR

Lexi

The moment I spot the sleek black sports car cruising down my street, my first thought is Deano, despite Connor's assurance that he's handled it. I pick up the pace, eyeing our run-down building longingly and wishing there were a handy manhole on this block I could disappear into.

As the car's dark tinted window slides down, my heart skips for a completely different reason. Connor's piercing eyes catch mine from the driver's seat.

"Lexi, hold up."

I halt reluctantly, bristling with nerves. "What are you doing here?"

He matches my pace, the engine humming softly. "Get in."

I bristle at his entitled command. "Um sorry, what? Why?"

It doesn't take long for passersby to start rubbernecking at the sight of Mr. Moneybags trailing me in his luxury ride.

When I remain glued to the sidewalk and don't immediately swoon into his passenger seat, he scrubs a tense hand over his stubbled jaw. "C'mon, just get in. Give a guy five minutes here."

"Don't answer a question with an order," I snap back, gripping my bag tighter and picking up my pace. Like hell am I in the mood for more emotional whiplash from him. "I'm not going to jump in just because you say so."

Even in a T-shirt and ballcap, he's unfairly attractive behind that expensive wheel. I staunchly ignore my pulse's opinion on the matter.

"Lexi, wait." His tone softens slightly, almost like he's just realized I'm not one of his people to order around. "I just want to talk, that's all. Please." He must be trying to give politeness a test drive.

"I'm pretty sure we covered it all, Connor. If this is about the care funds, I appreciate it, but my stance hasn't changed."

"It's not about the cash. Just get in before someone thinks I'm stalking you and calls the cops. We're drawing attention."

I let out an irritated huff. "If you didn't insist on trailing me in your flashy sports car, we wouldn't have drawn a crowd."

Seeing Connor again is like stirring up a

cocktail of feelings I do not want to deal with.

Why does he keep inserting himself back into my life after making it abundantly clear nothing real is possible for us?

I just want us to go our separate ways already. I need things to be calm and predictable, not this emotional rollercoaster he keeps dragging me onto.

I can almost hear that podcast psychologist's "helpful" dating advice echoing in my mind. Guys like Connor are all about power plays. I refused his offer of help and now here he is, likely trying to reassert his dominance over the situation.

"Lexi."

Connor's voice stops me in my tracks, stripped of its usual crisp authority. He sounds raw, almost vulnerable.

I turn warily, eyeing his flashy car like an alien invasion on my suburban street, my feelings all in knots.

"I need to see you. Please."

There's real urgency in his tone. What the hell has brought on this sudden change? His piercing eyes hold a ragged vulnerability that's messing with my head in ways I don't appreciate.

Letting out a sigh that feels way too much like I'm rolling over, I slide into the passenger seat, bracing myself.

"Mind if we just drive for a while?" he asks

hoarsely.

I check my watch with a small frown. "I've got ten minutes. Grace is waiting on me."

Ten endless minutes of charged proximity, his masculine scent enveloping me. I grip the leather beneath my legs.

He nods, easing the car into motion. His jaw is granite, eyes stormy and haunted like he's walked through hell. Dark stubble roughens his skin, and his T-shirt has definitely seen better days.

This isn't the polished, put-together Connor I know—Mister *GQ*, always picture-perfect. Now he's still got that magnetic vibe, but there's something off, something . . . broken.

Sadness. That's the word that keeps coming to mind. It's written all over him in the tightness of his mouth and the shadows in his eyes.

He shoots me a quick, hard-to-read glance before turning his attention back to the road.

The silence in the car feels thick, almost choking. Connor's usually so direct. But now he stays silent, jaw tight, leaving me in uneasy suspense about why he randomly showed up and what the hell he wants from me.

"I've been driving around for hours. Ended up here without realizing," he eventually says.

"Okay . . ." I reply slowly. "For someone who sees speed limits as mere suggestions, that's concerning."

He chuckles, but there's no real humor in it. "Seems recklessness is my MO these days."

I can't help but notice the tiredness shadowing his eyes. "You taking a day off?"

"Just needed some time to myself," he replies, his grip on the steering wheel betraying tension. "Look, I know you're not keen on accepting my help. But can I ask a favor?"

I eye him warily. "Depends. What are you asking?"

"Keep me company for a bit. Could really use the distraction right now." His eyes briefly meet mine. "Feel free to call me an asshole if it makes it easier for you."

"A distraction? I'm flattered," I reply, my voice dripping with sarcasm.

"That's not what I . . . damn." He exhales heavily, some of the fight leaving him. "You're a good distraction, Lexi. The only distraction I need right now."

"Sorry to burst your bubble, but I'm not up for a quickie at your hotel, Connor."

He looks genuinely taken aback. "No, that's not what I was getting at. What do you say to a drink at my place?"

I snort. "Thought your bachelor pad was a strict no-women zone."

"I'm making an exception because I want to see you," he says quietly.

My heart's racing like a fool, but my brain's on high alert. I can't let my guard down. This is the same guy who said he couldn't give me more. Now he's changing the rules, wanting more but only on his terms? Hell no.

"I can't do it, Connor. It's like one red flag after another with you. You told me you want nothing from me yet here you are. You kick me out right after we hook up—"

"I regret that," he cuts in, his voice low and edged with frustration.

"Oh I'm sure you do," I volley back. "Then you completely ignore me at that interview. Treat me like I'm invisible."

He has the audacity to look confused, or maybe he's forgotten. "What are you talking about? I didn't ignore you. Yeah, I was pissed you didn't pick up your phone that night we had sex, but that wasn't the time or place to get into it."

I let out a bitter laugh. "I tried talking to you and you turned right to Mason. Like I'm the invisible woman."

His expression darkens, a flash of something more intense in his eyes. "It wasn't intentional. Trust me."

"Sure looked intentional from where I stood."

His knuckles whiten on the steering wheel. "Look, I know I can be an asshole sometimes, and I'm sorry for that. But I don't mean to hurt you,

Lexi."

"You keep saying that, but your actions don't match." I glance at his handsome face, the same one that's haunted my thoughts and dreams for days, but I'm exhausted by this hot and cold act. "Can you just stop the car? I'm tired of whatever this is."

"Lexi, give me a minute here, okay? I'm trying."

"No, Connor. I need to get out, now."

He pulls over slowly, every muscle in his frame rigid.

I face him, trying to keep it light. "Look, I really do appreciate everything you've done—protecting me from Deano, offering to take care of my mom's medical bills. But there's no reason for us to keep seeing each other." My hand inches toward the door handle.

"Wait," he says roughly. "There's a reason I pushed you away that night."

I freeze at that. Against my better judgment, I turn back. "Okay. So why?"

He stares straight ahead, hands clenched on the wheel like he's ready to rip it off.

"That night, I rushed you out because I was hit with a wave of vertigo so bad it knocked me sideways. Probably why I didn't catch what you were saying back at the studio. And yeah, that's why the interview was a disaster. I've got some health issues going on."

My mind races to the darkest places. "What kind of health issues?"

A heavy silence fills the car, my anxiety skyrocketing.

Then he glances at me, catches the worry in my eyes. "I'm not on my deathbed, Lexi. Sorry, I didn't mean to scare you."

I exhale, a tiny bit relieved but still on edge.

"My hearing is fucked."

"Oh." I'm momentarily speechless, not expecting this revelation. "How?"

"It's an auto-immune condition."

My hand instinctively covers my mouth. "Oh, Connor, that's awful. I'm so sorry."

Uncertainty swirls within me, not fully understanding what this means for him or how severe it is. I have so many questions but tread lightly.

"Why didn't you just tell me that night in your office?" I ask gently.

"I was embarrassed, Lexi. We'd just had sex. Amazing sex. It's not exactly my normal move to fuck a woman then collapse on her."

He avoids my gaze, so I gently touch his shoulder. "Hey, there's no need to be embarrassed, okay?"

"I'm not telling you this for sympathy. I'm telling you because I want to see you again, and I know if I have any shot at that, I need to explain my behavior."

His honesty throws me off guard. "Thanks for opening up. I know that's not easy for you." Especially with how fiercely private he is. "So . . . what does this mean for you going forward?" I ask gently.

"Fuck if I know," he mutters. "Could go completely deaf, might just lose some hearing, or stay the same. They've got no way to predict. The uncertainty is a bitch."

I listen, trying to wrap my head around it all. "How long have you been dealing with this?"

"I first noticed symptoms about six months ago. Didn't think much of it. But lately it's gotten bad. Saw one doctor who seemed more interested in my bank account than my health. Didn't feel right. So I found the top guy in the field. He's in the state. Saw him today."

Knowing he came straight to me after that kind of day sends my heart into a flutter. But it's also a bit fucked up, especially considering what he said last time we talked. He can't give me more. And yet, here he is. I'm all over the place with my feelings.

I reach out, gently turning his face to look at me.

But he seems to shut down again, armor slamming back into place. "I've got it handled. No need to make a thing of this—people manage much worse."

I give him a slow nod, understanding the fine line we're walking here. I've been through the wringer before with my mom's sickness. There's a time to push and a time to hold back. And Connor is clearly a man who likes to handle things on his own terms.

"I'm trusting you with this, Lexi. I haven't even told Killian."

Wow, the weight of his trust lands like a ton of bricks. He hasn't told Killian? That's major. And kind of worrying. Why keep it from his brother?

"Why haven't you talked to Killian?" I ask, trying to keep it light.

"It's complicated. I'll get to it," he replies, sounding more like he's dodging the question than anything.

It just goes to show, money can't iron out every kink in family dynamics.

"I'm really sorry you're going through that. I'm glad I know. If you need a friend I'm here for you."

His lips curve into a half smile that could cause traffic jams. "Lexi Sullivan, you're something else," he murmurs. He glances away, the rugged lines of his jaw tightening. "But you've got Grace waiting."

I make a split-second decision. "Grace will manage without me tonight. How about we grab that drink at your place?"

His eyebrow arches. "You sure?"

"Totally. But just as friends. If we can even call ourselves that," I say, laying down the law.

Connor's condition is not a get-out-of-jail-free card. My heart's been through enough rollercoasters, and I'm not signing up for another ride, especially with Mr. Complicated here.

"Understood," he says with a grin. "Friends it is."

The term *friends* hangs in the air, feeling a bit off as we drive away.

As he drives, I try gently, "Do you want to talk about it?"

"No," he responds sharply, then softens, squeezing my knee. "Sorry, I just need to unwind tonight. There's no need to unpack all my problems right now."

"Of course. Whenever you're ready," I reply, letting it go for now.

The drive to his place is quiet as my mind races. I'm desperate to understand the full severity, but don't want to push too hard and shut him down.

He stormed out of a major interview over this, so it has to be serious enough. Is he in pain? Scared? How will this impact his future?

I want to comfort him, tell him it'll be okay, but I don't know that. Throwing around empty platitudes won't help right now.

He clearly doesn't want to discuss it further, so I resist pushing him. But I know from Mom that bottling things like this up isn't healthy. The more he can open up, the better for him.

I sneak peeks at his rigid profile as he keeps his eyes on the road.

I try to put myself in Connor's shoes, imagining being told I might lose my hearing. It's huge. Terrifying. Just thinking about surviving without a sense I've always relied on makes me feel panicked.

How do you even begin to adjust to something like that? Going to work, adulting, doing everything without hearing when it's been a constant your whole life? I can't fathom it.

And not knowing how bad it could get . . . or if it will get worse at all. That uncertainty might be the scariest part.

Would I want to tell Mom and Grace? I know they'd freak out, and that would only make me feel more anxious and overwhelmed. I'd want to tell Dad first, I think sadly.

I let my mind wander back through all the times Connor and I interacted.

Now when I look for them, I have lots of dots joining together.

I have to ask . . .

"That first night we met," I begin, hesitantly. "At the hotel."

He cuts in with a rough voice. "I'd just been to the doctor."

I wince, guilt hitting me. "Right, so my little hustle was the perfect ending to your already shitty day. I really earned your wrath, didn't I?"

Connor chuckles darkly. "Lexi, I didn't care about the car. Not really. Yeah, you pissed me off. But my anger went deeper than that. I was grappling with a lot of mixed feelings about you that I couldn't make sense of."

He pauses, letting the words linger in the air between us. "Maybe I'm still trying to figure them out."

"Oh," I manage to say, feeling my heart rate pick up. This open version of Connor scares me more than ruthless Connor, because caring Connor has the power to hurt me deeper.

I know his diagnosis doesn't excuse all his dick moves, like kicking me out of his office after we hooked up. We all have issues, but that's no excuse for hurting others.

Yet this is new for him. I'll extend some grace as he learns to handle it better.

His hand finds its way back to my leg, just resting there as if it's the most natural spot in the world.

But I can feel the weight of it, hyperaware of his touch.

I have no idea where we stand but hearing him open up like this feels like a breakthrough. Like there's something here beyond explosive fights

426

and mind-blowing sex.

But I need self-preservation. I absolutely cannot afford to give Connor another opportunity to shatter my heart into pieces.

THIRTY-FIVE

Lexi

I'm standing in one of New York's most expensive apartments. Fact. A few years back, Connor splurged an amount on this place that some countries earmark for their annual budget, grabbing headlines for the sheer cheek of it all.

Strolling down the hall, my chin's basically dragging on the shiny floors. The place is the ultimate shrine to bachelorhood. It's a deluxe man-cave aquarium, with skyscrapers peering in and helicopters doing nosy fly-bys outside the floor-to-ceiling windows.

The ceilings are insane. They've got to be three times the height of a normal apartment, with these massive, exposed beams that scream "urban oasis."

My nerves kick up a notch as I take in the sharp designs, tech that's probably too advanced for its own good, and artwork fitting for galleries, not someone's home. The whole place reeks of rich guy testosterone.

"I can't believe I let you inside Maison du Leak," I groan, doing a little twirl in his swanky living room.

His brow cocks in amusement. "Maison du Leak?"

"My place. Sounds way classier in French, doesn't it?"

"Got it. Though I'll admit, my focus wasn't really on the decor during my quick tour of your bedroom." That twinkle of amusement is back in his eyes.

He seems more relaxed now, like he's put his issues on the backburner for the moment. I can't brush them aside so easily though. But I'm honoring his request from the car ride—to have a relaxing night. I'm letting it go for now, waiting for the right time.

Connor's obviously struggling with his feelings about the diagnosis, stuck somewhere between denial and frustration. And from experience, forcing someone through those stages never goes well. Better to quietly do my homework and wait for the perfect moment to start chipping at his guard.

He watches me check out his living area, a smirk playing on his lips. "You know, you're the first woman who's ever kicked me out of her place."

"Because nobody has the guts to say no to Connor Quinn?"

He lifts a shoulder in a lazy shrug. "Sometimes a guy needs to be reminded of his place. Especially by certain fiery individuals."

His words, though tossed out casually, send this weird sensation zipping through me.

I turn away to hide my reaction, running my hand along the back of his fancy leather couch. "Here I was expecting the typical bachelor pad clichés—tiger skin rugs, mirrored ceilings, maybe a sex swing . . ." I tease.

He chuckles. "Come on, Lexi. I'm not trying to be the next Ron Jeremy."

With that massive cock of his, he might as well be.

"Can I get a grand tour and see for myself? Just to make sure you're not hiding any Playboy bunnies or playrooms," I say, mostly kidding. But with this guy's reputation, you never know.

"Be my guest." Taking my hand in his, he guides me through the sprawling space.

As we stroll deeper into the apartment, the sleek masculine style gives way to something more human—family photos and glimpses of his life beyond the billionaire persona.

There's a photo of him and Killian as kids, decked out in sports gear, grinning in front of what's unmistakably the building that would one day become the flagship NexiHub. He might play it cool, but it's obvious he's proud of what they've built together.

The place isn't giving off an overly sentimental vibe, but I spot at least three picture frames of his niece artfully blended into the sophisticated style.

"Has she forgiven you yet?" I nod at a photo of a young, grinning Connor with a tiny ginger girl on his shoulders—so cute it tugs my ovaries.

His mouth quirks. "We're getting there. Apparently, the secret formula is losing to her in *Fortnite* and a sugar overload. Works like a charm."

"She's beautiful."

"Yeah. She's got me wrapped around her little finger and knows it. Even as a sassy teenager." There's a warmth to his voice that suggests this playboy might just be a big softie.

"Can I open doors?" I ask, bouncing on my heels.

He chuckles. "Go ahead, make yourself at home."

I swing open the first mystery door, expecting a bedroom. Instead, it's a cedar-lined sauna with lava rocks. "Ooh, nice!" I squeal.

Connor grins, almost sheepish at my excitement.

The next room has a huge stainless-steel tub filled with ice water. I stop short, shooting him a look. Oh great, is this his version of a *Dexter* killing bath?

"My ice bath," he explains, like that's a perfectly normal thing for someone to have next to their living room. "Good for recovery after workouts."

Curiosity overpowers common sense, and I dip a finger in, instantly regretting it. "It's freezing!"

"You get used to it. The cold reduces inflammation, gets the blood flowing."

We continue down the hall as I take in this glimpse into his elite world. It feels like being on *Million Dollar Listing*.

"How many bedrooms?" I ask breezily, trying to sound as if I tour multimillion-dollar apartments every day.

"Seven." He says it like no biggie.

My breath catches as we round the corner to see this incredible, sprawling painting of a lush green landscape with mountains. "Is that Ireland?"

"Yeah, the Ring of Kerry," he confirms with a hint of nostalgia. "Mom took us there when we were kids. Only trip we ever went on as a family back then. She's Irish."

"Ireland's been on my bucket list forever." I smile, feeling uncultured and immature. "I haven't traveled much yet. My friend went years ago . . . I was supposed to go too . . ." I trail off, wondering why I'm even bringing up plans that never panned out.

One corner of his mouth lifts. "Don't worry, you'll make it there. If you start putting yourself first for once."

And then, the master bedroom. My pulse revs as we step inside.

This isn't just a bedroom; it's a shrine to raw sensuality. Deep red bedding, dark gray walls, a mix of leather and wood, and that bed—pure masculinity, dominating the room. Everything's arranged with military precision.

Suddenly, my own bed at home feels like it's from a Toys "R" Us catalog.

I can't stop picturing the bed's owner sprawled across it naked.

"So where's that famous crystal cock sculpture the tabloids were raving about?" I giggle, trying to bury my sudden nerves with jokes.

"I figured this place deserved some real art instead of my own massive crystal cock."

"People might start questioning that playboy image of yours if they knew." I sweep the dark, hyper-masculine space with widened eyes. "You're letting me in on quite a few secrets tonight."

He leans in the doorway, with a small smile. "Given you're the first woman who's not family or staff to step foot in here for ages, I'll know exactly who to blame if the gossip mill kicks into gear."

His words send a weird flutter through me.

He lingers in the doorway at a deliberate

distance, but his intense eyes dissect my every breathless reaction. "You seem on edge."

No shit. Between the killer views and über bachelor pad, this place has me buzzing out of my skin. But it's not the decor that's got me vibrating —it's him.

I remind myself we're keeping it light. Friendly.

"I'm good," I lie, pretty much bolting from his bedroom before my self-control snaps completely. "Let's grab that drink you owe me."

Escaping to the relative safety of his kitchen-lounge, he hands me a glass of wine that's definitely not from the bargain bin. My attention drifts to a Scrabble board on the table.

"Scrabble?" I tease. "There goes the billionaire bad boy image."

"Watch it now." A playful swat lands on my behind, a move so quick it's like he momentarily forgets we're just friends now.

"Sorry," he says sheepishly.

I push down a flutter of . . . something, reminding myself we're strictly in the friend zone. No funny business, no getting handsy.

We've tried lusting after each other. We've tried killing each other. We've tried fighting each other. And now here we are, venturing into the great unknown: just hanging out. No drama, no stress, just two people maybe having a good time together without all the extra emotional baggage.

He's told me about his diagnosis, he's let me into this house. He, dare I say it, *trusts* me.

It's a novel concept for us. I owe it to both our sanity to at least try the friendship thing.

I sidestep, putting a safe distance between us, and head toward the lounge area.

"I was playing with Teagan the other day," he admits with a small smile. "If you count making up nonsense slang teenage terms that aren't dictionary approved 'playing.'"

"A big softie for his niece," I tease. Might as well lean into this whole *just friends* thing. What could possibly be less sexy than a game of Scrabble? "Bet I can beat you."

"You wanna play Scrabble?" He cocks a brow, giving me a look that could make the strongest of women weak in the knees. "You sure that's how you wanna spend your evening with me?"

I stand firm. Barely. "Why not? Friends play Scrabble."

"All right, Lexi. But don't underestimate me. I'm more than just a pretty face," he says with a cocky grin that suggests he's already won. "I don't plan on going easy on you."

"Don't get ahead of yourself, Quinn. I've got some tricks up my sleeve," I shoot back, trying to match his swagger. "And don't even think about pulling any dirty moves."

He just laughs and saunters off, returning in

a T-shirt hugging those illegal muscles and shorts showcasing two of the sexiest legs I've ever seen.

Well fuck me, talk about playing dirty.

He proceeds to set up the board with the kind of enthusiasm you might reserve for, I don't know, something less dorky than Scrabble.

Catching me ogling all that bare skin, he winks. "Ready, angel?"

Oh, it's on. I plop down on the floor cushions, prepped for battle. "Bring it, hot shot."

He sits across from me, also on the floor, manspreading his big thighs around the board. I'm trying really hard not to think about what's between those thighs. We're just friends. Friends who play Scrabble and definitely don't think about each other's anatomy.

He's up first.

He confidently arranges E-L-U-S-I-V-E as his first word, looking pleased with himself.

"Show-off," I grumble.

My turn, and I lay down Z-O-I-N-K-S, barely stifling my giggles at his pursed lips.

"What the hell is that?" he grumbles.

"From *Scooby-Doo*! Shaggy says it all the time."

"Nice try. Not a word."

"It is!" I insist, pulling out my phone to prove my point, my faith in Shaggy and Scooby unwavering.

Of course, he's not going to take my word for it.

He checks his own phone and . . . "I'll be damned."

I blow on my nails. "Told you."

"Damn, Lexi. 'Zoinks' just scored you nineteen points." His handsome face contorts into a scowl as he stares at the Scrabble board.

I can't help but giggle at his deathly serious expression. "Suck on that, Quinn."

"You're good, angel. But don't get too comfortable. This just became an all-out war."

"Aww, is someone a sore loser?" I tease, finding his fierce competitiveness both amusing and, let's be honest, far too sexy. "Admit it, this is all about control for you."

"Getting ahead of yourself, aren't you?" His gaze pins me down with a challenge that's all but growled.

Jesus. Our Scrabble game has bizarrely become an intense showdown, filled with tension and wine disappearing at an alarming rate.

"I think we should add another layer to this—let's play the getting to know you game," I suggest with a smile. "After all, friends should know things about each other."

Connor raises a brow. "All right. What do you want to know?"

"What do you do all day?" I ask, genuinely curious.

"What do I *do* all day?" he repeats, his voice dripping with mock offense. "Your tone suggests you think just kicking back with a whiskey in hand."

"I'm serious! I have no idea what a guy who owns half the hotels in the States and a bunch of casinos actually does all day. Do you just play mini golf in your swanky office?"

He laughs, a deep and rugged sound that's way too sexy for Scrabble. "Afraid not. It's basically just one big hierarchy. I talk to the people below me, they talk to those below them. Things just go up and down the chain of command."

"Really? Sounds like a boring version of *Inception*."

Connor plays a word that's way too smart for someone drinking wine. Shit, he's good. And it's making me horny.

"All right, if you're really curious . . . Some days I'm overseeing new hotel constructions or checking out sites. Other times, it's back-to-back meetings—strategizing, looking over finances, you name it," he explains with a casual shrug. "Whatever fires need putting out."

I place J-I-N-X-E-D down, smirking at my cleverness. "Sounds exhausting. Well, you got a glimpse into my glamorous work life. It's nowhere near as fulfilling."

He turns serious, his gaze softening. "You should finish your psych course, Lexi. If it's about the money . . ."

"No," I cut him off, knowing where this is going.

Connor annoyingly outplays me word after word. The wine's making its presence felt, and my shoes are long gone. I have to up my game here.

A few rounds later, with the wine boldly speaking through me, I lay down L-I-C-K-A-T-H-O-N with feigned innocence.

"Interesting choice," he drawls. "For just two friends playing a harmless game of Scrabble."

I giggle because apparently that's my default reaction now. "Just playing to win. Your move, hotshot."

"Nice try, but that's not gonna fly. Not a real word."

I pout playfully, half jesting, half serious. "Come on, how about a few points for creativity?"

My leg stretches out, a spontaneous move that ends with my bare foot grazing the hot skin of his thigh. He reacts fast, fingers clamping my arch and pressing it to all that rock-hard muscle. A zip of electricity thrums through me at his assertive touch. Now he's really fighting dirty.

"Don't think I'm gonna go soft on you," he warns with a bit of a growl.

Is he still talking Scrabble? The room suddenly feels like a sauna.

"Fine then," my voice coming out huskier than planned. "Let's go with *LICK*."

"That's the best you've got?"

"Yes, considering the wine's taken over creative control."

His fingers work over my helpless foot. "Trust me. I can do way better than just lick."

Oh boy.

The innuendo settles hot in my belly, making me squirm on the cushion. Images of him between my legs in my bedroom flood my mind.

Judging by his smug look, he knows exactly where my mind just went.

I lick my suddenly dry lips, acting cool. "You're such a competitive jerk," I shoot back.

"You knew what you were getting into." He smirks, oozing the kind of confidence that says he's never been on the losing side of a Scrabble board—or much else, for that matter. "I don't lose, angel."

In a feeble attempt at rebellion, I try kicking free with my foot, but he catches it easily, thumb teasing my sensitive sole until I'm a giggling, writhing mess. "Jerk! That's not fair, cut it out!" My attempts to squirm away only fuel his cocky laughter.

"Gotta move faster than that," he teases with a wink.

I like this version of Connor. I'm having fun. Like, actual laugh-out-loud, forget-your-troubles kind of fun. With Connor Quinn, of all people.

So, are we friends now or . . . ?

Friends don't engage in unsolicited footsie, a little voice in my head points out as his thumb strokes lazy circles.

He glances over my tiles and grins. "Lotion."

Wait, what?

Oh right, my letters. I thought he meant what he wanted to do with my foot.

"You've got the letters for 'lotion' right there. Or . . . 'Colicky.'" He's suddenly the Scrabble mentor I never asked for. "I'm practically handing you the win."

"Colicky isn't a word!"

"Of course it is."

A quick check on my phone, and what do you know, I'm wrong. "Well, look at that. You're not just a pretty face after all."

"Someone once told me that the brain is the sexiest part of the body." He smirks. "My turn."

With one smooth, cocky move he plays S-E-N-S-U-A-L-I-T-Y.

I practically choke on my wine. I have to set my drink down before I spill it everywhere. Scrabble just got upgraded to strip poker territory.

"Not bad, fifteen points," he says casually.

"That's really sexy," I blurt.

He tilts his head at my sudden outburst, amusement pulling at his lips.

Feeling daring, I slide my captive foot higher up his thigh until I feel the unmistakable bulge of his cock swelling bigger under my toes. Well hello there, someone's enjoying himself at Scrabble.

I release an involuntary moan that surprises us both.

Connor's grip tightens on my wayward ankle, a warning for me to behave. "Hey now, I'm trying to be a good guy here," he says through gritted teeth, even as his bulge throbs encouragement. "Said you just wanted friendly tonight. And I respect that."

Oh shit, he's right. We're just friends.

But then it hits me. One tiny detail I forgot when I made that agreement: I'm absolutely soaked for this man.

I wonder if I have the finesse to pull off a foot job.

"Maybe we could be friends with benefits for the night," I throw out there, only halfway joking.

"You really think you can handle this?" he growls back, his grip tightening on my ankle as if to remind me of our friends-only agreement. "I don't want you waking up with regrets. I can't do a relationship, can't give you what you're looking for. And I know, even as we're laughing and kissing and things are about to escalate, that casual isn't really your style."

"I can totally do casual," I sound way more confident than I feel, as my foot moves over his cock.

"Lexi." He says my name like a warning,

struggling to keep his cool.

"It's fine," I reply, letting my lady parts do the talking instead of my brain. "We're both adults here."

Friends with benefits, no big deal.

I'm cool with it. Got too much on my plate right now anyway. Maybe I just need a little release too, to forget about my problems.

He watches, with hooded eyes under long lashes, as I crawl forward and climb onto his lap, lust swelling sharply as I straddle my thighs around him.

I can't hold back a shameless dirty moan at the feel of his rigid length pressed intimately against my soaked core.

That pesky inner voice keeps nagging about major trouble ahead, broken hearts and regret if I try getting frisky with this guy. That I'll only end up burned.

But right now, common sense can go fuck itself sideways. Friends be damned, all I want is Connor Quinn on top of me. Now.

He grips my waist possessively. "You sure about this?"

"Yeah," I breathe as his finger traces my parted lips, movements agonizingly slow.

"When we fucked in my office, I didn't get to properly enjoy the view." His gravel tone skates down my spine as he drags rough kisses along my jaw. "Tonight, I plan on exploring every incredible inch..."

This version of him makes me nervous in the most delicious way.

Without warning, he stands up, effortlessly lifting me in his arms. My stomach flips as I realize where he's taking us.

THIRTY-SIX

Lexi

"So that whole 'just friends' idea crashed and burned pretty quick, huh?" His eyes blaze trails of fire as he sets me by the massive bed, hands urgently working my shirt buttons.

"Hey, it's the thought that counts," I offer breathlessly, pulse hammering as fabric strains and a button pops free, skittering across the floor.

"Shit, sorry—" He wrestles the remaining buttons in a frenzy, usual composure cracking.

Holy fucking hell. I can't believe I'm actually seeing Mr. Cool and Confident in such a state of desperation.

A thrill shoots through me. *I'm* the one driving him wild . . .

Our hands both scrambling, my shirt finally falls away. With rough fingers, he unhooks my sheer bra, freeing my aching breasts to the cool air.

His blistering gaze devours my tits, and he

shudders. He actually physically shudders.

I don't think I've ever felt so sexy in all my life and if he doesn't put his cock inside me ASAP I'm going to pass out from arousal.

"You have no idea how bad I want you right now," he groans, forehead creasing as if he's in pain. "Couldn't even get through an innocent round of Scrabble without popping a damn tent in my shorts." He releases a rough, almost embarrassed laugh.

I trail my nails down his biceps, pushing my hardened nipples against his chest. He's still wearing a T-shirt and it's not fair.

"So quit talking and do something about it," I say in a shaky voice as his hard cock presses against my belly.

He lowers his head and presses his lips to my neck, kissing a tingly path so damn carefully down to my collarbone. I sense his restraint barely leashed, the effort to go slow difficult for him.

Strong hands wander my trembling stomach, inching closer to where I'm soaked and aching. My breasts are screaming for attention, but he's taking his sweet time getting there, teasing the hell out of me.

I moan and arch into him, my nails scraping his scalp.

He continues his torturous journey south, until finally his full, sexy lips land on my rock-hard nips.

"Gonna take my time with you, angel." His ragged drawl fans my heated flesh as he continues his relentless tease. "I'm trying so damn hard."

My moans reach porn star–level. Clearly, all it takes is a little nipple play to turn me into a quivering mess.

My moans seem to shred Connor's restraint. Suddenly he's devouring me, grunting as he sucks greedily like he's been unleashed after years of containment.

He breaks away only to yank off my jeans with impatient hands. At this point, I couldn't care less about my unflattering baggy boyfriend jeans. I step out of them, attempting to be sexy but probably failing miserably.

His fingers find their way into my panties next, tugging them down my hips until they hit his plush carpet. I'm too aroused to even care if they're on inside out or backward. All that matters is they're gone.

Straightening, his ocean-blue eyes rake every inch of my naked body possessively. I swear it's the most erotic moment of my life.

"Your turn now . . ." I say. "This isn't fair."

"All right." A sinful grin tugs his sensuous mouth. He slowly strips off his shirt, revealing a rock-hard chest and perfectly sculpted abs that make my mouth water. His shorts hit the floor next, exposing powerful thick thighs dusted in dark hair. Then his boxers follow and he straightens to his full towering height, buck naked and breathtakingly magnificent.

My breath hitches. This man is all fucking man. And he knows it. His hard cock stands proudly against his stomach, practically begging for release.

I run my hands greedily over his broad shoulders, down his sculpted chest and abs, relishing the sensation of his hot skin beneath my fingertips. That tattoo of his is so damn sexy.

My hand wraps around his erection, causing it to throb in response. Just feeling him gets me wet.

"Lexi," he groans, his eyes glazed with lust as I stroke him harder. "I won't be able to hold back much longer if you keep teasing me like this."

"Then fuck me already. I need you inside of me," I demand.

"With pleasure." He lifts and sets me on the expansive bed.

Gently, he parts my shaking thighs, eyes drinking in my exposed pussy.

"Quit staring at me like that," I whisper as he stands over the bed watching me. "You're making me nervous."

"I can't help it. I'm so attracted to you, I'm going out of my mind here."

I bite my lip, feeling my arousal skyrocket. This

man is intense in all the right ways.

After grabbing a condom, he climbs onto the bed, trapping me with his thick thighs and arms. It's the perfect cage.

The mattress dips under his weight as he spreads my legs wide, hoisting one over his shoulder. Holy shit, this is gonna be deep. I'm low-key terrified, because let's be real, this man is packing heat.

His eyes lock on mine as he slips his hand between my thighs. Fingers playfully glide up and down, teasing my clit just enough to make me crave more.

My pussy clenches with need, begging for friction.

Damn, I am so ready for him.

"Soaked," he groans as he sheaths himself up. "I haven't even started with you yet."

He lines up his massive cock with my dripping slit, and I shudder as he slides inside me. He's trying to be gentle, but let's face it, there's no way to ease into this kind of pleasure.

"Fuck," I moan loudly, unable to hold back as he fills me completely.

"You like that, angel?" he growls, lust dripping from his voice.

"Oh god, yes," I whimper.

He lets out a deep, guttural groan as he takes control of our rhythm. "Last time was quick. This time, we're taking our sweet time. Savoring every moment."

"Nice commentary," I quip, breathlessly.

His rough hand grips my ass and lifts me up for a good smack that makes me gasp and moan at the same time. "No backtalk."

"Okay, sir." My laugh turns into a moan as he grabs my hips and starts thrusting harder. How the hell does this guy know exactly how to fuck me in all the right ways to hit my sweet spot?

My hands flop onto the bed uselessly. He's got my leg pinned over his shoulder so I'm at his mercy. Fucking owning me right now.

"You're dripping wet for me," he growls, as our bodies collide with gloriously satisfying slaps. "God, your little cunt feels so good."

It feels like my vibrator on turbo mode. My tits are flying everywhere with each thrust, and my thighs are slapping against his rock-hard ones.

Oh.

My.

God.

"This . . . feels . . . so . . . amazing . . ." I gasp, barely coherent.

"Don't I fucking know it," he says through gritted teeth as he thrusts in and out of me. "I can't get enough of you. Your little sounds drive me wild. Sweet and sexy at the same time. I never wanna stop hearing them. Let me hear how much you want me. I can't stop hearing it. I can't."

The mix of pained pleasure on his beautiful face makes me ache.

"I'm gonna come inside you so hard, angel," he hisses through gritted teeth.

His name falls from my lips over and over again as he takes me to the brink of ecstasy.

With one final, primal groan that the doormen many floors below must hear, he comes hard inside me. My hips buck and my body shakes—I can't hold on any longer.

I milk every last drop from his cock, my muscles clenching around him as we both ride out our high together.

Damn.

It's only when he catches his breath and lies down on top of me that I realize he was talking about his hearing.

THIRTY-SEVEN

Connor

I watch Lexi passed out on my sheets, dead to the world. The opposite of me. My pulse is running a fucking million miles a minute like I just snorted a pound of blow.

I'm acting like I'm in a relationship. I'm acting like we're two lovebirds playing house here.

I invite Lexi back to my inner sanctum, bare my secrets piece by piece, make love to her six times. Thinking that'll scratch some damn itch. Yeah, I'm actually calling it making love because I stared dreamily into her eyes the whole time like a lovesick teen. Like I used to stare at Willow's mom's poster, my first crush.

But I know the score. Lexi's not built for flings —she catches feelings too quick. And me? I'm too dysfunctional to give anyone more of myself. Selfish bastard that I am.

She's the last thing I need complicating my

trainwreck of a life right now, but I can't stay away, and that's the goddamn problem.

But she's not just some fling I can send packing. I at least owe her basic human decency for Christ's sake.

All of this is meant to be making me feel more relaxed, and while I certainly love to lose myself in having sex with her, I can't damn well shake this feeling that we're heading straight for a steep drop.

I shocked myself by opening up to her about my condition. I hadn't planned to when I stopped in her street. I got desperate that she was going to walk away and leave me festering in my bad mood and dark thoughts.

Then I went further off script, bringing her here. The guy who wouldn't trust a barista with his coffee order is trusting someone in dire need of cash—who didn't take my money.

I do trust her though, as reckless as that sounds. Trust she'll keep her lips sealed even if I give her reason to despise me later on.

Although there's a realistic part of me that knows it's a risk. Everyone has the capacity to fuck someone over, it just depends how far they're pushed. I could make her try to sign an NDA, but I don't think that would go down too well. I guess I'll have to take the risk and trust her. It's too late now anyway.

I graze her cheek, ensuring she keeps sleeping.

I don't know how to play this.

I'm a selfish bastard for wanting her like this. Can't help it though. The way she melts under my touch, responds to my every move—it's like I've got total control over my body. That's the way it's supposed to be.

Her breath spills out in tiny chainsaw snores that make me grin. She's got a smudge of mascara or some shit on one cheek and her mouth hangs open like she doesn't have a worry in the world.

Now she's snoring loudly in my thousand thread count sheets, looking more at home than any woman before her. It sets off a weird panic in me, like it's highlighting how dangerously close we've veered into acting like a couple. Which is absurd.

And yet as the sheet slips off her bare thigh and she sprawls out, I realize I've never seen anything as sexy as busted-ass snoring Sleeping Beauty.

I can't stop my hand from reaching out and reverently trailing down the length of her body.

A thunderous snort jolts her awake. She blinks, dazed, catching my amused gaze.

"Was I snoring?" she asks, her voice thick with sleep.

"You? Never," I reply, the corners of my mouth twitching in a barely contained smile. "Sounded more like gentle doves billing and cooing."

A pillow thwacks my face. "Oh god, was it

bad?" She scrubs the sleep from her eyes. "Crap, what time is it? I didn't mean to fall asleep. I should jet . . ."

Christ. I'm supposed to agree with her, not do what I'm about to do.

"You hungry? How about I order us some food?"

Her eyes light up. "Like pizza?"

"I was thinking something more along the lines of Le Grand Cochen. They do have pizza, if that's what you're craving."

"That's one of your Michelin-star restaurants. That's an annual treat, not takeout." She eyes me. "So, I'm staying for dinner, then?"

The thought of her leaving now sends a wave of something I can't quite name through me. I'm not done with this night, not even close. Without thinking, I pull her closer. "Stay the night."

She meets my gaze, those gorgeous eyes holding some kind of struggle. "I can't deal with getting hurt, Connor. We can keep it casual, but you gotta keep those mood swings in check and not push me away. I want to be there for you, but you can't lash out at me."

"Message received loud and clear. I'll work on my mood control," I say, not missing a beat.

I smile, playing it cool. I don't know what the fuck is going on in my head, but I'll be damned if she leaves my bed tonight. I'll do whatever it takes to keep her here with me.

◆ ◆ ◆

I wake up with Lexi wrapped in my arms and a headache, like there's a bass drum in my ear. And a massive erection pressing against her sexy backside. It's a confusing mix of sensations.

The sunlight pours in through the window, casting a glow over her bare curves.

As much as I want to appreciate the view, I clamp my eyes shut, engaging in a silent battle with the pounding in my skull that's unfairly competing with my hard-on.

"Morning." Her voice breaks through the thumping. "This *view*. It's even more stunning in the morning. Can people see in here?"

"No," I mutter. "One-way glass."

Eyes still closed, I can tell she's moving, turning my way. Her sexy ass rubs against my arousal. My groan is both pleasure and pain.

"What's wrong?" she asks, concern lacing her words. "You're frowning."

"Just a headache," I mutter, my voice a gravelly mix of sleep and annoyance.

Her hands move to my temples, her touch soothing despite my mood. I pry my eyelids open to meet that hypnotic gaze brimming with sympathy I don't want.

"I'm fine, Lexi," I insist, a bit gruffer than intended. "It'll pass."

"What can I do to help?"

"You don't need to help," I say, getting more irritated by the second. Damn, why do I have to be such an ass? Instead of saying she's doing plenty just by sticking around, I let my annoyance win.

"You're not invincible, Connor," she says softly.

"Don't I fucking know it."

"I mean, you're human. It's okay to feel pain and ask for help." She pauses, giving me a small smile. "And to be afraid. Even tough guys can shed a tear."

"Lexi," I say, a warning growl in my tone. This is the last thing I wanted—for her to feel sorry for me. "Back off. I don't need fixing. I'm not some project for you."

Her eyebrows go up, clearly stung. "Isn't that what you're trying to do to me? Sending those hot builders to fix my messed-up floor?"

I can't resist a smirk despite the jackhammers behind my ears. "Hot, huh? Next time, I'll make sure the crew's a bunch of scruffy old guys with plumber's crack."

Her eyes narrow at my teasing. "I'm serious, Connor. Trying to cover my mom's care costs like I'm some charity case. Are you not treating me like your project?"

I'm about to shoot back a denial, but then, the

truth of her words land. "All right, you got me there."

And damn, why am I acting like some knight in shining armor? I'm anything but, and she's far from a damsel in distress.

"How about we strike a deal then?" I propose. "We're here to give each other a break, drown out the noise of our problems for a while."

Her lips quirk. "Deal."

I can't help but throw in, "Frustratingly, I do have the means to sort your issue if only you'd let me."

Because how the hell is she planning to tackle it? If she's desperate enough to be snatching rich guys' car keys, then what's her grand plan for coughing up the cash when the next due date rolls around? I don't voice these thoughts out loud. No need to shatter the moment we've got going here.

Her smile flickers with a touch of sadness. "And I wish I could fix yours."

I trace her jawline, rough fingers on smooth skin. "If you could, I'd be convinced you're a guardian angel."

"Doubtful. No miracles from me." Her eyes drop and she mutters, "Honestly, I half expected you to kick me out once you woke up."

I wouldn't have been that harsh. I'd have politely told her I had places to be and then organized for breakfast and a cab.

"I can be an ass, but I'm not completely heartless, Lexi."

She hums, skepticism in those hypnotic eyes.

A whiff of mint hits me. I raise a brow. "You brushed your teeth?"

Pink stains her cheeks. "Just with my finger—I didn't use your toothbrush!"

I chuckle. "Wasn't accusing you. Besides, you had my cock in your mouth last night. I don't think I can start arguing about swapping bodily fluids. I'll get you a proper brush in a minute."

At that, she lurches from the sheets like I lit them on fire. "I need to get going anyway."

Ah, fuck.

I catch her wrist. "No rush."

"I have things to be doing."

"Come on, stay for a while." What the fuck am I doing? "Enjoy the bath, the sauna—whatever you want." She's not out of my system yet. "I need to fuck you again. Let's forget about fixing our messed-up lives for a morning and have mind-blowing sex to take the edge off."

A shy smile spreads across her face as she gets out of bed. "Deal."

"Just give me ten minutes to shake off this headache."

"Or . . ." She pauses and stands awkwardly in the doorway, looking self-conscious. "We could share a bath; it might help with that tension."

Under normal circumstances, my Saturday mornings are reserved for the rugby pitch—me and a few guys from school, throwing ourselves into the game with the kind of reckless abandon only amateur enthusiasts can afford. It's the perfect way to blow off steam. It may not be as popular as American football, but it's the one good thing my old man passed down to me.

But who needs sports when there's a beautiful woman inviting you to bathe with her?

"I'll get it ready," Lexi murmurs before I can respond.

Five minutes later I follow, finding the tub filled with steaming, bubbly water. Smelly candles —good smelling ones, at that—flicker around the bathroom.

Didn't even know I had those. Must've been one of Clodagh or Teagan's attempts to inject a dose of femininity into my bachelor pad.

I cock a wry brow. "Yeah, a guy would definitely never light a bunch of candles first thing in the morning . . ."

She smirks. "They're lavender, for relaxation. Get in, Connor."

My hard-on is still raging, made worse by staring at her nude figure. I can't help but imagine flipping her around and bending her over this tub.

"Can we skip the relaxing part and get straight to fucking?" I suggest. "I'm not really a bath kind

460

of guy. Give me a couple of minutes in a cold room, and I'm sorted."

She lets out a playful laugh. "Guess it's time for a change. In you go, Connor. Do as you're told."

"Yes, ma'am." I chuckle.

Reluctantly, I step into the bath, admittedly enjoying the warmth of the water and the sensation of bubbles on my skin. "I never have the patience to run a bath."

"I don't either," she says, sliding in behind me. "But lately I've realized I need to slow down and take care of myself."

She wraps her legs around mine, her hands finding my shoulders, kneading the knots of tension with surprising finesse. "Relax," she urges, her voice soft yet commanding, "you're all tensed up."

Leaning back into her, I have to admit, this isn't half bad. The water's heat seeps deep, loosening muscles I didn't realize were tight. I put my hands around her ankles and let out a low, appreciative groan.

"What's with the pan pipes?" I ask, the airy tunes floating around, a stark contrast to my typical music.

"It's supposed to be calming. Spa vibes. Too much for you?"

I chuckle. "Not my usual taste."

I relax into her body, head lolling back onto

her shoulder as she works skilled fingers over my temples, neck, and head.

I push away the niggling anxieties I had last night. There's a high likelihood that this is all going to blow up in my face, what with the line between *casual* and *feelings* thinning by the minute, but damn, I can't remember the last time I let myself just . . . relax.

"Let me take care of you a little while," she says softly, breath tickling my ear.

"Keep this up and I might have to keep you here."

Her hands work magic on my skull, the kind of deep, skull-cracking massage that shoots sparks down my back. A deep, involuntary groan breaks from me when she nails that perfect spot, like she's got some kind of power surge straight into my spine.

"Damn, that's it. Keep it right there," I manage.

"Good," she replies, a smirk in her voice, clearly smug in her skill to unravel me.

Time loses meaning under her touch; minutes, hours—it's all the same when every muscle in my body is singing her praises. My eyes shutter closed, surrendering to the rhythm of her hands.

Eventually her sweet voice cuts through, yanking me from blissful oblivion. "How's that head now?"

"Like it's been touched by an angel," I grunt

out, only half joking.

Being under her care is not something I'd admit to needing, but damn does it feel right.

She laughs lightly. "That was almost romantic."

My eyes snap open, met with the damning scene—a bubble bath, surrounded by what can only be described as mood-setting candles, her body intertwined with mine as pan flutes echo romantically off the tiles.

Fuck. It couldn't get any more intimate if I brought in a string quartet to serenade us mid-soak.

As relaxing as this is, it's probably a bad idea.

Her foot presses against my half-hard cock.

My hands tighten on her ankles possessively. "Get on top of me."

"What?" she giggles. "In the tub?"

"Come on, you can't get me all worked up with your hands then leave me hanging."

I lean forward, giving her room to get out from behind me.

She swings a leg over me, splashing water everywhere as she settles into my lap. Her wild hair is drenched and tangled, but fuck if she isn't the sexiest thing I have ever laid eyes on.

"Sit on my fucking cock," I demand, unable to hold back any longer.

Her eyes widen. "But we're in the bathtub."

"No shit, angel."

"Smartass." She grinds against my hard-on teasingly. "You really want to have sex in the bath?"

My hips instinctively rise at her touch. "Hell fucking yeah."

"I don't think it'll work out logistics-wise."

"Trust me, it'll fucking work."

"But what about protection?" she questions, her eyes searching mine.

"I'm tested, clean. Are you on the pill? Tested?" I ask urgently.

"Yeah," she breathes out. "I'm trusting you here, Connor."

"Jesus, Lexi, I wouldn't lie to you about that. You don't think I'm trusting you more?"

Her face darkens at my implication, and I kick myself mentally for sounding like an asshole. But it's not the first time a woman has tried to trap me.

I soften my tone. "Sorry. Didn't mean it that way. We're both risking a lot here. Last thing either of us needs is a surprise pregnancy."

"It's okay, I understand. And you have nothing to worry about—I do *not* need another person to look after right now."

She hesitates for a moment then kisses me and slowly slides down onto my throbbing shaft.

I groan, my fingers digging into her skin. Fuck. Feels so damn good. I watch her face as she takes me inch by inch until I'm completely buried inside her.

"Oh fuck," she moans, tossing her head back in ecstasy.

"That's it, baby." I grip her waist, trying not to be too rough. "Show me how you want it."

She takes control, forcing my hands to stay on the edge of the bath as she rides me slow and steady.

Her face twists in ecstasy and her tits bounce at my eye line, begging for my mouth. I try to lean forward for a taste, but she's moving too much for me to get a good grip.

Her moans fill the steamy bathroom, mixing with the sound of our bodies slapping together and water splashing out of the tub.

"Damn, Lexi," I groan as she bounces on top of me.

More water spills out over the edge. "Shit. My bad," she pants.

"Forget about it," I growl. "Just keep fucking going."

Nothing else matters right now.

She picks up the pace, moving faster and harder.

I try to get my hands on her body, but she keeps them clamped on the bath with impressive strength.

It's clear that this is all about her pleasure, not

mine, and I'll be damned if it's not hot as hell. She's sexy when she takes charge like this.

"Connor, it's a tsunami in here," she gasps as water spills onto the floor with each thrust. It sounds like we're in a damn washing machine. This might be the messiest sex I've had in a while. And I can't get enough of it.

"Don't care," I grunt through clenched teeth. "Just keep fucking going."

All that matters is the intense pleasure coursing through my cock. I couldn't give two shits if we flooded the entire bathroom and water started pouring out the damn window. There might even be a bar of soap trying to enter my ass.

She rides me harder, faster, like the world is about to end, as the water sloshes around us.

Her head falls back with a loud moan as she quivers all over my cock. I hold her in place and keep thrusting until I'm exploding inside of her.

I come so hard in her that I might never stop. It feels fucking amazing to be bare inside of her.

"Holy shit," I exhale, leaning back against the tub, completely spent. "Looks like we'll have to make baths our thing."

Lexi

His offhand comments send my heart into a fluttery mess. I need to be careful not to read too much into this. But it's hard when he talks like that. He's not playing fair.

His head falls back against the tub, water trailing down his muscular chest. His eyes, half-closed and full of lust, lift to mine under those thick lashes as he fixes me with that infuriating smirk. Like a king in his tub, casually claiming ownership over my hips with those hands.

My stomach does a little somersault, even as my brain tries to blare alarm bells. This is just a temporary escape, a way to fuck our problems away.

But then, those thumbs of his start doing this maddening dance on my hip bones, and thinking rationally becomes difficult.

"You're thinking too hard," he grumbles, voice rough and deep.

I'm not thinking enough, I counter in my head as I lower myself onto his muscular body.

We stand shoulder to shoulder at his double sinks, gaze catching in the expansive mirror.

Well, more accurately, my shoulder is barely reaching his bicep, and my head comes just about to his shoulder.

It feels oddly intimate, sharing this private

morning ritual.

Connor even busted out a swanky new electric toothbrush for me, still in its packaging.

He winks at my reflection with a mouth full of froth, as if standing here buck-naked brushing teeth together is the most natural thing ever. But my pulse insists it feels strangely significant.

Connor spits and gargles with an unselfconscious swagger, like we do this every day. He leans across me—invading my personal space—to grab his very manly deodorant. Which he proceeds to generously apply while making unbroken eye contact in the mirror, like a cocky Gillette commercial model.

"There's female toiletries under your sink," he drops casually,

I make a face before I can stop myself. Of course he has a stockpile of random women's toiletries.

He catches my look in the mirror. "Relax. My housekeeper stocks them. Teagan's often here."

"You don't need to explain," I say, trying to sound cool and detached.

"Coulda fooled me."

Then he presses a casual kiss to my temple before sauntering out, leaving me standing there feeling confused as hell.

"It doesn't mean anything," I mutter at the flushed woman in the mirror. She's not convinced.

And if I'm honest, neither am I.

THIRTY-EIGHT

Lexi

I almost wish Connor let me do the walk of shame, instead of insisting on drive me home.

We've been sitting in awkward silence for twenty minutes, as if both of us suddenly forgot how to use words now that our rendezvous is coming to an end.

At this point, tuck and rolling from the moving sports car seems less painful than navigating whatever this post-hookup awkwardness is supposed to be.

The air's thick enough to slice through with things left unsaid. I've got the windows down, hoping the city noise might drown out the tension, but Connor's presence is just too overpowering. It's like I can't breathe.

Maybe it's just a hangover making everything seem worse. That must be why I'm so on edge.

I sneak a glance at Connor gripping the wheel.

His hardened jaw makes me think he regrets not keeping this a simple "thanks and goodbye" at the door.

My steamy tooth brushing with Connor somehow turned into breakfast which then spiraled into even more sex. I've set a new personal record for the filthiest night of my life.

I'm pretty sure my vagina has stretched to twice the size. It may never be the same again, but hey, at least it got to live its best life for one night.

Meanwhile, Gracie has been blowing up my phone with all sorts of apartment-related nonsense—Wi-Fi codes, the mystical whereabouts of the fuse box, the grand quest for towels, the works. Maybe solo time will toughen her up.

I try taming disastrous sex bed-hair in the visor mirror. He had all the toiletries a girl could want, except for the most crucial, given the circumstances: makeup.

"What's the matter?" he asks, shattering twelve blocks' worth of awkward silence. His voice sets my nerves jangling for some reason now. I need to get it the fuck together.

"I don't have my face on," I grumble, feeling pale and sallow without my trusty mascara and foundation. My eyes are giving off strong raisin vibes.

"Then whose face you got on now?" he quips, a question so ludicrous it demands an eye roll.

"Ha ha, so clever." I roll my eyes. "I know you date supermodels who wake up camera-ready."

"You're beautiful as you are, Lexi." To emphasize apparently, his hand wanders to my knee, squeezing.

"Both hands on the wheel, please, Speed Racer." I swat him away playfully.

We roll to a stop outside my building. "Thanks for the ride," I sigh out.

I got a glimpse behind that swaggering facade. Connor can be caring and passionate when walls are down.

A horrible part of me is relieved that there's an explanation for his abrasive behavior before. His diagnosis makes it less about him being an outright asshole. It's more complex than that. He didn't just shove me out the door post-hookup because he's uncaring.

"I enjoyed the company, Lexi," Connor murmurs.

"I had fun too." I smile back, ignoring the riot of butterflies doing acrobatics in my stomach. "You know you can open up to me . . . about everything you're dealing with . . ." I add bravely. "I really think you should talk to your family too. You need them right now."

Connor's face might as well be carved from marble for all the warmth it shows, making my heart sink.

Message received, Fort Knox.

He looks away, jaw locked in resolution. Clears his throat gravelly. "I gotta run. Killian's expecting me in thirty."

I force breeziness I don't feel, gathering my things. "Of course, no problem. Have a good one."

I move to leave when his voice snags me back. "Lexi—"

I pause, turning to face him.

"Thank you," he says gruffly.

He reaches out, brushing his knuckles along my cheek in a brief yet tender caress. Almost like he forgets himself for a moment. It says more than words could, hinting at a connection far beyond casual.

Just as quickly, his eyes shutter. Moment broken. With a gruff nod, he looks away. "See you around."

Connor

Monday morning hits like a heavyweight punch as Killian barges into my office, no knock, no warning, slamming down *The Enquirer* that features Willow and her waterworks.

So much for that serene weekend comedown.

Three pages of Willow weeping about how "Connor heartlessly shattered me," while a few pages later, her father mounts his soapbox to decry "unscrupulous businessmen who prey on young women for sport."

He makes no explicit accusations, but they might as well have included my photo with a bullseye superimposed on my forehead.

"Yeah, I saw that Pulitzer-worthy journalism already," I grumble back at Killian's fuming figure. "Thinking of suing for libel."

"And that's gonna make us look even better, right?" Sarcasm drips from him as he slaps another paper on my desk. "Your bullshit's cost us the Midtown project. Permits gone, thanks to some legal crap we're now neck-deep in. Build's on ice."

Fuck. My chest tightens with gutting disappointment. We've sunk a year of hard work into that build, and now it's in limbo because I couldn't keep my personal life from turning into a tabloid headline.

"Top marks, Connor," I silently chastise myself, picturing the demoralized faces of our crew. Our teams pour their blood, sweat, and tears into our ventures.

I've failed Killian and our crew.

I can't even get properly angry. That's a luxury I forfeited the moment I gave Willow carte blanche to drag my name through the mud when I ended our charade.

And to top it off, I've got the enviable job of convincing my niece and mom—who already see me as the screw-up thanks to recent drama—that I don't actually spend weekends preying on vulnerable women.

Killian's eyes flash. "Last strike, Connor."

"*Last strike?* What the fuck's that supposed to mean? Are you threatening me?"

"Yes," he snaps. "And hopefully it'll work. Get your shit together."

He storms out, door rattling the frame.

No way in hell am I telling him about my diagnosis. Not yet. Lexi might think confiding in family is best, but as much as Killian is the protective big brother, he's also the majority stakeholder in our company. As demonstrated here by that show of dominance.

Killian's the kind to mandate a time-out masqueraded as a long vacation, which is the exact opposite of what I need.

"You want to fully fund an entire research department devoted solely to Autoimmune Inner Ear Disease?" Dr. Hayes repeats incredulously over the phone.

Yeah, he thinks I've lost my mind, or have too much cash for my own good. Maybe both apply here.

Truth is I'm fucking desperate. The moment those words hit me—lifelong condition; no permanent cure yet—pragmatism didn't stand a chance.

Because I'll be damned if I surrender autonomy over my own body on some labcoat's defeated timetable. I need to regain control over my life, and this is the only way I know how. I'll hand the man a blank check.

"That's right," I state firmly. "My team will iron out the specifics and get it all down in writing. But to cut to the chase, yes—I'll fully finance and equip a dedicated team aimed solely at pioneering treatments for AIED."

Hayes responds with a series of spluttering noises, probably toggling between astonishment and the idea that he's the butt of some high-budget prank.

I barrel through any objections. "In return, I'll cover your clinic's full operating budget yearly. Crunch the numbers and get back to me."

I'll funnel capital into this until we have a cure. If modern medicine lacks solutions, then by god, I'll buy the future if that's what it takes.

"Hey," Lexi greets me, her smile cutting through

the crap of the day.

The moment I see those eyes, the edges soften on everything—the fight with Killian, the senator screwing us, the endless clinic calls and work squeezed into the chaos. It all fades into the background, losing its grip on me.

Fuck but I've missed her, and the revelation guts me.

And yeah, maybe it's a sign that I'm leaning on her presence like a crutch these days. My head's been split since she spent the night—one minute I'm shoving her away, the next I'm on her doorstep like a starved stray, pathetically grateful for any affection she offers.

It hasn't even been a damn week and here I am, dragging myself out to Yonkers on a random Wednesday.

She pulls me into her apartment, and I do my best not to trip over the small mountain range of shoes by the door.

I hold back a curse as I notice a dozen things in her apartment that need fixing.

"I've cooked," she announces, and that's when I notice the sauce stains on her shirt. "Nothing fancy, just some pasta. I know you're used to Michelin-star dining. This is more Lexi-star quality."

I let out a low chuckle, feeling the tension bleed out of me just from being near her. "I can already tell this is going be the best meal I've had in ages."

She shoots me a skeptical look. "I highly doubt that. Do you cook?"

"I've got a private chef. He comes in, works his magic in my kitchen, and disappears like a ghost. Yeah, I'm a demanding guy."

"You don't say."

My hand instinctively goes to her behind, giving it a playful smack. My blood's already pumping imagining claiming her later.

As we walk in, I catch sight of someone peeking out from another room.

"Hey there, Grace," I greet with a grin.

"Hi, Connor." She bounces out, like she's been itching for an excuse to make an appearance. "I've been told to make myself scarce."

"Which is a tough ask in our apartment," Lexi adds, rolling her eyes. "So I bribed her. She's heading out for dinner."

"I'm being sent to Taco Bell," Grace sulks. "Hardly fine dining."

I laugh, digging out a couple of fifties from my wallet. "Go on, treat yourself to something nicer, on me. Only fair since you're vacating the premises on account of my visit."

The moment the words leave my mouth, I catch a shift in Lexi's expression, a flicker of something I hadn't intended. Damn, I definitely miscalculated that one. But before I can even think to smooth over the awkwardness, Grace has already snagged the cash with a sly grin.

"Thanks! I'll be spending dinner cramming for this graphic design exam coming up," Grace announces, clearing her throat awkwardly. "I'm all in when it comes to my passions."

"Is that so?" I chuckle. The subtle plug hadn't gone unnoticed. "Good to know."

She holds my gaze, waiting for something. Lexi rolls her eyes in exasperation.

"Oh right, I almost forgot," Grace adds, her attempt at casualness falling flat. "I took a stab at redesigning the Quinn & Wolfe website for my coursework. Fancy a look . . . ?"

Lexi shoots her a scolding look. "Grace, honestly—"

"What?" Grace looks between us with wide, innocent eyes. "I've got the owner of my dream job in my living room. Call it seizing the opportunity." She fixes me with a look that's all determination. "I'm the kind of asset your company needs."

"It would seem so. All right then, opportunist, let's see what you've got," I say with a grin I can't suppress. Subtle she is not, but I admire the gall.

Grace conveniently has her laptop ready with the prototype site, and she's buzzing with anticipation. She shamelessly pitches her website redesign to me, explaining why it's the game-changer my company can't live without.

It's oddly calming. She's got that early-days hustle vibe, the kind where you're all in because, really, what's there to lose? Reminds me of my balls-to-the-wall younger self, chasing every opportunity. Part of me misses those days when I had nothing to lose.

Because now the stakes are so much higher. It feels like every time I puts a foot out of place some tower is going to collapse somewhere. I have my brother on my back, my mom. Not to mention a board of directors eyeballing my every move.

I'm not sold on the idea of a multimillion-dollar rebrand based on a student project, but I'm not about to crush her spirit. I give her design the attention it deserves, careful to give her some feedback without bringing her down.

"Make sure to showcase this in your interview. Our team will definitely appreciate your go-getter attitude," I suggest, genuinely impressed by her drive and enthusiasm.

Grace scampers off, a bounce in her step, satisfied that she has made a good impression.

I draw Lexi close, chuckling against that silken hair. "You've got to hand it to her—she really goes for it."

She lets out a sigh. "Sorry she ambushed you."

I smirk. "No need for apologies. I admire the hustle." I kiss the top of her head.

She studies me pensively. "Us being nice to

each other feels a bit strange," she admits.

I quirk a brow, amused. "You want us to go back to fighting then?"

"Fighting with you is pretty hot too. Although some of those arguments got too heated, and not in a good way."

Her words make me reflect grimly on some of our uglier clashes—all the hurtful shit I've thrown at her in anger, deliberately pushing her buttons to wound her.

I take her chin gently, regret churning inside. "I don't deserve your kindness, Lexi. Not after how I've treated you."

Her expression softens and she cups my cheek. "Of course you do. You deserve every bit of kindness, Connor. More now than ever." Her voice is firm, passionate. "I saw those articles. Damn, I was furious. That senator painted you as the sleaziest man alive. You can't let that slide."

"It's just noise. It'll pass."

It hits me like a sledgehammer that the only thing that truly matters right now is that she gives me her time. Even when I've done nothing to deserve it.

◆ ◆ ◆

I sink onto her minuscule mattress with a

martyred groan. "This bed's made for goddamn Smurfs, Lexi."

She climbs atop, baggy tee riding high on thighs I want wrapped around me and grinding.

I'll hand it to her; the girl can cook. Grace is still out, but I know we don't have much time.

"It fits normal folk just fine. You're the size of Godzilla," she teases, straddling my lap.

I attempt to fluff up her inadequate excuse for a pillow. "One pillow?"

"Is this not acceptable, your highness? Or do you require more padding for your royal head?" Her words drip with sarcasm. "It's not my fault your head weighs a ton."

"How many times do I have to tell you not to sass me?" I give her a stern look, my eyebrow raised.

In a flash I heave her over my knee. She squeals in surprise. "What the hell?"

I drag her shorts down and deliver a firm smack to her ass, savoring the satisfying sound it produces.

"Fuck!" She jumps, but there's breathless laughter too. "Shit, that stings!"

"It's meant to sting, angel," I reply, voice rough with lust.

Standing up, I bend her over the bed and gently push her forward.

"Spread your legs," I growl. "Now."

Reaching around, I tease her clit with my fingers, feeling it throb under my touch. She moans and lets her hands fall onto the mattress.

The sight of her naked body from behind, waiting for me, sends a surge of desire through me. No doubt about it, I'm an ass man.

"Wider," I command, nudging her legs apart with my foot.

I give that perfect ass another playful slap, relishing the way it jiggles under my touch.

She does as she's told, her laughter punctuated by a subtle shiver that reveals her nervousness.

Bending down, I press a reassuring kiss against her back.

I position myself behind her, my hands gripping her perfect backside. She lets out a soft gasp as I slide into her, feeling the tightness of her around me.

"Shit," I grunt. "You're so tight, I don't want to hurt you."

"Just give me a second," she pants.

I wait until I feel her relax before slowly pumping into that gorgeous pussy from behind. Each thrust sends a jolt of pleasure through my body as her cheeks smack against my thighs in perfect rhythm. I can't get enough of this view —her ass bouncing with every hard pump of my cock.

Our bodies collide, filling the room with the

sounds of our lustful moans and skin slapping together. I can't fucking hold on any longer.

I fuck her relentlessly, losing myself in pure bliss as sensations run up and down my cock. Her pussy has quickly become my favorite place in the world.

I grip her hips firmly, holding her in place as I continue to thrust harder and faster. She shivers at the sensation of my thumb moving in circles on her asshole.

I thrust harder and deeper until I can't take it anymore. With one final groan, I let go and explode inside her, filling her with every drop of pent-up pleasure.

And damn, does it feel incredible.

"Connor..."

With a nudge that feels like a gentle accusation, my eyes snap open to find Lexi hovering over me.

"You've been out cold for an hour, are you planning to go home?"

Damn, I actually dozed off. That wasn't on the agenda. I glance at my watch—eleven p.m. I was supposed to be long gone by now.

"Mmmph," I grunt, brain still groggy from

sleep.

Lexi shifts awkwardly. "I mean . . . you're welcome to crash here, I guess. Doubt my bed beats your luxe one though."

No fucking shit. The bed is more fitting for a dollhouse than a grown man. I think about the early session with my personal trainer tomorrow, a good ten miles from this very spot. Any sane man would've bolted by now, racing back to the sanctity of his Hästens Grand Vividus, a Swedish masterpiece of comfort that set me back two-hundred thousand but proves its worth every single night.

And then, out of nowhere, I hear myself saying, "It's comfy enough. I'll stay." We're both a little taken aback by that.

I lock eyes with her. "That work for you?"

"Sure." Her nonchalant shrug fools neither of us. I glimpse the shy flicker of excitement she swiftly smothers.

My back will hate me in the morning. Yet here I am, contemplating the night on what's essentially a glorified yoga mat.

I swore I'd keep things casual, and waking up in her home with her little sister in the next room is anything but fucking casual.

But dammit, I don't want to leave. Despite the imminent chiropractic appointment, the lure of staying tangled up in sheets that smell distinctly of her, with her body pressed up against mine, has a pull I can't shake off.

I glare up at the mold inching its way across the walls as Lexi curls into me. It pisses me off, her living in this dump. Her stubbornness about accepting help is admirable, sure, but damn if it doesn't make me crazy.

She burrows into my chest all sweet and innocent, even as her snores rev up to lawn mower levels.

Watching her, this tidal wave of protectiveness hits me out of nowhere. Every caveman instinct just roared to life.

I want her sleeping like a pampered princess on Egyptian cotton.

I want to see her genuinely beam with happiness.

To see her smile turned up to full wattage, in a way I suspect has been rare lately.

There's one thing I can do, since she won't take my help. A conversation we had lingers in my mind.

I'm toying with an idea. Something that might just knock her off her feet. And it'll kill two birds with one stone—it'll get Killian off my back for a while.

I want to give her that unforgettable date, that perfect moment. It's the least I can do. Lexi deserves that and more.

Maybe the only real thing I can offer her, even if it's all she ever gets from me.

THIRTY-NINE

Lexi

Connor's fingers graze my palm, tracing possessive circles that spike my pulse. I'm letting him whisk me away on a mystery date, only slightly vexed that he won't give me any hints.

Most guys do flowers. Billionaires show affection differently—by blindfolding you and sweeping you away in an SUV, apparently. It's kind of hot, if you ask me. I'm digging this this whole kidnapping vibe.

My best guesses are that impossible-to-book new Soho restaurant, or—based on his recent fascination with my ass—the Velvet Whip club.

Anxious excitement courses through me as I wonder where the hell we're headed. I white-knuckle the seatbelt, grinning like a fool, too amped to sit still.

After spending way too much time at Connor's swanky bachelor pad this past week, Grace accused me of moving out without telling her. We've been going at it like energizer bunnies on Viagra, and I am here for it. When I finally leave his apartment, my body buzzes for hours afterward.

Obviously, I've still got my laundry list of issues—Mom's care home bills, my empty bank account, Vicky piling on more work than any sane human can handle.

But you know what? Everything has a bit of a glow to it now. I've got an extra spring in my step, and I find myself grinning like a madwoman at random moments for no reason. Must be all the endorphins from the nonstop sex.

I'm trying not to overthink it too much.

I worry about Connor though. He shuts down whenever I try to bring up his hearing issues. Total brick wall. Says our time together is his escape from stress. So I've been researching on the sly about supporting someone with hearing issues.

Connor's thumb strokes that sensitive spot on my wrist. "Almost there," he murmurs.

My nerves jump as I strain to identify sounds. Curiosity is eating me alive. The loud roaring makes me think we're at an airport.

"Nervous?" Humor laces his voice.

"I feel so disoriented," I admit with an anxious laugh. Blindfolds tend to do that to a girl.

"It's okay, we're here now," he says. The SUV stops moving.

Cool air floods the car as Connor hops out. Butterflies swarm violently in my belly as he opens my door. His hands find mine, helping me out to more roaring sounds, like engines revving up. Maybe I'm not sold about the whole kidnapping thing after all ...

"Ready?" Connor asks, his fingers grazing my cheek before he slowly removes the blindfold.

Blinking against the sunlight, I see we're parked right in front of a sleek jet, with stairs leading up to the open door. Shock courses through me like I just licked a live wire.

"I don't understand," I stammer, my pulse doing the fucking Macarena. We can't seriously be about to ...

"I'm taking you to Ireland," Connor says, like whisking me away to Europe on a whim is normal behavior.

My hands cover my gaping mouth as I stare at the jet.

Glancing around, it's evident we're not at JFK— this is some high-class private airport. That plane is a private jet. And the pilot plus three fancy flight attendants are lined up on the aircraft stairs, all smiles, as though I'm the star of the show.

"What do you mean? I can't just hop on a plane to Ireland!" I practically screech.

"Yeah, you can," he says, infuriatingly calm and collected. "It's all taken care of."

I blink hard, my mind a whirlwind of emotions. Overwhelmed doesn't even begin to cover what's happening in my brain right now. I think it might actually short circuit and start smoking out the ears.

He shrugs. "Look, Killian's been on my case about taking a break. I figured I'd kill two birds with one stone. We have a cottage there that I've been meaning to visit." He chuckles, reaching out to tap my chin. "Close your mouth, Lexi. Relax, it's no big deal."

No big deal? It's a big fucking deal to me! This is just another example of how our lives are polar opposites.

Connor grins, retrieving a bouquet from the car. "For you, angel."

I accept the flowers in a daze.

The butterflies in my belly have now evolved into Riverdancing leprechauns, clicking and tapping so vigorously I'm concerned my navel might burst open and release a swarm of angry Irish fairies.

"I have work, Vicky will freak, Grace . . . Mom," I shout random protests at him because I'm incapable of forming coherent sentences.

"Vicky approved the time off. Grace gave me a shopping list for presents." His eyes glint with humor. "Your mom's thrilled for you."

"I don't have any clothes. Underwear. I thought

we were going for dinner, not going overseas!"

"Grace packed your bag. I told her Ireland could get chilly even at this time of year. Relax. If anything's missing, we'll sort it out when we get there. I can make a call on the flight."

I gape at him, feeling like I've stumbled onto the set of some elaborate prank show. Clearly, everyone's in on this except for me. I knew Grace was acting funny the last few days, watching me with that sly smirk. That little sneak.

"That means everybody knows about us." I'm not entirely sure what "us" even means. Are we friends with benefits still? Lovers?

"Not that it's anybody's fucking business, but Vicky thinks you're on a surprise family holiday. Your buddy Kayla helped me out."

The mere thought of my mom's reaction sends me into a preemptive cringe. "Mom's going to have a blast with this," I mutter. She'll be picking out wedding venues before we land in Ireland.

Only now do I really look at the flowers he's given me. Blue and brown blooms. And there's a note, with *Forest of Lexi* written in a fancy script. Are these freaking *custom flowers*?

He gives me a playful wink. "Matches your eyes."

"Pinch me," I breathe, half expecting to wake up any second now in my bed in Maison du Leak.

Connor, sensing I'm about two seconds away

from a full freak-out, gently smooths down my wind-wild hair. "Don't look so scared, Lexi. It's only four days. And the jet's very comfortable, so you won't miss any sleep. It'll feel like a long weekend away."

Going to Ireland on a whim obviously isn't as big a deal to him as it is me, in fact it doesn't sound to be a big deal at all.

The bombshell that he's orchestrated all this without my knowledge brings forth a mix of emotions. "You planned all this behind my back?"

He shrugs. "I didn't have to do that much." A hint of vulnerability peeks through his confident facade. "I know, I know—it's a gamble. If you're overwhelmed just say the word. I'm not forcing you, and don't feel bad if you want to pull the pin. I'll understand. But you'd get to see that view from my painting in the flesh."

Pressing palms to my flushed cheeks, I find myself whispering, "Guess I'm off to Ireland, then."

❖ ❖ ❖

We touch down after the best sleep of my life, thanks to the plush private bedroom and three flight attendants fawning over me. And I officially joined the mile-high club somewhere over the Atlantic. Twice. Bow chicka wow wow.

Now, we're cozied up in a quaint Irish bar, or should I say "pub," that feels like it's been plucked straight from a postcard, complete with a traditional band serenading us from the corner.

It's like nobody even knows who he is here, or if they do, they're doing an impressive job of playing it cool. Even the women who are discreetly eyeing him are playing it low-key.

Pinch me, I'm in Ireland. I still can't believe it. Just yesterday I was debating whether I could put off doing laundry for one more day, and now here I am., in Ireland.

Snuggling into him, I'm hit with a wave of . . . everything. "Honestly this is the most thoughtful thing anyone's ever done for me," I confess, voice wobbling traitorously.

Connor stiffens and clears his throat, shifting awkwardly. "It's nothing, Lexi. I needed a holiday too."

I probably wouldn't have been so open if I hadn't tried all the whiskeys.

He's trying to backpedal his romantic gesture, but I'm not buying it. Emotionally constipated or not, this man went out of his way to plan this surprise.

"I can't remember the last time I had this much fun," I sigh. That's when the harsh reality hits me. "It's made me realize how much of my life I've been putting on hold."

A couple decides to share our space, plopping down on the bench next to us.

Almost on instinct, Connor smoothly shifts me onto his lap, his muscular arms cradling me against his chest. "I see how much people lean on you, and that's admirable." He lifts my chin, his ocean-blue eyes locking with mine. "But you've gotta take care of yourself too. Prioritize your own happiness once in a while. Consider this trip permission to be a little selfish and do what feels good."

His words hit me hard, triggering a tsunami of fresh emotions. Maybe it's the Guinness talking, or the lilting tunes in the background, or perhaps it's the sheer reality of sitting here, in Ireland, on the lap of this absurdly handsome Irish American guy. Without warning, a snort-sob hybrid escapes me. Real attractive.

"Hey now, what's all this?" Connor's brow furrows, concern mixed with panic.

"Sorry," I choke out, trying to pull myself together. I can tell he's confused, as men often are by emotional outbursts.

He takes my face in his hands, using his thumbs to brush away my tears. "What is it?"

Through the sniffles, I admit, "I don't even know why I'm crying. I'm just . . . happy, I guess."

But even as I say it, I can't help but feel a twinge of fear deep inside. How gray and dull will life be

494

when this is over?

I'm waiting for him to inch away from the crazy, crying woman. His jaw tightens, but he wraps me in those strong, steady arms. And then he kisses me, not minding the tear-streaked mess that is my face.

"Hey, it's okay," he says, his voice hoarse. "Nothing wrong with a happy cry."

I let out a watery laugh. It doesn't matter when it ends. I'm here now and I'm going to live in the moment.

I wake after the second most incredible night's sleep ever, cocooned in our charming Irish cottage. I expected Connor to be all about the glitz of luxury hotels, but he surprised me with this cozy hideaway.

It's like Belle's corner in the Beast's castle, minus the enchanted furniture that talks back, of course.

Today we rented a car and drove the scenic Ring of Kerry, stopping at every beach and mountain view on the map. Seriously, it's like I've landed in my very own fairy tale, surrounded by jaw-dropping landscapes.

Now, back at our little hideout, I'm sprawled

on the comfiest couch known to mankind, toes buried deep in the fuzzy rug. Outside the cottage window, the wild sea pounds against a deserted beach.

The only thing that would make it perfect was if Connor were here. Where is he? He put on sweatpants and earplugs and said was he was going for a jog, but that was well over an hour ago.

I grab his jacket hanging on the stand, swamping myself in his scent and warmth. It's springtime, but apparently Ireland never got the memo.

I close my eyes, inhale the scent of the Irish sea air, and let it wash over me, soothing my frazzled New York nerves. The sand beneath my feet feels heavenly. The steady hush of the waves creates a soothing, unfamiliar lullaby.

I can't believe I'm really here—it's the most relaxed I've felt in ages.

I sit outside for what must be twenty minutes in the hammock, relaxing but also worried that after my emotional breakdown last night, Connor has checked into a hotel to escape the crying lady.

Then, I spot a figure coming along the far end of the beach. Shit, he's been running all this time? My god. I feel lazy now. I'm pretty sure I've broken a sweat just watching him from afar.

He's so into his running, he doesn't even see me.

He stops in the middle of the beach and . . . oh my god, this guy is completely nuts. He whips off his T-shirt and sneakers like he's in a *Baywatch* audition and dives into those big, white, frothy, *freezing* waves.

I know because I dipped my toe in them earlier and nearly lost my foot to frostbite.

I dash to the water's edge, watching him wrestle with the waves like some kind of sexy Aquaman warrior. His strong shoulders dipping in and out of the water, muscles rippling under glistening skin. Sweet baby Jesus.

Who in their right mind would want to be in that water?

It's like he needs to struggle, suffer, conquer. From the shoreline, I can practically see the stress and adrenaline ricocheting off his shoulders. Always battling some inner demon I can't see.

Then he spots me and waves. He strides out of the sea, dripping wet, water cascading down his chiseled abs and—oh my—clinging to his running shorts in all the right places. Every part of his body is fine-tuned, and I'm practically panting just drinking in the sight of him.

"You're crazy," I shout, hugging his coat tighter as he comes to drip beside me.

"It's good for you. Join me." He grins, running his hands through his hair, droplets rushing down his sculpted chest.

I can't help but smile. He's been much more playful and carefree since we got here, and it's intoxicating.

In my head, there's a rom-com montage happening, with Connor heroically swooping me up from the waves, all slow-mo and dramatic.

Here in Ireland, it's just Lexi and Connor, living our best lives on this beautiful beach. No billion-dollar empire between us, no power imbalance . . . Except for the fact that he literally owns this entire stretch of sand.

"Don't worry." His hot gaze trails down my fully covered body. "I'll warm you up real quick afterward."

Oh damn. He's using his horny voice. Now I'm imagining all the deliciously naughty ways he can "warm me up."

He arches an eyebrow, taunting me. "So, what's it gonna be, Sullivan? You gonna dive in and have the time of your life, or are you gonna be a bore?"

His playful challenge gets me. I don't want to look like a bore. Who knew getting hypothermia could be so enticing? "All right, you win. But if I freeze to death, I'm haunting your fancy plunge pool for eternity. Wait there."

I turn to go in and grab a swimsuit, hoping Grace has packed me a thick wetsuit, when he grabs my hand.

"Uh-uh," he drawls, grinning. "No need to get a

swimsuit. It's a private beach, Lexi. Just us."

"Wait, the beach comes with the cottage?" I blink in disbelief.

"Yeah, I own it. Well, Killian and I do." Connor says this casually, because of course he does. "We snagged it last year for the family to use as a holiday spot. But this is my first time checking it out."

He pauses, his forehead creasing in thought, and I have the sudden urge to smooth out those worry lines with my lips. "Come to think of it, this is my first real vacation in ages. Usually, it's just quick Vegas trips or work jaunts to check on our hotels."

I look at him incredulously. "You bought a beach house in Ireland without even seeing it first?"

He just shrugs. "Made sense for us. Killian, Clodagh, Tegan, and even Mom have all been here. I knew I'd make it out eventually."

I shake my head, marveling at the absurdity of it all. Then, before I can chicken out, I whip off his coat, the cold air hitting my skin like a thousand tiny needles. I kick off my flip-flops and shimmy out of my jeans and tee, standing there in nothing but my bra and panties.

Connor laughs, and that's not the reaction you want when you strip down to your underwear on a beach. "She really got behind the Irish theme, huh?"

"I'm having words with her when I get home," I mutter.

Grace has only packed underwear sets with strings and zero ass coverage. And to top it off —there are bedazzled leprechauns plastered on each tiny triangle of my bra. Jesus, it's like I'm auditioning for a bad St Patrick's Day porn flick.

Where the hell did she find this? I can't tell if she's trying to make me look hot or stupid.

To my shock, Connor drops his running shorts followed by his boxers. "Lose the underwear." Even playful it still seems like an order. Very bossy.

"Naked?" I can't help but burst into laughter, even though the wind steals the sound away. "You're joking, right?"

"Come on." He grins. "This is my private beach. No one's going to see us."

I try to laugh it off, but he's standing there with that look, like he's issued a challenge I'm too prudish to accept. God, I'm not exactly the naked-in-public type. I didn't grow up in a household where we pranced around in the buff.

However, I don't want to seem like a total nun either.

Connor strides back toward the water, bare ass on full display. The sun glistens off his muscular glutes.

As he reaches the shoreline, he turns and

crooks his finger at me, arrogantly beckoning. "I'm waiting, Lexi."

Okay, what the hell, right? It's not as if we have an audience, unless the seagulls are feeling particularly pervy today. Plus, I could use some vitamin D on these pasty ass cheeks.

I whip off my bra and shimmy out of my leprechaun-adorned underwear. I take off running toward Connor, attempting my best sexy beach sprint even though everything starts violently jiggling. Even though he's already seen me in various states of undress, this feels different, more exposed in the broad daylight. I suck in my stomach along with anything else suckable, and try to channel my inner Pamela Anderson as I reach him.

"Good girl." He winks, already knees deep in the water. "See, that wasn't so hard."

I cautiously dip my toes into the water, letting out a high-pitched squeal as I quickly retract my foot. "It's freezing, you psychopath!"

Is he trying to kill me?

But before I can stage a retreat, Connor lifts me up, bridal style, and I'm half laughing, half screaming, "What the—"

I shriek and swat his chest as he charges into the surf.

Connor's laughter fills the air as he playfully plunks me down into the water.

"Fuckkkk!" I scream, splashing away. "This is . . . so . . ."

HOLY MOTHER OF GOD. This water is glacial. I can't breathe. My organs feel like they're shutting down. We're going to die of hypothermia . . . They'll find our naked bodies washed up on the shore and wonder what kinky shit we were up to.

We must be in fucking Iceland not Ireland.

The shock sucks the air from my lungs and I burst up from the water, spluttering and smacking his laughing face. "You asshole!"

Okay . . .

I groan, adjusting to the cold. It's not so bad now. I can handle this.

"You okay?" he asks, grinning like a fool.

"Just about," I reply through gritted teeth, trying to keep them from chattering.

Connor runs his fingers through his wet hair, and like a man possessed, he dives under and resurfaces with a wild, boyish grin. "Feels amazing, yeah?"

"I hate you," I growl, smacking the water, even as my chest does that fluttery thing that I've come to associate with Connor's presence. I don't want to give the merman the satisfaction of telling him he's right.

Water droplets hang from his ridiculously long lashes, making him look like he's shooting for the cover of some steamy "Gods of the Sea" calendar. Not that I'm complaining. Seeing Connor so carefree and relaxed does strange flippy things to my heart.

It's as if Ireland has unveiled this other, more laid-back persona. He's miles away from the grumpy boardroom beast I've grown accustomed to.

But let's not kid ourselves; I know that side of him still lingers beneath the surface.

As yet another wave theatrically crashes over us, Connor wraps his arms around my shivering body. Despite the cold water and wind, I feel a surge of heat between my legs at being pressed against his hard muscles.

"You sure no one can see us?" I ask, attempting to keep my hair from slapping me in the face. I hope I look more *Baywatch* babe and less wet dog.

His eyes trace my lips hungrily.

"Positive."

He lifts me up and wraps my legs around his waist, holding me tightly by the ass. I cling to his unfairly warm shoulders for dear life, breasts smashed against his hard chest, nipples poking out like pencils, and not in a good way.

Then he goes in for a kiss, way too passionate for swimming in the chilly Atlantic Ocean. I cling to his shoulders, as we drift further out.

"You can't seriously be thinking of having sex here," I manage to say between breaths.

He chuckles against my lips. "As much as I'd love to show off my superhuman stamina, even my dick can't perform in these conditions."

"Good, because I'm freezing," I declare through chattering teeth, my voice an octave higher than usual. Christ, my bits are retreating inside themselves for warmth. "We need to get out of here before my nipples fall off and float to Canada."

He wheezes out a laugh, breathless from the cold. "All right, brave girl. Let's get you some lunch. We'll find some of that seafood chowder you wanted to try."

He leans in for another kiss, but movement on the beach catches my eye.

Is that . . . ?

"Hmm . . ." Squinting against the sun, I struggle to focus. It's tough without my glasses.

My arousal is swiftly replaced by a growing sense of dread as I peer back at the shoreline.

Oh my god.

People have congregated on the beach. And not just a few stragglers, but a whole freaking crowd. It's suddenly swarming with people.

Everyone's gazing out at the sea—or more accurately, at us, the naked idiots frolicking in the waves.

"Um, Connor?" I hiss, slapping his wandering hand away. "Why the hell are there people on your 'private' beach?! Did you forget to put up the 'No

Trespassing' sign or something?"

He turns his head. "What the hell?" he mutters, his brow furrowing.

I use his sturdy frame as a makeshift privacy screen, watching as what seems to be half the town gathers right by our abandoned clothes. *Oh no*. My leprechaun bra.

"What are they doing?" I ask, my voice choked with anxiety. They're looking at us. They're just standing there in a row, dressed in black, and staring at us, like some kind of bizarre cult.

"Shit," he hisses, his voice dripping with as much confusion as my mind. "I don't know."

Oh god. This is bad. Have they come to sacrifice us? I'm pretty sure Grace didn't pack for a séance.

"They definitely don't look like they're enjoying themselves," I panic-shriek. "Why are they just standing there staring out to sea? And why are they all wearing black? Are they goths?"

"Shit, is that a priest?" Connor mutters.

I squint and, to my utter horror, confirm the presence of a tall figure in long robes among the crowd. Oh my freaking god. Tell me we didn't just barge in on a funeral service.

No wonder there's a black-clad weeping woman in the mix. It makes a horrifying amount of sense.

As we drift closer, the priest holds up an ornate urn. Dread sinks into my stomach.

"Connor!" I choke out. "They're about to scatter ashes into the sea!"

"Fuck," he curses, his voice hushed in shock. We both fall silent for a moment, watching in disbelief as half the crowd bows their heads in somber reverence. This is really happening. We've accidentally crashed a funeral, and we're naked.

But the other half are staring at us, probably debating whether to call the cops. Garda, they're called in Ireland. *Indecent exposure at a funeral* is probably not something the Garda encounter every day.

"We need to head back," he says, his tone urgent.

"What?" I screech. I can't tear my eyes away from one woman's wrenching sobs. Guilt gnaws at my insides.

"We'll just make a discreet exit," Connor mutters, as if we can just dissolve into the sea mist.

For a super smart and ruthless businessman, he sure as hell can be dumb sometimes.

"Discreet? *How*? What do you expect us to do, just moonwalk out of the sea butt-naked?" I sputter incredulously. "I doubt 'sorry for streaking at your loved one's funeral' is going to cut it as an apology."

"Lexi," he growls. "We can't stay in here, for fuck's sake. They look like they're going to be there for a while."

I glare at him. "Don't you get bossy with me! You're the reason we're in this situation." I'm shivering, my teeth chattering a mile a minute. "I refuse. I would rather pass out and die right now than leave the water."

"That's not an option. I'll carry you out if I have to," he threatens, his eyes narrowing.

I glare back at him, my own eyes narrowing to slits. This is how I become an internet meme, isn't it? #FuneralFlashers.

But before I can argue further, he grabs my hand, hauls me into his arms like a sack of potatoes, and I let out a scream that could wake the dead. Which, ironically, draws even more attention to us. So much for discretion.

He shifts me around so I'm hanging onto his back like a koala while he powers towards the shore with strong strokes. I'm bobbing along behind him, my face smacking into his ripped back with every stroke.

Connor emerges from the water, muscled ass clenching as he strides ashore. I scamper gracelessly after him, cringing as everything bounces and jiggles violently. Less *goddess mermaid emerging* and more *sea creature on its first land walk*.

Now, everyone's eyes are locked on us, except for the priest who's still facing the congregation.

Jaws drop.

Eyes pop out of sockets.

Pearls and rosary beads are clutched so tightly, knuckles turn white.

More mourners whip their heads up.

Gasps fill the air.

Sand stubbornly sticks to my butt as it bounces violently as I sprint for cover.

Our clothes are conveniently nestled right next to the priest, who sounds like he's now in the midst of a heartfelt eulogy. Lovely.

The priest, in his booming, sermon-giving glory, remains blissfully unaware of the R-rated show behind him. ". . . and so may Eamon's spirit join the endless dance of the ocean waves . . . His spirit will rise from the sea . . ."

As we get closer, I realize with dawning horror that my leprechaun bra is lying right near the mourners, like some sort of kinky offering.

If embarrassment could kill, I'd be giving Eamon company in the afterlife.

Connor swoops our stuff up without missing a stride as I lunge unsuccessfully for my bra top, which seems to have become entangled under some old guy's foot. Great, just great. Now I'm playing tug-of-war with a geriatric over my own bra.

The priest turns, still cradling Eamon's urn. His expression freezes, a perfect snapshot of "this was not in the job description."

Every woman at the funeral, regardless of age, has her gaze fixed on Connor's cock. Most of the men too.

The mourning woman lets out a confused shriek.

"Sorry!" I bleat weakly, deciding to cut my losses and abandon my wayward bra. Really, what can you say in a situation like this? "Please, carry on."

Connor, the smug bastard, has the audacity to look composed, like he's not standing there with his parts on display for the entire congregation to gawk at. "Our apologies, Father," he says smoothly, his voice dripping with charm.

We sprint toward the cottage like our asses are on fire, desperate to put some much-needed distance between us and the astonished mourners.

"Sorry for your loss," I yell weakly over my shoulder. These poor people just wanted to say goodbye to Eamon, not get mooned by two idiots.

It'll probably become a legendary story told at family gatherings for generations to come. *"Do you remember Eamon's send-off? Yeah, the one with the streakers? What a way to go!"*

Hopefully for some of the ladies, the sight of Connor's swinging junk makes up for us crashing the funeral.

"Looks like Eamon got his dying wish after all!" one of the men calls out with a laugh.

We burst through the cottage doors in fits of mortified laughter. I collapse into the nearest chair, my legs giving out. Connor kneels down beside me, his big, strong hands rubbing warmth back into my frozen limbs.

"Jesus Christ," he chuckles, a grin lighting up his face. "That did not go as planned."

I drop my head with a groan as the giddiness subsides. "You think? We just crashed a funeral and ran across the beach in our birthday suits. We're definitely going to hell for that one."

Connor chuckles again, the sound rumbling from his chest as he scoops me up and carries me as if I weigh nothing at all.

Automatically I melt into him, tension dissipating, perfectly content in his arms.

"Thanks, Connor," I find myself whispering, the words more heartfelt than I'd expected.

He raises an eyebrow. "For what? Almost getting you arrested for public indecency?"

"For reminding me how to have fun."

I don't want my fairy tale to end.

◆ ◆ ◆

I once took a class that explored the fine line between making love and just plain having sex. Most of the time, "making love" is just tossed around as a polite term for getting down and dirty. Often a cheesy one at that.

But sex is just physical mechanics driven by our primal urges. It's all about rubbing, sucking, biting, and sticking things in holes.

Don't get me wrong, I'm all for it. It's what most of us spend our time daydreaming about, whether we're stuck in a boring work meeting, waiting in line at the DMV, or even during those important events like weddings and funerals.

Making love, however, is on a whole other level. It's intense and scary in its vulnerability. You're not just exposing your body, you're baring your heart and soul. It's terrifying and incredible all at once.

That's how I feel as Connor enters me again with a deep groan.

The sun has set, leaving us in the cozy glow of the fire.

We're sprawled out on a fluffy rug, gazing into each other's eyes as we fuck with deliberate slowness.

Our fingers are intertwined. Our gazes never break. Our chests expand and contract. Sweat beads on our skin as we move against each other.

He pulls out and slides back in, slow and deliberate, as he searches my face. I'm staring so hard at his eyes they're starting to look like stars. Shit, that was poetic. I can't help but notice the slight flicker of green in there too.

I arch my back and meet his thrusts, pleasure building at my core and radiating throughout my entire being. Every nerve buzzing with sensation from the man lying on top of me, from the feel of him inside me.

God, this is intense. I know he feels it too.

As we move together, I watch the orgasm build on his face and it's like nothing I've ever seen before. His hands grip mine tightly as he groans.

There's no dirty talk this time, just the sounds of our heavy breathing and quiet moans.

With every thrust, I feel myself edging closer to an orgasm so powerful it could make me cry.

And I'm scared. I almost don't want it to happen because I know it's going to shatter me into a million pieces. And I might never recover.

FORTY

Lexi

But like all good fairy tales, this one comes to an end.

The flight back is nothing like our carefree loved-up journey here.

Connor's pain begins the morning of our departure, right after breakfast. I'm guessing it's stress-related, maybe at the thought of going back to the real world?

There's all this research suggesting autoimmune diseases are tied to stress, or at least exacerbated by stress. But telling someone to stop stressing just fucks them up even more.

We had just found out from Killian that the so-called private beach was, in fact, not so private after all. Cue a good thirty minutes of us laughing our asses off.

Turns out, the Quinns only own half of it with the cottage, and there's more beach in the other direction. At least now that I'm leaving the country, I can find the humor in it. Hopefully they don't plaster my face all over the airport as a "do not let back in" warning.

But that was where the laughter stopped and the tension started.

For the first four hours of the flight, Connor barely speaks, doesn't sleep. Just stares broodingly out the window, muscles rigid as steel. And I can't drift off either, even with the comfort of our plush private bedroom suite in the clouds.

He makes sure that the crew is treating me like a princess, but he's too tense for any affection. It's like trying to cuddle a brick.

He attempts to distract himself with his laptop, but it's clear his mind is elsewhere. He just scowls at the screen, nursing a couple of scotches. Sure, flying can wreak havoc on anyone's system —popping ears, dry eyes—but it's clear Connor's battling more than just the usual air travel annoyances.

We've reclined the bed a bit now, and his eyes are shut tight, but I can see the pain etched into his handsome face. He's too wound up for sleep.

I'm pretty sure he popped more pills than what the label suggests, and he definitely shouldn't be pairing them with booze, but pointing that out would lead to major death glares.

"So, uh, did your doctor actually clear this trip?

With your ear stuff flaring and all . . . ?" I ask, treading on eggshells.

He barely grunts a response. "Didn't check. I'm taking the meds they gave me. I'll be fine."

I bite my tongue. He thinks he's invincible, that's the issue. Like being tall, built, and easy on the eyes somehow makes him bulletproof against the mundane rules of health.

Telling him that and pissing him off mid-flight doesn't seem like the best idea though.

So I trail my fingers over his chest, hoping my touch can work some kind of miracle. But every muscle stays agonizingly taut.

After endless strained quiet, Connor finally huffs out a ragged breath. I feel his fist clench and release where it rests on my hip, like he's trying to physically restrain his frustration.

"Any better . . . ?" I dare to whisper, praying he's found some relief.

"It's fine," he grits out. Subtext clear: Back off.

I hate seeing him in pain, but I know better than to push him when he's like this. Not until we've landed, anyway.

As we're descending the steps of the jet plane, with the crew waving at me like I'm Julia Roberts, I'm so lost in my own little world that it takes me a minute to realize there are photographers here. And not just one or two, but a whole swarm of them over by the waiting area.

I'm instantly thrown into panic mode.

I yank my hand away from Connor's. He turns on the step, raising a brow.

"There are photographers here," I hiss, eyes widening.

He glances over, shrugging like he couldn't care less. "So? They aren't looking at us. They're here for someone else."

He tries to take my hand again, but I barge past him down the steps. "Where's the car?" I ask.

He frowns, clearly not getting why I'm so worked up. "Over there, Lexi. What's the problem?"

I look over at the cameras with growing dread, because some of them have spotted Connor and are perking up like meerkats. "Haven't you had enough scandal?"

"I'm not doing anything wrong. The farce with Willow is over." He shrugs, and it pisses me off more. "And going out with you is hardly a scandal."

"That's fine for you. But what about me? I'm not exactly thrilled at the prospect of being plastered across every gossip rag as your flavor of the week!"

I stride toward the car, my heart pounding. All of this might be normal for him, just another day in the life. He might not give a flying fuck about the media circus, with his army of PR minions and an ego bigger than the damn plane we just got off. But for me? Being outed as the secret lover of one of the most notorious men in the country is kind of a big freaking deal. My god, what if Deano and his gang saw it?

We climb into the back of his SUV, and I slam the door.

"Come on, Lexi, I'm not in the mood for drama," he growls, like I'm a petulant child throwing a tantrum.

Oh, he did *not* just say that.

"*I'm* not in the mood to be featured on the front page of a tabloid because of you," I fire back. "What is this, Connor? Are we still friends with benefits? Because that's not worth public humiliation for me."

He nods at the driver then throws me a piercing glance. "You really want to do this now?"

"I need to know where we stand."

Connor shifts uncomfortably in his seat, his jaw clenching as he stares at me with an almost pained expression. I feel my heart stuttering in my chest, wondering what the hell he's going to say.

"I'm into you. I like spending time with you. I hope you feel the same about me."

It's not exactly a declaration of love, but coming from Mr. Emotionally Constipated, it's practically a sonnet. I can tell getting those words out was like pulling teeth for him.

"I think it's obvious I do," I say. "But you can't be so blasé about things that are important to me, like my privacy and my reputation."

He looks at me seriously, then nods, like he's finally getting it through his thick, beautiful skull. "Got it."

"And just to be clear, I don't share," I snap.

His blue eyes blaze with heat. "The thought never even entered my mind."

Despite the irritation still simmering under my skin, I feel a flutter of hope in my chest. Maybe, just maybe, this could be something real. If I'm willing to take the risk on a guy like Connor.

I don't make it through the week without seeing Connor again. When he texts, casually dropping an invite for Tuesday night, my pile of work suddenly seems less important.

So now I'm sprawled out on his couch, wearing nothing but his T-shirt that covers me like a dress.

"Are you sure you didn't have anything to do with Grace getting the job?" I ask him suspiciously.

Grace got news today that she secured the internship at Quinn & Wolfe's IT department, and needless to say, she's been happy-dancing around the apartment for hours.

He frowns. "No, Lexi. You think I would interfere with a young woman's career? You're not giving me much credit here. I sent over her résumé so of course she got an interview because it was coming from me, but the rest was all her."

"Sorry," I say sheepishly just as the doorbell rings.

He shoots me a look, miffed at me questioning his morals, then grumbles, "It's Killian."

"I'll give you guys some privacy—" I start to say, moving to get up.

"No need. He's only dropping something off." Connor waves me off, heading to the door.

Killian enters, leaning casually against the living room entrance. His eyes flash in a way that makes me nervous when he sees me. "Good to see you again, Lexi."

I wonder if he's still holding a grudge for the whole car hustle thing. Does he see me as a gold-digger, out to snag his brother's fortune?

"You too, Killian," I reply, acutely aware I'm wearing little more than Connor's shirt and an awkward smile.

Killian doesn't beat around the bush. "Connor, a word?"

I start to move from the sofa, feeling uncomfortable being present for whatever this is about, but Connor's expression stops me dead in my tracks.

"I said it's fine," he insists, effectively ending the discussion.

The air crackles with hostility and Killian looks like he's ready to throw punches. Yep, definitely not just a friendly brotherly visit.

"Care to explain why you bailed on the City Planning meeting and left staff to handle it?" Killian asks tightly. "Unacceptable, even for you."

Connor's response is equally stiff. "They handled it fine without me." He saunters to the fridge and grabs a beer with a casualness that doesn't fit the mood. "Want one?"

"No, I don't want a beer," Killian snaps.

"Suit yourself." Connor takes a long pull from his bottle.

I catch his eye by mistake and instantly regret it, wishing I could just blend into the couch.

"I want to know why you bailed on a meeting we planned for weeks, right when the senator is already screwing us on the hotel build," Killian snaps, crossing his arms. "What the hell are you playing at, Connor?"

"Jesus, relax," Connor snarls. "I said my piece at the meeting and had to be somewhere else."

Killian's eyes slit dangerously. "Like fucking where?"

My pulse spikes. Did Connor walk out of another meeting because of his hearing issue? I sense this is worse than he's making out and he's bottling it up.

"Are you spending all your time fucking?" Killian glares between us, his accusation landing like a blow. "Sorry, Lexi, this isn't personal."

Oh my god. Is he serious? Killian thinks this is about me?

"Watch yourself," Connor warns, a lethal edge to his voice. "Leave Lexi out of this. It has nothing to do with her."

Mortification floods my cheeks as I try to shrink into the couch cushions, wishing I could disappear like a fart in the wind.

Their argument escalates, each trying to assert their dominance over the other. Their poor mom must be a saint dealing with these two testosterone-fueled knuckleheads.

I want to make a run for it and escape this macho showdown, but I'm frozen in place.

Their argument feels like it goes on for hours, but it's probably only a few minutes.

"Get your act together, Connor. You're off your game, letting me down."

"I get that I've had a couple of bad weeks but get off my back," Connor snaps. "The last billion dollars this company made was off the back of my ideas and innovations, not yours."

They continue arguing until Killian decides he's had enough and storms out.

The silence that follows is suffocating.

521

"Sorry you had to see that pissing match," Connor finally murmurs, taking an aggressive swig of his beer.

I go over and stand beside him at the table, taking his free hand in mine. "Did you really have somewhere to be, or was it because of your hearing?" I ask gently.

"I had places to be."

He's lying. I can tell from the tension in his neck, the look in his eyes. My heart goes out to him.

"You should tell Killian the truth, Connor. He'd understand."

He just grunts and moves toward the couch, looking ready to start hurling furniture. I'm nervous when he's in this mood—I don't feel like I can get through to him.

But I have to.

Undeterred, or maybe just naive, I scoot closer, wrapping my arms around him in what I hope is a comforting hug, but his shoulders might as well be made of concrete.

"I've been doing some reading about what you're going through," I say. "Trying to understand, that's all. Even if I can't really help."

He stiffens further, scowl carved deep in his features. "You don't need to," he mutters. "I've got the best of the best on this. Nothing you can do about it."

My stomach twists. Connor is hard to push.

There's a part of me that's still on edge around him, especially after witnessing his wrath mere minutes ago. He's hardly the poster boy for open dialogue, especially about something as touchy as this.

But I can't just sit back and watch him self-destruct.

He's meant to be reducing his stress, but instead he's actively creating more and more of it for himself. If a house is burning to the ground, you don't turn your back on it or keep it a secret. You ask for help.

"Maybe you could talk to others further along in their diagnosis, see how they cope," I venture, trying to keep it as breezy as possible. Dead silence follows. So, I plow ahead. "Or maybe meeting people who've completely lost their hearing. Hearing loss communities maybe? Kind of like staring your biggest fear in the face . . ."

He levels me with an icy glare. It's clear he's not in the mood for what he sees as pity or unnecessary help.

"I'll go with you," I add quickly. "To appointments, or whatever you need. You don't have to do this alone, Connor."

"I'm handling it. I'm pouring funds into the best research team out there to find a cure."

I gnaw my lip, nerves frayed. Connor thinks he can wave his AmEx around until this disappears.

But from experience, it rarely works that way. Not with something like this.

But deep down, I know he's smarter than that. It's funny what we tell ourselves just to summon hope, though.

"Dad did the same when Mom got sick," I say gently. "We threw money at every possible cure, clinging to hope," I push, fully aware I'm treading on thin ice. "Even chased after some bizarre alternative treatments. It's one of the reasons we spiraled into debt. That magical cure never came."

"This isn't the fucking same," Connor snaps, his temper flaring. "This isn't some voodoo witch doctor shit, Lexi. I have the best doctors money can buy working on this."

"I know. I just mean facing your fears can help too."

He exhales, irritated.

I press on anyway. "What about trying some counseling? It really helped me after Dad. Just having someone outside the situation, you know?"

"I'm not going to a fucking shrink. You can see the shit I'm dealing with now, with Killian and work. Look, can we just have a nice night without the therapy session? I'm all talked out."

"Your way of handling this seems to be more about avoidance than acceptance. You can't do that forever."

His nostrils flare. "Lexi, once and for all, drop

it. Don't make me regret telling you. Respect my choice to handle my health condition the way I want to. Okay?"

He relents then and kisses my forehead, like he's trying to smooth over the cracks in our conversation, or maybe shut me up.

I nod weakly, ignoring the warning bells chiming in my mind. He's blocking me out at every turn. He needs to open up, not just to me, but to his family too. It's like he's his own worst enemy and doesn't even see it.

If he can't open up to me, where does that leave us?

FORTY-ONE

Lexi

Nothing puts me more on edge than an unannounced billionaire at my door. Even more so when it's the wrong one, looking thoroughly displeased.

"Hi," I say. What does he want?

"Who is it?" Grace yells from her room.

"Delivery for me," I call back, sizing up Killian and his resting bitch face.

"Hi." He tries for a smile, but it's as warm as an iceberg.

My brain jumps to catastrophic conclusions. "Is Connor okay?" Connor's been at mine three times in this last two weeks since we got back from Ireland, but I definitely wasn't expecting his brother to grace me with his presence.

"He's fine," Killian dismisses. "But you and I need to talk."

Looks like it's a family trait. Demands first,

pleasantries might follow, if you're lucky.

"I'm sorry for not calling ahead." He doesn't look very apologetic.

"That's okay. Come in. Umm, sorry it's not the fanciest place in the world." My apartment is barely fit for a rat, let alone another billionaire.

"The maid's got the day off," I joke as I lead him inside.

His reaction to my stab at humor is a whole lot of nada, not even a hint of a smile. Tough crowd. You'd think he'd at least pretend to find me funny, while standing in *my* living room.

Trying not to freak out, I rack my brain for why Killian could possibly be here. Something tells me it's not to plan a surprise party for Connor.

I wonder how long I can stall before Grace comes out. She's gaming though, so hopefully she'll be lost in virtual reality for hours.

Killian takes in the shabby, mismatched furniture and Target decor. Connor mentioned Killian lives in a Fifth Avenue townhouse—his "main home," he'd clarified casually. Of course the mega-rich have a roster of homes.

I scoop up the scattered underwear lying around the radiator before Killian catches a glimpse of my lacy intimates embarrassingly out in the open. Stuffing them into a storage bin in a rush, I flash him an awkward smile.

"Charming place," he comments. Translation:

this place is a dump.

I gesture to the couch. "Make yourself at home. Hmm, do you want a beer, wine or something?"

"No, thanks." Thank the gods for small mercies, because my wine collection is courtesy of Walmart's discount aisle.

He remains standing, gaze laser-focused on me. "Look, I'll get right to it. What exactly is going on with my brother lately, Lexi?"

"I, uh, I'm not sure . . ." I stammer, feeling my traitorous cheeks burn.

His raised eyebrow and disapproving stare make me feel like a scolded child. A gesture so reminiscent of Connor it disorients me for a second.

"I don't usually go to strangers for information. And let's just say your track record with my brother doesn't exactly inspire trust." He steps forward, the floorboard creaking under his polished loafer like it's screaming in terror. "I don't know you, Lexi, but your history with my brother makes me uneasy."

"I made a mistake, which was not in my character," I fire back. I'm not having a second Quinn judge me for crimes against billionaires.

"He told me. And I'm going to give you the benefit of the doubt. But I also want to protect my brother."

I resist the urge to warn him about the wonky

floor. Now's not the time.

"And Connor's been spending time with you," Killian continues. "So I'm coming to you for help."

I open my mouth but only manage incoherent stuttering.

Crap crap crap.

"He's distracted—walking out of pivotal negotiations, abandoning media appearances." Those glacial eyes drill into me, unrelenting. "Is it drugs? Alcohol addiction?"

I'm so thrown by the question that my mouth just hangs there. "What? No! It's nothing like that."

He folds his arms, looking every inch the older, slightly more world-weary version of his brother. There's a touch of gray in his brown locks, but those ice-blue eyes are exactly the same. A genetic Quinn family trademark, I imagine.

"There is something then," he deduces. "What is it?"

I gulp, feeling like I'm in a *Law & Order* interrogation.

"It's crucial you tell me."

This feels like a no-win situation. "Shouldn't you be talking to him about this?"

"I've tried repeatedly. He shuts me out." His jaw tightens, and I think I hear his teeth grinding from across the room. "I'm turning to you, Lexi . . . for his sake. Help me understand what's happening before he self-destructs. If you give a damn about him, you'll let me in on what's happening."

Wow, going right for emotional manipulation. Talk about being between a rock and a hard place in the shape of Quinn brothers.

Nervously, I shift on my feet. I have no idea how to handle this crisis. I'm damned if I do, damned if I don't.

I can't spill Connor's secrets, but part of me wants Killian to know the truth. Underneath it all, it feels like the right move for Connor. Killian may seem tough, but he's here because he cares. Connor loves his family deeply—by shutting them out, he's only hurting himself when he needs their support most.

"I . . . it's not really my call to make," I hedge feebly.

Killian leans on the table, gripping the edges hard. If he breaks it, he pays for it. "Lexi, I'm really concerned about my brother." Now I see genuine concern in his eyes. "Please, if you know what's going on, tell me."

The guy's pulling every heartstring with that appeal, but betraying Connor doesn't sit right with me either.

"Look," I say gently, tugging on a strand of hair like I'm trying to pluck it out. "I can't share details. It's Connor's story to tell. But he's under a lot of stress, not partying or anything bad. Ultimately though, he needs to open up to you himself."

He frowns. "If it's not drugs or alcohol, what is it? Something health related?"

I bite my lip, pulse racing with stress. Suffocating silence hangs between us.

Dread flashes in his eyes. "Christ. It is health related," he confirms grimly.

I keep my mouth shut.

"Dammit, give me something here."

I take a breath, trying to dial down the drama. "He's not on his deathbed or anything. But it is something he has to work through." I sigh. "This isn't fair, Killian. You're putting me in an awful position."

"Just tell me what it is," he demands.

I'm torn between loyalty and the urge to just spill it. "I can't betray his trust like that . . . lay off, will you?"

Killian gives a firm nod, his jaw set tight. "All right, sorry. But can you do me a favor instead? He's been giving me the runaround, always claiming he's swamped. If I can't get through to him, maybe Mom can. I'm inviting you to dinner at my place on Friday and I want you to make sure he comes, even if you have to drag him by the hair."

"What, like an intervention?"

"Call it what you want. I just need a conversation."

I gnaw my lip uncertainly. The thing is, I want Killian to know the truth. It's what Connor needs.

And Killian came to me, not the other way around. He stomped into my apartment demanding answers.

But ambushing Connor feels risky. He's not the intervention type.

Still, all I'd be doing is giving Killian a chance to talk to his brother. I'm not doing anything wrong here. Connor can't be mad about that, can he?

"Okay," I finally concede quietly.

Killian looks relieved. "Thanks, Lexi."

But the paranoid thought strikes me—what if I'm inadvertently setting the stage for a feud between the Quinn brothers?

❖ ❖ ❖

I check my watch for the millionth time. Tick fucking tock. I can't wait until this dinner is over. This waiting game is torture, almost on par with the time I was waiting for Deano's "mark" to show up at the hotel.

We're heading for a casual Friday night dinner at Killian's house. The story is Killian reached out to me to apologize and insisted that we attend dinner. I'm actually surprised he agreed at all, considering he thinks it's too soon. But I guess he wasn't ungentlemanly enough to put his foot down and say no when I acted offended at the mere thought of him refusing. All because I promised Killian I'd help.

A pigeon flies down in front of me on Fifth Avenue and I nearly jump out of my skin.

"Whoa, easy there, live wire. You okay?" Connor puts his hand on my back.

"Yeah, fine," I manage.

"Let's hear it. What's going on in that restless head of yours? For a pro hustler, you're bad at hiding things. Lucky for you, I was too gone to notice that night."

I force out another strained laugh. At least we can laugh about that now. "A pro? Yeah, right. That was my first and last dive into the criminal world. I'm fine, nothing's going on."

Connor's jaw tightens as if he doesn't believe me. "You don't need to do this, Lexi. We can cancel."

"No!" I say, a little too loudly. "No. Killian wants to clear the air with you. Don't ruin something nice before it even starts."

"He should have asked me himself, instead of conspiring with you behind my back," he grumbles.

"He wanted to apologize for the other night—with me stuck in the middle of your argument. Come on, Connor, it's only dinner. How bad can it be? Unless Killian's cooking is awful," I joke feebly.

I take his hand, my palm sweaty against his,

and tug him forward, toward Killian's sprawling townhouse.

All I want is for the brothers to hash it out, do the whole bro-hug routine and move past this. I'll feel relieved when everything is out in the open. It's hard being the only one carrying a secret, not knowing the right things to say or do.

Killian opens the door with a warm expression, like he's genuinely happy to see us. He gives me a kiss on the cheek then slaps Connor amicably on the back.

As we step inside, I can't help but gape at the sheer opulence. I've been to some pretty swanky places in my life, like the Met and the Guggenheim, but this townhouse puts them all to shame.

"Thanks, Lexi," Killian murmurs quietly.

I just nod and step back, not wanting Connor to catch us chatting.

"Mom." I hear Connor's voice ahead of me as Killian takes my coat. "What a nice surprise."

I enter the sprawling lounge area and stop at a dining table that could easily sit ten. My stomach flutters anxiously. I feel sick for some reason, like I've done something wrong when I haven't.

Connor's mom is clearly the source of the Quinn men's good looks. She's standing there, chatting with a knockout redhead who must be Clodagh. Like Yoda, but with a *Cl*, Connor told me. Apparently, Irish people don't believe in using their g's and h's.

"Lexi, meet my mom and Clodagh," Connor says, gesturing to the two women.

"Hi there." I beam. Oh god.

Their greetings hit me all at once. I slap on a smile, feeling like I've been thrown into the deep end. This is not how I wanted to meet Connor's mom.

"Lovely to meet you, Lexi," she says, giving me a kiss on the cheek. I wish it were under less stressful circumstances. "Connor's told us so much about you."

Oh fuck. I hope he left out the part about how we met. I don't think "she tried to steal my car" is the best first impression. "You too, Mrs. Quinn."

"Please, call me Mairead."

"I didn't know you were going to be here, Mom," Connor says. "Clodagh, I got these for you, now I look like a bad son not getting Mom any."

He hands over the bouquet of flowers, and Clodagh takes them with a grin.

"That's okay, sweetie, you can take me for dinner sometime soon." His mom winks, and now I know where he gets his charm from.

"Where's Teagan?" Connor asks.

Killian smiles smoothly but it's hard to miss the tension simmering beneath the surface. "She's at her friend's house."

Connor's brow furrows. "She's not avoiding

me, is she?"

"No, of course not," Clodagh jumps in, her smile bright as she pours us glasses of wine.

That seems to appease Connor, thankfully.

The attention turns to me as Clodagh and Mairead fuss around me.

It should be lovely, a momentous occasion. I'm meeting Connor's family, for crying out loud.

But instead of feeling all warm and fuzzy, I'm waiting for the other shoe to drop, or in this case, for Connor and Killian to start throwing punches over the canapés. I don't know what Killian's game plan is.

"I heard you stayed at our cottage in Ireland. Amazing spot, right?" Connor's mom offers me a bright smile.

"Yeah, it was absolutely incredible," I gush, shifting from foot to foot with nervous energy. "Is that where you're from?"

I can hardly detect an Irish accent, unlike Clodagh who sounds like she just stepped off the set of "*P.S. I Love You.*"

"No, I'm from Dublin." She smiles. "Maybe you and Connor will get there one day."

My smile stays frozen. Connor clears his throat awkwardly, and I can practically feel the discomfort radiating off him. This is all still a little premature in our relationship. Truth is, I would have said me being here is too soon myself if

Killian hadn't twisted my arm.

"The groundskeeper assured me that you two had a fabulous time. You got to do a bit of swimming in the wild Atlantic, yes?" His Mom smirks, and I feel my cheeks burst into flames.

My eyes widen to the size of Killian's dinner plates. Oh god.

"Yeah," I laugh nervously. I'm just going to have to own it. "When in Rome," I joke. "Or Ireland, in freezing cold conditions."

But then, something miraculous happens. Everyone starts laughing, including me. And not just polite, awkward chuckles, but real, genuine laughter. Like we're all in on some hilarious joke.

"We're going to have to sell up, Connor," his mom chides. "Eamon was a local fisherman. Very popular. The whole town was at that funeral."

This makes us laugh even harder. Connor grins at me.

Maybe this won't be so bad after all.

"Why don't we all take a seat?" Killian says. "Lunch is ready."

"It's Killian's signatory roast." Clodagh smiles. "He's been slaving away in the kitchen all evening."

I sit opposite Connor and thankfully, the atmosphere is relaxed. I can breathe easy.

Killian serves dinner, and my jaw nearly hits the floor. He must have a big oven because he comes out with enough meat to feed a small army.

We're talking lamb, beef, and turkey, like it's a medieval feast.

As we dig in, Connor's mom fires questions at me. She's got this breezy demeanor that puts me at ease, but I can tell she's trying to suss me out, to figure out if I'm worthy of her son.

They all seem like a really down-to-earth family, if you can forget that we're sitting in a multimillion-dollar house that has round-the-clock armed security surveillance.

"It's so good to see you smiling, Connor," his mom says as soon as there's a moment of silence. She grasps for his hand, diamond bracelets glinting. "We're worried about you, sweetheart."

The air is the room shifts, just a tad, but enough to make my heart race.

"Hmm? No need to worry about me," Connor dismisses with a rough edge to his voice.

"Darling, we're aware something's amiss. You can't just wall yourself off. In times like these, you need your family," she says, her voice laced with concern, but there's an underlying steel that suggests she's not going to back down easily.

Oh fuck. Oh fuck, oh fuck, oh fuck.

Connor's fork freezes halfway to his mouth. "What are you talking about, Mom?" he asks slowly—*too* slowly.

"Come on, man, enough's enough. Just tell us the truth," Killian says. "We're aware there's something you're not telling us about your health. Let us in, let us help."

Fuck, fuck, fuck. Why did he have to lead with the health thing? My throat goes dry as I swallow hard. Connor's going to put two and two together and realize Killian and I had a little chat.

Connor goes rigid, his shoulders tensing. "What 'truth' are you after?"

He puts down his knife and fork with a deliberate, almost ominous calmness, the silverware clinking against the plate.

He leans back in his chair, his eyes locked on Killian's. Blue on blue.

Suddenly, the massive dining area feels claustrophobic. I wish I could hide under the table, or better yet, disappear altogether.

I clutch my fork in a death grip, taking a bite of lamb just to have something to do, my unease growing by the second. Now I feel every bit the intruder in this excruciating family moment.

Killian's idea of an intervention is like a grenade with the pin pulled. No gentle prodding. Nope, he's taken the "health" pin out and rolled it into the room already, consequences be damned.

Why didn't I realize this would happen? Killian is no Dr. Phil when it comes to emotional intelligence.

And now, as I sit here, my heart in my throat, I'm almost positive agreeing to this dinner was a huge mistake.

"We need to tackle this head-on. Your wellbeing is our priority, not business or anything else," Killian declares, oblivious to the emotional shrapnel flying around him.

"I knew something wasn't right," his mom says. "You can't fool your own mother."

Oh god. This is the worst intervention in history.

"For fuck's sake," Connor growls, looking between them in utter disbelief, like he can't quite process what's happening. "Is this what this dinner is really about? Some kind of ambush?"

I try to nervous-eat another spoonful, but my hand is shaking so badly that a pea flies off my plate, hitting the floor with a pathetic little thud.

Connor turns his piercing gaze on me, his jaw tensing as if he's moments away from putting his fist through the wall.

"Lexi." The single word sounds like an accusation and a betrayal all wrapped up in one. His breathing is uneven, ragged, more like we're gearing up for a fight than a conversation. "You told them?"

I swallow hard. *I guess we're doing this.*

"No! I mean, not exactly," I manage to squeak out. "Everyone's just concerned about you. Maybe opening up wouldn't be the worst idea?"

He drags a hand over his jaw, his stubble

scratching audibly against his palm. "You thought it was your place to decide that for me?" he asks, his tone laced with such contempt that it sends a shiver down my spine.

Yeah, I'm scared now. Connor has this way of becoming even more imposing when he's angry.

"Ease up, this isn't on Lexi," Killian interjects, his voice sharp with annoyance. "Focus on what matters here."

"Stay out of this, Killian," Connor snaps, his eyes never leaving mine.

My face burns hot, like I've just been slapped. "But I didn't say anything! I wanted you to tell them yourself. I thought it would help," I mumble, my words stumbling over each other.

I hardly even know what I'm trying to say anymore. How did I become the villain in all of this?

"You had no damn right."

His eyes blaze with a fury that's both terrifying and heartbreaking, the full force of his anger directed solely at me now. It's even more intense than when I took his keys, a whole new level of wrath that I've never seen before.

My throat goes dry. What the hell? I'm too flustered to think straight, to figure out how I fucked up so badly and why he's so pissed at me.

"Fine. Since Lexi is so intent on this, I'll tell you—my hearing is fucked. I have an autoimmune disease." His tone is lethal. "Happy now?"

The room falls into a stunned silence.

His mom's eyes brim with concern. "Why hide this from the people who love you? We just want to help however we can."

"Because I'm handling it on my own terms," he bites out, his jaw clenched tight. "Maybe I wanted to tell you in my own time. Except Lexi thought she had the authority to fucking force this behind my back."

The disdain dripping from his voice makes me recoil in my chair. "Wait, no! That's not what—"

"I think you should leave." He glares at me.

"Connor, don't be an ass," Killian growls, interrupting his mom's chastising. "I approached Lexi."

"We'll discuss this when Lexi's leaves," Connor says.

My knife and fork hover in the air, my hands shaking so badly I'm afraid I might drop them.

"I'll walk you out." His words are clipped, his tone brooking no argument.

Is he serious? Is this really happening?

I hardly hear the others' angry words, their voices fading into the background as Connor stands up, his chair scraping harshly against the floor.

I set my knife and fork down, my cheeks burning with humiliation.

"It was nice to meet you all," I say in a low voice.

Killian gets up too, his expression pained. "Lexi, I'm so sorry about this."

"With me," Connor snaps, already striding off down the hall.

Stunned, I follow him out, feeling like I might be sick. Killian calls out another warning that Connor ignores, his voice fading into the distance as we walk away.

As soon as we're out of earshot, Connor rounds on me, his eyes blazing, every muscle in those powerful shoulders wound tight. "You really thought you could say my private shit to my family behind my damn back? You led me into this. This is why you were so adamant about making it today."

"It wasn't like that! Killian approached *me*, and all I did was agree to get you here." I fumble for the right words, trying not to piss him off more.

"You clearly told him I had health issues. You were the only person who knew." His jaw clenches visibly, the muscle jumping under his skin. "You had no right to go meddling in affairs that don't fucking concern you."

"Is it really so bad that they know?" I throw back, my desperation peaking. "They care about you, Connor. They just want to help."

"My call, not yours. You think batting those eyes at me and spending a couple of weeks together fucking gives you some sort of right?"

His words hit like a bucket of ice water, destroying any illusion of intimacy between us. I stare at him with a mix of shock and pain.

I reach for his arm but he jerks away like I've burned him, those blue eyes colder than I've ever seen them.

I feel like I'm in some twilight zone.

"I thought there was something between us. Your brother obviously did too, because he came to me."

"You shouldn't even be talking to my brother. For fuck's sake. This is exactly why I don't let women into my personal space."

He's looking at me like I'm some kind of psycho stalker. Confused and upset, I blink back tears.

"You should go," he states flatly.

Just an hour back, we were in stitches at his apartment, trying to level up his game in that one Teagan always kicks his ass at. Now he's kicking me out of his brother's house.

"I'll stick to my deal with Vicky. And I'll handle your mom's medical bills, if you let me. But that's it, Lexi, stay out of my business from now on."

I'm rooted to the spot, completely shell-shocked.

"Do you have any bags here?" he asks evenly.

My brain barely registers his question. "Yeah, just my backpack, by the couch."

"Stay put." A minute later, or maybe an hour, he returns holding my bag, his face an unreadable mask.

"Connor, please . . ." I reach for him again, desperate for the solid comfort of his frame. I know he's lashing out, but he's hotheaded—he'll come around . . .

Except he doesn't.

He steps toward me, all walls and barriers, creating an emotional distance that feels like a black hole.

With a face as hard as stone, he hands over my bag. His detached demeanor cuts deeper than any shouting match.

"I'm sure you can keep quiet about us. No NDA needed . . . right, Lexi?" he drawls.

I can't believe he's going there. His words drive the last nail into our relationship's coffin. Which apparently was nothing more than a fantasy in my head.

He opens the door, making it abundantly clear he expects me gone.

"You're actually doing this?" I rasp, barely able to speak past the lump in my throat, or maybe it's my heart. I clutch my backpack to my chest, feeling like it's the only thing holding me together.

How did we get here? How did everything go so wrong, so fast?

"I thought there was something real here," I

say in a trembling voice.

I thought I was falling in love with you.

"You thought wrong," he states flatly. "Now see yourself out. I have to deal with my family."

I swallow hard, my heart hammering in my chest.

"Fine," I say evenly, my voice steadier than I feel. "You send me out that door right now and I am never coming back, Connor. I mean it."

He narrows his eyes at me, his gaze hard and unreadable. But I don't flinch.

"Maybe I take things too far sometimes. Maybe I meddled where I shouldn't have. But I did it because I care for you, you asshole. I did it because I'm loyal."

I take a step closer, my eyes blazing into his, pouring every ounce of my hurt and heartbreak into my voice. "You know, I put up with a lot of crap every day. Vicky jerking me around at the office, Brenda hassling me for payments, my landlord refusing to repair my place, debt collectors breathing down my neck. That's my life, Connor. That's the shit I deal with on a daily basis. But you know what? I won't take crap from you. Not about us, and not about this."

I don't give him the option of deciding. I turn around and slam the door behind me.

And I mean it. This is the point of no return for me.

FORTY-TWO

Lexi

Let's get one thing straight: I've had my moments with rage.

Like when Grace got bullied in middle school by that mini sociopath Margo with her stupid Hello Kitty backpack.

Or when the school hottie called me a "freak show" over my heterochromia.

When Mom started puffing covert cigs after her diagnosis, flipping the bird at medical advice with each puff, I wanted to scream until my lungs bled.

When Vicky torpedoes my life with on a whim her absurd deadlines—torching my calendar and my sanity.

When Deano threatened Grace, sparking a kind of protective rage in me I didn't even know I had.

When the upstairs neighbors have naughty

time so loud I think they're going to come down on top of me and ask me to join in.

And then there was the time Dad died. Yeah, safe to say I was pretty pissed at the whole world about that one for a long time.

But this? This is a whole new level of rage.

Never in my twenty-six years on this earth have I felt sheer, unadulterated fury as when I storm away from that Fifth Avenue townhouse, making a beeline for the Central Park gates before I detonate.

No one has ever treated me so disgustingly as that jerk sitting up in that townhouse, probably swirling an espresso instead of, I don't know, maybe coming after me? Showing a shred of decency?

I know I screwed up and regret it deeply. But I also know my intentions were pure even if my methods were flawed.

All this drama stems from Connor hiding things in the first place. Killian was always going to confront him, with or without my involvement.

I'm so blinded by anger, I crash into what feels like a brick wall, only to snap back to reality when a gruff voice under a cap snaps, "Hey, watch it, lady!"

For a split, hopeful second my heart leaps. Is it Connor chasing after me, in some grand gesture, ready to apologize for being such a monumental asshole?

But it's not him. Of course it's not. Connor isn't coming. He's not going to chase after me, because he doesn't care. He never really did, did he? I was just a distraction, a shiny new toy for him to play with until he got bored. And when I became a nuisance, when I did something he didn't like, he ordered me out of his life.

In front of his family.

That was the most humiliating, soul-crushing moment of my life. To be treated like that, like I'm less than nothing, in front of the people he loves most in the world?

I have emotional scars.

He's still up there in that townhouse, finishing up dinner, while the Quinns make quick work of brushing any drama under their plush, expensive rug.

I hurl a halfhearted apology over my shoulder at Cap Guy and barrel through Central Park like I'm on a special ops mission, feeling my blood about to blow a gasket.

I could've hopped on a closer subway instead of stomping among the mime artists, buskers, joggers and Friday night party-goers. But I need to walk off this rage before I go full Stephen King's *Carrie* on Manhattan and telekinetically fling Connor Quinn into the Hudson.

A tear streaks down my cheek but I angrily karate-chop it away and keep marching forward.

How dare he treat me like that. Sure, he's got his bag of issues, but that doesn't give him a pass to treat me like trash, like I'm disposable. If our bridge wasn't burned before, it's up in fucking flames now.

I will never, ever forgive him for this.

"Never ever ever," I growl to myself. The joggers steer clear, giving me a wide berth.

He was a glaring red-flag button just begging to be pushed. And push I did, with all my might.

Hope is a fucking liar. It makes fools out of us.

The biggest mistake was believing there was something real between Connor and me. Because part of me did. I didn't admit it, not even to myself. I was falling in love with Connor Quinn—the good, the bad, and the broken parts.

Turns out, he's too broken, and not for the reasons he thinks. It's got less to do with his ears and more to do with the cold, dead cavity where a heart should beat.

I barely register getting on the subway, riding, getting off at my stop. It's all a numb blur.

When I stumble through the door, Grace takes one look at me and knows something's wrong. I can't even pretend. I wish I could muster the performance of a lifetime, like I did that infamous night for Deano's scam at the hotel.

Now . . . I just can't.

"Did dinner with the family not go well?" she

asks, eyes wide.

"No," I force out through clenched teeth. "It did not. Connor is a cunt." There's a musical ring to it, as if his parents, in their infinite wisdom, looked into his newborn baby eyes and thought "Ah yes, C for cunt, that's our boy."

"What happened?" Grace asks, worry lines creasing her forehead.

I should tell her the whole story after how he treated me. But I can't break his trust, even now, even after everything.

"Let's just say he acted like an entitled asshole. We won't be seeing each other anymore." My voice cracks on the last word.

Her mouth drops open dramatically.

"Don't stress," I assure, catching her panic. "It won't mess with your internship. Connor might hate me, but I think he has a soft spot for you."

"But seriously, what did he do?" she presses, her voice rising with indignation.

"I'd rather not replay the gory details. I've donated enough mind space to that guy."

Her expression crumbles for a mix of reasons. "I'm not gonna work for some jerk who messed with you!"

"Grace," I tell her, my tone dead serious, almost pleading. "You never see Connor in the office. This won't affect you. You love the people you work with and the work itself. Quitting won't even register to Connor, but it'll sure hurt you."

She grumbles unhappily but relents.

Her choice words for Connor suggest she's pegged him as the classic playboy, playing the field. The truth is so much weirder.

She stomps around the kitchen, brewing some bitter nettle concoction to "zen" me out. I'm thinking the only good those nettles would do is if they somehow find their way into Connor's Armani boxers.

I retreat to my room, needing to be alone, because I don't want my little sister to see me cry.

As the hours tick by, my rage simmers, sinking its claws in and gnawing from the inside. I'm just fucking sad and disappointed at this point.

God, I thought I was falling in love with this person. What was I thinking? No sane person jumps into a cage with a tiger not expecting to get mauled.

It wasn't just the suits and muscles and the sexy Christian Grey swagger reeling me in against my will. I was drawn to his broken pieces too. But time and again he's proved those jagged edges will slice my heart without remorse.

Deep down I guess I hoped I'd be the magical

exception. I could make a difference, be the one to finally get through his mile-high barriers. LOL. Idiotic pipe dream shared by countless ladies before me who also stupidly thought they could fix someone so damaged.

The same awful question hammers in my brain, mocking any chance of sleep. How could he treat me like this? Was I just nothing to him?

By 11 p.m., I'm still staring at the ceiling, battling the pathetic urge to text him and talk things out. Because clearly, I haven't been humiliated enough today.

But I said I was done and I meant it. There's no coming back from this. My pride would never allow it.

I fire my phone onto the table at a safe distance. It lands beside the bright-blue folder—the one I'd filled with resources I'd found about his health condition. I'd gathered information on support groups, therapies, anything that might help. I wanted to know he wasn't facing this alone.

What a fucking joke.

I might as well have been researching ways to communicate with ghosts for all the good it did.

Storming over, I shove that naive evidence of caring under old mail. Out of sight, out of mind. He doesn't deserve my help or sympathy.

He's not worth it.

◆ ◆ ◆

Four hours later, I'm still glaring daggers at my silent phone, as if my sheer willpower can magically will it to sprout legs, march itself to Connor's deluxe penthouse, and demand the groveling apology I richly deserve from that infuriating man currently sleeping sound in thousand count sheets instead of groveling desperately at my door.

I toss and turn, absolutely fuming.

Hating everything about him.

Hating that my stupid bed smells faintly of his aftershave.

Hating that there are too many pillows now, thanks to his giant blockhead requiring its own fluffy entourage. Huffing irritably, I grab one and hurl it across the room. It flops pathetically two whole feet.

Hating that he owes me the groveling of the century and isn't delivering.

Hating that I got in his stupid car that day and let him talk me into being his friend, to then be tricked into giving him my heart and my trust.

Hating that trip to Ireland, all romantic and fairy tale–like, that's nothing but a joke now.

And most of all, hating how he stared into my eyes and held my hand when we made love beside the fire, because that's what it was to me, even if it meant nothing to him. That's when he lied to me the most. With his fucking eyes. Making me believe I was special.

Now I know he bails at the first sign of something not going his way.

I deserve better than this.

The Quinn brothers are just arrogant bullies. I should have known better. I thought I was smarter than this.

I was mistaken.

No one, especially not Connor Quinn, will ever make me feel this way again.

Dragging my zombie ass out of bed, I stumble into the shower after another sleepless night. It's been two nights since Connor kicked me out of Killian's house. I thought I might feel a bit less shitty by now, but the pain is still as raw and fresh as ever. This has been such a horrible weekend, each minute dragging by.

Whoever spewed that crap about "things looking brighter by morning" clearly never had their heart mangled by an emotionless motherfucker who flips feelings off like a light switch.

So I hit the pavement to rage-run it off, stomping twenty blocks and trying to torch this anger and heartache from my cells.

In my head, I chew Connor out a dozen different ways. Verbally rip him to shreds with enough attitude and pissed-off monologues to make any grown dude bawl.

My make-believe world has him begging on his knees for mercy, spilling his guts on why he's such a dirtbag while I stand over him spitting fiery wrath like some scorned goddess of wrath.

"Come on angel," I mock in an exaggerated husky voice as I stomp down the sidewalk. "I know I'm an absolute jerk. But please, let me kiss your feet as I beg you to love me again!"

"You heartless dirtbag," I loudly proclaim to my imaginary groveling Connor. "Take your BS apologies and shove them right up your—oh, excuse me, sir!"

I quickly sidestep the alarmed businessman staring at me mid-expletive. Great, now I'm the lady ranting to herself on the street.

In his family's defense, all three of them—Killian, his mom, and Clodagh—got my number and messaged me to apologize. Which was sweet. It's nice to know that at least some members of the Quinn clan have a shred of human decency.

But every single time that stupid phone beeped, my traitorous heart skipped a beat too, thinking it was him.

"Fancy delivery for you," Grace calls out distractedly as I enter the apartment, her voice muffled by the sounds of her video game.

Despite my better judgment, my heart makes a hopeful leap. Connor trying to make amends?

As if. It's probably just some package for our neighbors who use our place as their personal post box.

I find Grace sprawled on the couch in her *Big Bang Theory* pj's and try not to look disapprovingly at her. It's past noon, Sunday or not.

But then I spot the delivery—a pricy-looking blue box, my name elegantly scrawled across it in gold cursive. No address.

My stomach flip flops uncomfortably. I don't know how to feel.

It only took him two whole fucking days. And now he's trying to make up for it with some flashy apology gift? As if throwing money at me will fix everything. The sheer arrogance of it makes my blood boil. He can't just buy my forgiveness and expect everything to be okay. He should be here groveling in person, begging for a chance to make it right.

I manage to keep my emotions under wraps, sneaking a glance at Grace who's too engrossed in her video game to notice anything awry.

The box looks so expensive, I'm almost

intimidated to open it. But it doesn't matter what it is.

"Who dropped this off?" I ask casually, wondering if Connor hand-delivered it.

"Some guy," she responds without tearing her eyes away from the screen, her fingers flying over the controller.

Super helpful, sis. Glad we cleared that up.

Better open alone in case it's something wildly inappropriate like racy lingerie. I swear, if he goes for cheeky charm instead of begging for mercy, I'll personally shove that smug gift right up his inconsiderate ass.

I hate the hopeful spark in my chest as I retreat to my room. No purchase on earth could smooth over his blunder.

My heart's going a mile a minute as I wrestle with the annoyingly stubborn lid.

And then, I see it.

A . . . sweater?

I blink, my brow furrowing as I lift the soft knit from its tissue paper nest. It's cute, sure, but hardly says *Please forgive me for being the world's biggest asshole*.

Hold up . . .

Confusion washes over me. My smile locks in place, icy and unmoving.

Could Connor have nailed my style so precisely he picked something identical to what I already own?

I shake my head, smile fading. No, something feels off. Flipping the sweater over, I notice a small stain on the hem.

My stomach drops.

This is *my* sweater. The one I left at his place.

This isn't some heartfelt, make-it-all-better present. It's not a peace offering or an olive branch.

It's a breakup package.

A clear-out. Of me.

Unfolding it further makes a note flutter to the ground. I grab it up.

Mr. Quinn requested these items be returned to you.

Signed with formal detachment by his housekeeper.

Another piece of fabric spills onto my bed.

My shawl! From that crazy night at the hotel when I swiped Connor's car keys. More damning evidence that we were doomed from the start.

"What the actual hell . . ." I hiss, my voice thick with unshed tears.

He hung on to this scrap of lace since that night without mentioning it? Just to suddenly dump it on my doorstep out of spite?

I crumple the note, tears stinging. The message couldn't be clearer if he'd stabbed me in the heart.

And he didn't even deliver it himself.

Even when we're done, he's still finding ways to hurt me.

FORTY-THREE

Connor

I flag the bartender for another Macallan, barely denting the first.

What the hell am I doing here? Chasing the good old days before everything went to shit?

I haven't been back here since Lexi's little hustle. Damn, it feels like both yesterday and a lifetime ago.

My doc's been on my case about keeping the stress levels low, but after that disaster of a dinner party at Killian's last week, even the small stuff's enough to set me off.

If I could have sat in an ice bath all fucking day, I would have. Only, that would have been the end of me, so I hit the streets instead. But I had to stop because my symptoms flared up and that really got to me. I reached out to my new doctor right away. The break did nothing for me. My irritation levels have been sky-high.

Case in point, the blond bombshell easing onto the stool next to mine. I vaguely remember feeding her some slick lines on the same night Lexi and I found our way into each other's arms in those bathrooms.

Now I've got zero patience for flirtation.

"Hey, Connor," she purrs, flashing a smile that I guess is meant to knock me dead. "Feels like forever since I've seen you. You holding up okay after things ended with Willow?" Her hand finds my arm, making itself at home. "I was so sorry to hear about you two."

It hits me then that she's sitting in the same stool where Lexi sat that night—where she sized me up and plotted how she could steal my keys. I can still see it crystal clear in my mind thanks to the damn security footage.

Maybe that's what drags me back here—chasing after some semblance of control. To scrub away her memory and spill out this pent-up rage into something, someone forgettable. To erase that night and start from scratch.

I muster the most unenthusiastic hello in history, keeping it clipped.

On any other night, I might've leaned into the distraction. But tonight, I'm my own enemy.

No women for me right now. Not even for a quick fuck. Too much drama, too much baggage.

Killian was right. I should have gone to Ireland

alone. Maybe then I wouldn't be feeling like this.

Even my apartment is still haunted with remnants of Lexi. I had to physically box up stuff she had left and get my housekeeper to send it to her, but I swear I can still hear her laugh, smell her perfume . . . she's everywhere—the bed, the bath, the goddamn couch. Might just move at this point.

"I'll join you for a drink," the blond decides, commandeering my Macallan and immediately regretting it, pretending not to grimace as she takes a sip.

I reclaim my glass, my jaw set hard. "I'd prefer to drink alone," I state flatly, leaving no room for debate.

She arches an eyebrow, clearly miffed, but forces a smile. "Fine, enjoy."

I catch a muttered "Jerk" as she walks off.

Tell me something I don't know.

The click-clack of heels has me bracing for another round of unwelcome advances. But then I catch a familiar floral scent wafting toward me.

"Ah hell," I mutter under my breath, recognizing that perfume anywhere.

I turn to see my mother gliding gracefully onto the now-vacant barstool, looking as elegant as ever.

"Mom," I say, the irritation melting into a reluctant smile. I haven't seen her since I left Killian's house.

"Connor," she replies curtly, dropping her designer purse on the bar with a decisive thump.

Hardly a moment passes before some old geezer at the bar has the balls to shoot her a sly wink, olive paused halfway to his mouth.

It takes monumental restraint not giving in to the primal urge to grab that leering letch by his ankles and forcibly eject him from the premises.

The gut reaction of any son worth his salt. Nobody eyes up my mother in front of me. But she takes no notice, unruffled as ever.

"Who'd you send to tail me? Cameron?" I ask wryly.

Cameron's the security guy ensuring she's protected. Can't be too careful.

"I don't need Cameron to track you down. You think I don't know my own son? A mother's intuition is like GPS," she says with a smile. Right. And Cameron just happens to be enjoying the ambiance of our lobby right now.

Ignoring my skeptical head tilt, she turns to the bartender and orders her drink. "Extra dry gin martini, sweetie. Whenever you're ready."

"Of course, Mrs. Quinn," the bartender replies, clearly charmed.

Mom's still got it, apparently. She hasn't aged a day in two decades—a dangerous topic to ever bring up.

"Why do I get the feeling I'm about to get

chewed out?" I grumble, leaning against the bar. "Reminds me of those nights sneaking into clubs with a fake ID, only for you to drag me out by my ear."

Mom gives me that look, the one that says she's put up with enough bullshit from me over the years. "You're never too old for a talking-to from your mother. Especially when she's worried about you."

I tap the coaster impatiently on the counter and lower my voice. "There's no need for you to be worried. I know what needs to be done now. I'm fronting a research department for this damn condition. And maybe I'll even give those support groups a try. You know, where everyone sits around, spills their guts to total strangers."

I attempt a smirk, trying to lighten the mood, but the words feel like I'm just throwing in the towel, admitting defeat to some unbeatable foe. Still, I push through, trying to sound more confident than I feel, hoping to ease her concerns.

She shakes her head. "Connor, I'm not just worried about your hearing, even though that's on my mind too. We'll tackle that challenge together, as a family. You're tough, I know that. But right now, you're being stubborn. You've got this, like you always do with any curveball life throws at you." She pauses to give me a sharp look. "What's really got me worried is the kind of person you're turning into. I didn't bring you up to treat a woman the way you did Alexa."

The moment she mentions Lexi, my back goes up. "Lexi isn't my girlfriend, she had no business interfering—"

"I don't want to hear it," Mom snaps in that unyielding voice that's had me toeing the line since I was a kid. "There's no excuse for how you acted."

That hits hard, right where it hurts. Looks like I'm on a winning streak of messing up with every woman in my life right now. Nothing quite like a maternal reality check to remind me I'm basically navigating life like an arrogant asshole.

"Believe it or not, I showed her the door with all the grace I could muster," I shoot back, irritation lacing my words.

Mom gives me a pointed look. "Really, Connor? Kicking her out in the middle of dinner was your idea of being a gentleman? Need I remind you, honey, that you can be a little intimidating."

"Lexi crossed a line, airing out my private stuff," I say with a rough edge. Lexi had no damn right. Not at all. And sure, I'm not laying it all on her—I'm livid with Killian for thinking that was a good move in front of Mom and Clodagh. But Lexi's involvement got under my skin the most.

Mom's lips press into a thin line, her disappointment hitting me like a wave. "Please.

You know your brother. Killian bulldozes through any subtlety when he's got his mind set on something. I have no doubt he railroaded Lexi into that. And no woman deserves the cruelty you showed her, even if she has quite a few sins of her own, from what I've heard."

I clench my jaw. "Sins?"

"She stole your car, didn't she? Bold move."

"Killian told you everything, huh? No secrets in this family, I guess."

Mom's comeback is swift. "Excuse me for wanting to stay informed about whether my son's girlfriend is potential in-law material."

I can't help but let out a sarcastic chuckle. "Dial it back, Mom. Lexi's neither a future in-law nor a Bonnie to my Clyde."

Her comeback is dry. "She did have a certain charm, though I'll be keeping an eye on the valuables next time she's around."

What the hell is she talking about? "Lexi's not some con artist. She's genuinely sweet and kind. You've met her, for crying out loud. How can you even question that?"

Mom arches an eyebrow. "But she did swipe your car. Seems she's got you pretty twisted up, especially now, with everything you're dealing with. Watch yourself, Connor."

"She's not like that. She made one mistake after being in a shitty situation. And let me tell you, she's got higher morals than anyone I know. She's taking care of her little sister and her mom all by herself. I offered to foot the bill for the medical costs, and she shot me down flat."

"Ah." Mom pauses, and I can almost hear the cogs turning in her head.

Now I see what's really going on.

"She sounds like a keeper," she remarks, a knowing smirk playing on her lips.

"Well played, Mom. Smooth."

She's pulling a move straight out of her old playbook. The one she always used on me and Killian when we were kids. I'd storm in, fuming about Killian hogging his games or ditching me for his older pals. Before I knew it, I'd be standing there, defending him till I was out of breath. Mom's tactics are slicker than Houdini on his best day.

She's grinning like she's already won the round. "So, after your passionate defense, you're really going to tell me you don't owe that girl an apology?"

I can't help but let out a frustrated sigh. This roundabout is endless. A thirty-five-year-old man being scolded by his ma. Some things never change. "You know what, you're right, I was a little out of line. I might've been harsher than Lexi deserved."

She beams at this. "Why don't you invite her over again? Let's make up for that disaster of a dinner."

I take another rough swallow of whiskey. "Not happening. I might owe her an apology, but ending things was the right move."

"Oh, Connor." Disappointment creases her face. "Are you that afraid of letting someone in? Take a look at Killian, all settled and content. Life's tough, you know. You've been bending it to your will, but it's not always going to bend back. In the tough times, having someone there, someone who loves you, that's what counts."

She hesitates, then hits me with a curveball. "I even wondered if you might be gay."

I shoot her a look. "You know I'm not."

"It's just . . . you've never looked at women as anything more than arm candy. But Lexi . . . she's gotten to you, and maybe that's not the worst thing in the world."

"She crossed a line," I retort, my anger flaring.

"Uh-huh," she replies, her lips pressing into a thin line. "And yet, here you are, gripping that glass until your knuckles turn white every time we mention her name. Maybe the very thing you're running from, the thing you're too stubborn to face, is exactly the thing that you should be paying attention to."

"Enough, Mom. I'm not in the mood."

"If you're lucky, she might still forgive you," she says, clinging to a sliver of hope she doesn't try to hide.

"Just drop it," I demand, finishing off my drink. "Lexi and I are done. That's the end of this conversation." Dwelling on the past is a waste of time.

I exhale heavily, catching the concerned look on Mom's face.

What was I thinking? Pulling Lexi into my world, inviting her to a family dinner? Now, it's like open season for everyone to pry into my affairs. This mess happened because I broke my usual rules and it blew up in my face.

Lexi thought she had the right to make calls about my life, and that's not how it works. No one —absolutely no one—gets to make decisions for me. Not Lexi, nobody. That's why she got hurt.

I know she's a good person, and I know she came from a good place. But my tolerance for people overstepping is low. This was never going to work out.

I'm no expert in love, but I understand business. Some guys get a kick out of stretching negotiations, playing mind games, flexing their power to make the other guy sweat. That's not my style. I don't mess around with people. If something's not working, I cut it off cleanly, move forward, and hunt down the next opportunity, ensuring freedom for the other party to do the same.

I owed Lexi that level of straightforwardness. Ending it wasn't the mistake—it was inevitable, a disaster waiting to happen. However, the manner in which I did it? That was off-mark. Lexi deserves better than that.

◆ ◆ ◆

I down my daily dose of steroids along with a protein-packed breakfast. Damn, this pill regimen sucks and it's not even effective half the time. The thing about my condition is that there's no long-term solution—one treatment might work wonders for six months, then taper off and become useless. And when that happens, you climb up another rung on the ladder of scary drugs with even more side effects.

I dial Lexi's number, figuring I'll have to ring her up a dozen times before she'd even think about answering.

But instead, I get nothing—just a constant busy signal.

I stride down to the IT team on the sixth, my eyes landing on some young guy lost in his oversized headphones. "Hey," I say.

The kid damn near launches himself through the ceiling. Do I really come off that intimidating?

"Sir! Uh—how can I assist you, Mr. Quinn?"

I shoot him a look that says *relax*. "Got a question I need IT expertise for. Let's say, hypothetically, a phone number's giving nothing but busy signals. Could that be someone riding the subway, out of reach, or is it a straight-up block?"

He furrows his brow, deep in thought. "Well, it kind of depends on the carrier. There's a distinct busy signal when you're blocked—more rapid, never lets up. It's pretty rare that it's just the network glitching, especially with the major providers." He shoots me a worried look. "Should we be looking into this, sir?"

Huh. So she's blocked me.

"It's fine," I say, already turning to leave.

I've had some time to cool down and reflect. Realized I may have handled things poorly in the heat of anger. Now it's time to own up and apologize for the way I showed her the door. Yeah, I could've kept my head cooler. I respect Lexi enough to see that. The things I said though? I'm not walking any of that back.

But the woman has blocked me. And I'm not about to show up at her doorstep or ambush her at work.

Seeing as I'm already making rounds on the IT floor, might as well take a shot at a different angle. And this way, the ball's in Lexi court.

I stroll over to the Web Development

department. The manager spots me and heads over. "Just need a sec with Grace," I tell him, then quickly add, "It's not about work," when I see the concern flash across his face. "I'm on her cousin's rugby team," I lie, internally rolling my eyes at myself. Now I'm getting creative with my excuses, Lexi-style.

Grace is zeroed in on her computer screen, clearly excited about whatever's going on there. Today, she's traded her usual quirky tees for a button-up that says *I have an adult job.*

I can't help but crack a grin at the sight.

Grace's expression flips completely when she spots me, looking like she just got caught by her dad at a party in front of all her friends. After the manager murmurs something to her, her shock turns from *caught red-handed* to *full-on panic mode.*

But she steels herself and meets me out in the hallway.

Seeing her up close, it strikes me—she's got Lexi's sweet button nose. The resemblance throws me for a loop and suddenly, I'm adjusting my tie, feeling unexpectedly out of place in front of the young intern.

"Hello, Mr. Quinn," she greets me, her tone overly formal.

"Grace, it's Connor. You don't have to stand on ceremony with me."

"I think I'll stick to Mr. Quinn."

"All right, if that's what makes you comfortable. First off, I want to assure you that your job here is secure. Your boss thinks I'm here to deliver some message to a 'cousin' of yours from my rugby team."

She gives me a suspicious nod.

"I need a favor," I tell her. "Could you pass on a message to your sister to call me?"

"Nope." Her voice takes on a protective edge. "She's done with you after the way things ended."

Looks like the little sister's picked up a thing or two about loyalty from Lexi. She's sticking to her guns, but she might rethink that stance once she's had a chance to cool down. She'll learn soon enough working with us that business isn't a place for emotions.

Lexi may think I'm an asshole, but there's nothing Grace could say to me to get her fired. It's fucking ironic that she might be the only one in this whole goddamn company with immunity.

"Look, Grace, I don't have time for games. Can you just pass along the message?"

Her gaze narrows. "I said no. Leave my sister alone."

Well, that's a first. Didn't expect to get sass from a college intern half my size.

I raise an eyebrow at her defiance. Same fire and attitude as her older sister. One of the few people who can stand up to me.

I exhale, trying to crank back my irritation. "Fine. I'll take it that even if you say you won't, you'll let Lexi know I'm trying to apologize."

She presses her lips together. "Is that all? I'm actually quite busy."

A laugh escapes me, despite myself. "Yeah, that's all."

Gonna miss this one, I realize with a tinge of sadness.

◆ ◆ ◆

"They're ready and waiting for you, boss," our events manager says, smiling.

I force an easy grin. "Looking forward to it," I reply before striding into the buzzing conference hall.

Today's a big day for our interns, their chance to shine in front of the company's veterans, showcasing their hard work and potential. We even encourage them to bring their families along, so long as their projects are on the right side of classified.

Events like this are my thing—I'm the charming, approachable face of the company, the guy who makes everyone feel at ease behind the cold corporate exterior. Supposedly. At least when my damn health cooperates.

There's a buzz of excitement mixed with nerves in the hall, especially from the interns up front. Can't blame the kids for looking anxious. The cavernous hall and theater seating is enough to intimidate anyone, whether they're new to the game or seasoned pros.

But they've got no reason to sweat. We only take the best. Some of these newbies even manage to steal the spotlight from our more seasoned staff, who might've gotten a bit too cozy in their roles.

My eyes find Grace among them, nerves betraying her as she fidgets with notecards. She's speaking today—to 300 people. It'll be the biggest crowd of her young career.

It's been a fortnight since we last crossed paths —no reason to.

My presence probably adds an extra layer of pressure. I doubt she's thrilled about it. But working with people you dislike is part of the job. She'll have to get used to it. Plenty can't stand their boss.

My jaw clenches as I make my way to the stage, fully aware that Lexi's out there in the crowd. She'd show, putting her love for her sister above her disdain for me.

I don't know why it fucking bothers me so much, but I'd lay down serious cash that Lexi will be glaring holes through me with those stunning eyes of hers the whole damn speech.

This is my first time hitting the stage at a big event since that godforsaken interview. Thank fuck there's no Q&A today—I say my piece then let the interns take the spotlight.

Following Killian's ridiculous intervention, my hearing's been out of whack, but I'm on some new experimental meds now.

I've been laying low, aiming for solid nights' sleep, and even ran a half marathon last Saturday to clear my head.

Need to find some way to calm this relentless mind.

Telling the family has been a mixed bag. Just like I figured, it's turned into everyone's pet project. Can't have a damn conversation without it being front and center.

Killian's been playing doctor now, throwing money at whatever he thinks will help. He's pushing for me to take a long break, kick back and relax, but I'm not having any of it.

Clodagh's been dropping by for coffee, probably checking I haven't spiraled into some wild bender, surrounded by champagne and hookers.

Mom's on my case nonstop, ringing me daily and harassing me with links to all sorts of witch-doctor stuff. Apparently, there's some guy in Ireland who can chant away my hearing problems with ancient Gaelic magic. Because that's exactly what modern medicine was missing.

And Teagan, she's taken to yelling, making damn sure I've caught every word she says.

I stride onto the stage and launch into my intro for the teams. Piece of cake compared to my day-to-day. Just spotlighting a bunch of eager twenty-one-year-olds.

"At Quinn and Wolfe, we empower young talent because you represent the future of this company," I project with ease. "I'm eager to see the effort you've poured into these projects. So, let's cut right to the chase . . ."

That's when I catch sight of Lexi in the crowd, her eyes spearing me like missiles. I freeze, momentarily knocked off balance under that withering glare. Yeah, she fucking hates me.

I've dealt with my share of cold looks and judgment in presentations. Occupational hazard. But damn, this really stops me in my tracks.

I muster a cough and barrel through the sudden knot in my throat, my usual eagerness to command the stage replaced by a sudden rush to escape it.

"Let's give a warm welcome to the future of Quinn and Wolfe." My signature grin is strained at best by the time I wrap up my stint and pass the torch to the interns. Their eager applause offers me a brief reprieve as I make a strategic exit.

From the wings, I pretend to focus on the presentations, yet my attention is hijacked by Lexi.

She doesn't glance my way again, her attention seemingly riveted on the young hopefuls parading their dreams across the stage.

I find myself scanning her, taking in the sight of her dark hair as it flows over her shoulders and that tight red dress that accentuates her figure. She looks stunning—perhaps making a statement, showing me exactly what I'm missing out on.

Good for her. Good for standing her ground in my territory, looking like a million bucks.

This is my chance to apologize. Now that Grace has wrapped up her presentation, Lexi will probably want to leave as soon as possible, especially to get away from me. But I'm not going to act childish and ignore her in my own conference hall.

As I approach, her body language screams she's acutely aware of me drawing near. Her spine straightens, shoulders bracing as if she's gearing up for a confrontation.

"Lexi," I interject through the buzz of conversation, pulling her focus away from Grace.

I turn to her sister, forcing a smile that feels more like a grimace. "Excellent work today, Grace. You should be proud. You really shone out there."

Grace gives me this nod, like she's not sure whether to thank me or slap me. "Thank you, Mr. Quinn," she replies, her tone clipped.

I shift my focus to Lexi, taking a step back to

avoid the sweet scent of her. "Got a minute?"

Her gaze hardens, annoyance crossing her face. But with Grace and her colleagues watching, she can't exactly tell me to go to hell. "One minute," she spits out.

I nod toward the hallway. "Follow me."

I lead her away from prying eyes and curious ears, acutely aware of the tension radiating off her in waves. This isn't a conversation for staff ears.

Once we're alone in an empty office, I turn to face her.

"Everything good with you?" I ask, though her folded arms and rigid posture scream otherwise.

"Better than ever," she fires back, tone icy. "What do you want, Connor?"

I clear my throat, the gritty sound loud in the tense quiet. Best get this over with. "Look, I regret how we left things. Asking you to leave that dinner was completely out of line. I'm not proud of it. I was a bad-tempered asshole and I owe you an apology. You deserve better than that."

She stares at me, caught off guard. Then her chin quivers, just a fraction, before she locks it down. "I told you, the second I walked out that door was the last time we'd ever speak. I have no interest in ever seeing you again."

A muscle in my jaw ticks, irritation flaring. I came here to make peace, dammit, but she's clearly uninterested, and it pisses me off more than I'll admit. "I'm trying to apologize here. I never should have taken things out on you like that. It was unfair and cruel, and I'm sorry. I'm not out to cause you more pain, I swear. Come on, Lexi. Can we please just be amicable?"

Her glare cuts through me, loaded with a venom I never thought her capable of. "*Amicable*? Are you fucking kidding me? You made me feel like crap by telling me to suck your cock in my own office for my freedom. Dangled my sister's future like a carrot, dragged me through your damn power plays. You turned me into your emotional punching bag whenever your issues flared up. You only wanted me around when it suited you, then pushed me away the moment you felt like you might lose control."

Her anger spills out, a torrent of emotions, a clear sign of how much she resents me. "So no, don't 'come on, Lexi' me."

My jaw clenches, molars grinding. "Seems you can't find a single redeeming quality in me."

"The little good there got buried by all the bad," she fires back, pain flashing through the anger. "But I do appreciate you not taking it out on Grace. She's happy here, and I don't want anything to jeopardize that. Just never speak to me again, please."

I give her a short, jerky nod. "Understood. Take care of yourself, Lexi."

She turns on her heel, heading back to the crowd in the conference hall.

My chest tightens. Lexi deserves to get her happiness. Even now, in our tense reunion, she's putting others first, worrying about her sister's well-being.

I hope she finds a man who can give her everything she needs. Everything she deserves.

But that man won't be me.

FORTY-FOUR

Lexi

I slide into my least sexy sweatpants and collapse onto the couch, balancing my laptop on my knees. Right next to me, there's a mug of what Grace calls her calming tea, sporting floaties that look a whole lot like backyard soil.

With a sigh, I open the files on our latest PR headache—a woman who became internet-famous for claiming she could see dead people on flights. Now she wants to rebrand as a wellness guru. Because that's the natural progression, obviously.

Just the mention of planes sends me hurtling back to that trip I've worked to repress. Ireland is now on my list of places ruined by association, all courtesy of one monumental jerk.

But you know what? Drowning in Vicky's work avalanche is a blessing in disguise. Keeps my mind from fixating on . . . everything.

Sometimes I'm deep into work, and BAM—this question just explodes in my brain: what the actual fuck was it all about?

Flying me out to Ireland, all the lovey-dovey acts, and then bam, dumped. He got under my skin, into my life. Mom knew about Ireland, so did Grace . . . Does he think my life is a fucking joke he can mess around with, coming in and out of it on a whim?

I forcefully slam those thoughts back into the mental lockbox labeled DO NOT OPEN.

These past couple of weeks since running into Connor at the intern presentations have been like living in a bubble of . . . calm. That's the perfect word for it.

The pain of running into him again was intense, and maybe the finality of that moment hit hard. We were both terse and definitive in our interaction. Dismissive of one another.

I broke down crying after seeing him . . . a lot. Ugly crying. The kind of sobs where your breathing is stuttered, you have snot all over your cheeks, your abs hurt like you've done a core class and you're exhausted just from the sheer physical exertion of all the body-shaking sobs. That type of crying.

But now everything's fine. Totally fine. We're all fucking fine.

Zero jerks in my life. Zero dating bullshit.

No more getting emotionally suckerpunched by deep blue eyes.

No more of my stomach flipping every time he smiles at me, like I'm the only girl in the world for him.

No more dealing with his moody tantrums or fucked-up mind games.

Single life is easy and drama-free. My time, my heart, my energy are all mine again, not at the mercy of Connor fucking Quinn's moody ass.

He's fading into a memory, right where he belongs. A mistake.

And the sleeping pills at least help me sleep through the nightmarish dreams. I know I can't depend on them forever, but I just need a bit more time because I hate waking up in the middle of the night feeling . . . sad.

Maybe someday, when I've settled down with a nice, normal guy, I'll tell him about my chaotic fling with the temperamental billionaire, and we'll laugh over what a bullet I dodged.

For now, I'm proud of myself for being strong and doing right by me for once. Connor Quinn is firmly in the rearview where he belongs.

I attack a stubborn pistachio shell, muttering, "C'mon, you little bastard. Open already."

The thing finally cracks open and goes flying from my hand, hitting the wall with a *smack*. Like it's giving me a "fuck you." A chip of paint flutters down, and I swear to god, I'm close to screaming.

Out of nowhere, an actual scream sounds from the bathroom, making me jump.

"What the hell?" I yell, heart racing as I imagine some horror scene with Grace facing off against Norman Bates. More likely, she's encountered a stray pube in the drain.

I rush the vast two-step distance to the bathroom. "Gracie, are you okay?"

"Oh my god!" she shrieks loudly from the other side of the door.

"What is it?" I demand, bracing for carnage.

"I got a job offer from Quinn & Wolfe," she screams. "Can you even believe it?"

My heart does this weird leap—not the good kind. It's ridiculous because she interns there. This is hardly a surprise.

Of course I'm happy for her. Statistically, only around 40 percent of interns land a job offer with them, but I knew she'd be one of the chosen ones. She worked so hard.

But hearing his name out of the blue still brings a sting of hurt. Time will continue to dull the pain . . . I hope.

"That's amazing, Grace," I manage to yell back, summoning every ounce of supportive sister I have in me.

I even manage a genuine smile, thinking of Dad's worn-out joke. Anytime "Amazing Grace" was mentioned, he'd launch into his own rendition. "... *how sweet my girl is*," he'd croon, then grin like he just nailed a stand-up set at the Comedy Cellar. It was equal parts endearing and cringeworthy.

"But obviously, I'm not gonna take it," she hollers. "Just wanted to see if I could do it."

"Sure," I say, playing along. She'll take it; I'll make sure of it. Even if I have to drag her to the office myself. "We can talk after you're done with your bath." And after I've had a stiff drink.

Grace is making a racket in the bath, likely trying to handle her phone with soapy hands. I'm mentally preparing to refuse another phone bailout. "Don't drop your phone in there," I holler, preempting the inevitable tech rescue mission.

"Yes, Mom," she quips.

Seriously?

"Let's get drinks to celebrate," I suggest, trying to be the cool sister. "But watch the bath, will you? Make sure it isn't too full."

"Yeah, yeah," she dismisses, probably with a soapy wave I can't see.

I'm starting to feel like the grumpy old caretaker of the house, always on her case. But if that bath water gets higher than the overflow drain, it's less "splashy bath time fun" and more "apologies and gift baskets to the downstairs crew." My diploma from YouTube's School of

Plumbing is definitely being put to the test.

Dragging myself back to my laptop, I'm ready to plow through work.

That is, until Sunnyhill decides to steal my breath with an email subject line that reads like a horror movie title:

Sunnyhill Care Facility Payment Update.

I hesitantly click, my trepidation morphing into outrage. Rates rising another 5 freaking percent in six months?! My blood pressure is skyrocketing by 500 percent right *now*.

Five percent might as well be a million. It's too much.

My chest tightens like icy hands have gripped my ribs and are pushing inward. Maybe the ghost of the vengeful plumber.

As I'm mentally drafting a venomous email, another shriek blasts from the bathroom.

"Lexi!"

What now? How many monumental discoveries can one have in a bathroom? Did she find the entrance to Narnia behind the toilet?

"The toilet," she yells.

Oh, brilliant.

I sprint back to the bathroom, and she bursts out the door, towel-clad, gesturing wildly at our new water feature.

The bathroom floor is a dirty water runway,

courtesy of our now-overflowing toilet. It's like a shit geyser.

"It overflowed," Grace states, as if it weren't glaringly obvious. "I flushed, and it just exploded back at me."

So, here we are. My life, in perfect sync with our plumbing: a complete, unadulterated shitshow.

◆ ◆ ◆

"Be honest—is my butt perkier?" Abigail asks, doing a little twirl in front of my desk. "Butt Buildr says to do a hundred donkey kicks a day, but I tapped out at fifty because I was bored out of my mind."

I tear my eyes away from the campaign I'm editing about the I-see-dead-people-on-a-plane woman, just in time to catch Abigail trying to channel her inner Nicki Minaj.

"Uh, yeah, definitely perkier," I say, trying to sound like I know what a perky butt looks like at nine a.m. on a Wednesday.

Over at her desk, Kayla is trying hard not to spit out her coffee from laughing.

"I'm going for the full Kardashian," Abigail elaborates, because clearly, I looked interested.

Never have I been more grateful for an

interruption than when Vicky strides by.

I jump up, following her down the aisle. She's been dodging my meeting requests for days. Time to pin her down.

"Hey, Vicky, got a minute?" I call out, hurrying to catch up. "Now that we've landed Quinn & Wolfe Hotels, I was hoping we could chat about my salary—"

She whirls around, one eyebrow arching sky-high. "Right, but we also lost Willow's account, didn't we?"

She's got me there, but still, I've worked my ass off for her, for years.

I feel my face catch fire with humiliation. "Connor's deal dwarfs anything Willow brought in.

Vicky smirks. "Oh we're on a first name basis now? Tell me, how cozy have you gotten with our latest star client?"

I blink, taken aback.

Her eyes gleam with undisguised triumph.

"Figured as much," she drawls, her voice dripping with sarcasm. "For someone supposedly so morally upright, you certainly use your assets well landing clients."

She just had to say it loud enough for the whole office to hear.

The place goes library-quiet, as though someone hit the mute button on life. Keyboards freeze mid-clack, phones suddenly become less interesting.

Abigail can't resist; she lets out an *ooh* that practically bounces off the walls,

I make a conscious effort not to make eye contact with anyone.

"No judgment, Lexi. Snag those clients by whatever means necessary. Just don't ruffle the feathers of their better halves, particularly if they're also cutting our checks."

My irritation spikes. "That relationship was fake, Vicky."

She gives me a *tsk*. "Well, Willow was still upset. Never mind, she'll forget you now that Connor's been seen cozying up to that hot new professor in town."

Professor? My stomach plummets as I struggle to keep my face straight.

This is the last place I wanted to hear about Connor moving on, surrounded by coworkers whose eyes bore into me, searching for a reaction.

I dig my fingernails into my palms. Truth is, I've banned myself from searching anything related to Connor.

"Anyway," Vicky breezes on, oblivious to my internal crisis. "I'll try to smooth things over with her. Oh, and by the way, Jenny's leaving. You'll do the handover this week."

I blink, her words barely cutting through the

thick Connor haze. "Why?"

"You're going to be taking on her workload from now on." She says it with such a light, airy tone, you'd think she was asking if I'd mind looking after her half-dead houseplants over the weekend.

She's got to be kidding. She expects me to handle the jobs of three people now?

Vicky pirouettes away, clearly done with this chat without even waiting for a response. Her heels click loudly through the tense silence.

Oh no she didn't. She can't just drop that kind of news and strut away.

"Vicky," I call out, pulse racing.

Ignoring me, she continues on her march, her ass swaying. That's it, I'm not going down without a fight.

"I'm not taking on Jenny's workload without a raise!" I yell out.

That snaps Vicky around with a death glare. "Excuse me?"

"You're excused," I toss back, willing my wobbly knees to stand strong. I'll be damned if I let her see me wobble.

Her mouth drops open as if I've just grown a second head.

We stare each other down. I swallow hard, pulse rocketing. The tension is so thick, you'd think we were two duelists in a western showdown, ready to draw our weapons.

"Just go and talk to Jenny," she finally spits out.

"You know what? I will talk to Jenny," I fire back, feeling oddly detached, like I'm watching myself from outside my body. "Maybe we can plan a joint farewell bash. Because I quit."

The words spill out before I can stop them. My brain screams *What did you just say?*

This might be my most epic mic drop ever, but oh god, it's terrifying. Blood rushes to my ears.

I don't have another job waiting. No Plan B. Just maxed out credit cards and debt up the wazoo.

I feel nauseous.

But staring at Vicky's sheer disbelief, something clicks. Forget the impending financial crisis; this is about self-respect. I can't work under this woman anymore.

I have to leave Vallure before I have no soul left at all.

Holy shit I'm actually doing this. Moonwalking right out.

My hands quiver faintly before I gather them into fists at my side. I hope no one notices.

The tension is knife-thick. All eyes are on us.

Vicky is floored. Speechless for once. And I want the final word.

I turn on my heel and walk away, feeling every gaze burning into my back.

I swear I can feel the silent cheers and rounds

of applause from my colleagues, a silent chorus of support—or maybe they're just thrilled to have some live drama to break up the monotony of the day.

Either way, I'm out.

FORTY-FIVE

Lexi

Obviously I had to come back.

Quitting your job isn't the mic-drop moment movies make it out to be when you're shackled by a notice period. I grabbed a coffee to gather my wits and then headed back to my desk.

I'm one week into my notice period at Vallure, which is just fabulous, considering Vicky's on a personal crusade to make each day as miserable as possible.

Now three interviews down and it's clear— Vallure PR is the skunk of the PR world. Just drop the name and watch people physically recoil as if they've just smelled something rotten. By now, HR's across the city are probably using my résumé as part of their morning comedy routine.

I'm doing a stellar job of pretending I'm not on the brink of a meltdown because I've quit without a backup plan. Panicking is off the table, so I've shoved that ball of anxiety into the deepest, darkest part of my psyche, right next to my dreams of ever finishing that psych course.

I haven't broken the news to Mom about quitting yet. I filled Grace in though, and had to slap on a smile despite her look of total alarm.

Grace peeks out from her room just as I'm kicking off my pointy heels, each one leaving a blister—trophies from the interview circuit.

"How'd it go?" she asks, eyes wide with sisterly concern. "Think you have a shot?"

"Maybe," I mutter, sinking into the couch. "They weren't exactly fans of Vallure." Talk about an understatement.

She plops down next to me, her face all scrunched up in worry. "Then they're missing out. You're the hardest worker I know. Any company would be lucky to have you. You're like a creativity ninja!"

A reluctant smile tugs at my lips. "You're biologically required to say that, but I'll take it. I'll take any compliment I can get at this point."

Grace scrubs at a hopeless stain on our coffee table, brows furrowed in concentration.

Then she stops, hitting me with that look—the kind that's either about to unveil some grand life plan or debate the merits of ordering General Tso's chicken again. With Grace, it's always a coin toss.

"So, about what Mom was talking about,

moving to Baltimore . . . hear me out. It's not the end of the world. They've opened up a NexiHub there, and I can transfer my final classes. My internship's done, and I've only got a few months of school left anyway. Plus, they have Taco Bell," she adds, like fast-food is a key factor in life decisions.

I stare at her, floored. "You can't be serious."

She just shrugs. "I'm kinda getting on board with it. You know the FBI's main office is there? I might land a job in their IT department! I could be like Penelope Garcia from *Criminal Minds*."

Her optimism makes me smile despite it all.

"Gracie," I start, voice catching. She's actually considering this crazy plan, for my sake. She has an amazing job offer from a prestigious company that will be gold dust on her CV. But here she is, ready to leave it all for some Taco Bell and a long shot at the FBI. That's real sister love.

I'm supposed to be protecting her, not the other way around. This role reversal guts me.

Tears betray me, rolling down my cheeks. I swipe at them angrily, pissed at my own vulnerability. "You're too kind, Gracie, trying to make things easier for me. But I'm the one who's supposed to be taking care of us. You're still in college, for crying out loud."

She scoots closer, giving my leg a comforting nudge. "That's total BS, and you know it. We're family; we got each other's backs, always. I'm not a kid anymore. Plus, think of all the hot feds we could meet in Baltimore."

She keeps nudging me until I let out a small, tearful laugh.

"We can't leave New York. You've got your job with Quinn & Wolfe lined up. It's a once in a lifetime opportunity, and I'm not letting you pass it up."

But she stands her ground with the same stubborn determination that once made her refuse to eat anything but Lucky Charms for a month. "There'll be other chances, sis."

The tears start flowing faster. Suddenly, the weight of everything I've been carrying hits me like a ton of bricks.

For so long, I've shouldered everything—the bills, taking care of Mom, being there for Grace. As the older sister, I convinced myself it was my responsibility to be the rock, the one who always had her shit together.

But here's Grace, considering flipping her whole world upside down just to make my load a bit lighter. And I've got to admit, there's a part of me that's embarrassingly relieved she's willing to throw her plans out the window to help me out.

Seems like Connor isn't the only one who's been building walls around himself.

The irony is that Connor would be the ideal

person to talk through my issues with. He's strong, logical, steady. Sometimes, you just need a solid rock to lean on. In Ireland, I felt like I had that, if only for a brief moment. He gave me that sense of security, then pulled it away.

I take a deep breath. But I realize, I do have a strong person to face this with. Grace.

◆ ◆ ◆

"Night, Grace," I call as she heads to bed.

I shift my laptop onto my knee, bracing myself. Time to rip off the Band-Aid and search Connor's new "professor" hookup. I've waited six days, but I'm ready now. Or at least as ready as I'll ever be. Better to see them together on my own terms than be blindsided by some glossy magazine pic while checking out at the grocery store.

The first one's gonna hurt like a bitch, and there'll be many more where that came from.

My fingers feel like they're made of lead as I type his name into the search bar, bracing myself for the flood of results. And boy do they come pouring in like salt on an open wound.

I was naive to think I was ready. It fucking hurts.

There he is—arm draped casually over a bar chair, cozied up with Miss Professor herself. The picture of ease.

The imaginary bandage over my wounded heart rips right off, taking a little bit of my bloody heart with it.

She's almost a mirror image of me, but somehow more polished, more . . . everything. Her name's Clarissa Miller, a shining star professor at Columbia. Beautiful, brilliant, and making waves. Girlfriend material. No, scratch that—wife material.

"You idiot," I whisper to myself as my heart cracks a little more. Seeing them together stings, even though it was inevitable. Even though I hate him with every fiber of my being. Even though a part of me is relieved I'll never have to see his stupid, perfect face again.

Bet he's already taken Professor Perfect back to his place. Shown her his ice baths where he probably bathes in the tears of the women he's hurt. His big bed where he sleeps like a baby after crushing hearts. And don't forget his bath, where he washes away the stench of his sins. He's probably even introduced her to his stupid Scrabble board.

Because professors are just so trustworthy, right? If he let me in, she probably already has a key made.

I bet he wouldn't dare send her packing in front of his mom, wouldn't dream of humiliating her the way he did me.

I hope he treats her better than that. Maybe she'll get the caring Connor I glimpsed in Ireland. She deserves that much.

But so do I.

A lump forms in my throat that I stubbornly swallow down. Refusing to let him win.

"Don't you dare cry over him," I sternly tell myself, even as my eyes start to water. "He's not worth shedding another tear over."

Everyone knows the old saying *No man is worth your tears, and those who are will never make you cry.*

No one seems to know where it came from, but it's practically the unofficial slogan for women who've been let down. Moms all over the world say it to their daughters, a futile attempt to shield them from the inevitable heartbreak that comes with falling in love with a complete and utter bastard.

But knowing that doesn't seem to keep the tears from spilling anyway.

FORTY-SIX

Lexi

"Why do you want to leave New York, Lexi?" Aaron asks, leaning back casually in his chair like he's about to offer me a beer instead of a job.

The question feels like a pinprick to the heart. Thinking about it too much threatens to unravel me.

Aaron, founding partner here at Ascend PR, exudes a laid-back vibe that instantly puts me at ease—a refreshing change from Vicky.

He's rocking jeans and a tee, tattoos peeking from rolled-up sleeves. He looks more like a hipster barista than a CEO. I'm probably the most overdressed person here. As Aaron explained, their dress code is casual except for client meetings.

This is the first interview in ages that's actually intrigued me—aside from the fact that it's located in Ellicott City, Maryland, which is about as close to New York as Mars. Okay, slight exaggeration since it's around five hours door to door. But realistically, I won't be zipping back to NYC often.

Just thinking about it stirs a pang in my chest. If Grace comes with me, like she says she wants to, there's nothing left for me in New York. I'll have zero reason to go back, save from visiting Kayla and my school friends who I never had time to see anyway.

I decide to just lay it out straight to Aaron—I'm done with lies and bullshit. "My mom might need to move into a nearby care facility, and I want to be there for her. Plus I'm over the city rat race. It grinds you down after a while."

Certain people have ground me down, that's for sure.

Aaron chuckles knowingly. "I did my New York time before starting Ascend here." He smiles. "It sounds like a solid work-life balance could really benefit you."

He nods out toward the open-plan office space where the team is working, or at least pretending to work. "The crew here get the job done without compromising real life too. You're welcome to chat with them to get a feel for the culture around here."

I peer out at the Laughing Happy People. "I'd love to meet the team, thanks."

"And you know, we've got some awesome hiking trails right by the Patapsco Valley State

Park, not to mention all the cool parks and natural spots nearby," he continues, "if that's your thing at all."

It feels like he's trying to sell me the position. Maybe I've got a real shot at this job.

A flicker of excitement stirs in me, a little beacon of hope in the dark journey of my job hunt. "That sounds perfect. I've missed the outdoors."

"You'll have time for hobbies here, that's for sure. Life's way more laid-back. It's got its pros and cons, but you're less likely to hit burnout."

I can see the good points already, even though the thought of leaving New York still makes me break out in hives. Even though I hyperventilated on the train ride here. The thought of a slower pace surprisingly appeals to me now.

Looking through the glass walls of the interview room, Ascend's office feels like a different universe. It's styled like a chic, modern warehouse with warm woods, plants everywhere, and the aroma of gourmet coffee in the air. People are actually laughing and chatting, enjoying themselves. Like they're in a commercial for job satisfaction. I know I'm seeing it through rose-tinted glasses because Aaron is nice compared to Vicky, but I can't help it. Sometimes you just get a vibe for a place.

I try to envision what my new life here could be. Easier, for sure.

A few plants and fancy coffee won't solve everything, but it's a start. I might be less anxious and wound up. Despite my panic earlier, hope flares now.

It's conveniently near the care home Mom proposed in her plan. I could easily visit her if needed—a huge weight off my shoulders.

"You'll love it here if you can handle a slightly slower pace," Aaron says warmly. "I know the PR firms in New York are more glamorous. We keep things pretty low-key and grounded here. But we really take care of our people." His eyes glint playfully. "And our famous Thursday night happy hours liven things up."

Pleasant possibilities unfold in my mind. PR Lead for their healthcare division could be amazing—no more peddling D-list celebs and their butts. I'd be working on stuff that actually matters, like hospital campaigns and mental health initiatives. Suddenly, I'm excited.

Maybe a slower pace is exactly what I need—somewhere my mind isn't constantly racing with stress and worry. A place where my heart doesn't tighten up thinking I might run into Connor around every corner.

I'd have more cash in my pocket, time on my hands, and maybe, just maybe, some peace of mind.

And living out here chops expenses by nearly

half. Plus, the care homes won't require me to sell my liver on eBay, which is always a bonus.

It makes sense.

It's not New York, though.

It's not home.

Though what is home, really? Home is where you feel content. Where you have the luxury of appreciating the world around you with the people you love and, most importantly, the people who love you back.

Home is a feeling, a vibe, not a place pinned on a map. It's where your heart finds peace. Where you can breathe and just be you.

I smile at Aaron, hoping he doesn't detect the sadness underneath. "It sounds like exactly what I'm looking for."

And it does. It really does.

A few days later

Grace lights up when I break the news—I landed the job in Baltimore.

She bubbles over with excitement. "When do we start packing? I'll start looking up jobs and—"

I inhale, bracing myself for the bomb I'm about to drop. "We don't."

Her brows knot in confusion.

For the first time ever, I'm actually nervous to

talk to Grace. Because of what I have to say next.

"I'm moving alone. You're staying here."

Her confusion turns to shock. "What? No! I'm coming with you!"

"No, Grace. You're not. You have an amazing opportunity in New York. I won't let you give that up. Not for me, for Mom, for anyone."

It's tough, watching her process this. Grace has grown up; she's not the little sister I used to watch over every moment. She's a woman now, strong, competent, and capable, even if she doesn't know how to use a washing machine without shrinking clothes.

We've never done the whole living separately thing. Our relationship has always been the classic big sister/little sister deal, and honestly, I wouldn't have had it any other way. But if I don't loosen our bond just a little, we're going to end up as those eccentric old ladies living together forever, with me nagging an eighty-year-old Grace about leaving puddles on the bathroom floor.

So, for the first time in our lives, we're taking separate paths. It's time to face a world where we don't have to sacrifice for each other, where we're both standing on our own two feet as adults. And that time is now.

Her face falls. She huffs sharply, emotion creasing her face. "We won't even be in the same city?" Hearing the hurt in her voice twists my heart, like I'm betraying her in the worst possible way.

I give her a gentle nudge, trying to ignore the tightness in my chest. "Come on, I'll just be a phone call away. Not disappearing off the face of the earth. But this is your chance to chase your dreams on your own."

She takes it in with a wobbly lip.

"Hey, it'll be fine. Whenever you need me, I'll come running, even if I have to hitchhike or steal a car."

Well, maybe not steal a car.

I hold her shoulders, forcing a smile even as tears threaten to spill down my cheeks. "Take the job at Quinn & Wolfe, Gracie. Connor swore he'd steer clear, and he's honored that. They're even throwing in a place to stay for new interns. This is your moment, amazing Gracie."

I smile, even as Grace's tears fall.

I always knew she would conquer New York in ways I never could. But I did one thing right— being the best big sister I could be.

I made sure Grace had all the opportunities I didn't have. And I'm proud of that. I'm proud of her.

She's going to soar at Quinn & Wolfe. She'll show them what she's made of.

Even though it feels like losing a limb, I know it's the right decision.

She wipes away angry tears. "I give you a year max before you settle down with some boring teacher in gray slacks, obsessing over your garden."

I laugh through my own sheen of tears. "Doubtful. I'm not heading to a retirement community. I might actually get to have some fun for a change."

She rolls her wet eyes at me. "Yeah, right. Ellicott City's idea of a wild night is probably playing Scrabble at the community center and being in bed by nine."

Just the mention of Scrabble sends a pang through my heart. Ridiculous, I know. Pathetic, even.

Ellicott City might not be the city that never sleeps, but it's a fresh start. A place devoid of Connors, Brendas, Vickys, and Deanos—and free from the ghosts of plumbing past. I'll take quiet over drama any day.

I know it won't be a fairy tale. But I found a cute house—yes, an actual fucking house with a yard and everything. A place where I won't have to perform a full-on bicep workout just to get the toilet to flush. I know; I tested it.

And for the first time in a long time, I feel . . . content.

It's a different kind of happy, one that doesn't come with dizzying highs and devastating lows.

Just a smooth ride. And it's really nice.

I've done what I needed to do in this city, and now it's time for me to move on. To start a new chapter in a new place. Someday, maybe I'll come back when I've made something of my career, when I can live in the city on my terms. But right now, New York isn't the place for me.

Grace wraps me in a fierce hug as we both cry.

"I'm so proud of you," I whisper, my voice cracking with emotion.

And I mean it more than anything else in my life.

My amazing Gracie.

FORTY-SEVEN

Three Months Later

Lexi

The birds are going all out, serenading us as the sun plays peek-a-boo through the pines, casting a glow over the trail.

Grace is visiting for the weekend, joining my Saturday morning ritual—hitting the Patapsco Valley State Park with the local hiking group my boss Aaron recommended.

I take a lungful of that spring zing—the kind that's petal-fresh and smog-free, making you thrilled to be alive. It's so nice to swap out cab honks and subway rumbles for actual, real-life bird tweets. In New York, even the pigeons have that stressed city-hustle energy, like they're late for a meeting with the mayor or something.

The air has that hint of Maryland humidity, but I'm all-in for the kind of sweat that only Mother Nature can induce, rather than the insomnia-induced sweat sessions you get at three a.m., stressing over stuff or people.

It's nice to have that deep-down happy feeling of just *being.*

Two months have flown by since I made the big move to Ellicott City. On paper at least, the skyscraper-sized problems from my New York days have shrunk down to more manageable, suburban-sized issues.

Mom's loving her new place, a care home that doesn't require a Wall Street salary. She's made more friends than me, ironically. And the manager is far less uptight than Brenda.

And I've made some new pals at work and at the hiking club—I'm going for quality over quantity.

For the first time in forever, I'm actually saving money and chipping away at debt. And sometimes, just to feel like I'm living on the edge, I go out for avocado toast for breakfast.

Grace is back in New York, making her way in the world. She's living in a cramped apartment with roommates but she's enjoying it. She's maturing, thriving at her job, and making a life for herself. I'm proud of her.

The move wasn't without its growing pains. Getting used to life without her around took some time. Sunday mornings were especially tough. But you know what? Now I'm totally fine flying solo.

I'm comfortable and happy in my own company, even if I sometimes talk to my houseplants.

And my PR role for Ascend proves more fulfilling than cleaning up after naughty celebs. I'm constantly finding myself smiling at my screen, totally unprovoked—that's new.

The health companies and topics we deal with are a breath of fresh air compared to dealing with divas claiming they can communicate with the spirit world mid-flight.

I actually look forward to work—sometimes I have to remind myself to log off at night. We've got deadlines and some can be brutal, but at least they're not dictated by the whims of someone who thinks mood swings are a valid management strategy. Aaron even threw me a little welcome BBQ, which was sweet.

I started a psych class at the community college, dipping my toe into figuring out this next chapter. I'm only twenty-six. No need to have it all mapped out yet. People reinvent themselves at forty or fifty all the time. Just look at Vera Wang. She was a figure skater before she became a fashion designer.

The neighborhood's got a suburban vibe but still keeps me connected to city life. I bought a cheap car since getting around here without one is a drag. Walking and public transport aren't the area's strong suits, sadly. Coming from New

York where everything was a subway away, it's an adjustment.

Grace shifts her fanny pack filled with Snickers into a comfier spot. "So peaceful out here," she sighs happily, swigging her water.

"Sure is," I chime back with a grin.

The word *peaceful* hangs sweetly between us as we meander on. Fits my life now—calm, smooth, predictable. No more dramatic pendulum swings, just a gentle coast.

Which is exactly what I craved when I hopped into Deano's car, driven by the kind of desperation that only comes from needing cash by any means necessary.

My soul feels like it's healing. And my heart has a protective bubble wrap layer of numbness because there's nothing or no one getting through to poke at the tender bits anymore.

Memories that dare pop up are quickly shoved back down into their mental box, stamped with a big red DANGER—DO NOT OPEN. They're long gone, hundreds of miles away in the city that never sleeps.

But sometimes the universe tests my newfound tranquility, throwing up images of him wearing that tux and that heart-stopping grin at some gala or function. And when that happens, the floodgates open. Emotions and memories spill in, before I wrestle them back in the box.

And sure, there are moments when I catch myself wondering about him. If his hearing's gotten worse and how he's coping. If he's in a meaningful relationship with the professor lady. But that's none of my business.

"Gorgeous out today, right?" Tom flashes me a grin. The sun's beaming down like a spotlight on his biceps, making them shimmer as he takes a swig from his water bottle.

Tom, the buff schoolteacher, is the only blip on my romantic radar these days.

Since joining the hiking group, I've gotten to know him a bit better. From what I can tell he's sweet, brainy, and refreshingly straightforward. Though, for all I know, he could be a Norman Bates in disguise, but so far, so good.

"It's great," I say. "I haven't tried this trail before. I love that we switch it up. I'd never tackle all these routes on my own."

"Yeah, this way you don't have to worry about the planning. Just kick back and enjoy the hike," he agrees. "No brainpower necessary."

"I bet you hardly find a moment to yourself at work with twenty kids all vying for your attention," I remark.

"You got that right. Sometimes I sneak off to eat my lunch in the supply closet just for a few minutes of quiet from the small humans' endless questions."

I smile. He's funny.

As the trail bends and begins to rise, I feel the burn in my glutes. There's something satisfying about going to bed physically exhausted from a hike instead of mentally drained from work.

"Hey, I was wondering," Tom says casually. "You got any plans tonight?"

My brow lifts. He's asking me on a date? "Grace and I booked that new Turkish restaurant everyone's raving about."

His face drops a notch, disappointment washing over it. "Ah, that's cool."

Cue Grace, subtlety of a foghorn. "You know, I'd rather we hit the Turkish joint tomorrow," she declares, volume cranked high. "I feel like sitting in. Lexi's night is wide open."

"Grace, you're visiting. I can't just ditch you."

"Maybe I *want* to read a book in the bath for hours."

My eyes can't roll hard enough.

She throws Tom a look that might as well be a flashing neon sign: *Ball's in Your Court, Buddy*.

I might strangle her for this.

Heat creeps into my cheeks.

"Fancy a drink then, Lexi?" Tom asks with an easy grin.

"Yeah, sure, I could do a quick one," I say, still catching my breath from the hike—and maybe the whole situation. If he's into this sweaty, makeup-free mess in front of him, then I'm counting it as a pretty big compliment.

Grabbing a drink with him sounds really nice.

Who knows, maybe Grace was on to something with her whole "you'll shack up with a teacher" prediction. This could be step one. It's nice. He's nice. I might actually shave my legs for it.

"We could catch a movie too if you get bored with me," Tom jokes. "New *Fast and Furious* is out, if you're into that."

I momentarily stiffen. Absolutely fucking not.

Blaming Vin Diesel for triggering flashbacks of Deano and Connor isn't rational, but tell that to my heart.

Unwanted memories and feelings bubble up, threatening to spoil the moment, that I quickly tamp down.

Memories threatening to escape their mind box.

Memories potent enough to send me into an ugly-crying session if I let them take hold.

"Maybe," I toss back, keeping it breezy. No need to come across as too fussy by dismissing the idea outright. I don't want him to think I'm some kind of movie snob.

My first date with a nice guy. Here's to fresh starts.

"Are you happy now, Lexi?" Grace probes as we wrap up the hike, her eyes scanning my face.

"Absolutely!" I respond, a bit too enthusiastically, maybe. "That route was killer, in the best way."

She hums that sound, the one that says she's buying it, but just barely.

And it's true—I am happy. Content at least.

The kind of 'content' that almost lets you sleep through the night, without jolting awake in a cold sweat, haunted by the ghosts of relationships past.

Almost.

It's a relief walking into Mom's care home without feeling like I'll be picked apart by a vulture.

Today we manage a slow stroll around the garden, with her leaning hard on her walker.

Just as she decisively drops into the wheelchair we brought "just in case," my phone buzzes. No caller ID.

My stomach lurches stupidly for a second before I answer. "Hello?"

"Lexi?" An all-too-familiar nasal sound rings out instead.

"Vicky?" My voice comes out a mix of horror and fascination. It's the devil wearing Prada, on the phone.

"How arrrrre youuuu?" she purrs with faux warmth. My bullshit meter starts beeping like crazy.

Suspicious is the truest answer because Vicky showing concern isn't something ever seen before. If I were on fire, she'd probably demand I finish some report for her before I stopped, dropped, and rolled.

"I'm great, how are you?" I reply evenly.

"Marvelous," she drawls, "Listen, I've got a little proposition for you."

Oh here we go. My Spidey-senses start tingling. "Uh-huh."

"How about coming back to your old job?" she sing-songs.

"No," I reply before she can even finish.

Vicky makes an irritated noise. "I'll give you a 20 percent raise. And free drinks at Vexo."

Tempting, if I was a masochist. "Sorry, Vicky, I'm not interested."

"Twenty-five percent. Final offer."

My head automatically starts shaking. "Nope, still a no-go. I'm all set with my new job.

"Fifty percent," she blurts out, desperation creeping into her tone. "You're practically robbing me, Lexi. People would kill for this."

My brow lifts. Christ, this is one hell of a hike. "Why do you think I deserve it now when you wouldn't give me a raise when I worked there?"

"Oh Lexi," she coos. "Don't throw away the opportunity of a lifetime."

I almost burst out laughing. "Hmm, I'm okay."

"I'll double your salary," she shouts.

"What?" I say slowly.

"Double," she repeats, and I swear I can hear her grinding her teeth.

I'm baffled. "What's the catch?"

"We just . . . need you."

As if.

"You lost Quinn & Wolfe, didn't you?" Silence. Bingo. "Vicky, I wouldn't be able to get the account back. I haven't spoken to Connor since I left." I swallow the painful lump. I hate even saying his name.

"Just consider it," she pleads, desperation oozing through the phone.

I let Vicky grovel a bit, savoring it more than I should, before ending the call.

For a dangerous moment, I let my mind wander to some alternate reality where I say yes to Vicky's offer and return to New York.

Somewhere in New York, a guy I try so hard not to think about is living his glamorous life.

Maybe at this precise moment, he's sharing a meal with his brainiac professor girlfriend, clinking glasses over some overpriced wine. Or perhaps they're indulging in a romantic soak in a tub made for two, her never-ending limbs all tangled up around him.

Maybe, he's introducing her to his mom,

showing her the respect he never quite managed to give me. Maybe he's taken her to Ireland, to that little cottage by the sea where he stared into her eyes and held her hand while he made love to her. Maybe he's telling her all the things he never quite managed to say to me.

And that's okay. Really, it is. Because we were never meant to be, Connor and I.

And I'm living my life too. Meeting normal guys like Tom who don't leave me an emotional wreck. We shared a sweet, solidly decent kiss after our date. Here's to the straightforward Toms of the world.

Men like Connor are too broken, too damaged to ever truly be happy. They expect the world to bend to their whims, never hearing the word no.

Not even buckets of money could get me working for Vicky again. I can already feel my soul trying to leave my body for entertaining the notion. She can keep her raise—I'll keep my peace of mind.

Still, it's weird she's making this last-ditch effort to get me back. Vicky knows I have zero sway with Connor now. She must be up against the wall.

"Everything okay, Lexi?" Mom's voice pulls me back.

"Vicky asked me to take my old job back," I tell her with a frown.

"Because you're so fabulous at what you do,"

Mom says, patting my hand loyally. "What did you say?"

"No, obviously," I reply quickly, the words tumbling out of my mouth before I can think about them.

Mom hums, a sound that's trying to be neutral but failing miserably.

We walk on in silence.

"Are you happy Lexi?" she asks softly.

I blink, surprised. "Yes, of course. I love my new job."

Why does everyone keep asking if I'm happy? I even told Mom about my nice date with Tom, about how he seems lovely and uncomplicated and exactly what I need right now.

I've got a great job, a cozy house, a work-life balance. It's perfect, exactly what I always wanted.

Right?

◆ ◆ ◆

As I scroll through the virtual lineup of rescue dogs, I'm bombarded with cuteness. How do you even choose one when every pair of puppy eyes is begging to be taken home?

I need to figure out what kind of furry roommate would vibe with my lifestyle. A pocket-sized, yappy chihuahua that could double as a fashion accessory? A noble sheepdog with more hair than sense? A refined greyhound, all class and long legs? That's not going to work in this house. Or perhaps a bulldog, with a face only a mother could love?

I eye my couch critically. It won't do well with dog hair. A switch to a leather one might be in the cards if I'm going to commit to this dog mom life.

This is going to be a challenge. Adopting a dog isn't just about the cuddles—it's a full-time commitment. But I have time now, which is priceless. Well, not quite priceless, but man, what a difference.

After work tomorrow I'll head to the shelter, if they're open. Maybe I'll even skip team drinks on Thursday for once. Decisions, decisions.

An email from Kayla interrupts my doggy daydream. She's summoning me back to New York to see her.

I smile scanning it, warmth rushing over me. I miss her so much—video calls just aren't the same.

Guess what, we lost the Quinn & Wolfe account!!!!

No shocker there based on Vicky's recent groveling.

And then, the plot thickens:

And the new company that snagged it? Get this, the owner is Vicky's Ex! She is LIVID.

She drops a link to the company's site, and curiosity gets the better of me. I click to see who would have the guts or insanity to have a relationship with Vicky—perhaps the lovechild of Hannibal Lecter and Satan.

Instead I'm greeted by a guy who looks too meek to say "boo" to a goose. Shy and nerdy, and not what I was expecting for Vicky at all.

As I scroll through their site, I stiffen like I've just been tasered.

There, in full defiance of my attempts to forget, is the face that keeps clawing its way back into my thoughts, dreams, and nightmares.

Their latest golden boy client, the one and only Connor Quinn.

My heart races, betraying the cool indifference I've worked hard on for months. I grip the laptop tighter, body instinctively leaning in like a moth drawn to a very dangerous flame.

"After all this time, you still affect me," I whisper sadly to my empty lounge. Talking to myself has become the norm.

When will looking at his picture stop hurting? Yeah, the pain's dulled—it's not the sharp stabbing sting it used to be. But god, I wish I could feel nothing at all.

Breathing deep, I click further, like I'm asking for heartache.

Instant regret, served up raw.

There they are—Connor and the professor, looking like they've stepped out of a magazine, all poised and perfect in the *Hello, New York* studio. Another couple's interview, but it's clear as day there's nothing staged about this. This is exactly where Connor wants to be.

This is the real deal, folks. Their genuine connection is on display for all to see.

My throat tightens, and the sensible part of me screams to just shut it down, close the tab and walk away. Watch that new true crime show on Netflix instead. At least the murderers on there can't break your heart.

But somehow I can't make my stubborn fingers obey.

He looks happy and relaxed, flashing an easy grin I haven't seen since Ireland. The familiar tension still lingers in his jaw if you know what to look for. But otherwise, he resembles his cool and confident public persona.

"Let's all remember not to take things at face value," Lucia says to the camera. "We're so quick to judge without really understanding what someone is going through." Her smile seems a bit too breezy for the heavy stuff she's saying.

I squint at the screen, totally lost. What the hell is she talking about?

Connor's grin spreads effortlessly across his

face. "Not offering an explanation probably wasn't my best move, letting everyone jump to their own conclusions. The paparazzi love to think the worst of me, and let's be honest, I've given them plenty of material over the years."

He chuckles, almost self-deprecatingly, drawing amused smiles from both women.

"And instead, you were silently struggling with a new hearing condition," Lucia coos, reaching to put a well-manicured hand over Connor's. "Do you want to talk about it, Connor?"

I suck in a breath. Connor's talking about his condition on national television? In front of the whole country?

"Not particularly," he says, chuckling it off, but there's a tightness around his eyes. "I'm not the kind of guy to air things like this. But when you're in my position, you have a responsibility to raise awareness about these kinds of things. There are a lot of people out there without the resources and support I have. An issue like this can be pretty isolating without the right help."

Lucia looks like she might swoon, eyes glimmering. "You're so brave to share this to us," she gushes.

Connor's jaw clenches for just a moment, revealing the sheer determination it takes for him to open up like that.

I'm frozen, my eyes glued to the screen without

blinking.

"Now, what's this revolutionary project you two are leading?" Lucia asks.

I hit pause, needing a second to emotionally regroup after Connor's unexpected oversharing. I consider pouring some wine.

But instead, I head over to the kitchen table, figuring maybe a new view will help me digest the shocker we just got on screen.

Deep breath in, I hit play once more.

"I've partnered with Columbia to fund some groundbreaking research into hearing loss," Connor reveals. "The team there is doing incredible work mapping out the mechanisms behind various auditory issues. The discoveries they're making could be game-changing."

There's a determined grit in his voice that makes my stomach flutter.

"But it's not just about funding scientists to push the envelope. I'm making sure we turn these discoveries into treatments that people can actually use. We're rolling out programs to get hearing aids and medical care to folks who don't have access, offering huge discounts or even free of charge when it's needed. I want to make real change here."

As he talks about the program, there's real fire in his eyes. He downplays it stoically, but I can tell how much the cause means to him.

"And the brilliant Professor Miller here is the genius driving all the research," he adds, grinning at her with unrestrained admiration.

The way he looks at her, as if she's behind every great thing in his world, as if she's the answer to every question he's ever had, makes my chest tighten. I hear a few faint pops in the protective bubble wrap around my heart.

They make quite the philanthropic power couple . . . if they are a couple. And not just charity collaborators. But who am I kidding? The chemistry between them is palpable.

I find myself glancing away, checking the sad state of my herb garden through the window. The basil's dead. It makes me want to cry, I tried so hard with it. Some things just aren't meant to thrive, I guess.

When I glance back at the screen, Connor and the stunning professor are bantering so easily, so effortlessly, that I hit pause, unsure if I can stomach more.

Despite the deep ache in my chest, I realize part of me is actually happy for him.

All this time, I've avoided thinking about him, pushed him out of my life and my heart. Yet he's still managed to find his way into my thoughts.

Is he drinking and partying? Is he alone? Is he isolated, pushing everyone away like he did with me? When I lay awake some nights and think about how he pushed me away, how he pushed his family away, I imagine his condition making matters worse.

I even wonder, pathetically, if he ever thinks of me anymore. If he's ever regretted how we fell apart or thought about what we could have been.

But seeing him now, I know he's not suffering at all. He looks fantastic—happy, relaxed, fulfilled.

He's making a real impact, leading the charge in this field. Using his power and privilege for positivity.

And I'm glad for him, I truly am.

Even as the tears stream down my face, even as the sobs break free from my throat, I'm happy for him.

I always knew he had the potential to step up and take ownership. This person was always in there, ready to connect with others.

I thought I was an idiot for holding on to that hope and seeing that potential. For believing in him.

And in fact, I wasn't an idiot at all. I was right. It was there all along, just waiting for someone to unlock it.

It's just that I wasn't the one to do it.

FORTY-EIGHT

Lexi

I'm on my way to my third date with Tom when Grace calls. When she asks me if I want to attend the glamorous Quinn & Wolfe annual summer party as her plus-one, my reaction is "Seriously, Grace? You're joking, right?"

"But there's free champagne," she practically shouts over the phone.

I can't help but roll my eyes. That eternal college mindset, still hanging on even though she has a job now. I guess it sticks with you for a while.

"No way, Grace. Not even for a lifetime supply of champagne."

"Awww."

I crack a smile. "But I'll come visit you that weekend. There's discounted train tickets. I'm due to meet Kayla too. So we can hang out during the day, and I'll see Kayla in the evening."

God. I'm not looking forward to sharing

Grace's bed. She'll be snoring those champagne bubbles back out, no doubt. She's such a bad snorer; gets it from Dad. Thank god I got the non-snoring gene from Mom.

And she's a kicker. But I sure as hell am not splurging on a hotel. I'd rather risk bruises than pay those exorbitant New York prices.

"Okay." Grace perks up.

My stomach does a weird flip. I'm heading back to the city for the first time in months, and I'm buzzing about it. I've missed it, strangely enough.

But then there's this gnawing feeling.

The nights Connor has invaded my thoughts, despite how hard I tried to drive him out with a mental pitchfork, I'd wonder what he was doing. Where he was.

When I'm in the city next, I'll have a pin on his exact location.

I swallow the lump in my throat. Well, at least I know exactly where to avoid.

Connor

I stand in front of the full-length mirror trying to get my bow tie straight, but my eyes keep getting drawn back to her silhouette framed by the city lights.

She's a vision in that tight black leather dress

that clings to every curve, her dark waves falling over her bare shoulders in a way that sends a sharp pang right through me.

She catches me staring in the reflection. She turns and gives me this hesitant, knowing smile. "Everything okay?" she asks softly.

I jerk my gaze away, fumbling with the tie again, trying to get my head on straight. "Yeah, I'm fine. Just gonna be a long night of small talk."

I watch her move from the window, those deep blue eyes looking concerned. She stops right by me. "I don't mind coming with you to the staff party, for support," she offers.

I turn to her, letting out a rough chuckle. "Thanks, but between all the meet-and-greets, I won't get two seconds with you. It'll be me doing the rounds for hours with the staff. You'd be bored out of your mind."

The Quinn & Wolfe ball is starting in thirty, meaning I'm in for four hours of nothing but chitchat with the staff. Which is great for me, but not a guest I bring. Even Clodagh knows better not to expect any one-on-one time with Killian tonight.

She steps closer and reaches up to straighten my bow tie. "You sure you're all right? You seem distracted," she murmurs, searching my face.

I clear my throat. "Just beat."

"Oh Connor." She smiles sadly at me as she

finishes my bowtie. "I can see your loneliness, even when you try so hard to bury it behind that charming grin. I know you well. It's okay to need people sometimes."

Before I can object, her lips are on mine, soft but insistent. Her hands slide around my neck, pulling me closer.

I tense up, totally thrown. I clench my jaw, holding her wrists gently to stop her. "Clarissa, wait." I let out a harsh breath. "Damn. I'm sorry if I gave you the wrong idea, but I don't feel that way about you."

Her eyebrows shoot up, all surprise and confusion. "Oh god, did I misread everything?" She laughs, but it's strained, and she's blushing from embarrassment. "This is mortifying."

I tilt her chin up firmly, forcing eye contact. "Hey. Don't go there. You're fucking incredible, Clarissa. Brilliant, gorgeous, the whole package. You gotta know how much I value our friendship. But I'm not in the market for romance. Not at all right now."

She studies my face, searching. "Not interested in general? Or just not with me?"

I give her an apologetic smile, feeling like a jerk. "General disinterest in romance these days."

"Connor, I've felt your eyes on me all night."

"Sorry. I didn't mean to. It's that dress." I swallow hard. "You remind me of someone." I step back, releasing a heavy sigh.

She holds my gaze, then offers a melancholic smile. "I thought I was good at reading signals. Guess I missed the mark this time."

"I'm really sorry. Last thing I want is to fuck up our friendship over this."

"We're good." She leans in, her kiss on my cheek gentle, leaving a trace of warmth. "It's curious, you've got this image, like you've got it all figured out, except when it comes to women. Then, you seem . . . lost."

I let out a short laugh, more out of discomfort than amusement. "You don't know the half of it."

Her curiosity piqued, she asks, "Who do I remind you of?"

"Someone I used to know," I say numbly.

My chest tightens.

Because the woman she's unintentionally channeling tonight? There's a very real chance she might be there in the flesh.

◆ ◆ ◆

One of the cons about coming out about my hearing condition is that people have taken to shouting at me, like I can't hear at all. It's enough to give me a headache worse than when I was straining to hear people.

634

Even the flirtatious attempt by the marketing department's latest addition, who loudly declared her single status and interest, felt more like a yell meant for a stadium than a failed-attempt at seduction. If there's one way to blow your career at my company, it's to think I'm interested in having a fling with someone on my staff.

Yet, there's one individual who seems determined to keep her distance, the young intern with the heart-shaped face from Yonkers. Our eyes have met several times, but each encounter is met with her quick retreat, a clear avoidance that speaks volumes more than the overt shouts I've grown accustomed to.

The grand ballroom at the Plaza is buzzing, everyone's looking sharp—tuxes, gowns, the whole nine yards. It's the usual chaos that kicks off when the crew gets unlimited access to drinks and a green light to forget who's boss for a night.

The majority are hanging on to their professional veneer by a thread. Already, at least five folks have blurted out things to me they'd never have the guts to say sober. Lucky for them, some of them are talking into my left ear, which has gotten progressively worse over the past few months.

I wouldn't be surprised if a couple of them, even the bosses, consider quitting after tonight's shenanigans.

I've always managed to keep it together in front of the staff, even back when I was drinking. Which, for the record, I'm not. Tonight, I'm sober as a judge, watching the spectacle unfold with a sort of detached amusement.

My gaze drifts back to Grace while the finance crew yaps in my ear. She's cracking up, right in the thick of it with a bunch of summer interns and newbies. By the looks of the empty bottles and shot glasses crowding their table, they're really leaning into the booze tonight. Guess their young livers can handle it.

My pulse kicks reflexively scanning her companions for a familiar face.

If Grace was going to bring anyone along, it'd be Lexi. Looks like she stayed back in Maryland. Is she avoiding me on purpose?

I grip my sparkling water a little tighter.

She's not showing up. She would've been here if she was coming.

I need to step out, get some air. "Excuse me," I grunt, edging past the finance crew's nonstop gab.

I duck out to the balcony, seeking refuge and maybe a bit of sanity. My hands grip the railings as I stare blankly at the traffic below, tension coiled tight in my chest area and shoulders. No one approaches me this time.

"You hiding out here?" Killian's voice cuts through the traffic, the sweet scent of whiskey trailing him.

I take a deep breath, a part of me missing the buzz that comes from a good quality whiskey.

Being sober makes you realize how much bullshit flows when lips are loosened by liquor.

Killian, clearly not wasted, has that relaxed vibe—just lightly buzzed, enough to take the edge off these social gatherings.

He leans against the railing next to me, his relaxed state evident by the abandoned bow tie.

I give a tired chuckle. "Figured I've worked the room long enough."

I try rolling my shoulders, hoping to shake off the tension that's been my constant companion tonight.

He eyes me, concern etched across his face. "Everything all right?"

"Just tight muscles."

I've been on edge all night. In fact, not just tonight but in the lead-up to this event.

"You make sure you take care of yourself. Hell, head home now if you've had enough."

"Come on now, Killian, I've got a reputation to uphold as the fun one between us." I chuckle.

"I bet nobody would even notice if we dipped out now. Half of them are too wasted to remember their own names. I've already had to tell the bar to cut some of them off."

He shifts his gaze to the street below, and we

settle into a comfortable silence.

"You know," he starts, his voice laced with a hesitation that's rare for him, "I don't think I've said how proud I am of you."

I raise an eyebrow, surprised, and crack a small smile.

Okay I had some major fuckups this year, meaning hotel builds stalled and revenue dipped. But I've done some good—three more hotels under our belt, revenue climbing this quarter, and now the team's pockets are heavier with well-deserved bonuses. "Yeah, the acquisitions were smooth sailing. Almost too smooth," I laugh.

But he's looking at me steadily. "I wasn't talking about the business side of things. This year's been rough on you. I'm proud of how you've handled it. You could've fallen back into some bad habits, but you've been damn strong. You've achieved so much in a short space of time."

"Guess I'm the only idiot who finds it harder to step back from work than to dive headfirst into it." I chuckle, the sound more rueful than amused. "You know how hard it is to unwind? It's a talent just learning how to do it."

"Of course I do," he says. "We're cut from the same cloth."

Handing off half my duties to lighten the load was no walk in the park at first. Turns out, I've got a bit of a control freak in me. Now, I've cut down to just three days a week at the grind. And once a month, I head out to the great outdoors for some solo camping.

When people say "just relax and chill," they don't understand that it takes skill to unwind when your natural state is being a pathologically driven workaholic.

I've started on a regimen of Immunosuppressive Therapy which, for now, is keeping my condition stable. I've quit drinking entirely, since the meds can be tough on the liver. That was fucking hard. I miss my scotch and wine. The medication sometimes gives me stomach ulcers, but I'm a grown man; I can handle it. People face far worse without the advantages I have.

The truth is, the immunosuppressants might not work indefinitely. They could lose their effectiveness in weeks, months, or years, and my doctors say my condition ranges from moderate to severe, so it's like living with a time bomb.

Once I approached my health as if it were a new hotel project, I found I could manage. I have the resources here to make a difference. And it feels pretty rewarding.

He clears his throat awkwardly. "I love you, Connor. I know I don't say it enough."

Ah, fucking hell, now he's lobbing emotional grenades at me?

I force a strained laugh. "Cut the sappy crap

before the staff overhears and we lose whatever shreds of respect we have left. And I love you too, by the way. Most of the time."

He laughs and gives me a solid thump on the back. "Fair enough. I'm heading back in. Stay out here as long as you need, yeah?"

I muster a halfhearted smile. "Go, enjoy your night."

"I'm dragging my lady home in thirty, if I can get her away, then heading straight to bed."

I'm happy for him. He's got everything he could possibly want in life.

Desperate for quiet time, I lean against the railing, eyes drifting to the street below.

Grace totters down the hotel steps, looking a little worse for wear. Huh. She's leaving early. Sensible girl.

I frown, uneasy seeing her walk toward a cab in those ridiculous heels. Maybe I should send one of my guys to make sure she gets back to her staff apartment safe and sound.

But then my gaze snags on something else, and the world grinds to a screeching halt.

Someone else.

The sight slams into me like a freight train at full speed.

The unmistakable dark mane of hair in the back of the cab.

Damn.

Lexi.

My heart kicks into overdrive, and I can't even see her damn face yet.

Turn around, I find myself silently willing, my hands clenching the railing so hard it's cutting into my skin. *Just turn around. Just once. Let me see your face.*

The universe decides to throw me a bone.

Lexi turns to hug her sister. That moment—catching sight of her heart-shaped face, the one I've tried to shove into the deepest corners of my memory—it hits me like a punch to the gut.

There she is. In the flesh. So damn close.

She smiles at Grace, says something that makes her laugh, and then throws her head back in laughter—a sound I can almost hear in my head.

Then she's gone. She's gone before I can do something reckless like vault over the balcony and shatter both legs getting to that taxi.

I slump against the railing, feeling this sharp pain in my chest, like I've been shot. After all this time, just catching a fleeting glimpse of her undoes me completely.

It felt like hours, drinking in every detail. But it must've only been a minute, maybe less.

I don't have many regrets in life, but the haunting memory of letting her walk away that night at Killian's house might just be my biggest.

It's a deep cut that won't heal, keeping me up

at night as I stare at the ceiling, my vision swirling with what-ifs. *What if I hadn't been so stubborn.*

I wonder what Lexi would think of the path I've chosen, of the projects I've poured my soul into. I wonder if she would be proud of me. It's ironic—out of everyone in my life, she's the one person I desperately want to share my triumphs with.

She looked so damn happy in the back of that cab, her smile lighting up her face as she laughed with her sister. Relaxed and glowing. A stark contrast to the exhausted, stressed woman I last saw, dark circles under her eyes from the toll of dealing with my bullshit.

I know she's happy. I still have some light protection on her, from a distance, making sure she's okay. And she's hiking, jogging, going out to bars.

She looks like that because I'm out of her life. Even when she was giving everything to helping me, I threw it back in her face. I took and took and gave nothing back but the superficial promise of money.

And as much as I want to jump in my car and track her down and tell her that I love her, that I made a terrible mistake . . . that vision of the sheer happiness on her face as she saw Grace, as they drove off together—that's the final proof I needed that she's better off without me.

I fooled myself into believing I was letting her go to spare her disappointment. But the harsh reality I refused to face is that I was never worthy of her love or her time. She was always too good for me, and I was too fucking arrogant to see it.

I was a complete asshole. Took me too long to realize I viewed myself as superior, believing she should feel honored I let her into my world. That's the message I sent embarrassing her in front of my family. As if *she* was the lucky one.

The way I humiliated her in front of my family rather than the treating her like the incredible woman she is . . . yeah, it makes me sick to my stomach.

Now, she's free to live her best life, the one she was always supposed to have.

Maybe there's something worse than losing my hearing. It's losing Lexi permanently, knowing I have no one to blame but myself.

But if I genuinely love her, the most selfless thing I can do is step aside, let her find someone who truly deserves her. The thought of her with someone else kills me, but I can't be that selfish, arrogant jerk to her again.

"Sir," Jim interrupts, materializing at my side. "There's a situation that requires your immediate attention."

FORTY-NINE

Lexi

"What are the bubbles made from anyway?" Grace asks as she stares into her giant mango bubble tea, her eyes wide with drunken wonder. "What's the point of them? It's weirdly satisfying when you suck 'em up the straw, right?"

I give her a smile, the kind you reserve for kids who ask why the sky is blue for the millionth time. I'm not sure if she's expecting me to reply to any of those deep questions, or if she's just drunkenly philosophizing.

Getting bubble tea was my attempt at sobering Grace up to avoid a killer hangover. Not just for her sake—I can't deal with the snoring. Plus, I'd rather not wake up to her head in the toilet in the morning. Now we're doing the short work back to Grace's apartment.

It's 11 p.m. on a Friday night in New York, and the city is alive. I inhale deeply, letting it fill my lungs, even the exhaust fumes and hot garbage. The beautiful stench of reality.

The city is buzzing with people coming and going from all sorts of weird and wonderful places —comedy clubs, jazz joints, poor suckers working late at the office, hospitals full of drama, all-night comic stores for the geeks, rooftop garden bars for the hipsters, vintage arcade bars for the nerds, strip clubs for the pervs, kink clubs for the adventurous. You name it, New York's got it.

In this city, seeing Batman stroll out of Pret A Manger doesn't even warrant a second glance.

That's what I love about New York —the stunning diversity, the exhilarating unpredictability. The heady rush of eight million folks going about their lives, each with their own story, their own soaring dreams and crushing letdowns, their own devastating heartbreaks and fleeting joys.

I know I'll come back someday. I feel it in my bones.

But right now, I've got a good thing going in Maryland, with my job, Mom in a nice care home, decent plumbing, and my life finally on track.

But being back, even just for a visit—seeing those dazzling lights, those towering skyscrapers, feeling that electrifying buzz that somehow kicks the tired right out of you—it's like a piece of my heart never really left.

It's funny, now that I'm not drowning in debt I can breathe easier, can feel a flicker of excitement at being back. I guess part of me wanted Grace to stay—beyond just looking out for her—so I could keep a connection to the city.

Grace's apartment is just ten blocks from Central Park, which is perfect. Buying earplugs for her snoring is cheaper than splurging on a hotel room in that neighborhood.

She's raved about the Quinn & Wolfe bash, and it sounds insane, like something ripped straight from the pages of *The Great Gatsby*.

They pulled out all the stops—magicians, poker tables, champagne fountains, acrobatic performers, even ice sculptures shaped like landmarks from cities where their hotels are.

Seems like the company is thriving. Because nothing says *we're loaded* quite like a giant ice sculpture of the Empire State Building slowly melting into a puddle.

I'm desperately trying not to picture him there, in his element, charming the room like the smooth-talking, charismatic asshole he is.

I'm attempting to block out the image of him in a perfectly tailored tux, his piercing blue eyes, his disarming smile.

And I'm also doing my best to ignore the thought of him with his arm around his professor girlfriend.

"Go ahead, ask me," Grace says, slurping her bubble tea.

"What?" I feign innocence.

I stab my straw into my honeydew bubble tea, trying to squash one of the tapioca balls, trying to squash the emotions swelling in my chest.

"Ask me about him. I won't mention him unless you do."

Fuck. She hasn't even said his name, and the pang is sharp. It's harder in New York than in Maryland. Because I know he's here, I know he's out there breathing the same New York air, gazing up at the same sky.

I could make a run for it, sprint those twenty blocks like my life depended on it, just to catch a glimpse of him. I know exactly where he is right now.

I could drag Grace back to her staff party and face my heartache head-on, because I'm a glutton for punishment. Maybe seeing him in the flesh would finally be the pain I need to forget him entirely. To stamp out that teeny tiny sliver of hope that's stubbornly clinging to my soul.

It's ridiculous. The dull pain has lasted longer now than the fling itself. It's not supposed to be that way. I'm supposed to be over him, moved on.

And Tom's great. Funny, handsome, uncomplicated. He's the antithesis of a brooding billionaire type. Tom is the kind of guy who

647

belongs in my world, the kind of normal guy a normal girl like me should be with.

"I don't care, Grace," I say, trying to convince myself as much as her as we cut through the park. "I knew he'd be there. He's technically your boss."

"Yeah, if by 'boss' you mean 'the guy on the top floor of my building.' There are fourteen levels between him and me."

I look at her and laugh, a real laugh this time. "Did you actually take the time to figure that out?"

"Yep. Obviously, the levels get more intense and harder to climb the closer you get to the Quinns and Wolfe. The Quinn & Wolfe version of Everest. And I'm still at base camp."

I laugh again, grateful for my sister's company. She takes a long sip of her bubble tea.

We fall silent. I let out a loaded breath, the type that feels like it's been gathering in my chest for weeks, maybe months, since I left New York. "Okay . . . so? Did you see him?"

Grace nods. "Yeah. He seemed on edge, actually. Kept glancing my way. I bet he was wondering if you'd show up."

"Grace," I sigh, my heart doing that stupid little flip flop thing. "He wasn't wondering about me. He really wasn't. A guy like him isn't going to care about you or me. No offense."

Grace hums. "I guess not."

Silence stretches between us. Then, softly,

Grace speaks again. "I'm sorry, Lexi."

I turn to her, confused. "For what?"

"I know how hurt you are, even after all these months. But it won't last forever, you know? Everything heals with time, Lexi. You'll get there."

I *will* get there.

The words echo in my head like a mantra.

As we stroll, I spot a couple glued to each other on a bench, engaging in what can only be described as a very enthusiastic, slurpy kiss. It's sweet, in that *Get a room* kind of way.

"I'm fine," I say, tearing my gaze away from the amorous couple.

"You are. And I don't believe that we only get one great love in our lives. You'll find a guy to love again."

"I don't love him," I lie horribly, the words cutting into my throat.

"I know," she says quietly, lying just as badly.

I glance over at her, sensing that she's about to say more.

"Don't," I say, my voice cracking. "You'll make me cry. Sorry, Grace."

"Okay." She nods.

For a second, I think the cold, hard thing pressing into my back is the pain from talking about him, like my body's giving me a physical reminder of the emotional shit-storm raging inside me.

But when I realize it's not, when I feel the hard metal digging into my spine, it hits me that there might be something worse than hurting over Connor.

I freeze, my breath caught in my throat. Slowly, I turn around, and the sight that greets me sends me stumbling back, a strangled gasp escaping.

"Hello, Lexi."

"Deano?" I blink rapidly, my brain struggling to catch up as I take another shaky step back.

"Fancy seeing you here," he growls, his voice dropping to a tone that sets my skin crawling like it's covered in spiders. "Back in the city for a little visit?"

What the actual fuck? Has he been following us?

I'm so shocked, caught so completely caught off guard, that I don't even register the gun until Grace screams, a high-pitched sound that pierces right through my brain.

She drops her bubble tea, and I'm dimly aware of the splash against my shoes.

"Shut the fuck up," Deano hisses at her, glaring between us, his eyes wild and unhinged. The gun in his hand is aimed right at my chest.

"What do you want?" I ask, my voice trembling so badly I can barely get the words out.

"Must've been nice, Lexi, living it up while I was locked up," he spits out. His beard is gone, exposing his weak chin that's been hiding under all that scruff. But what he's lacking in chin, he's more than making up for in bulk, as if he's done nothing but hit the gym.

"I had no idea you were in jail," I tell him, and it's the truth.

I almost feel bad for him. But then I remember that he's pointing a fucking gun at me.

My hands go up. "Deano, come on, put that down," I plead, my whole body quaking with fear.

Grace and I stand there, frozen like statues, scared shitless. It's dark, there's no one around. We're totally at his mercy.

I wonder how much it hurts to get shot. Do you feel everything or does the shock make you numb?

"Why ... what ..." I can't even string a sentence together. My body feels like it's been dunked in Connor's ice bath.

I feel like I might pass out or puke my guts out. I can't even scream. Fear's got me by the windpipe, muffling my cries, my breath, my ability to think straight.

But my sense of smell still works, and I can smell the stale cigarette stench coming off him. I hate that this might be the last thing I ever smell. Talk about adding insult to injury.

Grace clings to my side, her nails digging into my arm. I wrap her in my arms, holding her tight, in case she tries to run. The look on Deano's face says he's got nothing to lose. Maybe he wants us to give him an excuse, a reason to pull the trigger.

"While I was behind bars, thanks to you, you've been cozying up with your dream guy, right, darling? Looks like you really turned Quinn's world upside down that night, had him eating out of your hand. You think I'm clueless, that I don't know you had a hand in putting me in that cell?"

"What?" I whisper, my voice drowned out by the sound of my heart.

He inches closer, the gun pointed right between my eyes. I let out a whimper that sounds like a dying animal, a sound that I didn't even know I could make.

This is it. This is how I go out.

In a dark, empty park, at the hands of a man I think is a total moron, a guy I never should've gotten mixed up with in the first place. Oh my god, what would happen to Mom?

It's bizarre, you never really know how you'll react until you're staring down a moment like this. Turns out, I'm a beggar—a chatty one at that. While Grace is quietly panicking next to me, I'm spewing a stream of desperate pleas, my words jumbling together in a frantic prayer. "Please. No. Don't. God."

I squeeze my eyes shut, steeling myself for the sound of a gunshot, bracing for unimaginable pain.

But it doesn't come.

Instead, I hear a voice I never thought I'd hear again.

"I think you should be pointing that thing at me, don't you?"

The low, velvety voice I've replayed in my mind during countless sleepless hours, crafting conversations that never happened outside my own head.

"Connor," Grace squeaks.

"Connor," I rasp, staring at him.

He's here. In his tux. Looking like James Bond and the hot felon model guy rolled into one ridiculously handsome package.

"Don't hurt them," Connor says, his gaze fixed on Deano as if I'm not even there.

I want to run into his arms, to bury my face in his chest and just breathe him in. To replace the stench of Deano's stale cigarette breath with the intoxicating scent of Connor.

His chest rises and falls with each labored breath, his jaw locked tight, eyes burning with fierce resolve. "This has nothing to do with Lexi or Grace. I'm the one who got you locked up. Your problem's with me. Point that thing my way," he says slowly and deliberately.

He takes a step toward Deano, his hands raised in a gesture of surrender.

Deano keeps his gun aimed right at me.

"Shoot me. You know you want to. I'm right here, buddy, yours for the taking. Why go near Lexi when you can have me?" Connor's voice is steady, but I can hear the undercurrent of desperation.

Oh my god, he's goading him. He's actually trying to get Deano to shoot him instead of us.

"Connor, don't," I whisper. "*Don't.*"

"The second I move my gun from her, your guys are on me. You think I don't know there's about fifty ex-Special Forces waiting in the bushes?" Deano sneers.

Undeterred, Connor takes another step toward him. "Come on, man," he says, his voice low and steady, almost conversational. "We both know taking me down would be a lot more satisfying than hurting these girls."

"Get back," Deano snaps, eyes wild.

But Connor doesn't even flinch. With a calm that borders on surreal, he positions himself between us and the barrel of Deano's gun, his broad shoulders forming a shield.

"No, Connor," I cry, my heart breaking.

Deano's going to do it. It's written all over him —the determination in his eyes, the grim set of his jaw. He's going to pull the trigger, and Connor is going to die.

In a desperate bid, I reach out to grab Connor's shoulder, trying to yank him back, to shield him from his own heroic recklessness. But he's immovable, pushing me safely behind him.

"Please, Deano, don't do this," I plead.

But he isn't listening. He's not seeing me, not seeing Grace. All he sees now is Connor, the target of his wrath.

And then, in a moment that feels like it lasts forever, in a split second that I know I'll never forget as long as I live, I hear it. The sound of a gunshot.

The noise is so loud, it's like it's gone off inside my head.

I can't help it, I scream. A scream of sheer unadulterated terror.

But the bullet doesn't find its mark. It doesn't bury itself in Connor's heart.

Instead, it's Deano who drops, who falls to the ground.

"There's a sniper on a rooftop," Connor murmurs, like it's no big deal, like he hasn't just gone up against a gunman.

And Deano was right, men do rush in from the bushes, like some kind of secret agent squad.

Connor turns to face us, and I lose it. I let out this huge, ugly wail.

I don't know if it's sadness or happiness, relief or hysteria, or maybe all the emotions mixing together in a blender of feels to form the ultimate wail.

And then Grace starts in too, and together

we're like a fucking chorus of dying cats, just yowling and sobbing and generally making a scene.

Connor pulls us both in, wrapping us up in his arms. And even in the middle of this shit-show, I can't help but notice how good he smells.

"You c-c-came," I stammer. "Why is Deano . . . I-I-don't understand."

"Shush," Connor murmurs, his hand stroking my hair in a way that's so soft it nearly sets me off again. "You're both safe now. Deano got out of prison early. I just found out."

He looks down at me, his eyes filled with so much emotion that it makes my knees go weak.

Seeing him here, after all these months apart, after everything that's happened . . . it's like a fucking miracle.

I can hardly believe it's real, can hardly believe he's here, holding me. Protecting me and Grace.

"Grace, can you give us a moment, please?" he says. "My guys will take care of you for a minute. We're not going anywhere."

"I think I just pooed a little," Grace whimpers, her face pale as a ghost.

Connor lets out this little chuckle, which is so bizarre considering we were just staring down the barrel of a gun. "Hey, no worries. They've dealt with worse. As long as you're okay, that's all that matters."

"Grace, I'm right here," I say to her.

Grace nods, her legs wobbling as one of Connor's security team leads her away, probably to hose her down or something.

I barely register the sirens, the shouting, the chaos that's going on around us.

It's like tunnel vision. All I see is Connor.

I stare at him, my heart feeling like it's going to explode. There's so much emotion coursing through me, I don't know how to handle it.

"I can't believe you're really here," I whisper, my voice all shaky and lame.

He's still holding me, his arms wrapped around me like he never wants to let go. And god, I never want him to.

"I made you a promise. I promised I would never let him hurt you, and I'm here keeping that promise. I realized, when I saw you today in that cab—"

"Cab?" I interrupt, confused.

"Outside the party. I was so close to just letting you go, to convincing myself that I couldn't give you what you needed. But seeing you out there, in the world without me . . . it felt wrong. I'm meant to be there, to protect you, to love you. And I know now, without a doubt, that I have what it takes to be the man you need me to be. To put you first, to not take you for granted. I'm never letting go of you again."

I stare at him, doing backflips of joy in my head. "I'm never leaving your arms, Connor. I love you so much, it's insane. It's terrifying and overwhelming and just . . . a lot. I thought I wanted a quiet, normal life, and I tried it—it was great, but . . . I need you. I need this, us."

My heart feels like it might burst out of my chest, like that freaky scene from *Alien*. Except in a good way.

"But wait, what about the hot professor?" I ask.

Connor looks at me, confused. "What do you mean?"

"Don't you . . . aren't you in love with the professor lady?"

"Damn, the tabloids never quit. Lexi, no. Clarissa's a friend, a colleague. There is no other woman. There's only you. There's only ever been you. And you—do you have feelings for that teacher?"

I can't help but smirk. "You've been keeping tabs on me! He's a good guy, don't get me wrong. But he wouldn't take a bullet for me."

Connor chuckles, his eyes smoldering with intensity. "I love you so much, angel. Will you give me another shot? I want to do it right this time."

And I don't hesitate. I don't think. I just go for it. I launch myself into his arms like a koala, wrapping my legs around his waist and kissing him like my life depends on it. And in a way, it did.

The rest of the world fades away.

Never mind the fact that Deano is lying on the ground, groaning.

Never mind the sirens wailing, getting closer.

Never mind the fact that Grace is using this near-death experience as an opportunity to chat up one of Connor's security guys.

Never mind the couple from the bench, who are now gawking at the scene.

Never mind my bubble tea has spilled all over the ground.

Never mind I can now feel a hard length pressed against my core in what can only be described as a highly inappropriate time and place.

None of that matters. In this moment of chaos, there is only me and Connor.

Because why settle for peace and quiet when you can experience intense, life-changing, all-consuming love?

Peace and quiet is overrated.

EPILOGUE

Later That Night

Lexi

There's something about elevators that really gets me going. Makes me feel naughty.

It's the forced proximity, the way you're locked into this tiny metal cube with someone; your personal space nonexistent.

It's the sensation of that lurch in your stomach as you shoot up or drop down.

It's the fact that it's a moving box that feels like you're in a private little world while still being in a space that's open to anyone who has the audacity to hit the button and interrupt your moment.

But most of all, it's the fact that you're time-boxed. You've got forty seconds, if you're lucky, to do all the things you've been dying to do.

So when Connor and I finally escape the police investigation and step into the elevator that will take us to his penthouse, it's like every over-the-top movie elevator scene brought to life, where the characters can't keep their hands to themselves.

Our hands are all over each other, our mouths are all over each other, our noises are like two barnyard animals in heat.

He hoists me into his arms, and the kiss is like nothing I've ever tasted before. Desperate and dirty. Fucking with our tongues and our lips.

Meanwhile, Grace is safely tucked away in her apartment, playing house with Connor's security.

And by "playing house," I mean she's likely insisting that she can't possibly sleep alone after such a traumatic experience, and would he mind terribly if he got into bed with her and maybe even let her lie on top of him.

She insisted on choosing which protection guy would stay with her, and surprise surprise, it's the one she was making eyes at earlier. There's no real danger to us—Deano was acting alone—but still, having a gun aimed at you can shake you up, make you want to keep the night light on.

The elevator doors slide open to Connor's apartment far too slowly and we stumble out down the hall toward his apartment, still trying to devour each other's faces.

Connor breaks away from me long enough to dig around for his keycard in his back pocket. He swipes his key card, then presses his thumb to the scanner, then punches in a code that's seems longer than a barcode.

If he doesn't get this door open in the next five seconds, I swear I'll just have to roll up my sleeves and bust it down myself.

"Oh my god, this is too much," I groan, tugging at his belt like a woman possessed. "Let me in already. I'm dying here, Connor."

He lets out a lust-filled chuckle.

And then, finally, after what feels like an eternity of waiting, the lock gives way and the door swings wide open, dumping us into the sheer extravagance of Connor's penthouse.

I never thought I'd step foot in this place again.

We're barely through the door when our clothes start flying off. I'm ripping off his tux like a woman possessed.

But Connor gives as good as he gets. In his impatience he rips my T-shirt. Literally rips the damn shirt, and it was my favorite.

"Hey," I breathe, trying to sound indignant but my body is already betraying me, grinding against him. "I have to walk to Grace's tomorrow. I need something to wear on top, unless you want me to cause a scandal by strutting around Manhattan topless."

"What are you talking about? You're not leaving this apartment. Ever again," he growls, his voice rough with desire.

I laugh, a giddy sound that bubbles up from the

overwhelming rush of emotions.

I'll worry about my walk of shame tomorrow. Right now, I can't believe we are together. I'm with him. I have him. I have his love. I feel like my heart will burst with all the emotions spilling out.

I grabble with his dress shirt and trousers, desperate to get them all off, even though he looks like a million bucks in that tux. It's almost criminal to take it off.

But it looks better on the floor, and he looks better naked with them off. My god, I've missed that body. I used to think I imagined how good it was; now I realize it's better than I remember. Or maybe he's been working out even more.

He unhooks my bra. Our hands are all over each other, frantically undoing buttons and unzipping zippers.

He yanks off his boxers with the desperation of a man on fire, until he's completely naked and erect.

Oh. My. God.

And to think, just a few hours ago, I was staring down the barrel of a gun. Now I'm staring at something else loaded that could potentially kill me with pleasure.

This is what I've been craving since I left New York. This is what I've wanted every night since I left New York. I wouldn't admit it to myself, but I was sexually repressed, and no one could scratch that itch. Only him.

My hand finds his throbbing cock, and I let out a lustful moan at the feel of him pulsing in my grip.

He returns the favor by slipping a finger inside me, causing me to moan even louder. A sexy game of tit for tat.

"I've missed you so much, my angel," he growls with lust in his eyes as he starts going to town down there. "Missed those eyes. That heart-shaped face."

I'm his angel now. I like the addition.

We haven't even made it a foot from his front door yet.

"Me too," I rasp, but it comes out as another moan rather than coherent words.

"Baby, I can't wait," he breathes hotly against my skin. "I can't wait any fucking longer. I have to take you right here."

He presses me up against the wall, lifting me into his arms before thrusting himself inside me.

I gasp at the intense sensation of pleasure mixed with pain, my nails digging into his back for support.

He stills, waiting for me to relax.

I've never been banged against a wall before. Now I'm thinking we should bang against every wall of his house. Seven bedrooms means plenty of options.

Maybe not the plunge pool room though.

He thrusts into me, groaning like he's been dying for this for months—a feeling I can relate to.

All that built-up sexual frustration is finally being released for both of us, and it feels amazing.

"I love you, Alexa Sullivan," he grunts, his intense gaze piercing through me as he pounds into me.

"I . . . love . . . you . . . too," I pant, my tits bouncing with each thrust. From now on, I'm hitting the gym harder so I can multi-task talking and fucking simultaneously. Because I'm going to be doing a lot more of this.

My fingers dance over his stomach, tracing the lines of his abs and hipbones and the trail of hair that leads down to his cock.

He chuckles, his muscles jumping under my touch. "Hey, that tickles."

"Sorry," I laugh, but I'm not sorry at all.

I can't stop touching him. Or looking at him.

I want to watch him sleep all night. I want to see those long, giraffe-like lashes flutter, those lips part in silent dreams, and that ridiculously sexy wolf tattoo heave with every breath.

I'll be disappointed in myself if I fall asleep.

Christ, I sound like a psycho.

We've fucked maybe one billion times tonight, and it must be 4 a.m. What a night.

Connor looks just as exhausted but blissfully happy as me.

He's sprawled out next to me, one arm propped behind his head like he's posing for a Calvin Klein ad and the other slung possessively around me.

And I swear to god, I'm so happy to be in his arms, so content, that I could almost kiss his armpit with its dark fuzz.

That's how deeply I've fallen for this man. I've reached the point where I'm willing to nuzzle his underarm like it's the most erotic thing in the world.

That's when you know. When you've buried your face in the guy's armpit, it's love.

Because when you're in love, every inch of your partner's body is sexy.

Even the armpits.

Especially the armpits.

"You're tickling my armpit now," Connor chuckles, his voice rumbling through his chest and vibrating against my head.

"Sorry," I giggle, pulling my face out of Connor's armpit. I should probably keep the weirdo vibes at bay during the honeymoon period.

I rest my head on his chest, giving him the doe-eyed look as if I hadn't just been motorboating his underarm. "What now?" I ask.

"We should probably try to catch some sleep," he says with a smile.

"No, I mean about us," I clarify. I wish I could just leave this sensitive topic until tomorrow, but my brain won't let me. "I'm in Maryland, and you're here."

He looks taken aback, as if the thought hadn't crossed his mind. "Aren't you planning on coming back to New York?"

Shit shit shit.

"I thought you wanted to," he says, eyes drilling into me with that intense blue gaze.

I hate what I'm about to say.

"Connor, not yet. Mom's just settled in, and I don't want to disrupt her life any more than I already have. And I like my job, it's allowing me to save loads." I nervously bite my lip. "Realistically I think I'll be there a year before I can come back."

Will you wait for me?

Couldn't I have waited and let us bask in the afterglow of great sex for at least one night before dropping this bombshell of reality?

But Connor just shrugs, like it's no big deal. "It's okay. We'll work it out."

"Really?" I ask, my voice a mix of hope and incredulity. "Do you think we can do long-distance?"

He plants a kiss on my forehead, his lips tender,

his stubble scraping slightly. "I'm down to a three-day office week. I can make weekends in Maryland work."

I blink at him, surprised. Wow, I was not expecting that. "You're seriously okay with that? I'll come back to New York too, of course."

"Yeah, Lexi," he says, and the softness in his voice makes my heart squeeze. "I'm okay with whatever means we can be together."

I know the goofy smile spreading across my face isn't exactly sexy, but I can't help it.

"I'll give you room in my sock drawer in Maryland," I say.

Connor raises an eyebrow, a smirk tugging at his lips. "Christ, room in a sock drawer? In return for putting myself between you and a bullet? What do I need to do to get a full closest?"

"Go down on me for a few more hours, and I'll consider it." I smirk.

He chuckles again, the sound low and rough. With a playful glint in his eye, he starts to maneuver me off, then lays me down on my back.

He begins his descent. Oh boy, this is going to be good.

As he trails kisses down my body, igniting a fire wherever his lips touch, I can't help but giggle.

"Ticklish?" he teases, his lips dancing along my skin.

"No," I gasp, "Just . . . happy and horny."

It's wild how a few hours of craziness can flip your entire world upside down.

This morning, had you asked me about my grand plans for the night, I'd have confidently said I was destined for a meal and some drinks with Kayla, listening as she told me about her kinky sex with Justin. They've both come off the dating apps now.

Then I'd meet Grace and we'd go for some bubble tea before heading home, where I'd end up sleeping on the floor because she's kicking so hard.

But instead, here I am.

With New York's most notorious ex-playboy, his head nestled between my legs.

It's the kind of decision you make when you're totally, 100 percent thinking straight.

Now I'm in a long-distance relationship with the man of my dreams.

A man who's willing to travel hundreds of miles just to be with me.

A man who looks at me like I'm his guardian angel.

One Year Later

Connor

I guide Lexi along the street, her hand clutching

my arm as I lead her to the surprise. I'm not gonna lie, I'm a little on edge here.

"Connor, the last time you blindfolded me, we ended up on a different continent. I mean, don't get me wrong, it was amazing. But it'd be great if I could pack my bags for myself."

I smirk. "That's not entirely accurate. The last time I blindfolded you, I had you bent over my bed, begging for mercy."

"Okay, fine," she says, smirking under the blindfold. "The last time in public. I sure hope no one on the street heard you say that."

"Come on, just a few more steps."

I slowly slide the blindfold off, watching her face closely for her reaction.

She blinks, taking in the Fifth Avenue townhouse we're standing in front of.

"Wait, are we at Killian's place? No, hold on . . . Killian's is farther down, isn't it?"

I feel a grin tugging at my lips. "It's ours, Lexi. If you want it, that is."

Her eyes go wide, jaw dropping. "What? You bought this?"

"Not yet. I wanted to make sure you loved it first. No point in dropping millions on a place if my girl's not happy with it."

She shakes her head. "Connor, it's a townhouse on Fifth Avenue. Who in their right mind wouldn't love it?"

I pull out the keys. "Fair point. Ready to see the inside?"

We step through the door, and Lexi does a little twirl, her face lit up with wonder. "Wow. Just . . . wow."

But then she pauses, turning to me with a confused frown. "But I don't understand, you love your apartment."

I shrug. We've still being doing long-distance, if you can call it that. It's easy when you have someone you want to see at the end of the journey.

But still, it's not the same as having her here, with me, all the time. I spend at least three nights a week in Baltimore, or Lexi comes to New York. And yeah, it's great. But I miss her like crazy during the week. The only upside is that I actually get some sleep instead of spending all night fucking.

Last month I got a hearing aid for my left ear. It's been a game-changer. I can actually hear shit again, without feeling like someone's stuffed cotton balls in my ear. And the immunosuppressants I'm on right now seem to be stopping the inflammation and disease from advancing.

As much as I've loved relaxing, I'm ready to dive back into work, full throttle. Five days a week, no more half-assing it.

But I've also learned to listen to my body, to know when to push and when to back off. I've got an addictive personality when it comes to work and exercise. I get tunnel vision, obsessing over shit until I'm in too deep to see how far I've fallen.

It's a skill, learning to step back.

But Lexi has helped with that. She's given me something else more important than work and exercise.

I clear my throat, feeling a sudden surge of nerves. "Look, Lexi, I want us to do this for real. Live together, build a life together. So I'm trying to make that happen, to set us up for the future. I want to show you something."

"I can't believe this," she says. "This place. I can't imagine living here. It's beautiful."

I tuck a stray lock of hair behind her ear. "I'm not asking you to give up your life in Maryland, angel. We can figure this out together, make it work for both of us."

I take her hand and lead her through a door on the ground floor. "I had an architect look at it. Turns out, we can convert half of this floor into its own separate apartment. And the basement can be a self-contained unit too."

She looks at me, all puzzled but still smiling. "You're turning it into apartments? Like an investment property or something?"

"No, the rest of the house stays as is. But those two apartments will be one for your mom on the ground floor and then a carer's apartment in the basement."

I smile, trying to play it cool even as my heart hammers against my ribs.

"Connor . . ." Her hands fly to her mouth, tears welling up in those gorgeous eyes. "That's so incredibly thoughtful. But you really don't have to do that."

"I know I don't have to. I want to." I flash her a grin, attempting to lighten the mood. "But we get some say in who your mom's caregiver is, yeah? Can't have her hiring some Chippendale dancer."

Lexi shakes her head, a watery laugh breaking through. "Connor, you don't have to take on my whole family just because you're with me."

I raise an eyebrow, smirking. "Oh, really? Because you need to take on mine. My mom makes you go for lunch, stealing you away every time you're in New York."

Clodagh and Lexi have become thick as thieves too, and I've got to admit, it's pretty damn nice seeing my girl get along so well with my sister-in-law.

I take her hands in mine, looking deep into her eyes. "Lexi, I want us to build a life together. And that includes your family. Your mom, Grace, the whole package."

Lexi's tears stream down her face.

"Hey," I murmur, cupping her cheeks in my hands. "Those are happy tears, right?"

She nods, still sniffling.

I use my thumbs to gently wipe away her tears. "Nothing wrong with a little happy cry, angel. Let it out."

She throws her arms around me, hugging me so tight, it feels like she's trying to make us one.

I pull her in close, burying my face in her hair.

My hearing might get worse, and the hearing aid might not work forever. But that's okay. As long as she's with me, I can handle it. Just one look into those eyes, and I feel like I can take on the world.

Six Months Later

Lexi

I love visiting Connor's Irish cottage.

This place is special to me, and not just because it's where I accidentally flashed a funeral party. Sure, that's pretty unforgettable, but it's not the only reason this place holds a special place in my heart.

Streaking aside, this cottage is where Connor and I fell in love, even if it took a bit of separation anxiety to realize it.

Now, we're back for a mini-vacation, but this time we've brought the whole crew: Grace, Clodagh, Killian, Teagan, and Connor's mom.

We've just stuffed our faces with Guinness stew and bowls of seafood chowder, in a small quaint Irish pub, and everything feels perfect. My belly, my soul, and my heart are all content.

There's something about Irish pubs that sets them apart, making them the best in the world. The Irish sure know how to have a good time.

The traditional band is absolutely killing it tonight. The fiddler is playing like his life depends on it, and the guy with the tambourine-looking thing (which I learned is called a bodhrán, because apparently, I'm uncultured) is creating pure magic.

The whole pub is alive with laughter and chatter, and everything feels right in the world. I feel like I'm part of something special.

Grace still works at Quinn & Wolfe, but she's managed to get Connor and Killian to sign an agreement that anything she does or says on this trip is off-limits. It was a joke. I think. Connor jokes that she pretends not to know him at work, like he's some sort of embarrassing secret.

As for me, next week marks my last week at Ascend before I start my new job at a PR firm in New York City. I have mixed emotions about it —sad to leave my team but excited for this next chapter. Plus, I'll only be working three days a week so I can continue my psychology course.

As for the living situation, Mom is moving into Connor's new Fifth Avenue townhouse next month, and I'm making the move permanent after our Ireland trip. Connor initially wanted to cover the costs of Mom's carer, but I insisted on paying for it myself. He's not charging me rent, which allows me to afford it, so I guess we've found a good compromise.

Even though I'll be living in New York, I'll still go back to visit the team in Ellicott City. I made some good friends there, and I don't want to lose touch. Speaking of old friends, Tom is married now and has a kid. I'm genuinely happy for him and wish him all the best.

Connor and I have even talked about trying for kids ourselves when I'm around thirty. But for now, I just want to enjoy life and have some fun.

"I'm grabbing more drinks," Killian announces as the band wraps up their tune.

Oh god. At this rate of Guinness consumption, I'll need a dip in the cold Atlantic Sea to scare away my hangover. Connor and I agreed we'd make it our thing every time we come here, a sort of twisted tradition to commemorate our first visit. I still haven't decided whether I have the guts to skinny dip again, though.

As the band takes a break, the lead singer announces, "Okay folks, this next one is called Eamon's send-off. You'll know this one. Our good man Eamon who left us too early."

The pub erupts in cheers and whistles, pints of

Guinness raised high in salute.

Suddenly, I'm hit with a weird feeling, like an icy finger just poked my forehead.

I look at Connor and he has the same questioning look on his face, but he grins and gives a shrug, taking a sip of his beer.

Eamon . . . surely not. It's probably a different Eamon. It's a common name in Ireland. It's like the John Smith of Irish names. I'm sure lots of Eamons die all the time.

The song starts and it's clear that it's a crowd favorite. The locals are clapping and stomping along to the beat, like they've heard this tune a million times before. Maybe it's the town's "Sweet Caroline."

As soon as I hear that first lyric, I spray Guinness all over Grace's cheek in a mist of shock and disbelief.

"Hey!" she squawks, sputtering and wiping at her face with an indignant glare. "What the hell, Lexi? If I wanted a Guinness facial, I would have asked for one."

But I barely hear her. I'm too busy trying to process the words that just came out of the singer's mouth.

We were stood on the beach, all somber and sad,
Saying goodbye to Eamon, our dear old lad,

677

"Did he say the *beach*?" I yell to Connor, trying to be heard over the music and the growing chaos of the crowd.

He looks like he can't quite believe what he's hearing. *Sounded like it*, he mouths back, fighting off a grin.

Shit shit shit. This can't be real. There's no way this song is about what I think it's about.

But then, the next verse rolls in, and my worst fears are confirmed.

The priest had his urn, ready to chuck,
Eamon's ashes into the sea, oh what the fuck!

I grip the edge of the table, trying to steady myself. The heat in my cheeks could cook an egg.

The woman, she shrieked and tried to hide,
Her naughty bits from our startled eyes,
While the man strutted from the sea, proud as a cock,
His big mickey swinging free, like a proper bollock.

This is it. This is how I die. Not from a bullet by Deano or a freak hiking accident, but with me keeling over from pure, unadulterated mortification in a cozy Irish pub, surrounded by my boyfriend's family and a bunch of strangers singing (the worst song in history, I might add) about my naked ass coming out of the sea.

Clodagh is losing it. She's laughing so hard she's practically in tears, her whole body shaking as she leans in to share the hilarity with Teagan. Connor's mom is trying to hold it together, hand slapped over her mouth, but her eyes are watering.

I groan, facepalming as the bar erupts into raucous laughter and cheers. This is it, folks—my legacy. Forget about any career achievements or personal development.

No, I'll forever be known as the crazy American who flashed a funeral and inspired a fucking folk song.

Connor winks at me. "Maybe we should play this song on our wedding day."

"Our *wedding*?" I repeat.

He chuckles. "Don't worry, Lexi. I'm not proposing. Not yet, anyway." He leans in close, his lips brushing my ear. "For the record, when I do propose, it won't be in some packed bar with a tune about us in the buff blaring in the background."

Holy shit. He's thought about proposing.

In this moment, it may be the most romantic thing I've ever heard in my life.

He pulls me into another kiss, one that's thick with heat and lust and promises and the kind of love that I'm pretty sure comes with a lifetime warranty.

THE END

ABOUT ROSA

I'm Rosa, a contemporary romance author based in the UK.

I love crafting stories about strong, sassy heroines who aren't afraid to speak their minds. These fierce ladies are paired with alpha heroes who are as rugged as they are emotionally constipated.

I have a weakness for specific tropes, such as billionaire alphas with egos the size of their bank accounts, age gap romances that show love defies age, workplace romances that give "office politics" a whole new meaning, enemies-to-lovers stories that make you want to lock the characters in a room until they sort out their feelings, and grumpy-meets-sunshine matchups proving that even the most brooding of men can melt with the right woman by their side.

When I'm not lost in my writing world, you can find me roaming the countryside with my own Happily-Ever-After guy (who refuses to read my books, likely worried he'll see himself in them, or even worse, not see himself at all) looking for a great hike with a pub at the end.

Join the newsletter and get info on releases at: www.rosalucasauthor.com

ALSO BY ROSA

The London Mister Series

Have you met the grumpy London misters yet? Each one in the series is a standalone, dual-point-of-view romantic comedy with heat, banter and a happy ending.

Taming Mr. Walker

Resisting Mr. Kane

Fighting Mr. Knight

Billionaires In Charge

Fifth Avenue Fling

Manhattan State of Mind

Empire State Enemies

Made in the USA
Las Vegas, NV
24 April 2024